HEART COLD AS GOLD

FAE OF THE SUN AND MOON

JEWEL JEFFERS

Copyright © 2023 by Jewel Jeffers

All rights reserved.

No part of this publication may be reproduced, distributed, or transmitted in any form or by any means, including photocopying, recording, or other electronic or mechanical methods, without the prior written permission of the author, except in the case of brief quotations embodied in critical reviews and certain other non-commercial uses permitted by copyright law.

The characters and events portrayed in this book are fictitious. Any similarity to real persons, living or dead, is coincidental and not intended by the author.

Cover design by: Yanie Cadwell of **Real Life Design Covers**
www.reallifedesign.site

Edited by: Zainab M of Heart Full of Reads
www.heartfullofreads.com
Zoe Reading of https://www.zoereading-pa.com/

TRIGGER WARNINGS

Heart Cold as Gold is a Dark Fantasy Romance that contains Mature language, explicit sex, dubious consent, nonconsensual sex, aggressive sexual content, sadism/masochism, negative self-image, self-harm, drug use, suicidal thoughts and actions, panic attacks, graphic gore, graphic violence, and physical assault. The characters in this book act irrationally due to trauma, and the relationships within this book are toxic and are not to be depicted as healthy relationships.

HEART COLD AS GOLD PLAYLIST

Spotify: https://bit.ly/42hpNHZ

1. Nothing Breaks Like a Heart — Mark Ronson & Miley Cyrus (book theme)
2. Comfort Crowd — Conan Gray (Marie's theme)
3. Heartless — The Weekend (Karnelian's theme)
4. Broke Us — Cierra Ramirez Feat. Trevor Jackson (Corivina's theme)
5. Water Me — Parisalexa (chapter 1)
6. Cherry Flavoured — The Neighbourhood (chapter 2)
7. WYD Now? — Sadie Jean (chapter 3)
8. Too Late — Ruben Pol (chapter 4)
9. I Walk this Earth All by Myself — Ekkstacy (chapter 6)
10. 2 Cigarettes — Jack & Jack (chapter 7)

11. Met Him Last Night — Demi Lovato and Arianna Grande (chapter 8)
12. ARIZONA — Young Friend & Ella Jane (chapter 11)
13. MONTERO (call me by your name) — Lil Nas X (chapter 12)
14. We Belong Together — Mariah Carey (chapter 15)
15. Crazy — Zac Greer (chapter 18)
16. Fweaky — Miley Cyrus (chapter 20)
17. Sex Money Feelings Die (slowed version) — Lykke Li (chapter 21)
18. Disaster — Conan Gray (chapter 22)
19. Souvenir — Selena Gomez (chapter 23)
20. Would You — The Vamps (chapter 25)
21. Habit — Still Woozy (chapter 26)
22. Swim — Chase Atlantic (chapter 28)
23. Violets — Josh Golden (chapter 29)
24. More Than Enough — Alina Baraz (chapter 31)
25. Fangs — Matt Champion (chapter 32)
26. I Wanna Be Yours — Arctic Monkeys (chapter 35)
27. Alaska — Caiola (chapter 37)
28. Depression — DAX (chapter 39)
29. Constellations — Jade Lemac (chapter 40&41)
30. Yours — Conan Gray (chapter 41)

31. Void — The Neighbourhood (chapter 42)
32. 13 Missed Calls — Zach Hood (chapter 43)
33. Ghost Town — Benson Boone (chapter 44)
34. I Would Die For You — Miley Cyrus (chapter 45)
35. Calling My Phone — Lil Tjay and 6lack (chapter 46)
36. Out of the Blue — Rini (chapter 46)
37. If the World Was Ending — JP Saxe and Julia Micheals (chapter 47)
38. Better — Khalid (chapter 49)

You've heard a pen is a sword but truly it's a dagger.

It's not a pretty shiny dagger, it's rough cut and rusted.

When it slashes, it infects.

And when it stabs, it's brunt and raw.

It can kill.

But the dagger is also double ended.

Pen to a page.

Knife to a heart.

Some things should be left unsaid.

But sometimes they need to cut and kill.

Let the blood bleed from an infected wound.

Let it push out and drain and wash away the infection.

Life is a lesson, more so a combination of little tests.

So kill with absolute certainty,

Or die with unrest.

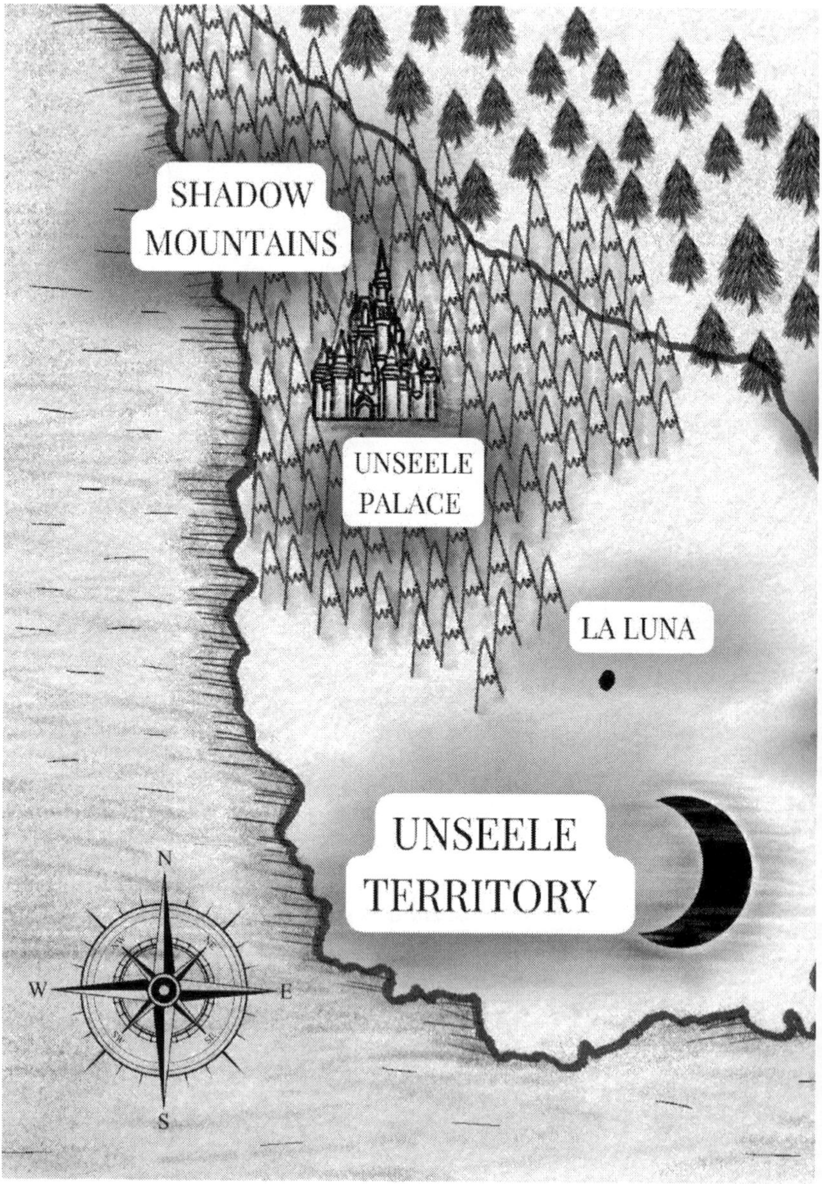
SHADOW MOUNTAINS
UNSEELE PALACE
LA LUNA
UNSEELE TERRITORY
N
W
E
S

HUMAN
TERRITORY
NEUTRAL
TERRITORY
CHARLOTTE
MANOR
LIGHTWOOD
FOREST
SOLARA
SEELE
PALACE
LIGHTWOOD
SEELE
TERRITORY

PROLOGUE

Karnelian
Two days after Winter Solstice.

There were two types of birds in the world. When faced with a threat, there were either birds that flocked away or birds that swooped and attacked. I knew by the look in her eyes that she was not the latter.

I'd never seen anything more broken in my hundred and forty-seven years of life. Broken wasn't even the correct word for it. Destroyed. Reduced to rubble, her pieces never to be put back together.

What a sad little bird she was.

It was the appropriate way to act in this type of situation. Half of her was missing. Her body was still whole, her mind still intact, her heart still beating, but her soul was connected to another's. Her soul had decided that she would spend this life with its other half, but the gods had other plans. Plans they tried to whisper in my ears, but I was known as another entity—one that went against the gods.

I was a male who wasn't kind, who loved to play games and make people squirm, but I would never put her through this. I didn't prey on the weak.

The Unseelie Princess spoke brokenly about her mate's death. Recounting in visceral detail every second of the event. She was lost in it, tranced in the memory. She recounted each thump of his heart, each gasping breath, the color of his dead eyes.

She didn't look at me or my father as she spoke, but her eyes were on us. Her stare penetrated through ours like a dull knife. She talked of the events prior, how the Unseelie King wanted to kill her mother, how she just wanted to save her life which cost her mate's as a price.

A shudder accompanied each word that left her mouth as if she didn't want to say them. To be fair, she hadn't had a choice. My magic bound her to speak the truth, but not in this much detail, not this graphic.

She wouldn't say his name. The *L* would start to leave her mouth, but she would quickly correct it to *my mate* as if saying his name would cause more damage to her psyche.

We were in my father's private throne room. Ridiculous as the rest of the Seelie Palace with its gold furnishings, but served purpose for when he wanted to do dirty dealings.

He was a king, so there were times when dirty dealings were inevitable, but my father held some honor. He didn't let the darkness sink into his bones, staying true and Seelie. Sticking to the light, pretending that the light didn't cast shadows.

He left most of the dirty dealing to me because I was as dirty as it could get with the fae. The Silver Blooded Devil, the Hybrid, the First—*the Original* Heir, Karnelian Lightfire.

A villain in the making if I said so myself. I had enough anger for it, enough power. They called me the devil for the many deals I'd dealt. For how I screwed over the arrogant and tricked the greedy, but I was the devil before I even dealt my first deal—before my baby brother took his first breath.

But my brother wasn't here, listening to a broken bird spew ramblings of the most tragic day of her life, I was. When it benefited my father—which it always did—my silver blood was seen as a *gift*.

Being of both bloods made my power boundless, and the gods had blessed me with an abundant power source. I never truly tested it, but I knew I was stronger than my father. Whose magic was artificial, being passed down from one king to the next. Even if people knew exactly how much power I held, no one would treat me with the same amount of respect. They saw me as an abomination, a cursed male, and they treated me as such. *Until* I grew into the devil who can grant one's deepest desires. *Until* they wanted power. *Until* they needed something, and I was there to aid, but for a price.

The tie around my neck grew tighter as I slid my tongue across my teeth in agitation. I was a monster, I would admit to that, but seeing this female cry was agonizing. Each shudder of her breath, I felt in my bones. Each hiccup stilled my heart. Each time her eyes flicked to mine, I felt my soul try to rip out of me to fill the hollowness within her.

I knew her. Not personally, but I had met her once about a year ago. I had probably seen her before, but that day, I had truly seen her. I remember thinking she embodied the sun, her skin sparkling a bronzy gold when light graced her. I remembered her eyes not looking as hollow as they did now.

Not able to stand there listening to the cracks that intercepted her ballad, I started toward her.

"*Karnelian*," my father hissed.

"I am a busy male, Father. I do not have the time to listen to this mess, I'll do what you need and be on my way."

"Karnelian, you will not leave until I say so." My father tried to use his king voice on me, and once upon a time, it would work. When my heart was filled to the brim with love for him, I'd do anything he asked. Though, now, my heart was a bitter blackened thing, filled with despair and fury.

I kneeled in front of the chair she sat in, knowing later my father would fuss about me kneeling. Princes don't do that, but even if I was his son, I wasn't a prince. Not anymore.

I was a tall male, above the average. Even being half-human, she was short for a person of fae blood—she was short for a human. I wouldn't hover over her. I wouldn't make this little bird feel smaller than she already was, so I kneeled, letting my eyes meet black orbs.

Their cold black depths were so deep it was endless. A pit of nothing. Her eyes looked to house no soul, like it had left her when her mate died. The darkness in those irises drew me in. The devilistic parts of me wanted to play with that darkness. I had the desire to drown in it. Bathe in her sorrow, swim in her pain. To dirty myself with their inky shadows because I loved dirty little things.

Her voice trailed off as I neared, her attention fixing on my form, her hollow gaze striking into me and connecting us.

I heard it again, the whispers of the night we first met, but I pushed those whispers away. I pushed everything away as my awareness settled on the soft chime of her angelic voice.

"Are you going to kill me?" she said, barely above a breath.

"Do you want me to?" My voice was normal, loud enough for everyone to hear.

She glanced at her parents, her lip trembling slightly, before she nodded. "*Please.*"

My hand found hers, her soft skin feeling nice against my rough palm. My fingers played with her clawed tipped ones; her rose gold ring looking misplaced with the Unseelie black of her clothes. "I'm sorry, little bird, but you are more valuable alive." I pulled up the sleeve of her dress, revealing the marks that adorned her body. I could sense she was probably covered in them, but I could also sense that her male was dead and of no threat to me. Not that any male or female was ever of threat to me.

She bit her lip as more tears started to line her eyes. "Please," she begged again.

Ignoring her, I continued to raise her sleeve and look for a free piece of skin before pulling out the dagger looped on my belt.

The silver blade glinted as a sharp stern voice pitched in my ears. "What do you think you are doing?"

I stifled a groan as I looked toward the female radiating hatred my way. "Did you not ask to keep her safe?"

She crossed her arms, the female's black eyes—similar to the princess but not the same kind of pain reflecting in their depths—boring into mine. "How is a dagger going to keep her safe?"

"*Vina*," the commander chided. The male never looked so heated. Normally, he was calm and breezy. Annoyingly happy all the fucking time, but nice. Today, he was swirling with anger, and I felt the flames of it choking down on his wife.

It was evident that this was all her fault, not fully, but it could have been avoided if she had spoken up. When she had relayed her side of the story, it was revealed that she was romantically involved with the Unseelie King, King Markos, and it ended badly. Badly enough for her to want to remove their child from her womb.

It was extremely uncommon for fae to do that. Frowned upon as well. Even if the babe was unwanted, someone would want it. Fae were infertile and the lack of being able to conceive a child made people desperate for one. Fae would rape for it. They'd steal others' babes. The cherry on top of it all is that we had an instinct to breed. The carnal need to fuck always imbedded into us.

Corivina couldn't speak of it, my magic not able to get past the deal she made with the king. The chill one felt from her gaze made it clear that what he did to her had slashed through a part of her soul and changed her forever.

We revealed the nature of the deal—she couldn't tell another being—but it was easy to tell what he did from the context clues. For him to cover his crime that well, meant it was appalling enough that he needed to make sure she kept quiet. It probably would have stayed quiet if he had not allowed her back in his palace. If he hadn't been so obsessed with her. If she didn't explode under the pressure of having her daughter mated to her rapist's son.

Corivina looked at the commander, her lips pressed into a thin line, their eyes passing messages that only lovers did. I could tell what they had was deep. I could feel his love for his wife through that blazing anger, but I could also sense the barricade she erected to shield herself from pain, from the world.

After a moment of their silent conversation, Corivina wilted, albeit begrudgingly, and her eyes met mine. "Continue," she muttered.

An amused smile tickled my lips, and I looked back at the princess. Calling upon my magic and accessing the deep well of power I had, silver veins started to permeate my skin. I brought the knife to my palm, a sting of pain lacing through me as I sliced into flesh.

I glanced over to Corivina, raising my eyebrows in taunt as I re-sheathed my dagger. Her eyes turned into slits, her jaw hard as stone.

A chuckle flittered under my breath before I focused back on the task at hand, letting my silver blood fall on the princess's caramel skin, slithering around with the guide of my magic.

The princess squirmed, jerking back a little. "What's happening?" she squeaked as the blood started to seep into her flesh.

I met her eyes as the magic formed into a silver eclipse tattoo—my personal brand. "I don't need to draw your blood to make a deal with you."

A crease formed on her forehead, the first time she had shown an emotion besides sorrow.

"You cannot cause harm or intentionally put yourself in harm's way until the brand is removed."

She paused, letting my words sink in, then asked, "What?"

"You cannot cause—"

"No!" Her eyes filled with panic, and she pulled at my arm, her claws ripping into my suit and finding purchase into my skin. "No, please, no. I want to die! I want to die!"

I pried her fingers off me, those whispers trying to flow in my mind again before I stood, looking down at the ruffled little bird. "And you will one day. No one lives forever. Just unfortunately for you, *little bird*, fae live close to forever."

ONE

CORIVINA
4 AND A HALF YEARS LATER.

"There will be a time when you feel like you have lost everything, Corivina. Though, you never lost anything at all. A darkness will come then, sweep you up and show you all its horrors. When those horrors come, let your darkness in. It will protect you from succumbing to madness."

A hand slid down my side, coming around my waist to brush my lower back. My chest was pushed against a naked torso, his hard abs twitching against the fabric of my blue satin dress.

"Corivina, you are so beautiful." His breath brushed across my skin.

I pulled back, putting a little space between us. "I know this, Dominick."

Dominick's fingers brushed the stray strands of black hair away from my face, his eyes gleaming with lust and devotion. "Corivina, I want you," he whispered; voice husked as he pushed his pelvis into me, his hard cock grinding into my front as we glided across the ballroom floor.

King Dominick Lightfire, the Seelie King, the Lion King, the Party King. Normal height for a fae male. Blond hair that came down to his shoulders and green, emerald eyes that threatened to steal a female's heart. Any female but me.

A seductive smile split my lips, though there was an edge to it. "I am spoken for, Dominick."

His hand slid down my back even further, coming to rest just above the swell of my ass. "Are you?"

"I am."

His face inched closer to me, his lips centimeters away from mine. "And where is the commander tonight?"

I tried to hide the tension that entered my body at his question, pressing my lower half into him to distract his keen mind. "At home watching our daughter."

"I thought General Kolvin took the night shift? Why isn't the commander here with you or every other night that you spend in my presence?"

My throat bobbed; emotion tried to wiggle its way into my presence. It was easy to ignore, my darkness secluding me off from the deeper pit of shadows that screamed of madness. Though, it did have its weak spots. Two people who I tried my best to keep a distance from. "He is tired."

Dominick hummed, his cocky ego smothering me with his unspoked accusations.

"He's a good husband." The same could not be said for the female pressed against the king almost every night, often in dresses that revealed more than she had ever shown.

Dominick leaned down and pressed a kiss on my shoulder. The act sent a shiver down my body, irritation following soon after. He wanted everyone to think we were fucking, that I was cheating on my male, my husband. I wouldn't fuck him, but I let him think differently. I needed to be close to him, to be the raven in the lion's ear.

Over the last four to five years, a war has started to brew. No attacks have been launched, but there was a restlessness amongst the people. It took little to get the fae riled for war. The Unseelie Prince's death and the withholding of information as to why Markos had killed his son drew tension from both the Unseelie and Seelie.

"Corivina, how does this marriage thing work?" Dominick mused. "I know I'm expected to choose a queen, but I still haven't done it. Is it normal for a pairing to be married and unclaimed?"

The downward quirk of my lips had my lust-filled mask falling. "Only I am unclaimed, and the reasons are between me and my husband."

The king raised a brow. "Darius wears no mark."

"Yes, he does."

"No, he doesn't. I saw him last week. He didn't wear your mark."

The world fell out from underneath me as I took his words, one of my weak spots being triggered. Frantically, I searched within for the subtle link between Darius and I and found it bare. How did I not fucking notice my mark had faded? Why didn't Darius tell me it had?

I knew the answer to that, but I also didn't want to acknowledge it. Acknowledging it would flip my darkness against me when it had finally started to become my ally.

Swallowing the lump in my throat, I plastered on a smile, hoping the king's sharp eye didn't detect my inner panic. "It doesn't matter that he doesn't, we are still married, and he is still my male."

"But are you really his? When was the last time he took you to bed? You haven't smelled of him in many months."

My body grew tighter in tension.

"I can smell your need to be fucked, Corivina." Dominick's breath fanned over my ear, making my nipples harden against his naked chest. The male was extremely attractive, and I couldn't remember exactly how long it had been since I had sex. "Let me sooth your ache."

I inhaled. "I am not here to fuck you."

He pulled back, his eyes glinting. "Why are you here every night, Corivina, if not to tease me with that beautiful body of yours?" He bit his lip, his canines grazing. "If you want me to kill Markos, why not just say it out right?"

"I want you to kill Markos."

He smiled, haughty and arrogant just like his devil son. "I know, and maybe I will."

"If I did let you fuck me, would it even persuade you?" A part of me hated that those words had even left my mouth, but I was becoming desperate. These past five years had felt like a thousand. Even though there was a wall of darkness holding me up, it didn't keep from things crumbling around me. I needed this done and over before I got swept up in a new darkness that would pull me under.

"The beast in me wants to say yes, so I could be buried in your sweet flesh. But I want more than just one night with you, more than just a meaningless fuck, so the answer is no."

"What would I have to do to persuade you?"

"The war hasn't even begun yet, Corivina."

"It will soon, and you know it."

"I do, but I cannot just kill him. There are steps and we will get there eventually."

I stayed silent, anger growing within, as he continued to glide me across the dance floor.

Dominick brushed a kiss to my head in placation. He had a soft spot for me, he always had it, and I was definitely exploiting it. We barely ever talked before, but he would comment and flirt. Treat me better than just the commander's wife. So when I started planning my ruin for Markos, I knew I could use Dominick to see my plans through.

"You should come to my family dinner tomorrow," he said, changing the subject.

"You have a family dinner?"

"Yes, me and my sons and their mothers have a family dinner once a month."

I gave a weak smile, trying to hold back the grimace that wanted to find purchase on my face. "No, thank you."

"Why not? Don't you want to be the puppet master who pulls my strings? A family dinner seems like a big step."

"I really prefer not to go to dinner with you and your other females."

"Jealous?" he cooed, nipping at my neck.

I pushed his face away from my throat. "No, I just don't want you to think it means something and I don't want people to talk."

"They already do."

"I don't want them to talk more than they do."

He rolled his eyes and huffed. "Corivina, you are great for a male's ego. If I wasn't a king with an overinflated one, I think you would wound mine."

I shook my head, not really in the mood to force a laugh out to soothe that ego. "Are you going to ask him?"

Dominick's hand cupped my cheek. The look in his eyes spoke of intensity and possession. A look I didn't reflect, would never reflect. "Yes, Corivina. I told you I would order him to."

My smile was genuine and pleased. "Thank you."

He pulled me in, kissing my cheek, way too close to my mouth. "When are you coming back?"

"The party this weekend."

He nodded. "Good."

It was late in the night when I arrived at the manor, quietly trying to climb the stairs to the bedroom, so as not to wake Darius. My efforts were useless because he was still awake, reading a book, waiting for me. He was a beam of light to my darkness, and I didn't want to lose that light, but I needed to be covered in shadows right now.

I set down my stuff on the vanity by the door before walking over to him and crawling into his lap. He barely had time to mark his page as I smashed my lips to his in desperation, pushing all my fears into the kiss.

Our marriage wasn't the same as it was. It hadn't been the same in twenty-five years, but over the last five, it felt like he was the one erecting the walls in our marriage instead of me, and I did little to stop him.

Darius wrapped his arms around me, and I moaned as that sense of home enveloped me. His lips pressed into mine, but I could still feel the disconnection between us, the block in the way. I wanted to break that block, but it would have to wait until after the war. Until after Markos was six feet under.

I rocked my hips into his, and he groaned as he began to thicken under me. My hips rocked more, my creature pushing me to move fast. There was an ache settled between my legs, and I only wanted him to soothe it.

I kneaded him through his trousers, trailing kisses down his neck. It was bare, my mark missing. My heart squeezed in agony, but I ignored the pain, knowing I could fill it with shadows when I wasn't being blazed by the sun. I pressed a few kisses to his throat before I let my teeth latch on to the now empty spot of his neck.

Then, I was pushed off him, landing in the softness of my side of the bed.

Darius wiped his mouth and stood. "I can't believe you were about to do that."

"Darius," I breathed, desperation seeping into my voice.

His eyes met mine. Where they were once a calm blue, now they always seemed to be lit with rage as he looked my way. "No, you don't get to do the shit anymore. I'm fucking tired of it."

"Darius—"

"It took you a fucking month to notice. A fucking month. Do you even know when the last time we had sex was? Four. We haven't had sex for four fucking months."

I stood, walking towards him. "I'm sorry."

"You're not or you wouldn't keep doing this shit."

"I was distracted, I have a lot on my plate. *We* have a lot on our plates, Darius."

"I get you want the war. You want your retribution from Markos, but we should come first. Our family should come first. When was the last time you even had a conversation with Marie that wasn't longer than two sentences?"

Marie. The other weak spot in my wall of shadows.

"She's not really the talkative type anymore."

"Who do you think she would talk to if she needed to? Who do you think she wants to wrap herself into when she gets triggered and combust into tears? She loves Kolvin and she loves me, but she loves you more than anyone and you fucking know that. But for some reason, you are never here when you say you will be." His voice was filled with anger, rough and ridged, but there was also a lining of hurt within it. Hurt that existed because of me, but I did nothing to soothe the pain. With hurt came distance, and that's what I needed. Distance.

"There is a war coming, a war that will result in her becoming queen. I need to make sure she is ready for it, that everything is handled before that happens."

He scoffed. "She is barely sane, Corivina." *Corivina*—he hadn't called me Vina in four years. Always Corivina, always formal and harsh, over pronouncing the V as if he spat out the last half of it.

"I am doing my best, Darius."

"And your best is sleeping with the king?"

"I haven't slept with him, and I would never do that."

"But you let him dry-hump you in front of the whole court? A court that I'm fucking a part of."

"He is the only one who can kill Markos. I need to make sure Markos pays for what he fucking did."

"I understand that you want revenge but why are you willing to destroy everything we've created for it? Why did you go to Dominick for help instead of me? I am the fucking commander, the male who orchestrates the war. Do I want one? No, but I would do anything to see Markos dead after what he did to you. I share your anger, and I shared your pain for two hundred years, Corivina, and you don't even consider including me in your efforts. Instead, you go and throw away our fucking marriage."

"I'm not throwing away our marriage, we are still married. I still love you. What I do with the king means nothing. I don't want him, you know I don't want him. You know I love you."

"No, I don't." He scrubbed his short beard. "You know, five years ago, you told Marie to not let someone mark her unless she was sure of her love. You haven't worn my mark for twenty-five years. I understood before why you didn't want it, but now, now I find myself questioning the same thing. Am I sure of our love? So, I let your mark fade and you didn't notice it was gone and the question answered itself. No, Corivina, I don't think I'm sure anymore."

My wall evaporated then, darkness swirling around me in a tornado of torture. "What?"

His fingers brushed through his toffee brown hair before he looked away from me with a sigh. "I'm going to sleep on the couch. Good night."

My teeth were gnashed together as I watched him leave, my heart burning from being set on fire. But I shook it off, taking a few deep breaths to calm myself. Without the sun, I was left in the dark again and I could reform my wall. Bargain with the darkness to give me more time before it consumed me whole.

I knew I would find my light again. Darius and I would work it out. He was my one, the person I wanted to spend this life with, and I would fix this, later. Now, I needed to kill Markos. Kill the creator of my shadows who haunted my dreams and probably haunted my daughter's as well.

TWO

MARIE

Blue-black eyes haunted my dreams, so I tried not to sleep. For if I did sleep, eventually, I would scream. Scream, and scream, and scream, until my throat was hoarse and my eyes had cried an ocean's worth of tears.

My parents tried everything to aid with the nightmares, but nothing helped. It was of my soul's doing, I was sure. A retaliation for its incarceration.

If my eyes were closed, he'd visit. I'd feel his love. I'd see his smile. His burnt pine scent would penetrate my nose. Midnight eyes would bore into me, feeling like a place that was home for my soul. Then those midnight eyes would be hollow, corrupted, and haunted. My being filled with fear, running and running, until I was caught. Then he delivered what my soul wished, what I wished, what he wished. My last breath.

So, I didn't sleep, or I tried not to. I may be half-fae, but even the angelic beasts need to sleep. I spent my days—that dragged into nights—tired, fighting the inevitable pull into a restless slumber. The cycle might have driven me to be a little bit mad, or I already was. Does one know exactly when the laughter starts to chime in your ears? Had it been there when he died, and all I could do was form tears?

My brain was slightly fired, but even in its charred state, it still wanted to work. Wanted to escape its tortures. For months after he died, I was stuck in the realm of nightmares. The same dream over and over on loop, no matter if I was awake or asleep. Months of my life trapped in my soul's torment. But then I registered the touching, they kept touching me, to feed me. I used that small tether to pull me back to life. Life was misery but a merciful misery.

A misery I desperately tried to end.

I was more mad then than I was now, doing everything to end my existence and failing over and over and over again.

The devil's brand on my arm kept me from doing so. I couldn't hurt physically—not intentionally. I could accidently stub my toe or cut my hand on shattered glass that pelted around me after I smashed the wine bottle or two in one of my episodes, but if harm was my goal, I couldn't do it.

And yes, I had tested this many times.

They thought one day I'd heal. I saw the smiles when I managed to do the smallest of things. Eat by myself, bathe, communicate with more than shakes of my head. I saw the hope that shimmered in their eyes. Was I functioning? Yes, unfortunately. Would I heal? No.

Destroyed. Ruined. Wrecked.

What was wrong with me could never be fixed. I was a porcelain cup that fell on a hardwood floor. Even if you managed to find all the pieces that made me, gluing them together wouldn't erase the damage. It would always be there. His absence would always be there. The madness would always be there.

My molars ground together as Kolvin's morning wood ground into me. They watched me in shifts. My mother—mornings, my father—afternoons, and Kolvin—nights. At least that was how it was supposed to be.

Kolvin slept in the bed because there wasn't anywhere else for him to sleep besides the wood floor. He didn't have to hold me as he did, but he thought holding me somehow held back the nightmares. What he didn't realize was that I never slept until my body crashed from exhaustion. He thought I enjoyed being smothered with his heat while my body was going through its own heat.

Apparently, fae went into heat. It was rare—everything was fucking rare—but if you were a mated female, it was almost a given. It was one of the reasons mates were so fertile. Even though I wasn't mated anymore, my body still thought it was, and it craved for my mate—or any male for that matter—to breed me.

I'm not fucking joking. *Breed me.*

I denied the heat the best I could, and eventually it would go away, but this time, it seemed my body was intent on having me break my heat the old-fashioned way—with dick. Not even my fingers could satisfy it, my attempts always ending in failure.

This current cycle had lasted about a full year. The heat seemed to grow worse each day and Kolvin and his cock weren't fucking helping.

Pushing away from him, I sat up on the side of the bed, breathing heavily. My stomach rolled, my core clenched, and cold sweats broke out all over my body.

Kolvin followed, his legs coming around my sides, arms wrapping around my waist, erection poking me in the back.

He didn't speak; there wasn't much he could say that hadn't been said before.

It will be okay.
You will get through this.
It will pass.

None of it true. None of it helping.

Tears welled in my eyes as my body betrayed me, craving to turn in his arms, push him back to the bed and take him inside me. My body urging me to betray my mate.

I would rather suffer than be with another. At least that was what I kept telling myself as my clit throbbed and begged for pleasure.

Kolvin pressed a kiss to my sweaty forehead. The sentiment wasn't overlooked. He had been there every step of the way, offering his comfort. I hated it, hated the smothering that not only he provided, but my father did as well.

My mother was rarely around. Her absence was a relief because she was more suffocating than Kolvin and my father combined. She kept a distance, features were pinned in stoicism, but her worry clogged the air.

I didn't want her worry. I didn't want anyone's worry, their pain, their sadness, their pity. They were all burdens I refused to carry because I refused to care.

A shudder stole over me as another wave of my heat coursed through my body. My mind now only on Kolvin's softening cock, disappointment filling me at its disappearance.

My panties were soaked and my nipples ached against the fabric that covered me neck to toe, but my scent was hidden from him.

A part of me, the mad and crazy part, wanted to rip off the necklace that held the reddish orange stone and let him breath in my arousal. Let it drive him as crazy as it drove me, and then have him plow me harder than he had once did before.

As if Kolvin could hear my thoughts, he whispered against my ear, his breath hot and tickling over my sensitive skin, "I could help you, Marie."

My teeth gritted together from screaming, *Yes! Please, Gods, yes!*

I shivered, standing from the bed, staring at the photo of my birth father that hung on the wall. "I couldn't do that, Kol."

"I'll make it fast. Then you can be done with this. So you don't have to suffer more than you do."

I wanted to laugh at how he made it seem like it was another duty he owed me. Like he didn't want to enjoy it, how he didn't still secretly wish I would let my mate go and settle for him. Like all he was worth was a broken, *ruined* female settling for him.

"I couldn't do that to *you*." My heart was cold—frozen, unable to beat, and though I broke his five years ago, I knew his was still intact. I also knew I was a big reason he hadn't tried to find another female. He wasn't celibate. I had smelled females on him, but he only kept them for a few weeks before he found another.

Kolvin would do anything for me. He had proven that over the last five years when he almost flunked out of school because he was caring for me. He only became general because he was years ahead of the other new recruits since my father had been training him since he was a young faeling. I knew that Kolvin would stay by my side for the rest of this dreaded forever if I asked. He would sacrifice his happiness for me. Which I rather he refrained from. He'd say he was happy to help, but it would tear him apart. He would hope. Let his hope protect his mind from the aches that came from his heart. I couldn't lie; the deep dark sadistic person I had become thought about it, but I already carried enough guilt.

"It's not about me. Marie, you feel like a fucking furnace. You literally have to change your underwear five times a day and you have moments when all you can focus on is trying not to jump my bones. I'm on the brew, we trust each other, and I will do everything possible to make sure that you are comfortable."

"It could come back right after."

Kolvin sighed heavily, the noise carrying a thousand thoughts that he wouldn't voice because I was too fragile. Everyone treated me like I was a violin. The instrument that played sorrowed songs, delicate and fragile and easily breakable. I wouldn't deny it, I felt like I was.

I went over to my dresser and grabbed some clothes. My mother had obtained my clothing from Unseelie. The clothing from my mate, and even though there was a fire in me, and the summer heat outside the fae territories intensified the Seelie Territory's temperature, I still wore them. But wasn't black the perfect color for one who was perpetually in morning?

Ignoring Kolvin's stare that attempted to burn against my back, I went into the bathroom, turned on the water to fill the tub, and placed my clothing on the counter. I removed my ring, taking in the rabbit and the wolf, their dance making my stomach sour, before I placed it next to my clothes. Then I crouched, my hand going under the sink in search for the leather pouch taped and hidden next to the basin.

My body slumped to the floor, and I carefully untied the pouch's strings. Sparkling blue power twinkled up at me as the bathroom light shone down on it.

The tension in my muscles dissipated, my lips almost turning up into a smile.

Faerie dust.

A substance that came from a poisonous plant that killed the fae if taken in large quantities. In low quantities, it had similar effects like venom, but instead of lust, there was chaos. Which was why it was popularly used as a party drug amongst the fae.

I scoped out a teaspoon's worth with one of my claws before bringing it to my nose and inhaling deeply.

Fire shot from the tip of my nostril traveling to the back of my throat and coating my lungs. Pain, an infrequent sensation to my physical body but an insistent sensation to my emotional one. The physical, raw and consuming, stealing my whole attention and canceling out the emotional.

The world went white as my senses went haywire. Nerves tingled; sparks prickled under my skin. My insides rotted and heaved. My tissues dying off giving me just the slightest taste of death before my body started healing itself. The healing was better than the dying, magic attempting to regenerate the damage, a sweet ruthless pain. My blood pumped faster, pushing the magic to my limbs, guts, and tissues. My muscles screaming at the sensation until all that was left was the white world that started to shift to black.

In that blackness, was pure bliss. A bliss where nothing else exists.

A quiet so silent it was sweet, sugary and filled with peace. I floated in that space, a space where nothing lived, my body and mind numb to the world.

This nothingness was addictive. I was addicted. Many fae were. How could a beast like us not love the chaos of bleeding the lines of death and life?

I started taking the dust soon after my mother stopped watching me in the mornings. Now that I'd started taking it, I couldn't bring myself to stop. It made me feel less and made the world somehow bright and dull at the same time. Even if I wanted to stop, I couldn't. The withdrawals brought my creature into a panic. It went unhinged, desperate, and with someone with a will as weak as mine, it would be nearly impossible for me to resist the call to a land of nothingness. I still managed to only take a little a day, right before my bath. If they noticed, they would take away the only peace I could manage to obtain in this miserable half-life.

My sense of smell was the first thing to come back, the subtle scent of plain soap tickling against the serrated flesh in my nose. Then my hearing, the dramatic sound of splashing water registering in my brain.

My eyes flung open, and quickly, I scrambled over to the tub to turn off the water. Doing this every day for the past four years,

I've learned to perfect the timing of my break away from life with the filling of the bath.

Nerves still prickling, head still fogged, I stood and shucked off my turtleneck and sweatpants. I didn't bother looking at my body in the gold lined mirror as I slipped into the white clawfoot tub. I already knew my once caramel skin was now ashened. My bronzy gold shimmer stood out against my skin instead of seamlessly blending, making me look like a haunted angel. Bags laid under my eyes, my irises a cold deep black that reflected my soul perfectly.

The warm water of the tub floated around my now cold body. The dust stunted healing, temporarily aiding with my heat, my heart having to work harder to circulate my blood.

I hope I die today.

I felt dead, living on borrowed time—wasted time. Me being alive without him was utterly pointless. We were meant to be together, for etr—

My hand rose from the bath, the trickling of water feeding into my ears, resetting the sweet silence.

There was a buzzing in my bones, and I sank into the feeling. I normally sat here until the water grew cold. Depending on how long it had been since I last slept gaged how high I would still be when I got out of the tub. Somedays, I could function; somedays, I stayed in bed and stared at the wall, not knowing where the fuck I was. Other days, I panicked, cried, and screamed, reflecting my soul's inner turmoil.

Today, I leaned more toward lost out of my mind.

They were never able to tell that I got high. Even before the dust, I spent most days not speaking, staring at the wall. Except, now I just wasn't counting the cracks in the wall, or the maids' footsteps as they passed, desperately trying to stave off the torments of my soul.

A knock sounded on the door. "Flower?" my mother's voice chimed.

An irritated inhalation accompanied the tensing in my muscles. I had heard my parents fighting last night, they did that more often now. Their voices were muffled, but I didn't have to guess what they were fighting about—me. Everything was unfortunately always about me.

"Flower, can I come in?"

"No," I snapped, standing from my bath. "I'll be out."

I dried off and dressed before re-taping the dust under the sink and checking to make sure my nose hadn't started to bleed.

Blinding light caused my head to throb. The curtains pulled wide in my bedroom, reminding me just how high I was. After adjusting to the room, I glanced at my mother who was sitting on the bed, Kolvin off to lead training as a general. Hard black eyes glued to me, catastrophe looming in the air around her.

My mother's claw tipped fingers brushed a strand of black hair away from her face, her blue icelike shimmer glinting against the sunlight.

She smiled; it was forced and didn't reach her eyes. The heaviness around her made me want to leave the room. A darkness to her—not like one that haunted your dreams, one that I don't even know if she was aware of but was ominous.

"How are you, flower?"

I didn't reply to her question, walking over to the dresser to pull out socks. She knew the answer.

She sighed ever so slightly. "Is the heat fading?"

"No," I said, rolling the black socks on.

"I talked to the king... he said there isn't much else we can do about it. If you want it gone, you'd have to... or wait."

I turned to look at her, my expression blank. I never offered much to them when they tried to speak to me. There wasn't much to offer. My nonreaction often affected a crease in their brows that my mother was now sporting.

She stared at me for a few moments, her eyes trying to bore into mine, but that intense feeling one gets when you connect eyes with someone never came. I felt hollow, partly because of the dust, mainly because my soul was shattered into shards.

After gathering nothing, she spoke again. "There are some things I want to talk about."

I moved to the bed, making her turn as I slid in and pulled the covers up. My body was still cold, and my head was still swimming too much to continue standing without throwing up the contents of my stomach.

"You are the heir to the Unseelie crown, you know what that means, don't you?"

I blinked. I knew it, but at the moment, I didn't really have the energy to grasp the meaning.

"If Markos—the Unseelie King, dies, his magic will be transferred to you." She paused to gauge, seeing if any sign of recognition flashed in my eyes, her mouth slightly quirking down when none was to be found. "A war is brewing. A lot of swords are aimed at Mar—the Unseelie King's head. When he dies, you will become queen. That amount of magic being transferred could be overwhelming. It could drive you crazy since you are untrained."

I am already crazy.

My mother's nostrils flared as if she could read my mind. "I want you to start training."

"I am of black blood." It was within reason that someone of gold blood wouldn't be able to properly train someone of black.

"Prince Karnelian will teach you."

That evoked a reaction from me, my brows slamming together and my nostrils flaring. The reaction was not because this male was the only reason I was alive. My life bound to his with the silver brand adoring my arm, but because... Well, he's... "The devil?"

She nodded.

The clouds were heavily fogging my mind and it took a moment for me to form a sentence. "Did you make a deal?"

"The Seelie King is arranging it. No blood needed to be spilled."

Silence once again filled the space. I had no other questions and I hoped she had nothing left to say.

"There is a ball this weekend."

"Mmhmm?"

"And I want you to attend."

I hoped my face accurately painted the fact that I did not want to attend a ball.

"Flower, you have a responsibility."

No reaction came from me, making her exhale heavily. "Look, I get it, Marie. I know what it's like to have demons dance on your shoulders. I know they are constantly whispering to you, and you'd do anything to make them go away. But while they drown you with their hypnotic songs, the rest of us are going to keep living. You are the heir, even if me and your father let you... let you be free of them." She paused to swallow an invisible lump in her throat. "You are valuable to more than just us. So we are going to the ball, we will meet the prince, and then maybe you will get lost in the music or at the very least the wine?" Her lips formed into a small smile, hope blossoming in her cold eyes. "Can you do that?"

I couldn't care for music, but I could definitely get lost in a bottle or two of wine. It wasn't like I had a choice. Much of my life had been choiceless, but now, I didn't really have the energy to try to fight it. They wanted me to go to a ball, I'd go to a ball. They want me to train, I'd train. Whatever got me closer to death, closer to him.

THREE

MARIE

*A*lone finally, I laid in bed, staring at the ceiling, letting my mind go blank. There was an urge to think of him, but that was a path into hysteria, filled with pain from the shards of my soul stabbing into my being. So I avoided it at all cost, even if I missed him.

An hour or so later, my mind was still foggy, but the silence from the dust dissipated. My mind attempting to find purchase in something. I didn't blame it; a mind's job was to think, but all my thoughts always led to him.

Getting up and leaving my room, I dodged the human servants as I made my way down the hall. They were afraid of me—within right. They had cleaned up many of my episodes that resulted in me tearing apart my room. Though they seemed to be more afraid of my eerie quiet than the manic outburst.

In the kitchen, I made a cup of coffee. I hated coffee, especially black. If old Marie was to have coffee, she would have had a handful of sugar cubes, milk, and vanilla bean added to it. That was too much work. Too much effort that I couldn't bring myself to care, so I drank it black. Plus, the rancid taste was a welcome suffering, as many other things were.

The alertness the coffee brought me, had me itching for another dose of dust. As well as my flaring heat. I didn't want to push it. If I ended up accidently poisoning myself, I was sure it would alert the devil. He would save me, and my family would find out. The only reason I was able to take the dust was because it classified as loophole. The brand kept me from harming myself, but I never took the dust with the intent to harm. The harm was just a byproduct.

Instead of dust, I made my way to the wine cellar. The place spanned rows and rows of aged fae wine that my father and mother had been collecting over the years. I grabbed a bottle made a few months ago, avoiding the stuff my Aunt Melinda made. My parents were too busy to notice if a newly acquired bottle went missing, but they would definitely notice my mother's favorites. Even if they did notice, it would be in a few years, and by then, I hoped to be gone.

I closed my eyes and readied my body, attempting to loosen my tense muscles. I wiggled my toes before focusing on my cold frozen heart. My heightened hearing let me hear the wet swishing sound of pumping blood. I called on my shadows, more so wrangled them into my grasp until they covered the wine bottle.

This was all I was able to do with my magic, a party trick, a really shitty party trick.

The bottle pushed tight into my stomach, shadows blending in with my clothes, I exited the cellar, careful to avoid any maids. They were human and easy to outsmart, but I wasn't always of keen mind, so sometimes, I slipped up, and the bitches were tattletales.

My grip on my shadows was weak and so I was practically running back to my room in the hopes I wouldn't get caught.

The door slammed behind me as I entered, and I released my hold on my magic, an ache now ringing in my head from dehydration, poor health, and strain on my magic.

HEART COLD AS GOLD

I ripped off the wax seal on the bottle, my claw piercing the cork, as I made my way over to the chair that sat in the corner of the room. I brought the wine to my mouth, chugging the contents, some of it slipping down my chin.

I didn't care. I didn't care for the sour taste that made me want to gag, nor that later my skin would be sticky from the spilt wine. I just wanted the bottle's contents in my body and pumping through my blood to numb out the horrid screams.

After a few gulps, my body relaxed, a heaviness settling over me. My soul's screams were still there but distant. The shards still cutting into me, but the ache dulled.

My plan for the day was to watch the animals play in the thick green bush of the Lightwood Forest and finish this bottle before my father came home in the afternoon and attempted conversation with me.

The wine was all gone by the time the sun hit the midpoint in the sky. The heaviness from earlier thickened and sunk my body into the push cushions. My mind muddied, my eyes weighted.

Blinking profusely, I sat up to stave off the pull of slumber. But in the next moment, I found myself slumped back in the chair, my head tilted to the side.

I stood with the intention of making another trip to the kitchen for a second cup of coffee, but instead, I was hit with a wave of dizziness halting my progression. A throb flared in my head, and my hand covered the area as an attempt to stave off the pain.

I took a step forward, trying to remember when the last time I slept was.

I scanned my brain, but the ache made it hard for me to think.
Another step.
My covered toes traveling across polished wood.
Another.
My head aching, my blood racing.
Another.

The world was lost to my feet. As well as lost to me, blackness filling my vision, shadows blanketing my brain.

The snow fell around us, my back against Levi's chest, as we sat under a pine tree. He had lit a fire for us, his cloak wrapped around me helped stave off any extra chill.

I snuggled back into him, and he growled, nipping at my ear.

"Mate, I'll fuck you here in the snow. Don't tempt me."

A giggle brewed in my chest and spilled out my lips. I turned to him, meeting midnight eyes, little balls of firelight glowing within. "You wouldn't."

"You know I would."

"I thought you loved me?"

His brow furrowed, seriousness coloring over his playful aura. "I do."

Another giggle left me, and I kissed his lips. "If you loved me, you wouldn't fuck me in the snow. You know I don't like the cold."

A sexy smirk lined his lips, and he pulled me closer to him, slightly pressing his hard cock into me. "I'll make you forget about the cold."

"I doubt it."

"Really?" A brow raised, mirth showing in his eyes.

"Really." I smiled.

"You want to bet?"

I kissed him in answer, and he consumed my lips. He turned me so I straddled his lap, his hands guiding my hips to grind into him.

Our beast came out and our kisses grew heated and then he rolled me so my back hit the ground.

A chill settled over me and it had nothing to do with the snow.

Something was wrong.

This was wrong.

"It's not wrong, Marie," Levi answered, his voice cold and menacing. "What is wrong is that you live without me. How could you do that to me, mate? How could you break our promise? For eternity, remember?"

I took a deep breath, staring up at my mate. His features sharpened, his eyes wild and raging.

"I remember."

"Good. Let's fix that, shall we?"

Then a blade appeared in his hand, his arm drawing back, before it surged down, aimed at my chest.

My body jerked with my scream, the sound scraping across my throat and exiting from my soul. Hands held me down and I fought against them, fought against him.

Marie.

Marie.

Marie.

My name on his lips, echoed from my dream.

For eternity.

For eternity.

For eternity.

Tears built in my eyes. I was going to die. He was going to kill me as he deserved.

I took a deep breath and relaxed into it. Ready for death, even if a part of me didn't want it. Ready to see him again, even if a part of me was haunted.

"Marie." A deep smooth octave sang out to me. "It's okay. I'm here, flower." Vanilla coated my nose and warmth filled my body as I was pulled into a chest. "Wake up, Marie."

Then everything became clear, but not as a crystal. It was clear like a well of tears poured from the truth of reality.

Clear that I was alive and missing a mate.

Clear that the only way to see him again was by fate.

The screams still sounded even though they weren't ripped from my throat. They sounded in my soul. Her sorrows a song of penalties, berating me on my many misdeeds.

They were loud and violent; a ballad of decay.

His body still and lifeless, fixed where my body should lay.

Shudders wracked me, and my tears flowed out along with my sobs.

I continued to cry out my anguished agony even as the picture of him fell fully away and all I had to do was open my eyes to see my father's warm blues.

I would rather be cold. When I was cold, *he'd* warm me. When I was cold, *he* was there. When I was cold, *for eternity* was still a promise I kept.

"Flower," my father whispered, his fingers trailing over my head.

My body jerked back as pain splintered over my skull and iron filtered through my nose. Blood, a lot of it. I brushed over my head, and I winced at another jolt of blissful pain.

I pulled my hand back and opened my eyes to see my hand tattooed with scarlet. Then I glanced to see my father's face taut with tension.

"It was an accident," I whimpered brokenly. My first sane thought was of preservation. All I could rationally focus on at this moment was that him seeing me like this could result in my small freedoms being taken away.

My father sighed, the sound weighted and full of pity. "I know, flower."

FOUR

CORIVINA

I made my way to the inn after my chat with Marie. My bones aching to be confined back into those four walls.

The inn held my hatred for Markos. My darkness stained into the walls just as my blood once stained the sheets.

It would be easy to just let Markos be, to ignore him as I'd always done, but that never aided me.

Markos took advantage of every freedom I gave him. He did everything to weasel his way back into my life. I wouldn't even be surprised if he commissioned a witch to bind my daughter to his son. What was it that he said again?

"You think we will be able to keep that a secret? They are mates, Cor. That means this *is forever."*

I wouldn't put it past him to stoop so low. So, there would be no more freedoms for him.

I hadn't contacted him, or even let him know I was coming, but I was sure he knew. I was sure the gods blanketed him with doom. Our children might have been fated together, but he and I were fated as well. Only, our fate was not of love but of blood and gore.

HEART COLD AS GOLD

This room fed the fire that burned within me. It kept the air of vengeance fresh and pumping into my veins. It kept my pain alive, and my darkness charred. I vowed that nothing would stop me from getting my revenge, and I meant it.

My partner in crime was not the king as Darius expected. I cared little for him outside this war. My darkness was my true partner. It had been with me most of my life, forming even before I was with Markos. It didn't want me anymore. No, now, it worked with me. The darkness still echoed out things in my ears, but now, they were whispers of retribution and revenge.

"A darkness will come then, sweep you up and show you all its horrors. When those horrors come, let your darkness in. It will protect you from succumbing to madness."

Another fated message. Another divine tragedy.

All my reckless actions were justified. My neglect for the people I cared for was justified. It was either this or madness. At least that was what I kept telling myself.

I pushed my worries away, walking over to the bed to reach under the pillow for the letter opener stained with Markos and I's blood. The blade was steel and the blood made it look rusted.

The sun streaming out of the window had the diamond on my finger glinting. Darius's words from the previous night floated in my ears, but I let them drift as I imagined the blood on the knife was real, and I was dressed in it.

I hadn't let myself break down, and my darkness held my worries in the confines of its walls, saving their tortures for a later date. When Marie crumbled, I erected those walls, and when she was whole again and Markos was dead, I'd let the horrors berate me. I had been drowned by the shadows over and over again and came out the other side. Even if I didn't come out the other side, it would be worth it. For my babe, it would be worth it.

Paper laid skewed across the desk in the corner of the room. I sat, keeping the letter opener close, and started reviewing my notes. The last five years had been spent calculating every which way possible for me to destroy Markos. To get good revenge was not about staying ten steps ahead of your enemy. To get good revenge was about staying in their blind spot, letting me be the last thing on Markos's mind.

He would never expect me to try to kill him. There was no denying that he knew me like no other did. He knew me when I was soft and fragile. He knew me before there were any walls erected. So he knew—more so, he thought he knew—that I would never kill a person, and I never had. He would be the first and the last.

As Markos knew me, I also knew him. I knew his strengths and his weaknesses. What he liked and what he loved. The load of useless information that was stored in my brain became useful again, and I was going to use it against him.

Besides his lust for me, King Dominick kept entertaining my drive for blood because of my intimate knowledge of Markos. Since the only person of equal power to Markos was Dominick, he would technically have to kill him, so I keep feeding him my trove of information to make that happen.

Killing a fae with magic often boiled down to their power level. If their system became too overwhelmed with magic, their body would fail and they would die—like what happened to the prince. There were the other ways, cutting an artery, the out flow of blood slowing the ability to heal, and poison, the berries from a faeshade plant—the plant used to create faerie dust—would do in a highly concentrated dose.

But Markos knew he had a target on his back, so he would be expecting that. Magic would be the only way, and one needed a great deal to go against a king.

I had a lot as I recently discovered over the last three years of training with Kolvin, but nowhere near enough, nor did I have great skill to use it.

I kept track of Markos's known movements over the last few years. The Unseelie Palace was once the hub for most all Unseelie fae. The Unseelie were pack people, a close-knit community with power divided somewhat evenly throughout the kingdom. Everyone lived either in the palace or in the Shadow Mountain Range. Over the last few years, Markos isolated himself, cutting away from the pack and forcing them out in the cold. The palace was closed off to all those who weren't of royal status or servants; even the students from the last sorting ceremony were being schooled in another part of the territory.

In my opinion, Markos closing himself from his people just made him look more guilty. The people on both sides wanted answers as to why he killed his son, and his refusal to speak on the subject just caused more tension between him and his people.

The Seelie were equally as agitated, but if we could turn the Unseelie people against Markos, this wouldn't be a war, it'd be a coup.

Accomplishing that would be a great feat. Even if the Unseelie were upset with their king, and the pack mentality being ingrained into them for generations, it would take a lot for them to go against him. Which was why this was leaning into another civil war.

The Seelie wanted answers, no matter what. King Dominick knew of the situation but for him to speak on it wouldn't be enough. Markos needed to be the one to speak on his crimes.

True to fae's nature to cause chaos, hate started to replace the peace that was settled between the fae, their beasts pacing within, ready for the fight. It took little reason for us to go to war and the small bloom of tension in the air had a lump sum of people joining the army to be a part of the blood bath.

Huffing, I tossed the notes back over the desk. Markos isolating himself made it hard to know what he was planning on, and then plan against it. It seemed like he was held up in a room somewhere in the palace, just waiting for the Seelie to strike.

Grabbing a fresh page of paper, I began plotting out strategies, taking inspiration from one of Darius's war books.

I spent the morning going over the text, looking for the secrets hidden between the lines of the page. I wanted this to go down in history, needed people to know my name and the wrath of a mother when her child is destroyed.

Fame was not my goal, but to demolish Markos as thoroughly as I desired. It would have to be so fucking grand that people had to talk about it. When they read about it, they would feel my fury, see my determination, smell the sweat and blood that I excreted. The whole ordeal being viscerally violent.

My fingers ached from writing by the time the sun was at its midpoint and I needed to move on with my day.

Changing into bland pants, a loose-fitting tunic and combat boots, I left the inn. The sun beat down harshly on my fragile skin as I followed the path to the training field. I was not one of the many fae to join the army in the hopes of blood. Ravens were solitary birds, and I didn't plan on joining a flock. Plus, it was a waste of time. If I was to join the war as a new recruit, I'd stay a private until the war was over. Darius wouldn't promote anyone until then, making sure one was serious about the army's efforts, and he knew I wasn't.

But if you are planning on killing someone who is stronger than you by both power and force, it would be dumb of you not to learn combat. I was shit at magic because I spent my training pining for that bastard to marry me and bring me home. I knew nothing about fighting because in Seelie, females had the option to opt out of physical training, and I thought I was going to be a queen one day, so why would I ever need to be physical?

I was an idiot as a faeling. I knew this.

Kolvin laid under one of the trees that boarded a field, reading a book on battles and snacking on an apple. Training had ended a couple hours ago, and I would meet him here after the fields had cleared. I didn't want anyone knowing I trained. I needed to be underestimated as I always had been. A weak female had no place in the war, but they all would pity me enough they'd let me in anyway. It was another reason to keep entertaining King Dominick. As of now, I was known as the Commander's Wife or the Seelie King's new whore. Both titles only value me as a docile female whose worth was only found between her legs.

"You're late, again," Kolvin muttered as he set his book down and stood. "Remind me why I am going behind Darius's back to train you, if you aren't even going to show up on time."

"You aren't going behind his back."

"You made me swear not to tell him, that seems like going behind someone's back."

"If he found out, he won't be pissed at you for not telling him. He'd just be mad at me for not asking him."

"And why didn't you ask him?"

Rolling my eyes, I pulled my hair back into a braid. "You are still young, your training is still fresh in your mind. You'd know all the shortcuts to gaining results in a fast amount of time. Plus, you're terrified of me, so I know you won't try and belittle or baby me because I'm a female."

Kolvin raised a finger. "One, I am not afraid of you. You just have that cold as fuck stare that no one wants to hold for too long. Two, what you just said was a load of bullshit. Darius trained me, meaning all the knowledge I know, he knows. We are preparing for war, training all the new recruits with a short timeline in mind, and Darius, *the most respectful person on this planet*, would never belittle anyone—let alone his wife."

An annoyed breath exited me. Spending all this time with Kolvin one-on-one meant there were a lot of barriers dropped between us. Before, Kolvin would never talk to me so openly, he'd stammer across his words before actually getting to the point. Now the male had grown a few balls, small ones, but they were big enough that he thought he could talk to me like one of his pals. "Kolvin, just stick to moping for my daughter and following her like a lost puppy, and stay the fuck out of my business if you want to keep your balls where they are."

His jaw tensed and his light-green eyes gleamed with malice. "I'm going to tell Darius, I don't like keeping shit from him. He's like a second father to me."

"Are you going to suck his dick too while you do it?"

"He needs it, since you are whoring yourself out to the king."

My eyes cut into him. I let my darkness flow within them just so that this boy could see how I wouldn't hesitate to drown him in it.

His throat bobbed before he hastily ran a hand through his hair. "Corivina, I didn't… I was just—"

I smirked. *Not afraid of me, my ass.* "It's a stressful time, Kolvin. It's hard to keep the façade that we are perfect beings at the moment. I won't hold it against you." I looked out to the horizon and the sun waning closer to the edge of the world. We only had a few hours before it tucked away, and the moon ruled the sky. "Let's start."

He rolled his neck, still uncomfortable with his past chosen words. What he said was uncalled for, but he loved Darius as much as I did. I wouldn't hold it against him for being on his side. He should be on his side. "Seriously, Kolvin, I could care less about my feelings at the moment. I want to train."

His lips pressed into a thin smile, and he gestured to the field. "Laps."

After training, Kolvin went back to the manor where he practically now lived. Instead of going with him, I decided to head back to the inn. I showered, changing back into my baby-blue sundress, and continued scouring through texts on past wars until the world was fully blanketed by the night and many slumbered in their beds.

A chill settled over me as I walked up the manor steps. It was summer so the territory was blazing, but an eerie feeling fell over me. I pulled out my key, glancing down to see a red rose lying down on the stoop. I kicked it to the side and opened the door.

The air was thick and pressing over my senses. Darius sat on one of the sofas in the main room, a drink in his hand. He wasn't much of a drinker; his extensive wine collection was actually a wedding gift to me. But the drink in his hand wasn't what had me sucking in a sharp breath, it was the blood, his white tunic covered in it.

I rushed over to him, my hands starting to scan his body, searching for any damage that was unable to heal. "What happened?"

Darius pushed my hands away, his angry eyes meeting mine. "Where were you today?" His tone was cold, detached, bordering on menacing.

I scanned the floor between us, avoiding the accusations churning in his eyes. He was my weak spot, and seeing him covered in blood blasted my darkness away. "I had some errands to do."

"They took the whole day?"

I brushed a strand of hair behind my ear. "Yes."

"And your errands were more important than your daughter?"

My eyes reconnected with his, the contact sending a sharp pain into my chest. "Did something happen?"

His answering chuckle was harsh. "Why do you think I'm covered in fucking blood, *Corivina*?"

Turning, I started my way to Marie's room, icelike fear starting to shoot in my veins, but before I could take another step toward her, Darius's hand wrapped around my arm in a bruising grip. "Don't pretend to care."

My eyes narrowed when I turned toward him. "I do care. She is everything to me."

He stepped closer to me, his face coming inches to mine, a muscle ticking in his jaw. "Then why the fuck weren't you here?"

I opened my mouth to reply, but all the excuses that ran through my head were just that, excuses.

He let go of my arm, turning away from me to grab his glass. He gulped back the rest of its contents before breathing out a heavy sigh. The sound made all my muscles tighten for some reason. "You are mornings, I am evenings, and Kolvin is nights. That's what we agreed upon five years ago when she wasn't even eating, but the second she showed signs of getting better, you left."

"I didn't leave. I'm still here."

He snorted, glaring at me. "Barely. You spend all your time out planning for your petty revenge."

"It's not petty. Markos destroyed our daughter. He needs to pay."

"Do you think she gives a shit about Markos when she can barely get through a week without having multiple breakdowns? Corivina, today I found her on the floor screaming and covered in blood. She got drunk on our wine, tripped and fell, cracking her head open. If you were here, instead of running *errands*, that would have never happened." He breathed in a guttural breath. "She could have died, Corivina, and you should have been here."

Staring off at the daisies that sat in a vase on the coffee table, I felt my darkness start to turn against me. The paint on those walls chipping, the bricks starting to fall. But I didn't let it consume me. Instead, my spine stiffened, and I ignored my feelings.

"A darkness will come then, sweep you up and show you all its horrors. When those horrors come, let your darkness in. It will protect you from succumbing to madness."

Vengeance grew profound, covering the pain that was etching itself deeper into my soul. The whispers probably would have worked if not for the whisper that exited Darius's mouth. "I want a divorce."

Nothing could have protected me from the pain that wrapped around my heart at those words. Not the walls that I kept up to keep me safe, not the promise of retaliation. Nothing.

My head snapped toward him. When I spoke, my voice was nothing but an exasperated breath. "What?"

Rather than repeating himself, Darius let the silence echo the words back to me.

Panic burned in my lungs, and I was falling, scrambling to stay up. "Darius… This…" My throat was filled with a gallon of honey, making it unable for me to breathe. "I know that things between us are fucked up right now… but it's temporary. After the war, everything will settle back to how things used to be."

He chuckled under his breath, the sound cold and stunted. "The way things used to be," he repeated. "Do you seriously think that the only problems in our marriage have occurred over the past few years? Corivina, our marriage has been fucked up for the past twenty-five."

Daggers cut into me, my emotions threatening to take me under. I shoved them back as far as I could, blinking back the tears that were trying to climb their way out of my eyes. "Darius, I just need—"

"What about what I fucking need, Corivina? I have always been there for you. You walked out on me, and I still stayed loyal to you. I worked to build our relationship back up for years, feeling immensely alone as you did everything to keep me shut out. I thought you would forgive me eventually and we could moved past the one time in our two-hundred years of marriage that I have ever fucked up. But you didn't forgive me. You said you did, but I realized that as time went on that you really hadn't. Then there was the shit with King Markos. You let me walk in there—you let our daughter live there—with the male that hurt you and you didn't tell anyone. Our daughter's life crumbled, and you stayed around until she started to talk again, then you left. I need you here, Corivina. I need you to help me keep our daughter alive. I need you to just—" He shook his head, his eyes shutting. "I can't do this anymore. I want a divorce."

"What about my daughter? Where is she—"

His eyes snapped open. "Our daughter. *Our daughter*, Corivina. I am her father; I have loved her as a daughter for her whole life. She is just as much mine as she is yours. This is her home, and she can stay here, and you can go to the palace and fuck the king like everyone already thinks, or you can go to the fucking inn. After all, this has never really been your home anyway."

His words were punches, stabs, hits, and jabs, having panic seeping its way through every orifice of my body. "Darius, I love you. This just isn't a good time for us, but after the war, we will work it out. After the war, I promise I will fix everything. I fucking promise."

"And what if I die in the war?"

My heart stilled and my eyes bored into those heated blues. "What?"

"Corivina, you are the one pushing for the war, but have you even stopped to think about how I will be the one fighting it? How I will be the one killing people all because you have a grudge with Markos?"

"It's not just me pushing for it."

His lips pressed into a thin line, his face shadowing in disappointment. "But in all your planning, you didn't think about me. You didn't think about what this could mean for me—your husband. I may be the commander, but I have never actually been in a war, Corivina. There's a chance we could lose, and a chance I might die, but that doesn't fucking matter to you as long as he dies as well."

I took a step toward him. "Darius—"

He held up a hand. "I'm tired, Corivina. Let's just sleep and talk about this when I'm not covered in our daughter's blood." His shoulders dropped like heavy weights pulled them down. He moved past me, making his way to the stairs, climbing them two at a time until he was out of sight, and I was left with his words still echoing in my ears.

I want a divorce.
I want a divorce.
I want a divorce.

FIVE

Karnelian

I stared at the gold grandfather clock, the ticking ringing in my ears, signifying every second I stand in here alone. *Tick, tick, tick.*

Whiskey burned in the back of my throat as I sipped on my third glass of the night.

Fifteen minutes. I showed up an hour late, and yet, that still seemed to not be late enough. Fifteen fucking minutes. I hated when people were late, but unfortunately, these people weren't ones I could demand to be on time and respect me, they were family after all.

The watch on my hand ticked a millisecond off from the clock and my senses gyrated at the inconsistency of it.

I was seconds away from letting my monster out to play and destroy the priceless artifact in front of me. But I wouldn't; instead, I took another sip of the whiskey, and I removed the watch I wore, crushing it in my palm before placing the crushed pieces in my pocket.

I made a mental note to show up an hour and a half later next month as I smoothed my blond hair back in the clean style I kept to maintain my image, but then the ticking continued to ring in my ears.

Snakes slithered in my lungs as I fought with myself. I was a monster. I might have been dressed in an impeccable suit and only drank the finest whiskeys, but I was a monster. Not enough alcohol could drown out what lurked under my skin. Every tick on that fucking clock reminded me of what I was, reminded me of why no one in my family respected my time—they weren't monsters. They didn't make shady deals and hold people under their mercy. They didn't do that—I did.

They were all sensible, their power wasn't gained, but in a way earned. Why would they respect the abomination they had to call a brother, or worse, *a son*.

My tongue slid across my mouth to my canine, and I bit down, letting my blood fuel my monster for just a second, and I made another mental note that I needed to let him play tonight. Locking him up more will just result in him acting out and adding to the chaos that the fae are already creating on a daily basis, and no one needed to see my monster pillaging the fae lands.

For the most part, I made sure to be connected to my monster, to see that side of me as not a separate being, but as myself. These stupid family dinners, though, just had a way of raising my blood pressure.

My family wasn't horrid, they were for the most part loving, but every time we were all together, it felt like all my muscles were being pulled from my body. The air was thicker, and the room heated to a boiling point that just had my monster pacing inside.

It always felt like there was another shoe about to drop, as if a demon was about to appear and cart me off to hell where everyone thought I belonged.

The click of the door unlatching had me turning my head to my brother entering the room.

I met the emerald-green eyes that mirrored our father's. A loose and lazy smile appeared on Fredrick's lips. "Brother!" He pulled me into one of his loving hugs, my body tight and rigid as he did so. I loved my brother, but I hated hugs. Still, I wouldn't be able to deny his hugs; he was my little brother after all.

He pulled away, looking up to me with that easy smile that was thankfully from his mother. Almost everything about him was from his mother, from his mahogany-colored skin to the tight black curls that he wore atop his head. Everything except those fucking eyes that alighted a slight rage every time I saw them. It's been sixty years since that rage fully flared within me and now it was just a flicker that I could easily douse when I remembered that these eyes were of my brother who I actually loved.

Fredrick walked over to get a drink from the cart, mixing some fancy drink he probably created that was extremely sweet and hid the taste of alcohol. His posture was slouched as he brought the pink foamy concoction to his mouth and took a sip. A drawn-out sigh escaped from him.

Fredrick embodied the title of *prince*. His clothing was luxurious and flashy, flaunting his wealth. His ego too big for most, bigger than his slender body that was not fit for battle but was perfect for gliding around the ballroom with his last conquest.

He wasn't a dick as one might assume by looks, but he was charming, too charming. That and the fact that he shared blood with me, made him one of my few soft spots.

"How are things, brother," I said in greeting.

"Annoying." He groaned, his eyes rolling, almost getting stuck in the back of his head. "Father is having me sit in during court. And after, he made me come up with a solution to everyone's problems. And, like, some people complain about the most ridiculous things! And I don't want to find a way to help annoying people, but then Father was like *this is what being a king is like and this will one day be my responsibility*. And stupidly, I replied with, 'But I didn't ask to be king!' and he made me scrub the whole courtroom floor with my toothbrush!"

I cocked my head to the side, ignoring the old pain that spiked in my chest at his words before speaking. "Fredrick, he has a point—"

"It's really annoying that you keep taking his side. You should be trying to plot our murder so you can rule!"

"If I murdered you, the people would be in an uproar."

He gave a wide princelike smile. "The people do love me, don't they?"

A light chuckle escaped me. "You are entertaining. I mean if you weren't around, who would sleep with the duke's son on the night of his wedding?"

He smirked, cocking his brow. "That is old news, brother. Have you not heard that I fucked the duke, and now he and his son are in a fight over me?"

"Son," my father said, entering the room. "You need to keep your dick in your pants."

Fredrick snorted. "I thought I was to create an heir for the throne?"

"Well, if you stuck your dick in females, then that would be useful in creating an heir, but you prefer males so all you're doing with that thing is causing problems in my court."

"It's not my fault your court lusts after my cock."

My father grumbled, walking over to the drink cart, and pouring a whiskey-neat—his preferred drink, another thing I inherited from him.

His head swung to me, his blond hair brushing his naked shoulders. "Karnelian, I have something I need you to do."

When does he not have something for me to do? "Hello to you too, Father. Yes, I've been well. How are you?" I said flatly, walking over to pour myself another drink to get me through this night.

"Karney, stop being a brat," Fredrick chimed. "That is my job as second-born."

My father ignored my comment as he always did and looked at Fredrick, changing the subject. "Is your mother coming?"

"No," Fredrick said as he plopped in a seat at the dining table that was covered with a gold cloth and set with fine glassware.

"Why this time?"

"She..." Fredrick tilted his head to one side, trying to find his words. "Hates you?"

The muscles in my father's back flexed with tension as he made his way to the head of the table. "Your mother doesn't hate me."

"Well, she doesn't love you." Fredrick's mother, Camila, despised my father because he never made her queen after she birthed my brother. She had a right to be mad because she was promised that, seconds before my father stuck his dick in her, but a whispered promise was still a promise, and if my father had any dignity when it came to others' feelings or worth, he would have upheld it.

"It's been seventy-seven years. She should be over it."

"Females hold grudges, Dominick," my mother said, entering the room. "You should really learn that before you end up with a knife in your heart."

My mother walked up to me, and I bent to press a light kiss in greeting to her freckled cheek. A piece of her chestnut-colored hair brushed against my skin that was dusted with those same freckles. Only, mine were lighter and barely noticeable, where hers were dark and gracefully scattered across her face.

"Maggie, you say it like it's bound to happen," my father replied.

My mother turned, making her way to the dining table, me following closely behind. "You aren't the best with females," I said, pulling out my mother's chair. "Aren't you fucking a married female who is clearly just using you to expedite the war?"

"We aren't fucking—yet—and their marriage has been crumbing for the last twenty or so years," my father refuted.

"And you think it's appropriate for you to be the pebble that makes them crumble?" my mother said as I took the seat next to her.

"You know I have these dinners to spend quality time with my family, but they always seem to be a way for all of you to accost me on my life decisions."

"Mommy number two has a point," Fredrick stated. "You talk about me keeping my dick in my pants when you're going to be the one who ruins the commander's marriage. Which is fucked up because marriage means, at one point, they really loved another, *deeply*."

My mother's brows raised to her hairline. "You're trying to bed the commander's wife?"

"Maggie, how do you not know this?" Fredrick asked.

"Well, I've been busy."

A sly grin cocked on my brother's lips. "Yes, riding Grayson's cock? Am I right?"

I choked on my whiskey, snapping my head to my mother, whose face was flushed red. "Grayson?" My eyes bore into her milky browns before they flicked away in embarrassment. My beast took the time to scent her, finding it scrubbed away with soap, but underneath, there were notes of my second-in-command that I never noticed. "Mother, him and I were sorted together. I've known him since I was a faeling, and he is my associate."

Her cheeks flushed red with embarrassment, a smile trying to break its way through her lips. "He is more than your associate, Karnelian. He is your second and you're his best friend. He's a nice male and I know it's weird, but... I've been thinking of settling down."

My father took in a sharp breath, it was subtle, but my eyes flicked to him, taking in his lips pressed together in a fake smile. My mother was his main female for about fifty years. I believe he was her first love since she was only twenty-five when she sired me. They would probably still be in love and if they hadn't had a hybrid freak for a son. My mother would have had a gold crown that matched my father's to adorn her head as well.

My father abruptly changed the subject again. "I need you to teach the princess magic." He wasn't looking at anyone directly as he took a drink of his whiskey, but everyone knew to whom he was talking to.

"Did you have another child we don't know about?" Fredrick asked.

My father scowled at my brother. "No, the Unseelie Princess."

My brain pinged with the image of a girl in a gold dress, but was quickly morphed into a female dressed in black from neck to toe, her face stained with tears, whispers sounding in my ears. "You mean the girl who last I saw was broken beyond repair because her mate died?"

"She isn't as broken now," my father retorted.

"And you want me to teach her?"

"You're the only one who could."

"You have Unseelie employees."

"Yes, but I don't trust them, nor are they as qualified."

I leaned back in my chair, my eyes turning to slits as they met dazzling emeralds. "Do I have any say in the matter?"

"I am asking you as my son, but if you say no, I will demand as your king. It's important that she knows magic, and I promised her mother I'd have you teach her."

A snort sounded from me as I finished the whiskey in my glass, letting it burn through me and settle the monster who wanted to rip those green orbs from their sockets. "That female better have the best pussy in the fucking world for you to be so whipped."

"*Karnelian,*" my mother hissed.

I rolled my shoulders, ignoring my mother and calming my beast before saying, "Fine, I'll do it, but what do I get in return?"

"The devil and his deals." My brother snickered, his grin sharp, probably relishing in the chaos that was about to brew. There was always a rush of excitement when one made a deal, especially if one had to give something of great value to get the other to yield.

My father eyed my brother, a muscle in his jaw flexing before he turned back to me. "What do you want?"

A wicked smile painted my lips. I had already been planning on this one for weeks. "Rico."

"You've got to be fucking kidding me," my father muttered.

"Rico or no deal."

"Karnelian, I'm your king, it's not a deal."

I cocked my head, my devil mask covering my face as I looked at my father. "Well, the quality of which I teach her depends on whether or not you give me Rico."

His inhale was sharp before he emptied his glass and leveled his eyes on me. They reflected the same thing they always did, the same word repeating in my head as I had to look within them. *Abomination.* "Fine."

With a mischievous smile on my face, I reached over the table to steal my brother's drink, taking a sip of the overly sweet concoction, and running my tongue across my teeth before saying, "Deal."

SIX

MARIE

The heels of my boots tapped the marble floor. The hallway I walked down was painted white to match the title, gold accents, and decals lining the walls. The royal Seelie emblem—two sunflowers overlaying a sun—a gold casting of it embedded on the walls every few paces.

The room was cold, not because it was magically cooled, but because there was something about gold that was just so cold, immovable, stiff, heavy. It was an ironic way to describe the Seelie because they are so weighted down by trying to be the perfect race, trying to force down their creatures and snuff out their chaos.

I hadn't been to one of the Seelie King's parties in years. From what I remember of them, they were a time when the Seelie fae succumbed to debauchery, letting their beast roam and creating chaos. Many scandals happen at these parties. Tons of bad decisions made, to be scrutinized over later. The memory of it was enough to perk up the beast within, my core squeezing tightly at the idea of getting drunk and letting loose, and also getting fucked.

The coldness of this hall and the stiff backs of my parents in front of me stifled those wants. Tonight, I was going to be watched, and pitied, and treated as a babe.

My arm was cinched in Kolvin's. He held me tight as if afraid to let me go. My father tense, pulling at his collar and fidgeting as we walked, not holding his usual soldier's emotionless persona. My mother silent but poised in her grace as if she always belonged in a palace, and I supposed she always did.

Kolvin's eyes flicked to me every few seconds, waiting for me to break down. I couldn't blame him. After my last breakdown, which led to a scar that was covered with powders at the moment because it hadn't healed fully, everyone watched me like a hawk as I predicted.

The air around me had thickened over the last few days, laying heavy on my shoulders, and clogging up my throat. They were always around, my only free time, my morning bath, and my only freedom was achieved from the quiet attained from blue shimmery powder.

My mother started staying home on her shift, sitting in the corner. A book rested in her hands, but her hard black eyes would never flick to it. They stayed pinned on me, my mother's thoughts loud, but never revealing. The room, physically peaceful, but energetically, a warzone. A warzone I had to endure every morning without any wine or extra dust to haze out the mayhem.

She would leave me feeling exhausted and my father would come to fill her empty space. His eyes warm and comforting but filled with pity. So much pity, too much pity. He shouldn't worry over me, for I cared very little of myself or my well-being and neither should he.

Thankfully, he didn't stare, but he talked. Sometimes of his day, or of times when he was younger, the stories always happy and uplifting. He talked and talked and talked, making my ears feel like they were about to bleed. The only plus side was that there was no way I'd fall asleep.

The night was the worst part. Kolvin would arrive and remove his shirt, his sculpted chest being revealed, along with his tan skin. He'd climb into bed and tuck me into that chest, my ass pressed up against his cock. It was always soft, but I wished for it to harden. Then guilt would plague me, along with the screams of my soul. Kolvin's soft snores would soon brush the hairs on my neck, tickling ever so slightly, sending shivers traveling down my spine, straight to my clit. Eight hours of battling my heat and tuning out the torments of my soul. Eight hours of his breaths, seven thousand two hundred and thirty-two of them would pass, then the sun would rise, and I would be forced to do it all again.

Which was why I was actually excited to be here at the palace. I hoped maybe my parents would need to talk to the king or something and leave me alone with Kolvin. He was much easier to sway than them, always willing to bend for me. A part of me hated his pining, hated the pain I knew it caused. Though, that part was buried under a thick sheet of ice that was wrapped around my heart, and so I couldn't bring myself to care. I'd use him tonight, not caring for the pinprick of guilt that would be added to my already massive debt. Tonight, I wanted to drown in the free wine my mother promised, and maybe see G and acquire a hit of dust.

Normally, my family would enter through the commoner's entrance. My father not really caring for his place amongst the court, or his high status. *But* I was a princess, so we had to enter from the top of the stairs and be announced like all the rest of the royalty.

My father and mother were announced. No one really turned their head to look at the commander, then it was our turn to step into view.

"The Unseelie Princess, Marie Shadawn, and General Kolvin Denmor!" My ears ringed at the announcer's dramatically loud voice, my body tensing and my creature wanting to attack, but as Kolvin guided me down, my senses focused on the crowd, every eye glued on me.

They'd see a girl who wore one of my dresses that my mate bought me, covering me neck to toe. The turtleneck collar and sleeves were a sheer netted material with snowflakes embroidered on them. The main slip of the dress, a thick black material that cinched in at the waist and trailed down my curves. Two slits cut through the sides, starting at the top of my thighs and exposed my sheer stockings that matched the other embroidered lace. And because I refused to wear heels, no matter how short I was, black combat boots were my shoe of choice.

Those eyes trailed my body, but most settled on the steel tiara that adorned my head. This wasn't my tiara, the style of it Seelie and delicate. A gift from the Seelie King. My tiara was left at home, in Unseelie, last seen on the floor of the royal dining room, after falling off my head from my excessive thrashing to escape my father's hold.

Many whispers were passed as those eyes stayed trained on me, rumors of what happened to me and my mate. They kept saying his name, over and over again.

Prince Levington.
Prince Levington.
Prince Levington.

My body grew tighter, claws digging into Kolvin's jacket. The over lit room burned my irises and my canines pierced into my tongue but unable to draw blood.

When my boots touched the ballroom floor, my eyes locked onto a waiter, carrying a tray of red magenta liquid akin to the color of blood.

The noise muffled, the eyes shadowed. I let go of Kolvin, letting my feet carry me to that waiter.

Throat dry, saliva lining my mouth, my fingers wrapped around a glass, and my mouth met the rim, gulping back the tart liquid until there was nothing left. The buzz that entered my body wasn't nearly enough to achieve the silence and bring me peace, but for now, it would do.

Quickly setting the glass on the waiter's tray, I grabbed another, hoping two was enough to drown my senses that were still peaked and wired.

"Marie." My mother's voice cut through, sharp and harsh, aggravating my beast immensely.

After a rough exhale, I turned back to see her, my father, and Kolvin standing next to the king and his two sons. All their eyes on me, but only my mother's hard and probing.

"That isn't any way to greet a king," she gritted through her teeth.

My feet dragged as I walked over to them. My fingers clutching the glass as I dreaded talking to anyone, let alone this king. He wore a gold crown. His straight blond hair shoulder-length and his tanned torso on display. He was known for never wearing a shirt along with his ridiculous pants. Today, he wore white leather pants, which wasn't as bad as I'd seen.

It was silent between everyone for a moment as I just stared at the king.

"You're supposed to show your respects to the king when he comes close to you." My eyes meet with steely hazel eyes that I remember cutting into me as I begged for death. Karnelian Lightfire, the Uncrowned Prince, the Silver Blooded Devil, the male willing to make a deal over anything.

A hybrid, a rare race of fae, rarer than fae mates, and a curse in the eyes of our people, an abomination.

My eyes flicked back to the king. "Why?"

"Because," my mother chimed in, voice polite but holding an edge. "The king allows you to live here from the graciousness of his heart. You are Unseelie and you aren't sworn to him, so it would be expected of you to show respect."

"Well." I took another sip of my wine. "I don't want to live at all, so his graciousness is really just a disturbance to me."

Tension settled in the air for a beat at my blatant disrespect to the king. The tension stemmed from my mother, but it didn't bother me. I mean, did they seriously think I would care to show anyone a modicum of respect when I didn't even care to get out of bed?

The king's chuckle rumbled, breaking the silence as he smiled down at me. The smile was forced, but not in an annoyed way. The smile was more as if he was desperate for me to like him, instead of the other way around. "It's nice to meet you, Marie."

I had already met him many times, but I guess before, I didn't really matter. I give a slight nod—a sign of respect between races—so this interaction could end, and I could down the glass of wine in my hand. Thankfully, the king got the memo and moved to my mother and father.

I took a huge drink, catching those hazel eyes again. A smirk painted on the male's lips as we shared a secret moment.

"Commander, Corivina, it's nice to see you again," the king said.

"Sir." My father nodded, which coming from him was a sign of disrespect. My father was the type of male who would give a proper greeting to those who he respected, but he didn't even offer the male his hand.

"Your Majesty." My mother bowed ever so gracefully and flawlessly, also out of character for her. She was not the type of person to bow low, normally a quick and short bow, respectful but not cajoling in anyway. Which by the greedy smile gracing the king's lips and his hooded eyes, she was doing a great job of flattery.

"You remember my sons," the king replied, talking directly to my mother. "Fredrick and Karnelian."

Fredrick stepped forward. My head cocked to the side as I took in his outfit. He... was wearing... a sheet. Or maybe a robe? White fabric wrapped across his body, clasped at certain areas with gold pins, showing off most of his flesh, his skin tone a shade or two darker than mine. He wore gold sandals with the sheet and his circlet, a gold branch that just wrapped around half of his head.

The prince said hello to my parents before stepping next up to me and extending out his hand. I let the male take it, tensing, as he brought it to his lips to press a soft kiss.

It took a deep breath in to settle my creature's need to jump this male, fuck him and tear that sheet into threads. I wiped the back of my palm on my dress. His sweet chuckle soon followed. "Don't worry, I don't play for your team." His emerald eyes gleamed as he took in Kolvin behind me. "But I do play for his. Are you two...?" The prince used his eyes to connect me and Kolvin together.

I snorted, almost smiling at the male. "Uhm, no."

His brows flicked up. "Fun."

"Fredrick, keep your dick in your pants." My eyes found the devil again, but this time, he didn't look at me. My eyes turned into slits as I realized he wore black—very unregular for Seelie. In fact, every time I had ever seen him, he wore black as if to remind the Seelie what other color swirled within his veins. He, unlike his father and brother, dressed normally in a plain suit. He didn't wear a crown over his short blond hair that was slightly longer on the top and shorter on the sides. As a prince, it was his right to wear one, but I suppose he chose not to. With or without a crown, they would all know who he was and the power he held.

The devil looked at my father, nodding in respect. "Commander." Their hands shook in greeting; my father's respect for this male more apparent by the soft smile on his face. The devil glanced to my mother, his head cocking to the side, a frown painting his lips. "Corivina, it's nice to see you not grinding against my father's dick."

My mother's head swung to me, her eyes bulging and studying me for a reaction I did not give because I did not care. Old Marie would care; I could feel her trying to replay the devil's words and try to see what filtered through my mother's eyes, but it was easy to shut her out. All I wanted was for this interaction to be over so I could grab another glass of wine and maybe find someone dealing dust.

The devil grunted. "You look to her," he hummed. "How interesting."

My mother broke eye contact with me to glare at him, her nostrils flaring, but she attempted a smile in a show of peace that ended up looking more like a grimace. "Karnelian," she said, her voice sharp and curt.

A grin broke across his face—wicked, doused in chaos that had my creature perking up and wanting to revel in it with him.

He moved on to me, towering over me with his large height. "Little bird, looks like we will be getting to know each other." His voice was sultry, coating a person lusciously and drawing my creature out further. Heat flared within me, brighter than any other male I'd interacted with since it began, the devil's madness calling out to mine.

I brought my unfinished glass of wine to my lips, downing it in seconds. The male had already thrown out pleasantries by outing my mother's adultery.

I licked my lips, tasting in the few droplets that fell before I replied, "I guess so."

He snickered, eyes churning with devilry or maybe his eyes always churned with it and that was why they called him the devil. "Care to dance?"

I glanced at everyone else, my mother's eyes screaming no, my father's reflecting his want to be anywhere else. The king looked annoyed with his son. Fredrick eyed Kolvin as Kolvin looked at me with a possession he had no right to.

My options—stay and continue in this annoyance, or dance with the devil?

Another server passed with wine, and I switched glasses, quickly downing the drink and handing it to Kolvin.

Then I met steely hazels and shrugged.

SEVEN

CORIVINA

I scowled as Marie walked away hand in hand with Prince Karnelian. Every time I interacted with that male, he made me hate him more and more. If he wasn't the only viable option to teach my flower magic, I wouldn't try to keep the pleasantries. Nor would I allow him anywhere near my daughter. The male called himself the devil, a human archetype that meant nothing to the fae. It was ridiculous and absurd, and I didn't want anything to do with him and his dealings, but the gods were cunts who loved to watch me suffer.

"Can I speak to you two in private?" Dominick's voice broke my brooding, and my head turned his way.

"Me and Darius?" I asked.

His emerald-green eyes sparkled, a slight smirk gracing his lips. "For now, yes."

Darius's irritated breath was low, his jaw set tight and eyes staring daggers at the king.

My reaction was purely instinct as I looped my hand through his arm, squeezing lightly in comfort. Those eyes met mine and I silently told him everything would be okay. We would be okay.

The king meant nothing to me; he had to know that. He had to know I loved him and only him and I wanted to spend my whole life with him. We just had to get through the war, and all would be right.

Those irises burned brighter in response. A blue flame that spoke words I never wished to hear again. *I want a divorce, Corivina.* They seared into me, trying to rip me apart, but that couldn't happen, not now.

Tearing my eyes from his, I met Dominick's, plastering on a fake smile and pushing down the emotions I felt from the blazing blues. "Lead the way."

We followed Dominick to a private room that held a three-dimensional map of the faerie territory atop a large table; little figurines scattered across the expanse.

Dominick walked over to the map. Darius shook off my arm and followed, his hand covering his mouth, eyebrows furrowing as he studied the contents.

"Darius, I just read your reports of more soldiers lining the wall," Dominick stated as he pointed at the diamond wall figurine, little black pieces standing near it on the Unseelie side. "And they seem to have more soldiers stationed around Lightwood and the Neutral Territory. Do you have any idea of what they could be planning?"

Darius rubbed the stubble on his chin. "Most of the army is stationed in Lightwood. Maybe they plan on taking a few of us out before war breaks."

"I thought that, but my spies tell me the males aren't normal soldiers. They are Neeki."

I frowned, moving over to Darius to get a better look at the map, him shifting slightly away from me as I asked, "The Neeki?"

Dominick looked at me, his eyes doting and patronizing. "They are fae who are skilled in magic and battle, expertly so. Not many know of them because they are often chosen directly by the king and go into intensive training. In fact, Darius was one."

My head turned to Darius. "You were?"

He inhaled heavily. "I am technically still one. I'm just also the commander. I was enlisted as one before my brother died, and well, when he did, I had to step up and leave. The Neeki and the army are separate entities. The Neeki are mostly only used during war or in disastrous times, so I wasn't able to stay and complete training. I've been teaching Kolvin most of their fighting techniques since he was fourteen or so when I gave up hope that Marie would be the one to relieve me of my position. The skill has definitely come in handy as commander and I think he should be selected as one, but I have no control over that." Darius gave Dominick a pointed look.

"Why didn't you ever tell me?"

That pointed look leveled on me. "Because our relationship was always about you."

I couldn't help the slight shiver that stole over me at his words. Was, not is, was. He talked as if we weren't still married, as if I still didn't wear his ring and him mine.

He stared at me for a moment, watching the shot land and stab into my cold heart, forcing it to beat with his blistering heat. A muscle ticked in his jaw as he saw me do what I'd done every time he tried to evoke a reaction from me for the past few years. I shoved the emotions down and rebuilt that wall, hoping that when I did finally let it down, I wouldn't implode.

"Anyways," he continued. "If they're Neeki, they are probably trying to figure a way around the wall without detection."

"They would need a lot of Seelie magic to balance themselves out. Especially with the number of soldiers reported there," Dominick pointed out.

"Or a lot of ore," Darius replied.

"What do you mean?"

"What are their top three trades? Rich soil, steel, and ore. I've been checking the trade reports for the last five years. The amount of steel and ore has gone down. That would make sense with more males joining the army and preparing for war, but the amount of soil has gone up. It's been slow. If you were just looking at the monthly reports, you wouldn't notice, but as a whole, you can see there might have been possible tampering. I wasn't sure of it, but with this new information…" Fae were designed to come together to balance out their magic, but we soon figured an alternative was using ore—crystals—that have the similar properties to our counterparts. Darius was suggesting that the Unseelie were pushing out other trades to keep us distracted as they slowly started to withhold the two trades most valuable in the war.

Dominick stared at Darius, his eyes calculating the information before he swiped at the table, knocking over a few figurines. "*Fuck.*" He looked out the window to the star scattered sky. "I need to get in contact with Markos immediately."

Darius shrugged. "Yeah, that might help."

"He hasn't fucking answered any of my portal mirror summons or any of my letters."

"Why do you need to contact him?" I interjected.

"He is about to attack our people, Corivina. I need to tell him not to," Dominick snapped.

"Isn't that what we want?"

"That is what you want." He started to make his way over to the desk that sat under the window. "I want to keep the peace like any good king would."

"What? But we've…"

Dominick searched through the drawers as he replied, "War isn't the best option for our people, Corivina. I do care for you, and I am sorry about what Markos has done to you and your family, but I would never willingly let my people die just for justice of one female I feel for." He pulled out a piece of parchment and a pen, beginning to scribble something on it.

My nostrils flared, blood heating my cheeks, my darkness whispering of vengeance and a female betrayed. "The war is going to fucking happen. The people are too antsy for it, not just Seelie but Unseelie too. Trying to stop it now will be just useless. Instead, we should be planning out a defense to the pending attack."

Darius snorted but remained quiet at my side.

Dominick brushed his hand through his hair. "My soldiers are sworn to me, they do not act unless I say so. No battles will riot without my word. Corivina, I am not arguing with you over this. As king, I will do everything in my power to protect my people before I declare war."

I crossed my arms, embarrassment coloring my face. I knew what he was saying was valid, but I didn't want to hear it. This was a way for me to see Markos dead. The vision of seeing his cold lifeless body on the ground was the only thing that kept me from succumbing to darkness when I saw Marie shatter. I needed him dead, and I was willing to let hundreds die for that to happen and I couldn't find it in myself to care.

Dominick glanced at me after he finished his writings. A breath exited him before he got up and walked over to me. Those green eyes stared into me, something akin to affection lighting them as he whispered, "We can talk about this later, okay?"

There definitely wouldn't be a later with us. Yes, I danced and flirted with him, but that was all for gain and he knew that. Dominick was a nice male, but I had no real interest.

Gritting my teeth, I let my eyes turn to their natural cold, no emotion reflecting in them. Dominick's eyes softened further, saying something that I couldn't decipher as I kept my detached stare aimed at him.

After a tense silence, he gave up and turned to Darius, whose features were hard, a mask covering the rage that simmered underneath. "We need to get this to Karnelian." Dominick waved the letter in his hands.

Darius nodded, getting to business like the good soldier he was, the two exiting out the door with me following close behind.

When we entered the ballroom, Kolvin spotted us and headed over. "I lost Marie."

Panic bubbled in my chest, my wall of darkness weakening. "How did you lose her?"

"I was watching her with the devil, and I got distracted for just a few moments. When I looked back, she was gone."

"She was with another male, and you got distracted? *You*, of all people, took your eyes off her while she was with another male?" I sneered.

"Corivina, he is not her guard dog," Darius interjected.

My head snapped to him. "You were just giving me shit about not watching her a few days ago, but your prized soldier doesn't even get a slap on the wrist when he loses our daughter in a place unknown to her?"

"You're her mother. He is just a friend doing us a favor."

I growled, irritation climbing up my throat. "The boy spends every second of his free time worshiping the ground she walks on, you'd think he wouldn't fucking lose her."

"Kolvin is a grown male, a general. I didn't give him the command to watch her while we were gone, and he was free to do as he pleased. We are at a party; he's allowed to live a little. He can't just throw his whole life away and for someone who doesn't even want to live."

My wall dropped then, and I pointed my finger at him. "Stop fucking saying that! She is not herself. She isn't the daughter I fucking birthed and gave everything to raise. She is not my flower or my babe. The girl who keeps saying she'd rather be dead is not her. Marie wants to live; I fucking know she does because she was my everything before Markos ruined her. *I will get her back*, Darius. So, stop fucking saying she wants death because she doesn't!"

Darius's hand curled around my pointed finger, pushing it down so it was no longer aimed at him. "Corivina, she is never going to be the girl we raised. The sooner you see that, the sooner you'll see that your efforts toward the war is just wrecking all that you had built over the last two hundred years. You may get what you want, his head detached from his body, but what will you be left with when it's over?"

My teeth ground together at his question. My emotions a storm, the clouds black and heavy. It took everything to rein the emotions back, but I did.

I hadn't lost everything, I hadn't. I just fucking needed more time. "We just need to find Marie right now and then you can lecture me later."

"I'm... right here." Marie's sweet voice chimed my ears. My head swung to hers, my body tensing as I saw those eyes, but it was overshadowed by immense relief as I saw my babe.

My feet were moving before I could even think, my arms wrapping around her. She stiffened but I didn't care because Darius was wrong. I hadn't fucking lost her. She was still there, and I would get her back.

EIGHT

MARIE

Karnelian's calloused hand held mine as he guided us to the center of the ballroom. People eyed us, whispering their gossip over me and the devil, the only two in this room dressed in black.

Music sounded in the background, a soft melody playing that was easy to sway to as Karnelian's other hand came around my waist and we started to move about the floor.

We didn't speak for a moment, the both of us studying another. Up close, I could see things easily overlooked about him. A light dusting of freckles adorned his nose and cheeks, making his gruff features less intimidating. His scent was of cinnamon and whiskey, sweet with a hint of sour. The scent clogging up my nose and shoving down my throat, my creature adoring every second of the torture. His hazel eyes, more green than brown, and that green shimmered with glimmers, just like his blood did the night he extended my life.

My body grew tighter with need. It would probably be impossible not to. He was more male than any other male in here, more powerful, strong, and handsome. All characteristics that would make any female's creature roll. But there was this sameness within him that was in me, that madness I recognized before. He wasn't insane like me, but he was erratic and that was noted by my beast, selecting him to be the perfect male to soothe my heat.

For the first time in five years, I was the one starting mindless chatter in the hopes to distract my brain from my sexually deprived body.

"Kar-kneel-ian." I tasted his name on my lips. "Who names their child after a stone?"

He smirked, looking up to think for a moment. "Onyx... Opal."

"Opal is a terrible name."

"True, but your name is Marie which means merry, and you're not a very merry person."

"It means marry, as in marriage, it's human. And I was... I was quite merry once," I said, feeling the echo of myself ring within my bones, reminding me that I lost more than just my mate when he died.

"Ah, yes. *Your whole personality*. You had a mate and being mated was the only thing you could possibly offer this world."

Anger flared in my chest, but it was soon placed with confusion and maybe a bit of awe as I realized that I hadn't felt anger in quite some time. Sadness, yes, but not anger. "You know, you're quite a dick."

"Yes, well. That's what I offer the world."

"Your dick?"

His lips twitched. "I suppose I have pleasured a few females in my days."

I gave a half snort in reply.

"You should thank me," he stated, expertly guiding me as the music changed tune.

"Why?"

"Because I saved you from that disaster."

"I'm pretty sure you are the one who caused it."

His smile was sinful, his eyes flashing with anarchy before he said, "Did I?"

"Yeah, you did."

"Your mother is the one entertaining another male," he remarked.

My brows knitted together. "Guess you're correct."

That smile turned cat-like, his eyes smoldering. "Looks like I win."

"What do you win?"

"You will owe me something."

My lips formed into a frown. "I didn't make a deal."

A small chuckle escaped him and gyrated against my bones. "Look at that, the little bird knows who she is dealing with."

I rolled my eyes at the nickname. It was the third time this night he called me that, and it was three times too many. "Everyone knows who you are."

He leaned down, his mouth brushing my ear as he whispered, "On the contrary, no one knows me. That's why they all get swindled and call me the devil."

I had to grit my teeth against the wave of arousal that overtook me as his heated breath caressed my skin. "So, what do you want?"

"I always want something, but this time, it will be simple."

I raised my brow, waiting for him to speak.

"A question."

"Those are free, you know."

"I can ask, and you can choose not to answer, or you can lie." His thumb slowly rubbed the back of my palm, stealing my focus. "I want the truth."

"Okay, so… what do you want to know?"

He raised a blond brow. "You'll answer honestly?"

"I might leave if you don't just get to the point."

He clicked his tongue. "Impatient little bird, you'd think you didn't have all the time in the world."

I growled, narrowing my eyes at the reminder of our first conversation five years ago.

His eyes shimmered with triumph, the ends of his lips tipping up. This male definitely liked pissing people off. "Do you want to be queen?"

My head cocked to one side. "Really? That's your question? All that buildup for that?"

He shrugged. "So, your answer?"

The answer was not hard. "No." Even before I was mated, I never desired to be queen, and when I was, I was only going forward with it because I had my mate at my side, and I knew it was something he wanted.

The devil cocked his head, thinking for a moment, then continued to move us along the dance floor.

"Nothing to retort my answer?"

"At a later date," he replied. "We will be seeing each other a lot, remember? I'm going to be teaching you magic."

"I'm so excited," I said, tone flat. "Considering how quickly you seem to get to the point, I might actually die before you teach me a single spell."

He laughed, my body growing tighter at the sound. He wasn't even trying to arouse me, but my creature didn't care who fucked us and as long as someone did, *soon*.

"I want to teach you combat."

"No."

"No?" He frowned playfully.

"No, I don't care to learn combat."

"Unfortunately, little bird." He let go of my waist and spun me, causing a gasp to escape from my mouth in surprise. I crushed into his hard body, my eyes locking with his and my core clenching painfully with need. I swallowed when his face came down only inches away from mine and he whispered, "I'm in charge."

I bit my lip in indecision. My brain fogged because my heat had grown scorching, overwhelmingly so. All my thoughts were on how close he was to me, how far away his lips were, how his scent was fully suffocating me and how I wanted to drown in it. He wasn't even my type, the exact opposite of my mate, but I think that's why I wanted him.

My brows crawled together, a frown forming on my lips. *I wanted him? No, I didn't want him. My creature did.*

"What is it, little bird?" he whispered. His voice was huskier than before, or maybe my imagination was making it seem that way.

I opened my mouth, but no words came out as I stared into his hazel eyes. My throat closed, locking, as I realized I did want him, and guilt, gut-wrenching guilt, consumed me.

How could I betray my mate like that? It felt like I was cheating on him, abandoning my promise to him to even truly consider taking another male, and I was doing it all night. In the back of my head, I was thinking of taking the devil to bed.

I don't truly want this male, I told myself. I just wanted to be free of the burning heat that was alive in my core. The deep arousal that only a male could soothe. I didn't want to bring my lips to his and fuck him deeply. I wanted my mate, only him, for—

I sucked in a harsh breath as tears built behind my eyes, panic crawling its way up my spine. My lip wobbled, my emotions escalating to new heights as I stared into the devil's eyes.

His brows furrowed, not understanding what was happening, but he didn't panic. Instead, he pulled me closer, looking around at the crowds of people. We had been dancing long enough for the gawkers to move on to the next thing, so no one noticed as we moved closer to an exit.

In the darkened hallway, which clearly wasn't meant for commoners to pursue, the devil loosened his hold, allowing me to walk on my own, but his arm remained around my waist, guiding me.

The devil used his magic to open the non-descript door. The room was small, lounge chairs and sofas in the middle, bookcases filled with dusty books lining the walls. The glow of the moon streaming through the windows the only light in the room.

I took a seat in one of the chairs, my head falling into my hands as my rapidly beating pulse became the only sound I could register.

The tears that filled my eyes started to spill, my soul's screams wailing as I did everything not to hear her turmoil. I was seconds from losing, from falling in her trap again.

Why the fuck didn't I bring dust with me?

The devil waved a glass in my face, the sweet-sour smell of whiskey filling my nose. "This will make it better."

I didn't believe him, but I took the glass, gulping down it back. Fire burned down my throat, the sensation seeping into my body and spreading through my limbs. I focused on the sensation, letting the pain be my anchor and the alcohol muddy my thoughts.

When I gained a semblance of myself, I realized how close he was. He crouched before me, like the time I begged him for death and he didn't deliver. That desperate feeling filled me, pushing to beg him again because now, only he could.

My mouth parted, ready to do so, but he stopped me, his finger coming over my lips, his eyes boring deeply into me. "What a pretty little bird in a pretty little cage. A cage you will not escape, Marie, not anytime soon."

His finger left my mouth, but his eyes still pierced into me, the moonlight making them shine silver. "This species is dependent on your survival. If you did kill yourself, the Unseelie King wouldn't have an heir with a war directed straight at him, and if he died, our people would be thrown out of balance. The kings hold way too much power unnaturally, and they need to stabilize each other. If you die and King Markos dies, then that magic will be lost, and my father will be unbalanced and extremely powerful. That power could corrupt him, or it could corrupt my brother when he becomes king or any of the future Seelie leaders. With one powerful king, the Seelie could overrun the Unseelie, killing them off. And if the Unseelie dies, the Seelie die as well. We are creatures of chaos, little bird. We aren't sensical when it comes to what we want. You want to die, but you don't see the destruction your mate's death alone has caused. I get it, everyone around you can see it, and they understand. We may have not met our mates, but we don't need to have been mated to understand. You ache without the other half of your soul. You feel incomplete and you don't want to live. But you cannot die. You have to wait till King Markos has an heir or you have to kill him and have an heir yourself."

My nostrils flared, more tears falling on my cheeks at the thought of being forced to live another day.

Karnelian wiped them, his fingers featherlight and gentle. Something so unexpected from a male who called himself the devil. He pulled the glass out of my hand, replacing it with another that he had placed on the side table. "You need to keep busy. Sitting around all day will just keep reminding you of the loss. The training and combat will help. At times, it hurts, but there are goals you can focus on."

I sniffled. "It will hurt?"

His brows pulled together. "Yes."

"Will you teach me to use my claws?"

His face scrunched up more.

"Anyone who has ever trained me has never let me use my claws in combat."

He smiled, the smile soft and lacking his devilish persona I met in the ballroom. "Okay, but you owe me."

A growl exited me, annoyance clouding my sadness. "I'm doing what you asked of me in order for you to teach me with my claws. That seems like a fair deal."

"That is a fair deal, but you owe me for getting you out of the ballroom when you were going to break down and also stopping said breakdown from happening. So really you owe me two things, but I'll only take one because you are feeling a bit under the weather." He smirked, the devilry unfortunately coming back to the surface.

My scowl deepened. "It was your fault I was going to break down. You were making me—" I cut off.

Curiosity etched into his features, his head tipping to one side. "I was making you what?"

I blew out an annoyed breath. "Fine, what do you want?"

He grinned wide and bright, his canines flashing before he spoke. "To be determined at a later date."

"To be determined at a later date?" I gritted out through my teeth, irritation building in my middle.

He nodded, that smug smile still ghosting his lips.

"I think I absolutely hate you," I said.

He snorted. "Wouldn't be the first, little bird, and won't be the last."

NINE

MARIE

The devil and I exited the study, walking down the hall, no words being exchanged. I noticed that he didn't seem uncomfortable by the silence, nor uncomfortable with me. I had bawled my eyes out in front of the male twice, and he didn't feel the need to swaddle me like my family did. He just handled it as if it meant nothing to him, which I guess as the devil, he wasn't one to care, but something about his stoicism was refreshing.

We walked back into the ballroom, the noise the same level of loud, but for some reason less jarring as I walked with the devil. It was easy to spot my parents, who were joined with the king, because they were arguing. As we grew closer, it was apparent that they were arguing over me.

"We just need to find Marie right now and then you can lecture me later." An old pain tried to sting in my chest. The reminder of how many fights my parents had because of me. The guilt filled me, my conversation with the devil piling on the fact that my existence was a great pain to many. I hurt others alive, and I hurt others dead. Me and my mate were designed to create the most chaos a fae could, so it wouldn't make sense if that wasn't the case.

"I'm... right here," I said, my voice dry, the burn of whiskey still in my throat, giving me something to focus on as the guilt swirled within.

Next thing I knew, I was wrapped in my mother's arms, the smell of sweet rose filling my nose. A scent my creature loved dearly.

The surprise of her holding me, something that only happened a few precious times in my life, was almost enough for the old me to break through for a mere second and wrap my arms around her but then my mother pulled back, her eyes connecting with mine, a slight shudder racking her frame.

Tears lined her eyes as she looked at me, and it pierced through me. My mother rarely cried in front of me, in front of anyone. To see her with tears was a punch to the gut that had me ripping my eyes from hers to look at my fathers. His blue eyes, heated, but also swirling with the familiar pity I was used to.

My mother brushed some invisible lint off my shoulder, drawing my eyes back to her now tearless ones. "Sorry, flower. I was just worried about you."

At her distance, my current self returned, and I tucked a curl behind my ear, shuffling a little to my right where the devil happened to be standing.

At the action, a scowl promptly formed on my mother's face. "What were you doing alone with him?"

Her tone revived something in me to cower and answer her immediately. "We were just talking, mother."

She crossed her arms, a brow raising on her face. "About?"

"Confidential," the devil spoke then, popping a grape into his mouth. Where he got the grape from, I had no idea because the tables of food were far from us.

My mother's eyes narrowed on him. "Everything that Marie is involved in, I am as well, so clue me in."

"It was nothing, Mother." My voice carried a weight of embarrassment within it. "He just talked to me about training. A training you are forcing me to do, remember?"

She schooled her features, returning to her graceful, detached look. "That's it?" She eyed me.

"Yes, Mother."

"Good, don't go off again without telling someone."

I nodded, sighing internally because I wanted to get some freedom tonight, but my near breakdown with the devil, probably was a good example of why I shouldn't be left alone.

"Karnelian," the king said.

My head turned to the devil, his hazel eyes meeting mine before he looked at the king. "*Yes, Father.*" His tone was three notches too high, his face slightly pouted in submission. The whole charade in mock of me, and it was confirmed when he looked back at me, a smirk gracing his face, my lips twitching in reaction.

"War room." The king waved to the door that was a few feet away from us.

The devil rolled his eyes. "I wish I wasn't your son."

The comment was in jest, but the king stiffened slightly before starting towards the door, my father following and mother grabbing my arm to pull me with them. "If you weren't my son, I would demand you pledge yourself to my loyalty and do everything I said if you wanted to live here with silver blood."

The devil shrugged as if the comment meant nothing to him. "I could have chosen to go to Unseelie. I think I like it better than here. The weather isn't scorching all the time and they have a king who makes better fashion decisions."

The king inhaled deeply. "Whatever, Karnelian."

I shook off my mother's arm, walking faster to catch up with the devil a few paces in front of me.

The male was tall. He was taller than his father by a few inches, his shoulders were broad, his frame in between lean and bulky, a six-pack probably hidden under that suit. His appearance, though large, didn't go with his devil persona. No, that was in his eyes. His eyes held a mischievous twinkle within, but the twinkle was a trick, distracting you from the hardness hidden with those irises. A hardness that carried a deadly energy, a reminder of what he could do to you with the power he carried.

"You've been to Unseelie," I asked, slightly breathless from trying to catch up to him, my hair coming into my face as I tried to keep his pace.

The devil brushed the curls out of my view, his finger sliding across my skin, my heat making itself known as I felt my dampened panties become soaked with my arousal. "Yeah, little bird. I had to learn Unseelie magic somewhere."

"Did you go to training there?"

He had slowed his walking when I approached, matching my strides, everyone else unintentionally following his lead, his beast the biggest and probably the most mean. "Yes, a little after my training here."

"What was it like?"

There was a tension in the air, eyes burning into the back of my head. Turning to look, I took in the wide eyes of my parents and Kolvin as they stared at me like I had grown a second head.

"Probably the same as you experienced."

I tore my gaze from them, not reading much into their expression and frowned at the devil. "I doubt that."

"Did you study, party all night, and have a ton of sex?"

I thought for a moment. "I guess so, but I probably had more sex than you did."

He laughed, a sound my creature was really beginning to like. "What do I have to offer the world, little bird?"

My lips twitched, the sweet tension in my muscles pushing me to laugh, but I didn't let it become a sound.

The devil smirked, raising a brown in challenge. Those muscles tightened further as my stomach swirled with the want to voice the feeling. I snubbed it out, because I shouldn't laugh, but a small snort managed to escape me as I did.

He rolled his eyes as if he knew what I had done and turned his head to the door as we approached the war room.

After everyone had entered, the king handed his son an envelope. "I need you to get this to Markos."

The devil raised a brow, a look of surprise filling his eyes. "That is highly illegal, and you know it."

"It's urgent and I doubt he will do anything about it after he reads the contents."

"I don't know." The devil rubbed the back of his neck. "It is a lofty request. You are going to have to offer me something just as weighted in return."

"Karnelian." Irritation sounded heavy in the king's voice. "This is important. Can you drop your devil act for one gods-damned second and just do your duty for your king and your people?"

"*You* and *your* people made me this devil after *you,* and *your* people decided that *my* abilities were a disgrace, but of course when until *you* and *your* people need something from me, it's a fucking gift." Karnelian's eyes bore into his father's. "You want me to violate the law, so you can get your letter past the diamond wall and into Markos's hand, you need to give me something in return."

A muscle ticked in the king's jaw, his green eyes a mix of emotions as he looked into his son's. "Fine. What do you want this time, going to steal another one of my top chefs?"

"No, I want Charlotte."

"You already have Charlotte." My brows furrowed on who this Charlotte was and why she was so valuable. Maybe she was his lover? He didn't wear a mark, which was one of the reasons my creature was ecstatic to jump his bones, but that didn't mean he didn't have a female he kept as his.

"I want you out of my business. I want Charlotte to myself, and for you to stop poking your nose into my affairs."

"Not only are you my son, but I am your king. As a father, I worry about the shit you are fucking dealing in, and as a king, I worry about the damage you could cause."

Karnelian scoffed, the easy, carefree mood he had earlier fully abandoned as his features became more tense, that deadly gleam showing more in his eyes. "No one is more dangerous than me, Father. You don't need to pretend you're worried for me when we both know you're worried about me and the power I acquire when *your people* come begging to me to fix their problems when you can't. I want you out of my hair. Give me Charlotte and leave me alone or find another hybrid with the power to cheat the law."

The king clenched his jaw, closing his eyes to settle himself before he spoke next. "Fine, but—"

"No buts. This is what I want. Take it or leave it."

"Deals are meant to be negotiated, Karnelian."

"You aren't really in the position to demand anything from me, Dominick."

The king gritted his teeth. "My court members, you still report when they deal with you."

"You act like I would go against you, Father."

"Isn't that your goal as the Silver Blooded Devil?"

"Father, if I wanted you dead, you would be. If I wanted your power, I would have killed Fredrick then you. Fortunately for you, I love my brother."

The king rolled his shoulders, trying to dispel the tension that refused to leave his bronzed body. "It's a deal?"

"I want this one bound."

"You act like I would go against you, son."

"You already have."

The king's nostrils flared, but he held out his hand, extending it out to the devil. "You are insufferable, Karnelian."

"The apple doesn't fall far from the tree, Father." The devil smiled, pulling out his silver dagger, the one he drew when he placed his brand on me.

He grasped his father's hand, cutting into his palm before doing the same to his own.

"I, Dominick Lightfire, promise to let you, Karnelian Lightfire, own the deed to Charlotte, and I promise to pull all my personnel from your dealings, including my spies."

The devil snorted before reciting, "I, Karnelian Lightfire, promise to tell you, Dominick Lightfire, about all the dealings I make with the members of your court."

The males shook, silver veins traveling up the king's arm and gold veins disappearing underneath the devil's sleeve.

The devil pulled out a silver handkerchief from his coat pocket, wiping his hand but leaving his father to deal with his own mess. "Okay let's get this over with. I have places to be." He cracked his neck, shaking his limbs out before holding out a hand for the letter.

The king handed it to him, and the devil closed his eyes, silver veins flooded his whole body, the room quiet as everyone stared at the anomaly.

A few moments passed before nothing happened, the devil's brows creasing as he opened his eyes, cocking his head as he inspected the letter. "That's odd."

"What?" the king questioned.

"I can't find him."

"What do you mean you can't find him?"

"It's like he's dead."

The king glanced at me, confusion filling his face.

When I offered nothing in reply, he looked back to his son. "If he were dead, we would know about it."

"I know he isn't dead," the devil said, annoyance ringing in his tone. "It's like he is blocked or veiled. I could normally call upon his energy, like a portal mirror and tell you where he was exactly or who he was with, but now when I search for him, he isn't there to receive my call."

"Like he left Faerie?" my mother questioned.

The devil shook his head. "I would still be able to find him even if he did leave our lands. No, he is using magic to block me from finding him. A lot of it and it's not his magic being used to create the veil."

"Whose could he be using? Can you tell that?" the king asked.

"No. It's probably multiple people. The only person who would be strong enough to do that would be you. I would say it's at the maximum twenty to thirty other fae, ten to fifteen if they are all skilled with magic."

"Then we know where he is," my father interjected.

The devil cocked his brow. "Where?"

"The Neeki are gathering along the border. Wouldn't they need to be near him to block him?"

"He could have Neeki that aren't there," the king supplied.

"Yes, but we can't ignore the threat," my father stated. "Markos is probably with his people, so he can easily give out orders. Meaning he is probably planning something, and it either has to do with the Neutral Territory or Lightwood."

The king walked over to the map, studying the contents. "Well, Corivina, looks like things may be going your way. Markos is setting up for an attack."

TEN

MARIE

*T*he devil didn't speak when he came to pick me up. It was the next day, mid-afternoon, the sun due to set in a few hours. When I opened the door, he offered no hi or hello, just a nod in gesture for me to follow. His face masked in stoicism, maybe contemplation, as we walked the path from my father's manor to town.

Normally, I wanted silence, craved it. Especially when the silence wasn't painted with one's woes or worries. This silence let me listen to the cicadas' beautiful songs and the bird's chirping their afternoon tunes, but the devil's silence felt too airy, too quiet.

Something about his silence felt like a game. His disengagement on our trek feeling forced. Gracefully forced, but still forced. There was a hold in the air as if there was something to come, but the thing never did.

"Are you going to tell me what we are doing today?"

He turned to me, a smirk lacing his plush lips. "Nothing."

"Nothing?"

A tiny glimmer of delight entered his eye before he replied, "Well... something technically, but more or less... nothing."

I rolled my eyes which pulled his mouth into a goading smile. "What does this something that is more or less nothing consist of?"

"A walk around Lightwood."

"A walk around Lightwood? You know as the commander's daughter I have lived here my whole life." Lightwood wasn't just a small town, it was the army town. Most who lived here served the army in one way, or they had moved here for a small town life that had little to do with farming as most all the other towns in Seelie did.

"I am very aware of whose daughter you are, but from what I've read from your father's reports, you have spent the last five years indoors and lying in bed." He raised a brow as if asking a question.

I nodded, though stiff and with weariness in my eye.

"I don't want to jump into combat. Yes, we have limited time and I'll try my best to teach you what you need to know before war breaks out. But I doubt it will break out this week. I don't want you to pull a muscle or anything, that would just deter your training. You need to get used to being active, so a stroll through Lightwood will do and, in a week or so, we will start light training."

"Okay, so... we are just going to walk?"

He hummed in answer. "And maybe talk a bit."

"About?"

"Whatever you fancy."

"I haven't fancied talking in some time."

He nodded and turned to look ahead as we approached the town square. "That is fine as well."

Being dinner time, the square was bustling with people. The town still decorated with old Lughnasadh décor—a harvest sabbat with the main dish being centered around corn. The people smiled greeting me with their, *Oh Marie, it's so nice to see you. Oh Marie, are you feeling better? Oh Marie, it's too hot to be wearing that.*

Thankfully the devil scared people away, and I didn't have to deal with as many oh Marie's as I was surely promised.

"The people seem to love you here."

"I used to be known as Sunshine, but no one calls me that anymore." Except G after he heard Alirick say it in passing.

"Yeah, now they should call you shadow, or ghost. Much more fitting."

My head snapped to him, a spark of rage building in my chest when I was met with his arrogant smirk and taunting brows.

"You are too sensitive, little bird. You need extra feathers to deal with the winter chill when you become queen."

My shoulders rolled, a heavy weight falling on me with thoughts of the future. Thoughts of the things I'd have to do that would just add more guilt to my plate. "You said we didn't have to talk."

"You don't, but I enjoy a bit of banter." His thumb came to smooth out my forehead. "Enjoy the little crease in your brow when you scowl."

A wave of heat flared in me, my creature enjoying his touch, his attention, enjoying his sardonic voice, and chaotic jests.

I huffed, continuing my walk, his chuckle following close behind.

It took him two strides to catch up to me, and he snagged a curl in his fingers. The tug ever light, but a welcomed pain that flared my arousal even more. My eyes met his, the hazel softer than moments before, but still wicked and devilistic. "You hungry?" he asked.

I pulled my curl from his grasp before I shook my head in answer.

In reply, he held out his hand, which made me furrow my brows again.

We stood there for a few moments, the lively town roaring around in cheer, until I slipped my hand in his. His skin, rough and calloused, scraping across my smooth and soft. My eyes asked if this was the intended reaction, and he nodded his head in reply.

I frowned, and he frowned, then I realized it was another game, another mock of me that had my lips twitching, butterflies blooming in my belly.

But my soul slashed the wings off those butterflies and my mirth quickly left.

With a roll of his eyes, he interlaced our fingers and pulled me along. His direction intent.

"Where are we going?"

"To get food."

"But I said I wasn't hungry."

He looked back at me, that devilry illuminating his face. "Well, maybe not everything is about you, little bird." He chuckled. "And technically, you didn't say anything."

My lips pursed together. "Why didn't you eat before you picked me up?"

"I'm a busy male, I tend to skip a few meals." Before I could reply, he tugged me along, entering Ma Mason's.

Ma Mason's was a restaurant that was very jovial. The music upbeat and cheerful. The tables along the walls opened up to a dance floor where people let loose, freeing their beasts to the rhythm of the beats. The freedom was nothing like King Dominick's parties; there was no debauchery or stiff regality. This place felt like Seelie, how Seelie truly should be. Warm and full of life. The restaurant was decorated with plants and all the tables were made from wood sourced here in Lightwood. The food wasn't elegant or sophisticated; it was homely and comfortable, perfect for a calm summer's night.

At this time there was a line of people, but Karnelian walked straight up to the hostess. Not one being bothered to call him out on cutting because they knew who he was, or they sensed his dominance, and the act had my nipples rock-hard and core throbbing.

"Excuse me," Karnelian said to the female.

She smiled wide, the smile genuine because the staff actually enjoyed working here. There was legitimately a waitlist for being a server here. "Yes, sir?"

"Could I see Cecelia?"

I tugged his hand, making him turn toward me. "You know Cecelia?"

"I do."

Cecelia Mason, AKA Mama Mason, the owner of Ma Mason's, was the oldest fae I knew personally. Most fae retired around a thousand or so years of age though many could live to be around twenty, sometimes even thirty thousand years old. Retirement meant one of three things. One, traveling the world and seeing what life was like in other territories. Two, settling down in a town such as Lightwood and lying low for the rest of your days. Three, suicide. The retirement I would like to take as soon as possible and the option many fae who lived tortured lives—because being a creature of chaos doesn't seem so fun after thousands of years of disarray—chose. But there were some people like Ma Mason who never wanted to retire and has been running this restaurant since she was about six hundred or so.

"Uh yes, sir. One moment."

"How do you know her?" I asked.

Karnelian smiled, then gestured to himself like that would suffice my curiosity. When I didn't get it, his eyebrow quirked up and he said, "I am the devil who makes many deals, little bird. Ma Mason isn't exempt from that list."

"She made a deal with you?"

He put his finger to his lips, wickedness brewing in his silvery eyes. "Shhh."

"Kar-Nelian Light-Fire!" Ma Mason swirled his name in her thick, rowdy accent.

Karnelian let go of my hand, which I hadn't remembered he held, to pull her into a hug.

Fae aged slowly, truly slowly, so though Ma Mason was eight thousand years old, she looked close to a forty-year-old human. She still held youth in her cheeks but there were some fine lines in her dark skin, but to be fair it made her more beautiful because fae loved flaws. She had long silvery hair that I found out was genetic and not from old age, and she was a fae who also had claws, but hers weren't black, they were a brownish white that blended nicely with her skin.

My eye twitched when she stroked his back twice, my teeth gnashing together at her friendly and bubbly personality.

Karnelian kept the hug short, pulling back quickly and Ma Mason turned to me, her smile wide and bright. "Little Marie!"

She went in for a hug, and I stiffened in her hold. My beast did not like her. It had in the past, but now something made me want to rip her eyes out.

Karnelian interjected, and thankfully ended the five-second embrace. "Do you mind getting us a private place to convene?"

She smiled, not at all bothered by him stopping her. "Of course, sugar."

We followed her throughout the restaurant, going up the stairs to the upper balcony where the bar was placed. Ma gave us a table that sat right next to the railing looking down on the dance floor.

"Don't get any ideas," Karnelian said as we sat.

My eyes turned to slits, my expression scowling. Which was met with a deep chuckle, that even over the music I felt vibrate through my bones.

"So, what can I get you, honey?"

Sugar. Honey. Words normal coming from Ma but I found them irritating tonight.

"Whiskey."

She laughed deep in her belly, laying her hand on his shoulder. "Any food, *Mr. Devil?*"

"Steak is fine and..." He flipped through the menu. "Do you know what her favorite is?"

Before Ma answered, I interjected, "I told you I wasn't hungry."

"Little bird, your current diet consists of coffee, fruits, whatever your chef makes for dinner, and the spare bottle of wine when you can get your hands on it. You need to have fuel to burn if you're going to train."

My nose scrunched. "How do you know that?"

"I think you miscalculated how important you are, little bird. There are eyes on you. Your family, the maids, *my brand*."

"Your brand tells you what I eat?"

Karnelian ignored me, turning back to Ma. "Do you know what she normally has?"

"She loves the roast."

Karnelian closed the menu, gathering mine up before handing it to her. "She'll have the roast and a water, thank you."

After a show of gratitude, Ma Mason left to tell the kitchen our order, and I narrowed my eyes on Karnelian.

"You're not about to throw a fit about me buying you a meal, are you?"

"The brand tells you when I eat?"

He smiled, slow and full of arrogance. "You think I care if you eat? I have more important things to do than pay attention to your diet."

A growl built in my chest, but I repressed it, hoping that the music drowned out my creature's bitterness. "You just said I was important."

"You are, but not *that* important. The brand tells me when you are close to death. But your family reported your eating habits in the file I leafed through."

A small sense of disappointment fell over me at his worlds, and I didn't analyze it or poke.

Soon, a server dropped off our drinks and Karnelian nudged the water toward me in a nonverbal command. For the first time in a while, I thought about resisting. It was a brief second of my beast feeling riled for chaos, but then I submitted and sipped on the water.

I studied the place, noting the dancers moving with the music, freed and vibrant. Opposite to how I felt with the eye's glues to us—to Karnelian. He didn't seem to care, or he was used to males glaring and females gawking. He just sat there drinking his whiskey, his finger tapping against the table to the beat of the tune.

Again, he didn't initiate conversation, making me feel obligated to. "So, what are the plans after we eat?"

"We continue our walk."

"And after our walk?"

He snorted, shaking his head at me. "We will do what we do after our walk."

An irritated breath left me. "I just want to know what your plan is."

He leaned forward, eyes intent and piercing. "You want to know my plans for you?"

There was something dark in his voice that made me shiver. My beast remembering the male who sat across from us was no ordinary male. My shiver should have been from fear, but it was from arousal, and I took a few more sips of the ice-cold water to tamper down my heat. "I do."

He sat back in his chair, studying me before he said, "You'll need to trust me if we are to do dealings."

"Dealings? I thought we were doing magic?"

"And is our magic not bound with blood? Each spell a deal with divine, with nature?"

I chewed on my lips, forehead creasing. "Yes…?"

"It's not a trick question. Though your weariness is good because I am known for trickery." He sipped on his drink, smirking. "Your energy is tight, closed off. You need to open up more if you are to do magic at the level expected of you."

"I can call upon my shadows."

"But can you hold them?"

I frowned at myself, shame filling me. "Kind of?"

"Magic is energy and you're closed off. I figured fresh air, a nice comforting meal would help open you up. You need to breathe a little more, birdy."

I fixated my gaze on the dancers without reply. I couldn't live. Not even just a tiny breath. I didn't want to tell him my soul berated me every chance it got whenever I did. That if I tried to live without him, it would possibly lead me to be trapped in a damnation of my own making. I didn't want to say that living felt like a betrayal to him, especially since my dreams were of him bringing me to death.

Ma Mason dropped off our food, chatting a bit with Karnelian before continuing to work. We didn't speak while we ate, and I mostly picked at the food, but ate enough that it didn't go to waste.

When we were finished, Karnelian stood, cocking his head to come. "Let's dance."

"We danced yesterday."

"And it was cut short. Plus, it was stiff ballroom dancing, not like this."

"Karnelian, I don't want to dance."

A look passed over his face, his eyes locking on me for a second before he said, "Okay." Then held out his hand.

I took it using it to aid me to stand, but he took it a step further, pulling me into his chest. My sense of gravity lost as the world swept out from underneath me, my stomach flipping and the restaurant disappearing from view.

ELEVEN

Karnelian

Claws dug into my back, ripping into my tunic, and piercing my flesh as I portaled the little bird. The second we were on solid ground, I let go of her, taking a few generous steps back. I had learned quickly to give someone space after being vomited on too many times from the abrupt travel.

Marie bent over dry heaving, proving my point. It took her a moment before she straightened and took in the new scenery. A smile adoring my lips as at her shocked expression, eyes wide and mouth slightly agape. She blinked a few times as if she could not believe her view. "We're... at the beach," she stated though it was said as more of a question.

"We are, little bird."

A crease formed in between her brows. "How are we at the beach?"

I looked out towards the waves, the setting sky coloring it a dark blue, little flecks of pink and orange skimming the top. The sound of the water crashing into itself settling deep within me, relaxing my muscles, and soothing my soul. "Magic."

She didn't speak and I turned back to her, tensing as I took her in. The golden sun filled her skin, her shimmer refracting the light and making her caramel skin glow. She looked… better, throwing me off from how dead, lifeless she looked moments before.

The whispers sounded, not the first of the night. No, the first was when she said my name as if she was my friend, not a pawn in my game as she was.

Her expression held confusion still, not grasping my meaning so I explained, "I have both magics, little bird. I can create a portal at will."

Her eyes widened more, almost popping out of their sockets. "The beach is like a two-hour ride from my home."

I shook my head, unable to hold the chuckle at how odd shock looked on her. "Take off your shoes." That crease formed between her brows again. "I want to show you something, trust me."

She grumbled but kneeled and started to undo her boots. A smile, a genuine smile, formed on my face as I watched her. I hadn't expected her to be *lively*. Everyone acted like she was lifeless. But over the few occasions I'd spent with her, I learned that wasn't the case. There was still a soul attached to her body. Was she broken, yes, but she was still living. Still a being who desired, even if that desire was to die.

And I hoped she desired other things, for my plan depended on that.

Kneeling, I removed my shoes and placed them next to her smaller ones.

She was so small. Her body was full and curved but everything else about her was small. Her feet adorned with black manicured nails, I figured were naturally that color like her claws, were small. Her hands, one of which I held in mine as I walked us to the edge of the beach, were so much smaller in mine. Her height, only coming up mid-chest level to me, had me bending down so I could look into the abyss of her eyes.

Others flinched when they looked her in the eyes, but those eyes drew me in. They were different than the first time I saw them. Dark and deep, filled with pain, agonizing pain. I didn't feel sad when I looked at them or pity or fear. No, I wanted to drown in her eyes, play with her demons, suck the darkness out of her soul.

I was like that because I was a monster.

I didn't dive very deep into that feeling, or how I was enjoying her company, or how, for some reason, I just wanted to make her smile and see it one more time. I had another agenda, as the devil I always did.

She was a key piece in the upcoming war. With war came power, and I craved power.

It was my birthright, and my revenge.

If I had her in my corner, I had that power, but getting her to work with me would be tricky. The devil finds your deepest desire and uses it against you. Her desire for death wasn't going to aid me one bit. I needed her alive. One of the reasons I even agreed to teach her was so I could figure out who she was, find her desire and exploit it for my gain.

I wanted to be her ally, more so, I wanted her to be my ally. Markos always projected that stiff darkness that made me feel suffocated in his presence so I never attempted a partnership with him and, well... he was drinking buddies with my father. My deals let me own most of the wealthy in Seelie and too many of the poor, but my reach in Unseelie was restricted, so partnering with the little bird now offered great gain in the future. Well, it would if she wasn't mad, but I was a bit mad too so maybe the devil and the little bird would be a good pairing.

"Why are we here?"

Laying my suit jacket out for her, I sat at the shoreline, pulling her down with me. Our toes poked into the sand, our bodies close, fingers still entwined. "Your magic is tied to the moon. The ocean's current is as well."

The water rushed up to us, and she let go of my hand to pull her knees into her chest and avoid the waves.

"Put your feet in the water, little bird."

Her head snapped to me, frowning, her bottom lip jutting out in the cutest way as she did. "Birds don't like to get wet."

I laughed, feeling it deep within my stomach. Her eyes locked on to my mouth, the urge to join me apparent by the twitch in her lips. She had been more grumpy today, more agitated and moody, but now that we were alone, I could already feel her aura lightening, and becoming less hidden to me. "This is a part of the lesson. Put your feet in the water."

Her nostrils flared in irritation, brows slanted down and an annoyed stare aimed at me. "I don't see how putting my toes in the water is going to help. We definitely didn't go to the beach in Unseelie." The waves came back, and she gave the water a scathing look as she drew her knees even closer to her chest, inching back as the water kept coming. She was about a foot back when she realized that I was using my magic to get the water to move towards her.

"Stop!" she squealed, the sound loud and vibrant.

"*Little bird.*" My look was demanding, causing something to flare in her eyes. She squirmed, shivering in ninety-degree heat before she submitted, scooting back to where I sat, leaving her feet out to be brushed by the waves.

The water came back, splashing over our toes, another squeal sounding in her voice as she immediately pulled her feet back. "It's cold!"

Her cute little squeals brought a smile to my face. "It's water."

She narrowed her eyes on me in that cute little scowl, her beast attempting to be scary and failing miserably. "Are you going to actually teach me anything?"

I sighed heavily. "Magic is more about your feelings, your energy, your aura. Not the mechanics they teach in school. You are tied to the moon. You are her child and she gifted you with the shadows she spends her nights with."

She cocked her head to one side, ruminating over my words. "I never thought you'd be so poetic about this."

I chuckled. "I'm not. I read that in a book once."

Her lips twitched but she didn't smile. "So, why are we here?"

"To connect to the ocean, find the current within and let it guide you to the moon."

"And when I reach the moon?"

"Become one with her and be the force that drives the waves."

She rolled her eyes. "That's bullshit and you know it."

I shrugged. "Maybe. Maybe I just wanted to come to the beach today, but I had to teach this depressed female magic. She clearly doesn't want to work with me so why bother, or maybe I'm telling the truth and offering you the best advice in the world. You'll never know until you try, little bird."

She huffed but opened her palms on her knees, closing her eyes and tuning into the crashing waves of the sea. Her aura opened up, gliding against my nerves for me to read.

I didn't though, didn't need to. I knew what she would discover when she dived within the depths of her shadows. Many people thought magic was something they had to take and pull from, but if you opened yourself up to the body that governed your magic, it would just simply flow through you, offering you a wealthy supply.

Marie gasped as she felt the divine connection she had with the moon. The moon was cold, silent, and stern. She was rough and harsh, but she was also calm, wise, and loving. When you connected with her, all those attributes spread through you at once, filling your chest with her energy, unlocking the shadows within.

Marie opened her eyes to black veins crawling across her skin, then she released the shadows through her palms, those eyes sparking as the last rays of sun illuminated her.

I moved closer, my body inches away from hers, and whispered, "Let more in."

She took a shuddering breath and let the moon fill her more as more shadows saturated her palms. My hand came close to hers as I let the moon fill me, so our shadows could play with one another.

I guided them, allowing them to snake around our hands and crawl up our arms. The tendrils cold and icy as they brushed up skin.

She trembled, her connection wavering before she lost it completely.

Turning to me, wonderment filled her cold eyes, and the tiniest ghost of a smile lined her lips. "That felt... amazing," she breathed.

I smirked, letting my shadows fall on the sand and freeze the crashing waves before they returned to the sea. "Told you, little bird."

TWELVE

MARIE

*T*he heated sun pounded down on me as Karnelian, and I walked the city of Solara. It was probably the most ridiculous Seelie name out of all the cities. It was also the most populated, and the dirtiest. This place was for the people who wanted to work all day and party all night, the city being known to never sleep. I'd never been here before, my mother would never allow that, but I heard about it from Kolvin. Apparently, at night the place was covered with fae lights, said to be almost able to bring day to night.

The cobblestone streets were littered with people. Being just after lunchtime, all were hurrying their ways back to work or wherever their days carried them. Despite the fact that my body grew in temperature when near him, I stayed close to Karnelian's side. The people knew him here, the second their eyes caught on his tall silhouette, they cleared a path for him, trampling over another like he carried a deadly plague.

We approached a building, Karnelian holding open the door for me. The small respectful gesture riled my creature and had my body tightening a fraction. The breath in through my nose to calm myself was a mistake when I entered the tavern that smelled of stale beer and piss.

I couldn't fathom why he would bring me here. The past week we had done the same thing, a walk with small talk, then toes in the sea and connecting to the moon. Sometimes we would eat, we always went to Ma Mason's and Karnelian would always pester her about what I liked and order it for me. And in truth, I was beginning to enjoy my time with him. The walks were refreshing, the food was savory, the beach was nice and mellow. Connecting to my magic was my favorite part. The ocean's soft waves, the setting sun and Karnelian's gruff but somehow smooth voice, guiding me through calling the shadows, an harmonious scene. My soul hated the small sparkle of joy, but her screams weren't as loud over the ocean's waves.

Karnelian's hand found my upper back, and he guided me to a lone table in the tavern. He never hesitated to touch me. He did it often, but in a way where he never crossed that line that would make one uncomfortable. It was always slight, like a hand on my back or shoulder, or his fingers twirling the end of one of my misplaced curls before placing it back, or his hand grazing mine when I cast shadows to aid me with control.

All the little touches too soft for such an erratic male, but that was what made them all the more pleasing; my body yearning for them, craving them, longing for more.

We sat, and a female, eyes filled with hunger for Karnelian, came by to receive our drink order. Karnelian ordered us whiskeys over wine, and I didn't hesitate to gulp back the burning amber liquid, enjoying my extra dose of pain for the day.

Karnelian surveyed the room, his silver hazel eyes keen like a cat.

"Why are we here?" I asked when he hadn't spoken.

He took his time sampling his drink before his eyes met mine. "I'm going to teach you to use your magic as a weapon."

"Shouldn't we be on the training grounds if you're going to teach me battle magic?"

"I'm not teaching you battle magic. I'm teaching you how to use your magic as a weapon, two different things."

My head cocked to the side in confusion.

His eyes leveled on the action, a sigh exiting his mouth before he spoke. "Weapons are crafted. They are pieces of art, curated by blacksmiths and metal workers, who spend hours shaping the tool. In battle, the sword is no longer art, but a means to survival, there is no place for craftsmanship. The welder slashes to kill, not maim, not injure, *kill*. The only art on a battlefield is the abstract splatterings of blood on one's uniform."

"Morbid, but what's your point?" I said, twirling my empty glass on the table.

A cocky smile appeared on his lips, my eyes locking on it, my mouth watering at the sight. His canines poked out, showing the dangerous beast, the almighty powerful beast. "You're so impatient, little bird."

My thighs pressed together to stifle my ever-growing arousal towards this male. My heat was worsening every hour, doubling in need each day. My creature eager to break it with the best male it could find, and she had set her sight on the devil. "Just tell me."

He rolled his eyes, that smile not leaving his lips. "Today, you are going to be a blacksmith, not a soldier. It would be rare for you to be in a position where you would need to fight. But you may be placed in a predicament where you'd need to evade an attack and you'd need to be able to craft a weapon for your defense."

"If a blacksmith was in danger, do you really think he would start making a blade? Why not just use the hammer or something, or better yet, one of his other blades?"

Karnelian laughed, the sound rolling through my body and traveling straight down to my pulsating clit. "Okay, maybe the metaphor is getting a bit out of hand." He took a drink of his whiskey. "I'm going to teach you to poison someone."

I leaned closer to him. "*What?*"

"What are Unseelie?"

"The fae of the moon."

"Yes, but what do they represent?"

"Darkness, death, and decay."

"Exactly. The Seelie breed life, which makes them gifted with healing, but the Unseelie breed death, making them gifted in killing. Don't be fooled though; the Seelie can kill just as easily, and the Unseelie can also heal in a way. You know not to be naïve about the light equals good and darkness equals bad narrative, I assume." His eyes narrowed on me, assessing me like a child.

"I know the Seelie are just as bad as the Unseelie."

That malevolent smile curled his lips, and he nodded as if praising me. "Give me your hand."

Swallowing the lump in my throat, I extended my hand out to him, my fingers brushing against the calluses on his, my mind wondering where he got them if he spent his days in suits and taverns.

He turned my palm over, his thumb brushing against the inside of my wrist. "Your pulse is fast," he whispered, smoothing over the area. "Always."

Another horrid breath in, I pulled at my turtleneck. "I'm just hot."

Instead of commenting on my clothes, Karnelian's hands shifted just a fraction. A coolness slithered over my body, seeping into my pores, and bringing my skin to a pebble.

A shiver accompanied my reply. "Thank you." Karnelian's eyes connected with mine, penetrating deep, something passing between us, but I had no idea what.

His finger ran across my pulse point which hadn't calmed. In fact, I was sure it had doubled. *"You're welcome."*

His eyes went back to our joined hands, black veins starting to line his fingers that soon transferred over to mine. My pulse was forced to slow, my stomach starting to turn, and a heavy weight poured over me. The feeling intensified the longer Karnelian held my hand, and I was moments away from vomiting before gold veins replaced the black and balanced out the sensation.

"Did you just poison me?" I said, removing my hand from his.

An unapologetic smile appeared on his face as his eyes lifted to mine, carrying a wicked gleam. "Want to learn how?"

"No..." I lied.

That smile widened.

A growl rumbled from me, mostly a reaction from the war between my body and soul when it came to him. "Why are we in a bar? It's not the best place to concentrate and the people are side eyeing us because we look Unseelie."

"You are Unseelie, but that is not why they eye us. And these patrons, little bird." He gestured at the packed bar. "Are your subjects."

My mouth parted. "You want me to poison them?"

He finished off his drink and waved for a server. "How are you going to learn to poison someone, if you don't poison a being?"

"Uh, I don't know. Maybe we could start with a squirrel or another animal, but not a fae who can talk and speak and notice?"

His upper lip rose in disgust. "You'd kill a harmless squirrel. You are truly heartless."

My face fell blank as I just stared at him.

A low chuckle reverberated from him before he said, "One, I would have to catch a squirrel if we did use them. Two, the goal is not to kill anyone, just give them a little stomach bug, which their revitalizing fae bodies will heal within a few moments."

"But how are they not going to notice?"

A finger to his mouth to shush me was his only response as the same female server from before approached us.

"*Hello*," Karnelian drawled, his voice filled with charm. My spine stiffened, my creature perking up to attention, eyes keen on the female.

She smiled, her cheeks staining red. "Hello."

He tipped his glass toward her. "Do you mind getting me another... I'm sorry, what is your name again? I forgot." Karnelian tapped his head. "Busy male and all."

"Yeah, I know. Uh, it's Carmen."

Karnelian fingers trailed over her skin, my beast ready to pounce the female but then I noticed the small black veins dancing on his digits.

The female's eyes were caught in the steely hazel of Karnelian's, so she didn't notice the shadows entering her skin. "Do you mind getting me another drink, *Carmen*? It would mean the world to me." His voice was husked, running against my skin, and probably punching into Carmen who was starting to look overly flushed.

Her brow began to sweat, but she was trapped in Karnelian's façade and unable to see her body starting to fail. "Yeah... Mr... Um, Devil, I can do that."

"Good, you do that now." He let go of her, dismissing her with a wave of his hand.

She nodded her head a little too eagerly and scurried off.

My eyes met Karnelian's, but he shook his head. "Watch her."

Observing the waitress as she brought the drink tray to the bar. She hurriedly told the barkeep the order, her hand holding her stomach, sweat dripping down the side of her face. She excused herself, then ran to the back hall where I assumed the bathroom was located.

Turning back to Karnelian, I was met with a look of devilry. Malicious and chaotic, wicked with trickery.

"Is she?" I asked.

He nodded.

My mouth twitched and I could feel a laugh wanting to leave me, but my soul thrashed inside, reminding me of my penalties.

Karnelian's eyes narrowed, before he let out a defeated sigh. "You ready?"

"I am not really the best flirt."

"Your subject just needs to be distracted. I can help you with that if you need. You just work on the poisoning."

"And how do I do that?"

"We aren't trying to kill anyone."

"Obviously." I blinked, voice dripping with sarcasm.

"You're such a delight, little bird," he mused before continuing, "Anyways, you just need to call upon your shadows, focus on them entering one's blood stream. Once it enters another's, the shadows will naturally do the rest."

"Really?" I said with disbelief.

He nodded.

I didn't know the Unseelie were that dangerous. "And how do I get into their bloodstream?"

His fingers wrapped around my wrist, my muscles tensing. He flipped my palm, tapping my pulse point. "Just like with the ocean, follow the flow until you get to the heart."

I pulled away, tucking a curl and trying to will my pulse to slow. "Where do we begin?"

That smile flashed. "Pick your poison."

Scanning the room, I stumbled across a male sitting at the bar. He seemed to be on a date with a female but wasn't paying attention to a word she said. Instead, his eyes were glued to another female's revealing cleavage.

"I don't think you'll need my help with that one, little bird."

The waitress came back with our drinks then, looking a bit rough for wear but normal in color. She tried to flirt with Karnelian again, but he waved her off the second our drinks were on the table.

HEART COLD AS GOLD

I hammered back the whiskey, letting it calm my nerves and dull my senses before I got up and headed to the bar.

Next to the male, I sat, ordering a wine. My hand laid casually next to his, our skin inches away from touching. It took me a few moments to access the power of the moon. It was day, making it harder for me to find her. I was also on day four of no sleep, so it took a little longer than usual for my veins to color black.

My wine came and I brought the glass to my lips, trying not to look suspicious as my hand drifted closer to his. A small sliver of our flesh touching. I hated it, and it became known to me that there was only one male I wanted to touch.

I tried not to think about the shift from lusting for all males to just one, focusing on the faint pulse beating against the back of my hand. The loud tavern and my body's yearning for me to go back to the male it wanted was all I could think about and my connection to the moon fizzled out of my grasp.

I tried to call back to her, again, and again, with no luck. Eventually, the male moved his hand, got up, swung his arm around the female he didn't give a shit about and exited the bar.

My walk of shame back to the table was only made worse by a chuckling Karnelian.

I stood between his legs with a frown, his hand absently finding mine and caressing the back of my palm. "Don't pout, little bird."

I folded my arms, growling at his sardonic tone. "It's too loud in here."

"You probably won't be doing this under easy circumstances." He handed me his drink. "Here."

Bringing the glass to my lips was subconscious. My creature secretly wanted to put our mouth where his had been, and we only took a sip before handing the glass back because we wanted his lips where ours was.

He finished the glass, before pointing out towards the room. "Who's next?"

The next hour was spent with failure—almost getting caught, but Karnelian swooping in to save me—and more failure.

Slouching back in the chair across from Karnelian, I huffed. "Can we be done now?"

He shook his head. "Not until you get one."

My eyes cut into Karnelian's screaming murder. I was exhausted, annoyed, and overly aroused. I wanted to go home, change my drenched underwear, and bathe this dirty bar away, but Karnelian's eyes offered no relenting, so I sighed and got up.

The main part of this exercise is the distraction. All I needed to do was create a distraction that lasted long enough for me to connect with the moon and was big enough for me to not have to worry too much about being subtle. As I swirled my second glass of wine at the bar—the bartender was definitely a bit curious as to what I had been doing, but my association with Karnelian kept them from interjecting—I got an idea.

The liquid in my wine glass glinted, and I glanced at the male sitting next to me. Placing my drink right next to him, I purposely fumbled my execution and the glass tipped, spilling red liquid all over him.

"Oh, my gods! I'm so sorry," I said, using old Marie's caring voice, standing as I grabbed a few napkins off the bar and started aiding the male in cleaning the wine.

My other hand wrapped around his wrist, not tight enough to cause alarm, in the way someone would show concern. His pulse was easy to find at this location, and he was perfectly distracted with trying to salvage his ruined shirt.

I opened up to the moon, easier to do, now that I had been doing so for the last hour, and then I let my shadows sink into the male's bloodstream.

It was a few moments of cleaning him up before it was time to let go, and I reached into my pocket to grab a few coin, offering it for the ruined shirt because that was definitely something old Marie would do. "I'm *so* sorry."

The male grunted, wet and malicious. "I don't need your Unseelie whore money. Go back to your slut king."

I was left speechless. I knew it wasn't the best time to be Unseelie and living in Seelie, but I hadn't had any problems with it until now.

Before I could even grasp at a reply, smooth baritones that were pitched with a malevolent edge interjected, "What did you just say to my friend?"

The male turned, then paled.

Karnelian loomed over us, his energy dark and venomous.

"Mr. Devil, s-s-sir."

Karnelian placed his hand on the male's shoulder, causing him to flinch. "The one and only," he said, a bit annoyed. "Now, why don't you repeat what you just said. I must have misheard you because it sounded like you just called my friend a whore."

"I didn't…" The male looked to me for help, but I kept my face blank. I wasn't going to come to his rescue even the old me wouldn't have done that.

The male started sweating, the gurgles of his stomach able to be heard in the now deadly silent tavern. He was a few moments from shitting himself if this didn't end quickly.

"Are you lying to me?" Karnelian's eyes flicked to me, wild with chaos, his madness calling out to mine. "Is he lying to me?"

My creature perked up to answer his call, eager to play this game. "He is."

"No. No. She is—"

Karnelian's hand wrapped in the male's collar, pulling him to his feet as the bar stool crashed to the ground. The male's toes were tipped, not even close to reaching Karnelian's fierce gaze.

The male's hold on his bowels went lax and not only did I ruin his shirt, but I was pretty sure his pants were now ruined as well.

The smell had me scooting off to the side, but it was so bad I ended up needing to plug my nose.

Karnelian glowered at the male. "Seriously?"

The male's face reddened. "I... I'm—"

"Shut it. I want you to apologize to my friend *and mean it*."

The male's face turned towards me, his temples dripping with sweat. "I'm sorry. So, so, very sorry."

Karnelian cocked his head, his face a mask of seriousness but that sparkle shining in his eyes told a different story. "You believe him?"

Laughter bubbled within me but the hand plugging my nose kept it from exploding out as I nodded.

"She believes it." Karnelian dropped the male, shoving him into the bar. A bone cracking sound released as his back hit the wood.

Karnelian pulled out his handkerchief, wiping his hands before extending a palm out to me. "We are done."

My hand slipped into his, my eyes locking with those silver eyes before the world fell out around us.

THIRTEEN

Marie

There were many things that reminded me of my mate. The obvious things—snow, pinecones, and wolves. There were also random things like strawberries and buttons. They had no relation to him, but my insane brain would at times find any reason to break. So, they deemed strawberries and buttons unsafe.

There was one thing in particular that reminded me of him more than anything else and I avoided it at all costs—Books.

Just the idea of them had me breaking, so I wouldn't go near my father's library. If I saw a stray book laid about in the main room, I would leave the room before letting anything settle in my mind. I wasn't a huge reader before my mate, so it was never really a problem, well, of course until today.

Rain poured down outside, pelting the Seelie Territory with hot, heavy droplets. Friction built in the air and thunder boomed in the background, sounding the doom of my cautious steps toward the library.

Normally I liked rain, especially as of late. The perfect background to my dreary state. A welcome reprieve from the stifling heat. Today, though, the rain was not my friend. It washed over Lightwood unpleasantly, and any plans to spend outside were canceled or rearranged, much like my walk with Karnelian and our evenings at the beach.

Karnelian's statement about training becoming a distraction for me was true. When I was with Karnelian, the screams weren't so loud and the time didn't seem to stretch. With the rain, I thought it would wash away my distraction, but instead, my distraction was here in my home, in the library.

I could hear the distant chatters of my father and Karnelian. Their words lost to me as my focus was on my feet, the creaks in the wood floor scratching against my senses. Each screech competed with the wails of my soul. That friction in the air had seeped inside me and I was one crack of lightning away from releasing a downpour.

In the open door, the smell hit me. The comforting scent of books, like cotton and vanilla had a babe.

A shudder stole over me as the scent filled my being, building a well of tears to cover my vision.

"Marie." My father's voice a tone I had come to befriend. The pity voice. The saddened voice. The placating voice.

I took a step back; my body prepared to run and hide until the storm fully subsided. Before I could, a shadowed figure came to me, a blob blurred by my tears. Cinnamon swirled through the stifled air cut with a soured edge of whiskey before rough hands grasped my cheeks.

The darkened figure was revealed when their thumbs softly brushed away my tears. There was a smidge of relief when I saw his face. A pinch of joy when I met those silvery hazel eyes.

Maybe it was because there wasn't an ounce of pity in those eyes. Or maybe it was how his features were firm but calm. Or maybe it was because a tiny part of me was just glad to see him.

"What is it, little bird?" Karnelian's voice was smooth but strong and it soothed over my sorrow.

"The books."

His thumbs brushed away a new set of tears. "What about the books?"

"The smell."

He nodded, quick and curt. Then his veins flared silver. A dome of starlight spread out from him, flaring bigger and higher until it covered the room completely and disappeared through the wall. "That better?"

I sniffled and smelled nothing but him, a scent that brought my creature out and scared away my soul. "Yeah."

He took a few steps back, his hazels holding me, grounding me as I took a cautious step forward. Then another and another, until I was deep into the library.

"Good because I would rather you not ruin your father's beautiful collection."

I blinked, sadness falling away and a frown lining my lips. "I wouldn't have ruined the books."

"The reports of you tearing rooms apart say different."

I glared at him, and he smiled, wide and wicked and full of arrogance.

"Flower, are you okay?" my father said, voice soft and full of his worry.

My eyes averted away from his, shielding myself from his pain I didn't wish to carry as mine. "Yes, Father. It was a false alarm, I guess."

He walked up to me, placing his hand on my shoulder and pressing a kiss to my head. He was the only male I could stand to be around without my heat acting up. Something I was ever grateful for, my beast recognizing him as my father even though we weren't of the same blood.

"Do you want me to stay just in case?"

I shook my head, and he waited a moment for more. For a reaction old Marie would have given, like a hug or a smile, maybe even a kiss on the cheek. That reaction wouldn't come, not when I truly wanted to move away, but stayed still only so it didn't add to his pain.

With another soft kiss to my head, he left, and carried his heavy cloud of concern with him.

My eyes connected with Karnelian's, worriless swirls of silvery green shining in the dim light of the library. He jerked his head, gesturing me to sit at the table with books laid out on it.

Warily, I walked over and pulled out a chair. "How did you do that?"

"The shield?"

"Is that what is keeping me from smelling them? I can still smell you and my father but not the books."

Karnelian sat down next to me. "I shielded the room. Anything that is of normal essence in this general vicinity is covered with that shield. I tweaked it to mask the scent, but also nothing will be harmed while we are in here."

He was the hybrid. His magic held no bounds. He didn't need to balance his energy with another or use a crystal like the other fae did. The sun and the moon were both connected to him. Energy already balanced and ready to be manipulated. "Thank you."

Silence followed my gratitude, and eventually, I gained the courage to reach for a book. The cream pages looked up at me, triggering the shards of shattered soul to pin prick into my being.

I fisted the edges of the book, ready to burst, but then Karnelian's hand found my back, drawing my attention to him.

"He was known for being studious."

My snort was sad. "He loved knowledge, history, magic." I sniffled as a fresh set of tears welled in my eyes. "He rarely ever read fiction, always wanting to learn something new that he would spend hours talking about. He was like an encyclopedia." I wiped at my face, turning to Karnelian. "I don't know if I can do this."

"You can, and you will." He said, eyes strong, voice intent.

"Karnelian, they—"

"Little bird, you have to do this. They are just books. So, your mate read. Your father reads as well. I read and I bet before this you read. Everyone likes to pass the time with some escapism every now and then. I need you to get over this, you need to get over this. So I'm giving you homework."

"Homework?"

He gestured to the stacks of books in front of us. "I'm going to need you to read these."

My frown deepened. "You said that magic was based on feelings."

"Marie." Karnelian leveled his eyes on me. "Your feelings are erratic. To be capable of performing a spell you need to be able to be centered. From what I have gathered from your father and others, you were once a very gentle person energetically. You don't oppress people with your energy and from being around you these last two weeks, I've gathered that you'd be best at technical magic. Which means your unpredictable, explosive feelings are of no benefit to you. Your connection with the moon is one that needs you to be fully aware of her. She doesn't naturally come to you. Instead, she asks you to seek her out."

"Is that your nice way of saying I'm weak?"

Karnelian chuckled. The hand I forgot rested on my back gliding up my spine and calling out to my heat. "Your well of power isn't the biggest, little bird. But it doesn't mean you're weak."

He continued to guide his hand up and down my back, soft strokes that at times would twirl the end of my curls when they brushed his fingers. His pettings loosen up my body and made me primed for his cock.

"Look at it this way, little bird," Karnelian continued, misjudging my silence. "The moon wants you to connect to her, to call to her and ask for access to her shadows. She wants a light tether between you that is consistent. It's like she wants to spend time with you, so she made your access to her something that will need your constant attention." His hand left my back, and he maneuvered through the stacks of books, pulling one out. "You should start with this one. It talks about our connection with divine, and the elements. It theorizes that when we carnate, the gods assign us to energetic forces. Like how nymphs are defined to certain elements. Fae are connected to the figures of duality. Positive and negative, light and dark, cold and hot, sun and moon. It's theorized that the forces are actually gods but of course we don't know for sure."

Humans were the only kind to personify their gods. Other beings such as fae thought it was disrespectful, especially since humans often used their personified gods to keep others in compliance. Other beings believed that if we were supposed to know the gods by face, they would be visible on this plane, and if we were supposed to be in servitude to them and worship them at an altar, we would have incarnated as witches.

We only honored that of which we knew because when you lived as long as us, you learned never to assume. The gods were not perfect beings as humans idealized. They were flawed just as us, their wrath was brutal, and their karmas were worse than sins. If you angered them, they'd retaliate and if you honored them, then they'd manipulate. It was best to just flow with whatever they dealt you, and stay true to the path that you were guided.

"Are we just going to read today?"

Karnelian shook his head with contempt. "You can do that on your time. Today, we are going to work on balancing energy." He stood. "Come."

I followed him to the part of the library where the two couches laid next to a fireplace. Karnelian stopped when his shoes touched the rug in the center, taking off his jacket, and tossing it on the couch. He began to roll up the sleeves of his button up, revealing forearms that had yet to grace my eyes. The skin tanned with a light dusting of blond hairs, enlarged veins popping out against taut muscles.

I attempted to bite into my lips at the site, only to be stopped by Karnelian's brand.

His eyes met mine, brows furrowed, and I quickly acted to divert his attention. "So... how do we do this?"

His eyes stayed pinned on me for a few moments before he shifted and moved to lay on the floor.

I stared down at him, incredulous.

He smiled, soft and full of absurdity. It made me want to mirror one back, but I didn't, couldn't, shouldn't.

Karnelian patted the place beside him. "Lie with me, little bird."

My thighs squeezed together to ease my throbbing core before I stiffly lowered to the ground. "Why are we on the floor?"

He scooted closer to me, his body heat adding to mine. "Because."

Instead of trying to get him to tell me, I just huffed, rolling my eyes.

His answering chuckle vibrated against my skin, making my body stiffer and my panties wetter. "Call upon your shadows, little bird."

With a deep breath, I called out to the moon, her cold icy energy a welcomed feeling to my heated body. Black veins laced my palms and soon black tendrils swirled in my hands.

Karnelian moved closer, whispering, "Good." His smooth voice almost making me lose my connection.

Raising his palm, his arm lit with gold veins, and he formed a ball of light. He pushed outward and the ball floated up in the air. "Another reason for the shield, I don't want to destroy the books as we practice."

My focus was on him when I said, "Practice what?"

"Not getting burned." He smiled wickedly, devilry entering his eye.

It took me a moment to realize what he meant before I looked up to see the ball falling down, aimed straight for me.

A scream exited me as I covered my face, anticipating getting burned, but after moments of nothing I opened my eyes to see shadows formed in front of me—his shadows.

"You would die if you were wild," Karnelian said, dispelling his shadows.

My eyes narrowed on him as I released a growl.

He laughed at me in pity. Not the pity that showed in my family's eyes. The pity brewed from condescension. "You sound like a puppy, little bird. I should call you pup instead."

"Don't call me pup," I snarled.

His eyes widened with delight, his lips pressing together to stifle the laughter that bloomed in his chest.

I frowned. "Nelian, Stop."

And he did, his body stilling, his eyes falling to my lips. He stayed like that for a bit before he looked back up at the ceiling and sighed. "Fine… but this time, try to dispel the ball with your shadows." Then without warning, he threw the one into the air.

We spent the whole afternoon on the ground like that. Him throwing the ball of light in the air, me extinguishing it with my shadows. At first, it would be milliseconds of me trying to build enough shadows to douse the ball before it nearly singed my being, but as the time passed, I got better, able to dispel the light at least one full second before it burned my face.

"Why are we doing this again?" I said, throwing out my shadows.

"It will help with harmonizing later. As well as practice for if a Seelie rogue decides to try and attack you."

"Hmm. What will we do after I can harmonize?"

"I doubt you will be able to harmonize for a while. It's quite hard, especially if you aren't open to it. But... the goal is to get you comfortable crafting shields."

"Like the one you cast earlier?"

"Yep."

I couldn't help but realize how comfortable I felt on the floor with him. Yes, my heat was flared and my aura tight, but besides that, I felt peace. It had been a thing that had been building over the last two weeks, a sense of balance settling over me the more time I spent with Karnelian.

I pushed out my shadows before turning to look at him. His face was angular, but there was a roughness to it, a maleness to it. His blond hair was always styled back, making him seem more intimidating, and his neck... his neck was bare and he never smelled of anyone else. That didn't mean he didn't do something to hide their scent, like my necklace, but I didn't sense a mark anywhere else on his body.

I wondered about Charlotte. Who she was to him. Was she just busy this last month and they hadn't seen each other, and that was why he didn't smell of her?

The idea of him smelling like another female had my creature stiffening. I didn't get time to analyze why because next thing I knew my face was burning, and I was yelping in pain.

"Marie?" Karnelian shifted to hover over me, cupping my face.

I gritted my teeth from the searing agony. The shock of the blast didn't allow me to enjoy the pain. Instead, tears built in my eyes, and whimpers exited me.

Karnelian tilted my face, inspecting the damage. "What happened?" His thumb brushed the area, causing me to squeal and flinch away.

"I'll heal it, just stay still."

I nodded, staring up at him through my tears and his hand hovered over the area, light streamed from his palm. The same light that burned me but no pain came, just warmth.

When he was done, both his hands cupped my face and he brushed away my tears. "You okay?"

I sniffled, nodding. "Yeah. I got distracted, sorry."

He shrugged, a soft smirk carving his lips. "When you have the almighty hybrid training you, chaos is bound to ensue. That's why they call me the devil. I'm more wicked than the rest of them."

I snorted, shaking my head. "You're wicked but not evil."

Karnelian tsked, his smile widening. "You're going to get yourself caught in a trap if you go around believing I'm not always up to no good."

I sat up, positioning our faces inches apart. "You healed me. I'm sure that would be deemed as good."

With his hands still cupped around my face he brushed his finger across my cheek. "It was selfish."

My brows furrowed. "Selfish?"

"I enjoy looking at pretty things."

My core clenched, my eyes piercing into his, my beast set to attack and maul his body.

"Marie?"

My muscles tensed as I broke away from Karnelian's hold to see Kolvin standing a few paces away. His honey green eyes churned with accusation, his presence pulling me out of the lust filled trance I was caught in. My soul flared to life, washing me with guilt and berating me with her screams.

"Yes?" I answered, tucking a curl behind my ear to avoid his gaze.

"Dinner is ready."

"Oh." I turned to Karnelian who didn't even look a little bit frazzled. "Do you want to eat with us?"

Karnelian gazed at Kolvin whose eyes churned with raging jealousy before he looked back to me, his smile light and full of arrogance. "I'd better go. I'll see you tomorrow when I take you out for physical training."

I frowned and his smile widened before he stood and grabbed his suit jacket.

"Bye," I called out.

He smirked at me. "Bye, little bird." Then he was gone, portaling out of the room.

That was when I noticed the smell. The room's scent didn't change when he left. The smell of books didn't overwhelm me at all. No, it was just there, a pleasant smell that lingered in the air. I realized that the scent had been there for a while, meaning Karnelian had let the shield down long ago; I was just too distracted to even notice.

FOURTEEN

MARIE

$\mathcal{B}$ooks, another distraction Karnelian gave me. They weren't as powerful as his presence or dust, but the second I opened this book last night, I hadn't stopped. My mind would drift, and my soul would scream, but it was easy to come back to the inked pages, let my mind catalog the information on the page for later.

My father was busy this afternoon, I'd guessed with planning for the war, so Kolvin was filling in for him today. I laid on the couch in the main room, twirling a curl around my finger, starting on the second book Karnelian had assigned me. My feet were propped up on Kolvin's lap—his choice, not mine.

"So, you're going with the prince soon?" Kolvin stated, his fingers playing with the hem of my dress as he studied the papers in his hand.

"Yeah, in an hour probably."

"Probably?"

"He didn't give an exact time." There was a pause, silence forming around us in a beautiful harmony. I might have had a second hit of dust today and that may also be why it was easier to ignore my soul. My heat had grown in strength, my body boiling with lust, and I just needed another to get through the day. Unfortunately, taking two hits a day, while blissful, depleted my supply faster and with my mother watching me in the mornings again it was going to be hard to sneak out and meet up with G.

"You two talked a lot," Kolvin mumbled.

"Hmmm?"

"You talked to him. You barely talk to me or your parents."

"I didn't notice." And I hadn't. I also hadn't stopped thinking about him either—another reason for the second dose of dust.

Kolvin sat his paper down, moving closer to me, causing me to sit up and move slightly back. His hands came around my waist, my body tensing as he pulled me into his lap, so I straddled his thighs.

My mind went blank, and not in the good way as heat settled in my core and my nipples pebbled under my dress.

One of his hands left my waist to cup my face. "You know I will never leave you, Marie."

"Unless you die before me."

His eyes closed, his jaw flexing as he took in a breath. "You know what I mean. I will be by your side for the rest of my days. You are still my best friend."

"Thank you," I whispered, my throat dry and my body taut. "I thought you would hate me forever after what I did. It hurt me to hurt you like that, and I am sorry I did."

He leaned in, placing a soft kiss on my temple. "I forgive you. It just wasn't our time."

A heavy breath left me. I knew what he was going to say next. I opened my mouth to refute it, but he spoke before me. "Marie, I know you won't ever be the same, but maybe things won't be so bad in a couple more years. Even if the heat goes away on its own this time, it's going to come back. Every time it has, it's been worse, and you may need someone to relieve it eventually. That should be someone who cares about you, and I care about you. I lov—"

The doorbell chimed then.

Kolvin rested his head against mine. Exhaustion coloring him, not physically, but spiritually. These past five years have been hard on him, he's given more of himself to me within those years than anyone. I knew he loved me, but I hated to see his love for me. I hated that he was trying to waste his life to care for me. Kolvin was the perfect male, he was. I knew he loved me broken just as much as he loved me whole, but I couldn't be with him. I couldn't watch him live half a life with me when he deserved the whole thing. I couldn't add that wrongdoing to my conscious.

Leaning forward, I brought my lips to his, holding my breath as they connected so as not to aggravate my heat. I did this simply because this was what old Marie would do. Kolvin needed something, some type of closure. A last kiss. I couldn't be with him ever, not even to relieve my heat, and this kiss would tell him that. Tell him that there was nothing there between us, that my heart was cold, frozen, lifeless and it would never beat again. Not for him, not for anyone.

After the emotionless kiss, I met his honey-green eyes, eyes that did nothing for my soul. It didn't even scream, not a cry to be heard. "That's probably Karnelian."

Kolvin gave a tight smile, his eyes tracing my features, hopefully realizing that all I would ever do was bring him pain.

I got up from his lap, maneuvering my dress to brush out the wrinkles before I answered the door.

Karnelian stood, wearing a black short-sleeve tunic tucked into black cargo pants and combat boots. He leaned against the door frame, not speaking as his eyes roamed over my body.

There wasn't heat in his gaze, but the action made my already heated body scorching. I was glad the dress was thicker in material, so it covered my aching nipples that really just wanted to be sucked into his mouth, and it took everything in me to stop myself from begging this male to do so.

Karnelian's brows pulled together, and he shifted his weight to his other side, his eyes landing on mine. "You're wearing a dress."

I looked at the item in question. It was black and lacy, covering me from neck to toe. "Yes, I am."

"You will have a hard time training in that. Go change."

The command made my body go taut. I was a sick freak for a male who was demanding, especially a powerful one as he.

A growl sounded from me, the action coming straight from my beast. A challenge to his authority that was disguised as a plea for him to ravish me. "No please?"

"I am not one to ask for something unless I need it. I don't need to train you. You need me to train you. So, you will do as I say. Go change, little bird, you're wasting time."

I grumbled, but obeyed and went upstairs. I needed to change my undergarments anyways and do more dust to deal with him.

When I came back down, Kolvin and Karnelian weren't in the main room. I followed their scents to the kitchen, Karnelian looking through our magically chilled cabinet, popping grapes into his mouth as Kolvin stood aside, staring daggers at him.

I cleared my throat, getting the males' attention.

"Little bird, how is that any better?" Karnelian asked.

The outfit I picked out was a turtleneck and sweatpants that I tucked into combat boots, like Karnelian had done to his pants.

I lifted my foot. "What? You don't like me stealing your thunder?"

Karnelian snorted, using his free hand to trail through his hair. The reaction was a bit less than I expected. I picked these clothes thinking he'd laugh his thick deep laugh or smile, maybe even smirk but all I got was a measly snort, leaving me feeling a little disappointed.

"It's a thousand degrees outside. You'll fry in that outfit."

I crossed my arms, my eyes meeting his. "If I change, it would look very similar to this."

"You're wearing a turtleneck in the forever summer."

I held his gaze, using my look as a reply. We stared at each other for a few moments, battling wills, but I wouldn't change my mind. This was a ground I would stand on until it crumbled.

He must have seen that in my gaze because he sighed, turning to Kolvin. "What was your name again?"

"Kolvin. General Kolvin Denmor," he grunted.

"Well, Kolvin, General Kolvin Denmor, if she dies of a heat stroke, it is not my fault."

"If she dies, you die." Kolvin seethed.

Karnelian glanced at me, his lips pressing together, eyes wide. "Well… we shall be going. See you later, Kolvin, General Kolvin Denmor."

He walked out the kitchen and I followed closely behind, and when we were outside walking toward the Lightwood Forest, Karnelian spoke. "That male wants to fuck you."

"He has fucked me, twice."

He raised a brow. "Recently?"

I shook my head. "No, before my mate."

"Ah, and you broke his heart when you left him for your mate?"

I gnawed on my lip in answer, looking away to take in the trees that surrounded us.

"I didn't peg you as a heartbreaker, little bird."

"Are you not a heartbreaker, devil?"

"No one trusts a devil with their heart, so I haven't had the chance," he replied.

My brows furrowed at the statement, confused. I was twenty-four and have been in love twice and this male was at least a hundred and hadn't been in love once. "Why?"

"Why what?"

"Why have you never been in love?"

He smirked, but the action was bitter. "It's a general rule of thumb that when you are rich or powerful, the people who want you, only want what you have. When I was younger before I had sorted, there were a few females who were like that, but I used them right back for sex, so there wasn't any harm done. Then, I sorted, and no one wanted me anymore. My father hadn't had Fredrick, so I was still the heir. I still had power and money, but I was an abomination. I learned then that love is really only meant for those who aren't cursed because love is a curse itself, is it not?"

One could say I was cursed being mated to a prince, then having that mate be killed and have to be forced to live because you are now the heir, but… "It's not a curse."

"Really?" His voice was dry, dripping with sarcasm.

"Loving my mate was not the curse. The curse is losing the people you love. Is it inevitable? Yeah. But when you're bonded to them like that, you don't really lose them. My sadness is not because he's gone, it's because we are separated, and I yearn to be with him again."

Karnelian pondered it for a moment before arguing, "If you would have never loved, you would have never lost."

"If you never love, you have nothing to lose."

"There are other things to have."

I snorted, my lips twitching at his stubbornness. "What do you have?"

"Power," Karnelian breathed, the sound haunted and chanting through the summer air.

"I can't argue with you on that one, I have none."

"Everyone has power. They just don't know how to manipulate it in ways that get them where they want to go."

"Like a devil who's made a thousand deals?"

He chuckled low and my ears preened to hear it. "I've made way over a thousand, but yeah, those deals made me the male I am today. Someone who is valued, if not also feared."

"You were feared before."

"Because of the power I already held, but I wasn't respected."

I thought on that for a moment, cocking my head to one side. "Why are you telling me this?"

"What?"

"You're so... open... why?"

He studied me for a moment, eyes saying something I could almost read if I had a little more time before he looked ahead and replied, "The Seelie try to hide their demons to make others comfortable. I like to watch others squirm, little bird." The pet name rolled off his tongue, sensually rolling through my body and making me shiver.

He smiled then, it was purely devilish, sharp, hard, and incredibly sexy.

Tearing my eyes from his, I looked straight ahead, a dark chuckle following as we continued through the forest.

We approached the training ground, vacant at this time of the day, the sun due to set in a couple hours, illuminating the sky with a golden hue.

"What do you remember from your earlier training?" Karnelian asked.

"I didn't physically train when I was in Unseelie."

He frowned, blond brows pinching together. "At all?"

I looked down at my claws, fiddling with them as a memory of my time there flashed through my brain and my shattered soul pin pricked my being. "No, everyone was too afraid of my mate to comfortably come near me. I would sit out so they could train without the fear of accidentally hurting me and getting reprimanded for it."

Karnelian hummed, a knowing look on his face. "Do you know anything when it comes to physical combat?"

I shook my head.

A sigh expelled from him. "With the war so close, we don't have enough time for me to properly teach you combat. Instead, we'll focus on self-defense and quick easy kills."

My eyes widened. "You are going to teach me to kill people?"

"If someone is coming for you specifically, little bird, it is because they are trying to kill you and you cannot die, not now. Not until you birth an heir."

The shards pushed deeper into me, the screams ringing in my ear. "I won't birth an heir that's not his."

"Then you won't be dying." Karnelian shrugged as if his words meant nothing, but that wasn't true, they meant everything to me. I would not die until I birthed another male's babe. I couldn't die without leaving an heir or it could lead to a catastrophe amongst the fae, and though I wanted death more than anything, I wouldn't want to wipe out our whole race to achieve it. I had to birth an heir; another choice taken from me. If I wanted to be with my mate again and keep the fae balanced, I had to birth another male's babe.

The thought had my teeth gritting together. Before all of this, having a babe was something I was looking forward to. I imagined a life where Kolvin and I were together and we had a babe. That changed when I met my mate, and the want intensified. One of the things that was deeply set in a mated being's bones was the need to procreate, and I was extremely excited to have children with mine. Now, I was forced to have a babe. A babe I didn't want. A babe that would grow up without their mother's love because, horribly, I would probably choose to return to my mate the second it was born.

The tears bubbled up in the back of my eyes with that one. I had wanted to be a good mother to a child, like my mother was to me. Now, I would be the worst mother in the world, choosing death rather than to stay and see that child grow. That child would grow up with demons, I was sure of it. I was sure the demons would tell them how unworthy they were because their mother would rather be dead than stay and love them.

My body jerked, shuddering. Tears pooling and ready to spill, but a warm, calloused hand cupped my face, sparking my heat to throb back to life in my body as my head was lifted to meet hazel eyes. "Could you cry about this later?" Karnelian's tone sarcastic. "We're kind of on a tight schedule."

I snorted hard, pressing my head into his chest, his muscles flexing under his tunic as I connected. His cinnamon scent wafted around me, soothing me as I blinked back the tears. It took me a second to realize what I had done, and I took a step back. "Sorry."

Karnelian looked down at me, his face blank, my action exhibiting no effect over him. "You're okay?"

"Yeah," I whispered. I realized that was the third time he'd stopped me from having a breakdown, saying the perfect thing to distract my mind from my impending flood.

"Good, let's begin. First, we will go over the places for you to kill quickly and efficiently. If we go over them daily and get them ingrained in your brain, you will act without thought in the sense of danger." Karnelian brushed his fingers across my neck. Even though there was fabric baring his skin from mine, the action still sent shivers through my body straight to my core. "You may have found that when your creature is riled, your eyes are drawn to the neck of others. That's your instincts telling you to kill. Biting, though instinctual for us, isn't very effective when someone has a dagger or sword. You'll need to disarm them, which we will work on later. First, we need to retrain your survival instinct. You're smaller so if in danger your first thoughts are probably to defend, maybe even flee, instead of kill."

I nodded because true as I knew my beast was submissive in nature.

"Right, so self-defense and disarming will probably come naturally to you. Killing will take more time, you'll need to memorize ways to kill, practice it until it becomes natural." Karnelian's fingers moved to the soft spot where my chin met my neck, my muscles tightening to repress the shiver. "Slash here."

"Slash?"

"With your claws. You wanted me to teach you how to use them. Slash here. If you hit an artery, you kill them in seconds, their healing won't be able to kick in fast enough."

"Okay. The neck. Got it." Or at least I tried too, but my clit was pulsing, and my body was buzzing with need.

Karnelian chuckled, then I was turned, my back pressing into his chest, his hand along my throat. He bent down so his breath brushed across my ear as he spoke next. "It will also be the place that others will try to strike."

A wave of arousal flushed over me, a whimper caught in my throat, and I gulped it down, giving a stiff nod in reply.

Karnelian's other hand found mine and he pulled it up, placing it on the hand wrapped around my neck. "The wrist has an artery as well." He tapped the place where his thumb met the arm. "If one is trained to kill, they'll know of it, but never think of it. You appear helpless, they won't think of your claws as a threat. Cut here." His finger held one of mine, using my claw to pass over the weak spot, careful not to break skin. "They might not die but they will scramble to cover it up. That's when you go for the neck."

He let go of my neck, his hands trailing my sides aimlessly before he took a step back.

Immediately I acted, turning and lifting up on my toes to grasp his neck. His flesh hot under my palm, his pulse steady.

Karnelian smiled, anarchy flaring in his eyes. "Good. You learned quick."

My lips twitched, a blush tenting my cheeks at his praise.

His lips pursed, eyes narrowing on my lips for a moment before he backed up. "Let's do it again."

The next hour was spent with Karnelian trying to grasp me, and me getting out of that hold and faux killing him but failing at it. The touching just made my body more taut, and my mind wasn't able to focus on anything, but the throb settled between my thighs. Karnelian didn't hold back either, he never hurt me, but he was rough with his handling, his ruggedness exciting me in the craziest of ways, throwing my mind off even more.

At one point, after getting loose from his hold, I stumbled back, falling hard on the ground. The sting of that pain, not doing shit for me. Instead, I looked up at the male who was trying to hold in his laugh, and scowled.

At my look, he couldn't hold it in and a laugh burst from him, not a slight chuckle either. He fucking guffawed, each laugh thick and deep, which only had my scowl deepening. Partially because of his reaction, another part because that laugh sparked something in my chest, begging me to join in.

After he calmed down, he walked over, offering his hand. "Stop pouting. We are done today, little bird."

FIFTEEN

Corivina

There was a change in Marie. It wasn't huge but it was noticeable. Before she spent her days in bed staring at the ceiling, but now she spent her time reading books on magic. Marie wasn't the biggest reader before her incident but the ones she did read were often romance of a certain variety. Now I spent my mornings in the library, watching as she went to the magic section and pulled out a mountain of books to read. That was all she seemed to do now, going through each book like wildfire until she read all of the ones her father had, and started moving on to the combat section.

The change was welcomed, sparking hope within me that my little girl would once again come back. I found myself smiling as I watched her, the occurrence distracting me from my own research for the war. I had to rein my hope back behind the wall when she continued to break down, and I was reminded that I had a job to do.

The annoying part of the sudden change was Prince Karnelian was behind it. That male was insufferable and yet Marie appeared to like his brazenness. She seemed excited when Karnelian would pick her up. Though he would come and get her at despicable times, often around supper and he wouldn't bring her back until late in the night. It caused Kolvin to stay up waiting for her, making him tired and sluggish during our trainings.

It was mid-day, past my shift with Marie, when I went to the library to grab some of Darius's war strategy books. I was faced with Marie laying on the couch, her head in Karnelian's lap, casting shadows in the air. With one hand Karnelian distinguished them with light, his other twirling her curls.

The pair was focused on their magic play, not noticing me enter, nor did they notice Kolvin who sat in the corner glaring at them.

Marie's brows were firmly pressed together, her mouth pinched tight as she concentrated on forming the shadow and fighting against Karnelian, who easily extinguished the tendril. She huffed and tried again, growling when Karnelian overpowered her.

"Nelian, this isn't really a fair fight. You're an extremely powerful hybrid with fancy-ass magic, who could probably do this in his sleep."

Nelian?

His hand in her hair moved to brush softly across her forehead. The action seemed subconscious as if he was used to closely touching her like that. "Strength is built, little bird," he said, casting her shadow away.

"Yeah, but don't you start with the smaller weights when building muscle? Maybe, I should be taking on someone my size?"

"No one is your size."

"Are you commenting on my weight?"

He chuckled lightly, Marie's attention straying from her tendril to his mouth. "Fuck you." His thumb swiped across her forehead again. "You knew what I meant."

Marie focused back on her finger, casting another. "When can we do spells?"

"When you overpower my light."

"Isn't light more powerful than darkness?"

"Light only burns for so long before the energy runs out. Darkness is forever. It takes a lot of light to completely get rid of all the shadows."

They continued to talk idly, mostly focusing on their magic play. Karnelian's body language relaxed, but I knew that male had no care in the world, so it was not much of a surprise. Marie, on the other hand, seemed comfortable near him, though it was clear her heat was disturbing their peace on her end.

It was insane how much they talked. How familiar they had grown over a few short weeks. They might even be friends, though they talked about really nothing, but Marie never talked to anyone this much, not with me, not with Darius, not with Kolvin. She only spoke a sentence or two at a time to us, but with Karnelian, she replied verbally to almost everything he said.

I cleared my throat to alert them of my presence. "Do you two really think it's safe for you to be practicing in here?"

They didn't stop their play, nor did they glance at me. "It's extremely hot outside today and Marie refuses to wear weather appropriate clothing," Karnelian stated.

His cocky, arrogant tone had me gritting my teeth. "There are other rooms."

"Father was in the main room with Jacoby..." Marie trailed off as she focused on holding her tendril of shadow longer.

"What about the books?"

Karnelian waved his free hand in the air. "I cast a barrier spell," he mumbled as he fought her.

I pressed my lips together, a fierce sense of jealousy coming over me as I watched the two bond. Marie's face was stressed, Karnelian relaxed but concentrated. Then finally, Marie won, and joy filled her face.

Joy filled her face.

She didn't smile, but she gasped in surprise, her eyes flicking to Karnelian's, wide and bright as he smirked down at her. "Look at that, little bird."

Her joy vanished to suspicion, her eyes narrowing on him. "Did you let me win?"

He cocked his head to the side. "Depends on how you see it."

Her nose crinkled. "What does that mean?"

"Does it matter? Tomorrow, you get to learn a spell." Her eyes sparkled at his words and his smirk grew wider before he pushed her head up and stood. "I have to go."

Marie sat up, kneeling on the couch, looking at him with disappointment. "But you just got here?"

He looked at his watch. "I've been here four hours, little bird. Two hours too late. I missed a meeting with a client."

His devil persona was ridiculous and over the top. Fae didn't believe in the devil! And I was quite sure the King of Demons would take personal offense to this devil complex.

Marie's lips turned down as she looked at his watch, the disbelief clear on her face.

Karnelian used his fingers to tip her chin up, giving her a cocky smile, his canines flashing. "I'll see you tomorrow, *little bird.*"

Marie's throat bobbed, his voice obviously affecting her. "Bye."

His eyebrows raised and then he was gone, teleporting out of the room.

Marie sighed, in relief or disappointment, I couldn't tell. It might have been a mix of both. Then, like she was a candle, the flame of life left her and she turned cold and distant, lying back on the couch, grabbing a book nearby and flicking through it.

Kolvin came over to the sofa, sitting and pulling Marie's head in his lap, his fingers playing with her curls. It took about five seconds for Marie to pull her curls from his fingers and re-situate herself to where her feet were in his lap, her head on a pillow.

Kolvin stared at her intensely. He looked like he was moments away from claiming her as his and proving to her that he was the male she needed.

I grunted, his eyes snapping to me. My look said he better not fuck with my babe, or I would kill him brutally, which caused him to gulp and pull his beast back.

Marie paid no attention to this, her eyes trailing the words on the page. She probably wouldn't interact with anyone again until Karnelian returned tomorrow.

Disappointment filled me, sorrow I didn't—couldn't feel, and I fixed my wall of darkness, grabbing a few books on war before leaving Kolvin and Marie to their silence.

Down the hall, laughter sounded. *His laughter*, warm and rolled over you like a fire on a summer's night.

I entered the main room to see Darius with Jacoby—Kolvin's father, the First Lieutenant of the Seelie Army and Darius's best friend. They were playing chess on the coffee table in the main room, drinking wine and laughing carefree. I could see from here Darius's soft blue eyes. Eyes I hadn't seen in five years.

Seeing them caught me off guard. My already weakened wall shattered and caused me to stumble, dropping my books in the process. I cursed myself, quickly bending to pick them up.

"Corivina, is that you?" Jacoby chimed.

I straightened, meeting Darius's burning angry eyes, eyes he seemed to save only for me. "Yeah, Jac, I didn't mean to disturb."

He gave a wide smile. "Oh, come on, this is your house. You don't have to tiptoe around because I'm here."

I nodded, giving a tight smile. "Thank you."

"I feel like I haven't seen you in forever. I know with Marie, things are hard, but Dare tells me things are getting better each day. We miss you. We especially miss your cooking. Can we come over this Mabon? You know Sariah can't cook for shit."

"I'd have to see if Marie was okay with it, but I don't see the problem. Not the whole family though, just you, Sariah, and Kolvin. Finn and Lerien have families of their own and that might be too much for her."

He smiled nice and wide. "Why don't you sit with us and help Darius out. He's losing bad without you whispering in his ear."

I swallowed, plastering a tight smile on my face. "I can't, sorry."

"Come on, Vina. we haven't spent any time with you in the last few years. I miss you. We need to spend time together before the war has me and Darius spending all our time away from our ladies."

"She'll be fine, Jac," Darius grunted. "We are getting a divorce anyways. So, it's not like she will be waiting around here for me to come home."

Jacoby stiffened, flicking his eyes between Darius and I. "Oh, I didn't know."

Darius sipped on his wine. "It's fine. We are fae. We grow tired of our lovers and move on to the next. That's why we don't get married in the first place. Nothing lasts forever."

21 YEARS AGO.

"Mommy! Mommy!" Marie's tiny hands pushed at my sides, an unnecessary action as her squeals were enough to wake me.

Rubbing my eyes from tiredness, I took in my babe standing next to the bed. "Good morning, flower."

Marie smiled, bright as the sun, her shimmer reflecting the light from the window. "It's my birthday!"

I pinched at her nose. "It is, my flower, and how old are you today?"

She raised three fingers.

"And how many is that?"

"Th-ree?"

A smile lined my lips. Even if I felt despair in my heart, I'd never show that to her. "Three whole years old! You're growing so fast!"

Marie's face painted a frown. "I'm still small though, Mommy. When am I going to be as big as you?"

"Hopefully, not for a long time." I sat up, grabbing my babe and pulling her into my lap. She was growing so fast. It seemed like just yesterday I gave birth to her in this very room.

We still stayed at the inn for the moment. I was busy with watching her and the shop that I hadn't gotten around to looking for another place for us. I was pushing it off because moving meant more than a change of scenery, it meant a change of name. Which I was also pushing off.

"Are you excited for today, flower?"

"Yes! Park! And Kol!"

"*Kol-vin*." Unfortunately, the only child around Marie's age in our village was Jacoby's—Darius's best friend—son, Kolvin. Sariah—Jac's female, spent most of our playdates subtly bringing up Darius. I hated even thinking of the male, but I sucked it up, so my child could properly form good social skills. Not to say that the five-year-old boy was all that bright.

"Kolvin! Park! Mommy! Park!"

"We are going to the park, but *later*. First, we need to get you fed, then bathed and dressed."

A small, cute grumble sounded from my babe. "Mommy, I don't want to take a bath."

"Don't you want to look pretty for your birthday?"

"Yes! You said you'd do my hair in pig-tales, and I can wear my ellow dress."

"*Yellow*. And you have to take a bath if you want me to do your hair or wear that dress."

"Okay…"

I pressed a kiss on her head before getting out of the bed with her in my arms and starting to get us ready for the day.

Marie had cake on her dress. She was running about the park, screaming at the top of her lungs as Kolvin chased behind her in their game of tag.

The summer sun beat down on Sariah and me as we sat on the park bench. My eyes intent on my babe, Sariah's intent on her needlepoint.

Sariah was the type of female who did needlepoint. Not really my thing which is why we were never really that close of friends, but she was nice and a good mother.

"They really need to update this park," she muttered.

"You could always donate to have it renovated."

She huffed, tossing back her blond hair over her shoulder, bringing the hooped canvas closer to her face. She often got frustrated while working because she was quite terrible at needlepoint, but since her male provided everything for her, she needed a mindless task to take up her time. "You have more money than me."

My teeth knitted together. I didn't have more money; *Darius* had more money.

Before I could respond with a very tactful comment, Sariah was lifted out of her seat and pressed against the lips of Jacoby.

"Daddy!" Kolvin screamed, running toward the bench.

Jacoby broke from Sariah, his eyes locking on me and widening a bit. His head snapped behind him, at a male, my male, Darius.

A cave opened up in my heart, loss and sorrow filling it. I had to rip my eyes from him to be able to take my next breath, settling them on the whole reason he was even here—Jacoby and Sariah.

Jacoby looked down at his screaming child and pulled him into his arms carting him off to the playground. Sariah sighed, lifting her shoulder in a shrug. "I didn't tell him we were here with you..." She looked between Darius and I, then with another shrug, she was off to join her male and babe.

My eyes reconnected with Darius's; his body always steady when he looked upon me. Even if his eyes were red from tiredness, his gaze to me was solid and firm.

His steps were unsure as he approached the bench, looming over me in a sweaty tunic, dirtied from training. "Corivina," he breathed.

My nod in reply was stiff. "Darius."

There was a parting between his lips, as if he was about to say something but had no words to form, or maybe there were too many. But without needing to speak them, all his words rambled through my mind as I stared into those soft blue eyes. A gentle sky, perfect for a raven to soar in.

Those eyes were probably taking in my differences. My hair pulled into a bun, the hairstyle I'd been resorting to most since Marie was born. My sunburnt skin from when I forgot to apply the preventative salve before spending hours in the garden harvesting with Marie. The extra bit of frost that had entered my eyes after I left him.

"Mommy!" His blues snapped to my babe. The tight ringlets in her pigtails bouncing as she ran up to me.

My smile was never forced when it came to her. To others, yes, but I could always find it in my heart to give her more. It was just the slightest tip of my lips, but it was filled with more love than I had ever given to anyone. "Flower."

"Who are you talking to?" Her head was tilted up to Darius, her eyes turning into slits as she took him in.

"Flower, this is my husband."

She glanced at me, cocking her cute little head. "Us-ban? What's that?"

"Hu-sban-d. It's a person you marry."

"Marry? What's that?"

A small chuckle came from under my breath. "Next, you are going to ask me where babes come from."

"Where do babes come from?"

My upturned lips spread to flash my teeth. It was not hard for me to push back my darkness when she was around. She may not be my sun, but she was just as bright as any star.

Darius kneeled, his face nowhere near level next to my small babe. "Hi, I'm Darius."

Marie smiled, a little sparkle dazzling in her coffee-blacks. "I'm Marie."

"Marie," Darius repeated under his breath, a ghost of a smile on his lips.

She nodded eagerly, her curls springing up and down with each shake of her head. "Yes! Today's my birthday!"

Darius's nostrils flared slightly, but his lips bloomed into that easy smile, filling it with all the warmth he possibly could. "And how old are you?" A question he already knew.

She raised her fingers.

"Marie, how old are you?" My voice stern but loving.

She looked at me and raised a brow. "Tree?"

"Th-ree," I offered.

"Th-ree."

I flicked her nose, and she giggled before turning to Darius. "Do you want to play? Mommy never wants to play."

I scoffed, tugging on her ear, causing her to squeal. "I play with you all the time, flower."

"Yeah, but you don't play tag."

Placing a kiss to her head, I fixed a few curls before saying, "Go play, my babe. You said you wanted to go to the park today and you aren't even enjoying it."

She looked out to the park where Kolvin was playing tag with Jacoby, my heart panging because she wouldn't have that, a father. She turned back to me quickly, pulling me into a hug. "I love you, Mommy."

"I love you too." Then she was off, leaving me and Darius alone.

He stayed on the ground, shifting, so he was kneeling in front of me. "She is beautiful."

"She is."

There was a pause, stilted with the jumbled words.

"So, I'm still your husband?" Darius finally said.

"We are still married." My tone was stiff and a bit harsh now that my babe was gone.

There was a slight shift in his eyes, and a small tick in his jaw, frustration and sorrow filling the air between us. "You haven't made any movement to change that."

"Marie and the shop have all my attention at the moment."

A tiny nod brought his sight to the hands tucked in my lap. Tentatively, his fingers found mine. The roughness of his scraping against the braveness of mine. My skin ice cold against his warmth. "You cut your claws."

"I didn't want to accidentally cut my babe. They'll grow back." I tugged away but his fingers interlaced with mine, a feeling familiar but foreign and I didn't know which part I hated more.

Darius lifted his eyes. Those irises ripping into me and crashing through the first few walls I had built to keep my darkness at bay these last few years. "Come back," he whispered. "I am sorry, Vina. What I did was atrocious, and it will haunt me forever, but I do not want it to haunt us."

I straightened my spine, rebuilding those walls one at a time. "I have a child now, Darius."

My efforts were useless because he kept breaking through them getting deeper and deeper till he found my soul. "I have a room ready for her. Painted it purple."

That hole in my heart started to be plastered over, but the darkness was still in corners echoing my fears. "It's not about space, Darius. It's about the fact that I don't know if you are fit to be around a child."

"Vina, haven't I proven to you that I am a good male? I know what I did was fucked up, but other than that, haven't I been a good male to you? There is nothing I wouldn't do for you. Nothing I wouldn't give up for you. You are the love of my life, my one. And I know I've tried to be my best for you, as you tried to be your best for me."

He was my sun, lighting me up in my darkness, but as the moon I knew that eventually I would be swallowed in darkness again doomed to repeat the cycle. "I don't want to do this now, Darius. Nor is it appropriate. It's my daughter's birthday."

His fingers brushed through toffee brown hair wet with sweat, the movement drifting his vanilla scent into my nose, my beast straining to take a deeper whiff. "I wasn't planning on interrupting your day, but I haven't seen you in almost four years, Vina. I haven't heard your voice or seen your smile, and I couldn't miss the opportunity to try. You haven't replied to my letters."

"I've read them." Over and over again, almost every night until I was breaking apart while my babe slept a foot away from me.

"What do you need, Vina? What can I do to make us, us again?"

Tears lined his blues, making the sky turn into a sea. A sea that was sure to destroy me, so I wiped those tears.

I hated hurting him, I hated that all his pain was caused by me. I stopped trying to rebuild the walls, letting him see the raw, dark and wretchedness of myself. "I don't know."

"Do you want a divorce?"

"I don't know." A truth because I hadn't forgiven him, but I hadn't condemned him either.

A shuddering breath ripped from him before he stood, bending halfway to brush a kiss over my head. The warmth of him seeping into my bones.

He pulled away, eyes finding mine, talking without needing a breath, without needing any of those words. Then he turned and went on his way.

His words tore through my wall viscerally, having me bite into my cheek, blood filling my mouth as my canine seared through the flesh. I inhaled, heading towards the kitchen. "It was nice to see you, Jac," I mumbled as I passed them.

My emotions high and threatening to tear me down, I slammed my books onto the kitchen counter, starting to pull out the food for dinner.

My shop was closed because I hadn't had the time to maintain it with the situations that had occurred over the last few years. All

I had left to keep the thoughts from crashing down on me was cooking, which I barely had time for anyways.

I needed it in the moment because with my walls ripped down, my darkness had turned on me.

My knife ready and sharp, I grabbed a random vegetable for tonight's dinner, cleaning it off before placing it on the cutting board. Each chop of my knife accompanied with my darkness echoing Darius's past words.

Am I sure of our love? So, I let your mark fade and you didn't notice it was gone and the question answered itself, no. No, Corivina, I don't think I'm sure anymore.

Corivina, our marriage has been fucked up for the past twenty-five.

I can't do this anymore. I want a divorce.

It's not like she will be waiting around here for me to come home.

We are fae. We grow tired of our lovers.

A sharp pain burned through my hand as the knife sliced deep into my flesh instead of the food.

"Fuck!"

I rushed over to the sink, washing the wound, blood streaming from my palm as tears streamed down my face.

"Corivina?" Darius called from behind my back.

I kept my body turned toward the sink, hiding my face as I took in a deep breath. A shudder wracked me as a sob tried to come out, but I pushed it down and kept my voice steady. "I'm fine, I just nicked my thumb."

"There's blood everywhere, Vina. Are you sure?"

A whimper exited me, my teeth gritting together as the nickname punched through me.

Today, the day he told his best friend that he was divorcing me, is the day he calls me that.

The pain from my thumb was nothing compared to that, leaving my soul in blistering agony, more tears spilling down my face. "It's fine. I'll clean it up in a second."

"Are you sure? I can call Jean-Luc if you need." Jean-Luc was our new cook.

"No. It's fine, Darius. I got it."

"Vina, you don't need to cook if you're too busy. That's why we have Jean-Luc."

The extra blow to my heart had me whirling on Darius. "I said it's fucking fine! It's just a nick. I'll clean it up. Now just leave me the fuck alone."

Darius's eyes took in my tear-stained face, and for the first time in five fucking years, his blue eyes were warm and pointed at me. They softened more at the sight of me, the look filled with love. Hurt love, but *love*.

I shook my head, not able to handle it anymore. "Call him," I said, grabbing a towel to soak up the blood on my hand, walking past Darius toward the door. "I'll be back later."

SIXTEEN

Karnelian

There was a throbbing pain in my cock that woke me an hour before I normally rose. It stood up straight, hard as a rock, screaming for me to relieve it, but I wouldn't. That would be a trap I wouldn't get lost in again.

I didn't need to torture myself with hopes, or dreams, or fantasies. I already had enough trauma piled on my back; I didn't need to inflict myself with more. No matter how hard my cock grew every morning, begging for me to give in, and no matter how badly my monster urged me to, I wasn't going to be lost in it again. I couldn't.

I was going to have to fuck something soon though. I didn't like being separated from the beastly side of myself, but currently, our wants didn't align. It needed to be satiated though, a female who could calm him down a bit, so I wasn't distracted from my plans.

My teeth gnashed together as I sat up from the bed, my cock scraping against the sheets, a strangled moan ripping from my mouth. My cock calmed when I stepped into the cold spray of the shower. The water doing nothing to aid with my agitated mood, I could handle water at all temperatures but I still didn't enjoy freezing cold, but eventually my beast relaxed into it, centered enough within me that I was sure I could go through my morning without whispers.

I dressed for the day in one of my impeccably fine suits, and portaled to Solara. My office was nowhere near my home, and I preferred it that way. Creatures would line up at my door ready to plead for a deal if they had access to my home. As well as Solara was the perfect place for my dealings. Greedy fae lived in the dirty city, my office a beacon to them to exchange their soiled souls for petty possessions.

With an extra hour before my day began, I settled in my desk chair and opened the file that had been lying on my desk for the last month—*her file*.

At my father's request, Darius was to report her health once a month. For the first few months, they were practically the same until she started participating in life again. With her current progress, Darius predicted she wouldn't be able to ascend to the throne for at least another five years. Unfortunately for the little bird, I don't think she had five years, which meant neither did I.

Over the last month, I had learned very little about the little bird, her aura not as clear to me. The little bird kept her energy wrapped up—which is why when she broke down it was a torrent of emotions that filled the air around her and crawled against my skin. Though I could read auras better than an average fae, I couldn't prod deeper than what was littered in the air, like my mother could.

I had gathered that her beast was in survival mode but with a twisted altercation. Her beast was in a frightened frigid state, but if faced with danger I knew it would jump into the fire. She desired death, she desired her mate. Two things I couldn't bring her.

She was also coping with the tragedy, trying her best to avoid breaking down in tears. It was hard to know the little bird when she was just trying to avoid him, which I assume was an extension of herself. I had talked to a few people about who she was before him.

They talked of *Sunshine*.

She wasn't that female now. She had become someone new. The only way for me to know the new her, was to continue as we were, spending the afternoons slowly getting to know another.

It was a time I hated to enjoy, the whispers would become too incessant and clouding, if I did let myself like her too much. It was a good radar though at when and where I needed to put distance between us. She was not actually my friend, she was a pawn. I was spending time with her because I was forced to and not because I wanted to.

A lesson that was ingrained in my head many years ago was to plan. To be the greediest, you needed to have many plans on how to swindle others for your gain. I wrote out the strategies for the day. What I did and didn't know about her. What would help me know what she deeply desired, so I could get her on my side.

It may sound a bit sinful, but I wasn't playing the little bird. I had no intentions of harming her or setting a deal that would cause her tribulations. No, I was just looking for what I could offer her that would bind her to my side during the war. I didn't extend this kindness to everyone, I was given the name devil for a reason.

When my hour of planning was over, one of my henchmales walked in—Merrick.

His little sister suffered from a rare disease where her magic disagreed with her body and slowly killed her. Just as the little bird, I made a deal with him that aided me but didn't punish him. He worked for me, and was paid handsomely with actual coin and every few months I would siphon her magic—a dangerous task to perform if not skilled—so she could live.

One of my many rules was I only employed people who were honest at heart, something I could sense in their energetic field. My people weren't going to let their greed speak too loudly in their ears and be led to try and overthrow me, or something even more stupid like steal from me. Employing people with dirty intentions such as my clientele would just get unnecessary blood on my hands that I didn't need. Merrick loved his sister, and he wanted her to stay alive, and I treated him kindly, so he had little reason to ever betray me.

"Who am I going to swindle today, Merrick?"

A small smile spread across his lips. "The duke."

I didn't hold back the groan that escaped me as I pulled open my desk drawer and brought out a glass and a bottle of whiskey.

"Already, boss?"

Pouring myself a glass, I replied, "We are on the brink of war. I don't have the patience to deal with this shit."

He snorted. "You don't even know why he's here."

"Let me guess? Fredrick?"

"Yep. He wants him to stop fucking his son."

I scoffed. "My brother's dick is not something I can or will control."

"Well, the duke is still here and he paid Grayson to bump up his slot."

"Let him in," I said, taking a savory drink of my whiskey.

The clacking of posh boots sounded against the old dingy wood of my office floor. The duke walked with his face poised in a grimace, his body language screaming his distaste in my choice of location. The devil needed a den, not a pristine office to do his dealings. I thrived off of my clients' discomfort, thrived off shoving their demons in their face.

"I can't control my brother, Zander."

"He's fucking my son who just got married."

"Are you sure this isn't about how you have been with my brother too? Last I recall, you were also married."

The male's features flatted, his bravado wavering. "I want him to stay away from him."

"You have better luck controlling your son than I do my brother."

"You're the devil, I'm sure you can figure it out."

"Funny because the devil is a known advocate of free will."

"I have money, Karnelian, all the money you could ever want."

"You act like I am not a richer than you, more powerful than you, and I don't give a fuck if my brother prefers to fuck your son over you."

A small growl vibrated from his chest, his beast small and meek compared to mine. "What do you want?"

"I want you to get out of my office and stop wasting my time."

"I paid for this meeting."

"That you did, and any sane and unentitled being would have told you that your spendings were in vain. As well as a lost cause. I don't negotiate deals of someone's will. Plus, slavery is illegal. You'd be lucky if I don't decide to report you to my father."

"You're putting words in my mouth, devil."

"And you're attempting to try to force someone's will, duke."

He didn't contain his growl then, his beast fully agitated and willing to force his point. He was that type of creature, submissive but unable to see it, so he acted out to prove his dominance. Only to get kicked down like the useless puppy he was. "You act as if it is so lowly of you to do that. You're the hybrid, an abomination."

Abomination.

129 YEARS AGO.

I would turn twenty-four in five days. The sun had waited almost 6 years to cross paths with the moon, making me wait until my veins were practically buzzing with my magic to get sorted.

With my age and status, I stood first in line. I'd prefer any other position, but every other faeling was shitting their pants, and used me being a prince as an excuse to be first.

I didn't want to be scared or have my hands tremble as I took the cautious steps to the ceremonial knives, but I was.

I had more to lose than these other faelings. A crown, a kingdom. In truth though, I didn't care to lose those. I cared to lose the two most precious people in my life. My mother and my father. I feared to lose, my mother as my advocate and my father as my base. Lose the peace that was attained when it was just us. Our family dinners or casual mornings when my father took off. Being ripped apart from them was my biggest fear, and today would be the day that I could be faced with that.

The elixir that turned my blood from its burgundy red resting color to its magical state added an extra buzz to my body that was hard to hold back as I grasped the ceremonial knife.

"Prince Karnelian Lightfire," I stated before placing the blade on my palm and pulling back.

The pain was sharp and rang through my body, alerting my beast to a challenge, but it didn't hurt as much as what had me stopping the blade mid cut, my blood pooling in my hand.

Not gold.

Not black.

But the color that shined when dark mixed with light.

Silver.

Like when the moon eclipsed the sun and a tiny ring of starlight sparkled around.

In tragic events, they say that time stops. That was not the case for me. I stopped, my body taut and my heart stilled, but the world still moved, time still passed.

"*Hybrid.*" The whisper sounded behind me, inciting my pulse to race and my head to snap up to the bowls.

Black, gold, and green, not a place for me.

"*Hybrid?*" An echoed query.

"*Yeah, he's an abomination.*"

My knife clattered to the floor as I turned around and ran. The faelings backed away like I carried a plague.

Abomination! they screamed.

That was what I was. A Seelie infected with the Unseelie. An Unseelie bleached with the Seelie. An abomination in both of the races' eyes.

Once I was out of the sorting building, I continued running. I entered Lightwood, and then I went to the portal hub, navigating my way to the palace. Hastily climbing the steps until I reached the war room. My father was there making last-minute plans just in case a war broke out while the gates were raised during the eclipse. He was never one to act without plan.

"Father," I choked out when I saw him, my body jerking with my suppressed sob.

"Karnelian?" he said, eyes alarmed, brows worried.

I raised my hand showing the silver-stained blood, shame coursing threw me as I hiccupped. "Father…"

His strides were haste, but his face still showed with strength. He took my hand in his, studied it before his emeralds locked on to me, solid, confident, and safe.

I was pulled into his embrace, my nose falling into the crook of his neck, his familiar scent a triggering drug that had me pouring out tears.

"Father…"

"Shhh… Karnelian, everything will be okay." He patted my back, lulling me. "I'll make sure everything will be okay."

I held him tighter, believing his word. He was my father, my king, and I had always known him to be a male of honor.

At least that was what he had always appeared to be.

I didn't respond to the duke as I was sure he thought I would. His beast was out ready for violence, he'd expect the same from mine. Instead, I ignored him, sipping from my whiskey, letting my monster settle in the smoothness, then revel in the burn.

Standing, I walked around to the front of my desk, leaning against the table top. The male didn't even bother to sit, an attempt to placate me before requesting me to bend the law for him. He chose to stand and try to assert dominance he didn't have. He had been with my brother, and unfortunately, I knew my brother was a top.

I studied him as I sipped, in no rush to state my dominance. In truth, there was no need. Just leaning against the desk, I already won.

"Zander," I said, voice calm, eyes intent. He tensed, prepared for a treat—not prepared to fight—prepared to flee because he was a weak male. A weak male who thought he could control people with his money and gluttonous greed. "I am an abomination." I smiled, smug with an edge of villainy. "That's why they call me the devil. That's why when I walk into a room, people stare. That's why males' arms tighten around their females and females clutch their pearls. They know I am an abomination, I know I am an abomination, but the true question is, do you?"

"Do I?" A slight tremble began to distribute through his frame.

I finished my drink, placing it on the desk, my eyes never leaving his. "Do you know I'm an abomination?"

As soon as I asked the question, his body stiffened like prey caught in a trap. I straightened, walking the two paces to him so we were only inches apart. His ability to maintain eye contact with me was admirable. A good little prey needed to keep their eyes on predators if they wanted to survive.

"Zander, I could kill you without even blinking, you know that, right? That's in the terms and conditions for abominations such as I. *But* I won't kill you. You know why?"

His throat bobbed. "Why?"

"Because it wouldn't work in my favor. That's why, and that's it. As the devil, I don't care about your petty lovers' quarrel with your son and my brother. I don't care about your money, or your blackened morals. What I do care about is my image. As the devil, I need to be dark, a male who will dance with demons, but I can't be so bad that people want to ban against me. So, you get to live on that technicality for now."

"For now?" he asked, voice choked.

"Yes, because no matter how many times your son takes my brother's cock. He got married a few months ago, which is a requirement in the Quintin's trust, is it not? Section 4 article C? The heir of the Quintin line must marry to take the position of duke or duchess? Well, Zain did marry." I raise a finger, making the duke flinch. "In fact, I think I should request a meeting with him. I'm sure he's just as greedy as his father. I mean I am my father's son, so I understand inheriting wicked traits. I'm sure he's eager to stop being seen as a boy and extremely willing to get you out of his hair and off my brother's cock. *That* would give me reason to kill you, and not one soul would care for a washed up duke once your son is head of the Quintin line."

I took a few steps back letting him get a full look at the devil, silver blooded and dressed in black. "So, Zander, should I do that? Should I call up your son and strike up a deal that ends up with you at the bottom of a hill? Or… should you turn around and go home, and never bring your trivial affairs to my door again?"

He opened his mouth to reply but I put my hand up to stop him. "This decision requires no words."

He nodded hastily, before turning and briskly walking out the door.

My breath out was annoyed before I called out through the still opened door. "*Merrick.*"

He entered, a smug smile on his lips, most probably a product from seeing the duke scurry off with his tail tucked behind his legs. "Yeah, boss?"

Day was well into afternoon when Fredrick arrived, sauntering into my office with no care in the world.

"Brother!" he chanted. "You called?"

I leveled a look on him, but he brushed it off, plopping down in the chair with no sense of worry. He'd had years to deal with my weathering looks, and he knew I wouldn't dare ever hurt him, often using his immunity to press my buttons.

"I had a visit from the duke today."

A black brow rose against his darkened skin. "You did?"

"Unfortunately, yes, I did. Could you guess what he wanted?"

"My dick?" He smiled arrogantly.

I closed my eyes, taking in a much-needed breath. "Fredrick, could you not settle down with a male? You know, claim someone, so I don't have to deal with your vindictive ex-lovers?"

"Oh, Zander isn't an ex-lover, he took me last night."

I pinched the bridge of my nose. "Fredrick, you are going to be the king. You should be looking for a partner to rule at your side. Both Zander and Zain Quintin are married and are great at causing disturbances."

My brother sighed with that princely smile on his face. "Creatures of chaos. It is a beautiful thing, Karney."

"Fredrick, you need to keep your affairs private. It doesn't look good for your image. The people view you as a scandalous boy prince, and they will never see you as a king if you don't start tightening your image."

Fredrick waved a hand. "Or... Or... father will realize that you are the one fit for the throne and I was, and always will be, the second born fit for lavish lunacy?"

"You could be a great king if you tried."

"You are the one who should be king."

"If that was true, I wouldn't be in this chair and you wouldn't exist."

"Well, maybe I shouldn't."

I worked my jaw, eyeing my little brother. "Frederick, just stay away from the Quintins. They are spoiled piss sports who think they can walk up in here and demand me to control your sexual interactions."

"And are you not attempting to do that right now, brother?"

"If Zander is stupid enough to come to me, then he might be stupid enough to go to a witch. Witches' morals are not sound. If the gods deem that you deserve to learn a lesson, then they will craft up a love potion, and you'll find yourself drugged and caged. Beast don't like to be caged, Fredrick."

He huffed. "Fine. By the way, Father sent me with a message."

"What does he want?"

"There's a party tomorrow, and all the court members that aren't on the committee for war are required to come."

"And?"

Fredrick smiled with mockery. "And he wants you on the dais."

I glanced at my watch, noticing the afternoon sun was a few hours away from night. "He knows my answer to that request." I stood, walking around to meet my brother who embraced me as he always did. "I'll see you tomorrow."

He pulled away, saluting with jest. "Tomorrow."

SEVENTEEN

MARIE

*S*uffocated—that was the best word to describe how I felt at the moment. I laid in my bed; Kolvin's body wrapped around mine. His chest bare, his hot breath brushing against my ear. Me dressed neck to toe and my body sweating profusely, legs pressed so tightly together to attempt to relieve the aching throb settled there. My nipples hard and scraping against the fabric of my dress.

I was wide awake, not able to sleep if I even desired to. The need to turn over and press my mouth to Kolvin cutting deeply into me. A few days ago, my beast made it clear she didn't want him to relieve her, she had her sights set on the devil. Today though, she didn't care, she ached, and she was ready to go wild.

Kolvin had gotten more clingy over the last month, spending every free second he had with me. Sometimes he would sit in on me and Karnelian's sessions. I cared for Kolvin deeply, but his presence was beginning to annoy the fuck out of me. I was seconds away from fucking him, then cutting his throat out like Karnelian had taught me for being such a nuisance.

It had been three days without sleep. I could last five or six, seven or eight days on occasion. Lately, my energy had lessened with my heat pressing down on me, wearing out my body.

Karnelian noticed my dip in energy. He was the first and only person to notice. His questioning had me panicked. If he figured out I didn't sleep, he'd tell my parents and they might make me take a tonic to go to bed. Which I seriously didn't want to happen. No matter, dust, wine, whiskey, or tonic, if I fell into slumber, I always woke up screaming, midnight eyes haunting my dreams before he put me into a forever sleep.

I tried to up my caffeine intake, so I appeared more energetic, but it ended up aggravating my heat more, and exhausting me further. When I fell asleep last, it was only four days in before I passed out, thankfully it was at night and I woke up screaming with Kolvin, instead of during the day with Karnelian.

My heat was at a point of lust filled pain. My dress was soaked with sweat, my panties suctioned to my clit. If I so much as breathed too hard, the fabric would scrape across my sensitive flesh, causing my whole body to shudder.

At the first brush of bronzing yellow across the morning sky, I got out of bed, Kolvin still sleeping peacefully.

The walk to my dresser was a slow waddle, bringing exacerbated breaths from my lungs. I grabbed a dress, something of light material that flowed while still covering me in full and a new set of panties before I took more labored steps to the bathroom.

With cold water filling the tub, I slid down to the chilled floor, happy to call this my new home if need be. I unlatched the leather pouch from under the sink, untying the satchel to reveal an empty bottom.

Every shard of my shattered soul made itself known in that moment, cutting into me with its wailing screams.

Unable to process what the empty bag meant; I closed it, only to open it again as if that would change the result.

It didn't.

"No."

It was known to me that I was running low, but not that I was completely out. I tried to remember the last time I took a dose. If it pinged in my brain that I was completely out but the heat had started to muddy my mind. Yesterday was so much like today, and today was so much like tomorrow, and tomorrow was like yesterday which was the same as today.

The past days had blended together, my focus completely on my throbbing core, making me unable to process the passing of time.

Of course, my brain was able to remember Karnelian's concerns about my change in focus. How his blond brows furrowed, and his silver eyes sharpened in worry that was pitiless. A primal reaction to kneel at his feet and worship his cock for simply noticing me, muddling my mind even more.

The splashing of water hitting the tiled floor kept my mind from spiraling with thoughts of him. I rushed to turn the faucet off, and I resumed my spot on the floor. The quiet becoming loud, the hollow feeling within making itself known. The fibers of my being vibrated, panic rising with each hymn.

I was about to go through withdrawal.

Dust wasn't a drug; it was poison that altered the mind, giving a faux high. If that high went away, the damage that was done to your body was still there, now able to shine. I could already feel my stomach starting to turn and my body temperature rising from heated to blistering.

I peeled off my clothes, sinking into the freezing cold water in hopes it would diminish my rising temperatures.

It didn't.

The cold temperature made my skin taut, the tiny hairs standing and my nipples becoming tight sensitive peaks. The water made my tender flesh raw, the slight ripples within caressing me and bringing more full body shudders.

I quickly washed up. Whimpers emanated from my throat as the rough abrasions from the washcloth scraped my skin.

Exiting the bathroom was a slow process, the microscopic movements of my dress halting my steps, my panties already starting to be saturated with my arousal.

My mother was there, her looming presence more grave than it had been before or the lack of dust made me more aware of it. She suggested we spend the day in the library, and I didn't object.

I sat on the leather couch, staring at the page of one of the current books I was reading. My focus on my throbbing core, the pulse of which I could hear thundering in my ears.

I needed to figure a way to see G as soon as possible, or I would definitely be breaking my heat within the next few days, if not hours. The problem was that my mother was now watching me during the day so I couldn't sneak out to meet him. I didn't even know if he would be in town. He didn't live in Lightwood; just visited from time to time so there was a chance he wouldn't be here all week and I definitely knew I couldn't last that long.

Chewing on one of my claws, I pondered solutions. I could sneak out at night, but Kolvin was a light sleeper, and he'd eventually notice my absence from bed if I was gone too long. I could make up an excuse that I just went for a night walk to aid with my heat. But, I could only use that excuse once, and there was still the chance that G wouldn't even be there tonight. Another option was to ask Karnelian.

He was my best option but the most complicated one. Firstly, he aggravated my heat more than any other male and I was dreading him showing up later today. I would even go as far as saying that the reason my heat was so bad was because of him. Secondly, there was a big chance he'd tell someone or make me stop. Snorting poison went against the whole staying alive thing and I doubted he'd be on board with that. If I made a deal with him, I could ask him not to tell, but I also had nothing to offer him in exchange. I would have to settle for just asking and hope he'd be in a giving mood today.

The day stretched; each second known to me from the pulsing of my clit. My body felt like it was filled with lava. So, I stared at the page in misery. My limbs tight with tension, an ache developing in my back because I didn't dare to even shift an inch the whole day.

My father eventually relieved my mother from watching me. Thankfully, he didn't seem to be in the mood to chat, busy working on something I didn't really care to know what. His pen scribbles gyrated against my nerves and aggravated my already riled beast. I was a few moments away from ripping out the male's carotid.

Karnelian really shouldn't have taught me that.

The leftover residuals of dust were fully gone by this time, revealing my rotted and tattered insides. The wails of my soul were loud, and it fought against my body's heat. The strange mix of sadness, arousal and nausea, a chaos that didn't appeal to my beast one bit.

I focused on counting my breaths, the deep inhalations enough for me to drown out everything outside of myself. I wouldn't say it was better because it was like being trapped within myself again—but I didn't have any more thoughts of killing my father.

A slight tremble entered my body, panic creeping its way up my spine. I couldn't last like this, confined inside myself. The thoughts of him were just lingering behind a very thin veil and if that broke was going to be a sobbing, horny mess.

"Little bird."

My eyes snapped to silvery hazel, cinnamon filling my nose and pushing everything but my arousal back.

"Karnelian." My voice a wispy rasp.

A cocky smile formed against his soft bronzed skin, his canines peeking through.

Fuck me.

Karnelian was here with that smile and my father had left.

A tremor filtered through my body. A result of my creature trying to pounce the male and myself holding back with the last bit of restraint I had.

He was the best male. Perfect in the most primal ways. He wasn't my mate but that didn't mean he wasn't perfect. A prize any female would be proud to win. He was powerful, intelligent, with a roughly sculpted frame that was sure to ruin soft curves. I could break my heat with anyone, but he was the best choice. He'd give healthy babes. He'd be a good provider, able to fetch us game easily, and defend against threats.

Karnelian sat next to me. Raised my legs into his lap, his fingers stroking my covered calves.

I pressed my lips together to hold back the moans that wanted to escape. My core tightened, the ache within spreading.

My eyes were trained on his magical fingers, that knew exactly where my strained muscles were and rubbed out the soreness. His scent wrapped around me like a warm blanket and the rumblings of his voice rolled over my body.

My panties were soaked, and my mind jumbled in a fight between jumping him and holding back. I couldn't even remember what I was going to say to him or what it was even about. All I could do was think about him, him, him.

"Marie." Karnelian's voice was rough as he called to me. A harsh shock to my senses that had a gush of my arousal seeping into my wet panties.

A curious but unengaged hum exited from me.

"Did you hear me?"

I gave a shake of my head—mostly to clear my mind.

He sighed. The sound of disappointment emanating from him had my creature ultra-focused on him then. We didn't want him disappointed, we wanted him happy, *pleased* with us.

His glorious fingers trailed down my legs to my sockless feet. I normally wore stockings to cover myself but today I forgot. He didn't massage my feet, thankfully, but his fingers brushed over the skin curiously. His eyes trained on the action.

"I'm not stopping by tomorrow."

My body stiffened further. "*Why?*"

His head swirled to me; a brow raised.

The reply bordered on harsh and desperate, so I understood the look. I tried to relax my features and tilted my head in question—a horrible attempt to downplay my response.

Karnelian didn't pry, re-focusing his attention on the back-and-forth sway of his fingers on my legs. A small mercy that he didn't go back to my feet.

"My father is hosting a party."

I took a measured breath in, nearly moaning it out with the new whiff of his delicious scent. "Your father is always hosting a party."

His chuckle was low and a bit harsh. "This one is to divert people from the looming war and placate their worries. He needs his lap dog there to play as a fear tactic to impede anyone from stepping out of line."

"Lap dog? You mean, you?"

He gave a smile, but it was dark and shadowed with sadness. "I am the devil of many deals."

He continued to torture me with the gentle press of his fingers. Each stroke sent blots of pleasure to my clit. The roughness of his calloused fingers grating against the fabric of my dress, adding to the pleasure.

He'd be so perfect to fuck. Not only for my creature but for me too. I felt comfortable around him. He was a strong male, not just physically, but emotionally. He was able to handle my breakdown without an ounce of panic entering his eyes and he even knew how to distract me from spiraling. He didn't believe in love either so I didn't fear that he would fall for me, only to be crushed later when I chose my mate over him.

The best fucking option.

"Where are you today, little bird?" Karnelian's smooth baritones broke through my foggy mind. I realized I had probably spaced out again.

My eyes met his, a mistake, as they cut into me with concern again. "I'm... just... not as well today."

"I know. You're extremely tense and your pulse is faster than usual." His thumbs pressed more into my stiff muscles. "You want to talk about it?"

That was the final straw.

I couldn't fucking hold back anymore, not when he showed concern for me. It was basic, almost nothing, the bear fucking minimum, but my beast was already on the edge with this male and that was what pushed us over.

I lunged for him then, my legs straddling his lap, my mouth pressing against his.

Instead of pushing me away, his hands wrapped around me, and he deepened the kiss.

Equally pained moans sounded from us.

I didn't know why he sounded pained, but I knew why I did.

Kissing him caused a battle within me. I wanted him like a starved animal wanted food, but it ripped me to shreds with guilt.

My body verses my soul. My hips grinding into Karnelian, my spirit thrashing away.

A betrayal to my mate that continued with each stroke of Karnelian's tongue against mine. He tasted of sin and savagery. Wicked and dark just like the inners of my being, his madness the same as mine.

I wanted more of it, but I hated that I wanted more.

There was a dryness that itched behind my eyelids before they filled with tears. I ignored them as best I could, deepening the kiss further, my hands traveling down Karnelian's face to his neck.

I ignored the shudders that wracked my body, pretending they were shudders from the pleasure of this kiss. My fingers traveled to the collar to his tie-less button-up, tears streaming down my face as I undid the first button.

That was when Karnelian snapped out of it and pulled away. "Little bird?"

My fingers brushed my freshly bruised lips, a shiver rippling through me as I realized what I had done. I kissed a male who was not my mate, more than that.

My eyes locked with Karnelian's shock and confusion showing through in his hazels as the tears fell from mine in a flood.

"I'm sorry," I whispered before I scrambled off him, almost falling to the floor.

"Marie," Karnelian said, trying to catch me, but I caught myself and ran out of the library through the manor. Sprinting as if I could outrun the hurricane emotions that was coming after me.

"Marie," Karnelian called out close behind.

I sped up the stairs, probably the first and only time I'd ever manage to take three at a time. Then I was in my room, slamming the door shut, my back coming flush with the wood as a sob was stolen from my throat.

"Marie." Karnelian's voice was muffled, but I could hear the concern within it, the concern that my creature adored. The sound that made me betray my mate.

I slid down the door, my cries matching the ones that were sung by my soul.

I kissed a male. I kissed him and I liked it, more than liked it, I craved it. I still wanted to open the door, press my lips to his and pull him to my bed to do more.

The guilt was all-consuming, my soul flashing me with images of my mate dead on the floor in punishment for this act.

The shards of my spirit cut into me deep. I could feel the metaphorical blood oozing within and filling me up, spurring the tears from my eyes.

It lasted hours, me sitting there tormented by my soul as Karnelian stayed on the other side of the door. He didn't speak, just sat there listening to my cries in condolence. His scent filtering through, adding to my pain but equally soothing it.

His stoic presence was an anchor I could hold on to and eventually the storm subsided to a drizzle and then clear skies.

I didn't open the door, and he didn't speak. He stayed though. Stayed when the day turned to night, there for me as I pieced myself together the best I could. He only left when my mother came. Her harsh words to Karnelian had me standing, realizing the door was still unlocked.

Latching it, I made my way to the bathroom. Once again filling the tub, checking the satchel to see if dust magically appeared and could be an answer to my pending problem, then stepping into the cold water to find no relief.

New tears came but these were not of the sorrows of my soul, these were from frustration.

I just wanted peace. Peace from my maddened mind. Peace from my frozen, hollow heart. Peace from my shattered, wailing soul. Peace from my heated, aching body.

Death would end the hell within, but I couldn't die, the silver brand on my arm glimmering in the dim bathroom light.

Out of all the ailments within my being, my body's screams were the loudest. They were aggressive scathing things, and I couldn't take it anymore.

My fingers found my clit without much thought, circling the little bud, and creating shock waves of pleasure through me.

I had tried this many times and failed many times, my mind conjuring images of my mate, making the cries of my soul shriller, and my body taut with tension.

My mind was done with my soul's torment, and I quickly found silver eyes shining like moons in the sky of my imagination.

The devil haunted me with his masculine aura and devious smiles.

There was a freedom with letting the devil through my door. All my dark desires spilled in with him, probably because they were all of him.

His hands in replacement of mine. His cock in my mouth. His voice in my ears.

It didn't take long for my orgasm to come. My first in five years and it was what you'd expect if you hadn't come in five years. An amazing accomplishment but still not fully satisfying.

It was still enough to offer that tiny bit of relief I needed to clear my head.

When I opened my eyes and met the white plain ceiling of my bathroom, my thoughts on Karnelian and what I had just done.

The guilt was there, but behind a veil. Like my fractured psyche created a barrier between me and it. The thing was, while I was lost in my thoughts of Karnelian, I didn't feel it at all. I had fully given into my desires of him, and he distracted me away from the pain. A reprieve better than any drug.

Like a drug, all the dark and dirty parts of him corrupted my mind, his hellfire burning through everything else and only leaving him amongst the ashes. With the peace that settled over my mind, I could evaluate how whenever he was around, all I thought about was him. I didn't know if it was just my desire brought on from the heat or if he was just the ultimate distraction I needed. Overall, when I was with him, I only thought of him, there was nothing else but him. Maybe, maybe, if I relieved my heat, it could stay that way. The burning in my body would be gone and maybe I could escape the guilt from cheating.

Maybe.

In my mind, I had already betrayed my mate. Sleeping with the male might make it worse but the guilt was already there. It wasn't going to go away, and at the very least I could break my heat and dose myself with enough dust that wouldn't kill me, but would still drown out the howls of my soul.

Exiting the tub, I decided to remain naked for the night since I would be spending it alone. My curtains were opened, the sky littered with stars and a silvery moon.

I contemplated everything in the small, cleared space of my mind. Weighing if I could go another week of my heat. When the next time I would be able to see G. If I could actually go through with breaking my heat.

The stars soon disappeared, and the sun was blazing in the morning sky, and I decided what I would do.

Dressing, I opened the door, ready to walk down to the kitchen where I was sure to find my mother, but she was sitting against the wall opposite my door. The pillow and strewn blanket an indication she had slept there last night.

Black eyes met mine, filled with pitiful worry. "Flower, are you okay?"

I nodded, clearing my throat. "I'd like to go to the ball tonight."

EIGHTEEN

Karnelian

*T*he taste of death and heartbreak was stained on my tongue, and it was fucking delicious.

I couldn't fathom why she did it. Why she pressed her pillowy lips to mine with hunger. Why soft moans exited that sweet mouth. Why her round hips ground into my cock.

I lost myself to her the second her tongue swirled with mine. Unable to process the situation as my cock became steel and my hand gripped her plush curves.

For a second, for just a fucking second, I gave into the whispers that rang in mind when I laid eyes on her. Let myself get lost in her lust. It was a slip up, she had caught me off guard, and it was a mistake on my part. I should have pushed her away the second I tasted her because no matter how sweet she tasted, how soft she felt against me, I couldn't get lost in a delusion. Not again.

There were tears in her soulless eyes, regret etched into her features. The look, a needle stabbing into my dead heart. A heart that I wished to keep lifeless.

A third glass of whiskey scorched my throat. An attempt to erase her taste from my tongue, and to drown out my father's deceitfulness to his court.

Lying to the fae was absurd. We were creatures of corruption; we could taste lies in the air. Not one of the court members in the ballroom believed his assurance that all was well between the fae. If we could taste lies on the wind, we could feel anarchy in our bones. Carnage between the races was soon to approach, and while I understood my father's attempt to keep the people at bay, I also knew the people. They were all wretched, greed filled beasts that would kill their own for a chance to create chaos.

My brother stood on the dais with my father, his face disinterested and bored. My father knew my answer to stand up there before he had Fredrick ask. It was why he had Fredrick ask. If anyone could sway me, it would be him. I'd rip my heart out for my little brother, but my father knew that even if I was a part of this court, I was not a prince, and I wouldn't stand behind him and be the puppet as I once was.

My eyes drifted through the fae on the ballroom floor, landing upon a female who looked at me with faux lust. A mask that covered up the greed that permeated her being.

I, as of late, avoided the opposite sex. I didn't hate females; I just grew tired of them, thinking their pussies were gold, and a cheap, meaningless fuck was bargainable in a deal. My needs were satiated when need be. Often by one of those greedy females, but I didn't trade in sex. I may let her believe I would—I was a monster, that I do not hide—but I would often just fuck her until she lay boneless and leave before she could utter a word. If I wasn't feared by the fae, I would have many angry females at my office door, screaming about how I wronged them, though they thought to deceive me with the sex in the first place.

Tonight, I was considering using this female who planned to use me. The little bird had ruffled my feathers, and the whiskey wasn't washing her away. My cock twitched at every thought of her, something that was doomed to become habit if I didn't do something about it.

A sensual smirk formed on my lips; eyes hooded in artificial desire. I was going to break this female in half. Fuck my rage and frustration out on her. Not all of it. Unfortunately, she was a frail thing, beautiful, but frail. Breaking her was a possibility if I fully let my beast out—something I'd never do with a partner. And for weathering my storm, I'd be nice enough to broker a deal after—skewed in my favor, of course.

My monster hated the idea of attempting to wash away the little bird. He was reading into the true lust hidden behind the tears in her obsidian eyes, reminding me of the fact that she kissed me simply because she wanted to.

She didn't want to. There were tears in her eyes, and she spent hours crying after.

Then why did she do it?

Chastising myself for getting wrapped up in her nest again, I started toward the female with disingenuous lust. The gods though, were not on my side—not that they ever were—because my father intercepted my approach.

"Karnelian."

I hadn't noticed the ending of his speech, another reason why I needed to get the bird out of my head.

Lips pressed together, I turned to my father. "Yes?" Another swig from my glass, to tamper down the blazing rage when forced to meet those green greedy eyes.

"I wanted to talk to you about a few things."

My groan was loud enough to draw eyes, eyes that quickly snapped away when their irises landed on me. "Do I have much of a choice?"

"No."

Finishing my drink, I followed my father to the war room. It wouldn't be wrong of me to assume he picked this room for its sentimental value in hopes to rekindle our bond. He could talk to me anywhere, the private throne room, his fuck room to right of the dais, we could even just talk in the hall, and I could cast a sound barrier against prying ears.

My father did nothing without reason. He wanted to talk in the war room because that was the room he taught me to be king. The room where we spent many days bonding as father and son do. The room he lied to me day after day, telling me my silver blood wasn't going to be a problem when I ascended to the throne as he fucked any female he could to make sure I never had to.

My father's greatest weakness was his inability to see things from the angles of others. He did things for the good of the people, not the good of his family, or his heart. If the good of the people went against the good of his family, he expected that his family would bend to his decisions. Which didn't happen when he torched the bond between us in favor of appeasing the people. So, for me, this room would always be a reminder of the breaking of us, not the building, doing more to dissuade me of his favor.

My father made his way to the cabinets near his desk, grabbing a bottle of wine and a glass. "Would you like some?"

"I'm fine."

"When was the last time you had a glass?"

I leaned against his desk, his eyes pin pointing to where my body met the wood before flicking them back to mine. "I don't see why that would matter?"

"We are beasts, Karnelian. Creatures who crave to kill, fuck, and feast. It's important that you make sure your urges are taken care of."

With a cocky roll of my eyes, I flashed my canines in a devious smile. "Who's to say I don't let my beast out to play every once in a while, father?"

His nostrils flared ever so slightly, and irritation he covered by sipping his drink. "Karnelian, if you deny your urges, it will eat at you until you are ready to explode. It is crucially important that you, your brother, and I never lose control."

I didn't hold back the snort that emanated from me. "Father, I am not a child, no need to parent me. As well as I will never be king, no reason for you to carry on with your king lessons. Thanks for your artificial concern, but I am able to handle myself. So, what do you need?"

A muscle in his jaw clenched. He let emotion swirl into his eyes, and I was sure that he was pushing out his aura for me to read—two of his exploitative tactics. "Karnelian, I do care about you. You are my son and I do love you."

"You really shouldn't let others know your kindness; they may abuse them." My smile turned wicked; my eyes gleaming with mayhem. "Is that all? I was about to lure a female to my bed and let my beast have its way with her before you graciously interrupted."

The roll of his naked shoulders meant he was done trying to rebuild something that was tarnished, and his sigh meant he was soon to stop wasting my time. "No, how is the princess?"

My cock jerked at the reminder of her, bringing awareness to her haunting taste on my tongue. "She is fine."

"Her progress with magic?"

"She is ready to start some small spells. She has a general idea of how to handle her shadows."

"How long do you think it would take for her to be ready to rise to the throne?"

"A couple months if we continue at this rate but she is unpredictable." *Extremely unpredictable.* "One day she can be fine, and other days…"

"Keep working with her. The commander reported she was doing better these past couple weeks. Says she seems to be enjoying training."

"You know I can be quite entertaining." I smirked, and his eyes narrowed on me. "What are your plans after her magic is matured?" My father had not learned that I wasn't a trusted ally. In ways I was. I would never betray him like he did I, but that didn't mean I wasn't trying to twist the plot to favor me. My father made a grave mistake putting me in the little bird's orbit. If I got her under my wing, my power in faerie could potentially double, something I was certain he didn't want to happen.

"I plan to marry her off."

Fire flared in my middle, the reaction was potent enough to flicker across my face, but I quickly covered it with disbelief. "You plan on marrying her off? The mated female? And to whom do you think to marry her off to?"

"Grayson would be a good fit, or another nobleman in our circle."

"Grayson? From what I recall, he isn't anywhere near noble, and he is in my circle, not yours."

My father waved a hand. "He was noble. His family is still a part of the Unseelie Court. He grew up in that world before he was sorted, so he would be of good help to her."

"Did you specifically pick Grayson because he is fucking my mother?"

He kept his face controlled at my comment but there was a gleam in his eye that revealed the truth. "It doesn't have to be him. Just a male, preferably someone fully fae who is trusted."

"Why does he have to be fully fae?"

"She's half-fae and the people don't like the royal line to be diluted. She'll need to fuck someone of full blood to produce a worthy heir."

I scoffed at him and his hypocrisy. "You want her to not only marry someone who isn't her mate, but fuck them too?"

"Yes."

"She would never agree to that." There was an edge in my words. An unwanted feeling of possession bubbling up in me. While her taste still stained my tongue, my monster didn't even want to consider her with another male.

"She would."

My arms folded in an attempt to stifle my rising agitation. "How? You can't demand her to fuck someone because you're king."

His next sip of wine was slow and savory. "She's in heat."

I gawked; my brows pushing together. A fae female being in heat was extremely uncommon since fertility was a struggle amongst our people. "What?"

"She's in heat. She had a few cycles before that dissipated on their own, but this current one hasn't gone away yet. It's looking like it won't go away unless she fucks someone. I'll offer someone and after she marries and bares a babe, she can finally get what she wants."

Death. Though that didn't need to be stated. "I think I'd notice if she was in heat. As well as it wasn't in the file you gave me."

My father smiled, a horrid rendition of my devilish grin. "She wears a necklace that covers her scent. You made it. And it wasn't like you needed to know that to teach her magic."

A frown painted upon my face, my rage filling every pore in my body. I had kept my view of Marie very analytical, looking at her like an object over a person. A puzzle to be solved. It was purposeful. Not only because she was barely alive, but the whispers of a delusional destiny clogged my ears, growing in volume if I got too close to her. Scenting out a female was something you'd do if you planned to fuck her, and I had no such plans. So, I didn't pay attention to the fact she didn't offer a clear scent.

"It's a good plan." One I needed to intercept as soon as possible.

HEART COLD AS GOLD

That needle of pain in my chest grew to a spike. The little bird didn't want to kiss me as I suspected. She was using me just as the others, but at the very least I discovered the thing she truly desired—sex.

My monster paced back and forth within, angry at my father for ruining my plans, angry with the little bird for being just like everyone else, and angry with myself for fantasizing even for a second. I needed to fuck something or break something, and I needed to pound down a thousand more drinks, all of which I couldn't do in this fucking room.

"Is that all?" I asked.

"I have one more thing." He walked behind his desk, opening a drawer and pulling out a wooden box. "With the war coming, you know it could end badly."

"What is war without bloodshed?" I said, doing my best to hide my irritation.

He shook his head, opening the non-descript box, his eyes roaming over the contents. "I do love you, Karnelian. You know that."

It was an easy thing to keep my face blank.

His green eyes stayed latched onto mine, waiting for a response that would not come. He knew that, but still he had hope.

Giving in, he sighed. In his hands, he lifted the gold crown from the box—my crown. The crown I gave back to him when I told him I wanted nothing to do with him. "I want you to start wearing it again."

"Is that an order?"

"No, but—"

"Then, no."

"Karnelian…"

"If it's not an order, then I'm not fucking wearing it." I couldn't hold back the callousness of my tone. I was already raging within and then he tried to pull this. No wonder we are in this room.

"Do you want to make a deal over it?"

A grunt exited me, paired with a sinister sneer. "Father, I only make deals if it benefits me, and wearing that crown will bring me nothing but shame."

"Karnelian, what I did wasn't intended to hurt you. I didn't intend—"

"Father, I don't care what you have to say. You did what you did, and the damage is done. You chose your crown over your family. And I chose to renounce my title. Even if you reject it, it's only a title. A title I do not care to keep."

Vulnerability waved in those greedy greens, swirling with many unsaid things. Things I had never allowed him to say. He didn't get the right to apologize. Even if I allowed it, I wouldn't forgive him. You don't spend seventy years lying to someone you claim to love and get pardoned from it.

"Is that it?" I asked again, but it was more of a growl.

His lips pressed tightly together before he nodded, and I was turning my back, walking out of there.

Back in the ballroom, I scanned the floor for that female with greed in her heart and lust in her eyes, but then black fabric caught my eye and there was the little bird.

Her dark abysses found me, drowning me in their agony. My feet were moving before I could register it in my mind. But when I reached her, my thoughts were precise. I needed to find out what she desired, and I did. Now to strike a deal.

NINETEEN

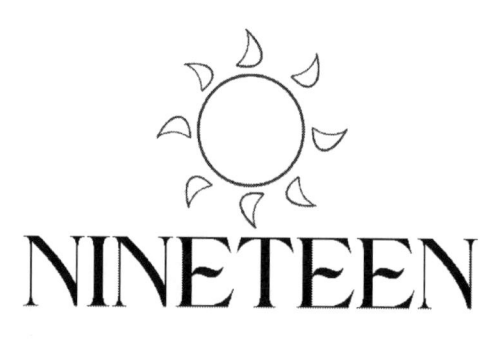

CORIVINA

The ballroom was bustling with people, their energy loud and filled with delight. But it wasn't them that blasted away the darkness that kept me sane. No, it was that light that burned into my being was standing near, too near, and dressed in his commander's uniform.

"Do you want a drink?" Darius asked.

A shake of my head was my reply.

Marie didn't tell me why she wanted to come to the ball tonight. I figured it was about that blasted male. I knew he was not the reason for her breakdown yesterday, but I still blamed him. He had fired a light in my flower, which sparked hope in my heart. Silly of me to think she wouldn't be blanketed in my darkness as well. Stupid of me to think a candle could fully cast away the night.

Darius's gentle fingers brushed across the dip in my back. It was an involuntary action when my body leaned into him to seek his warmth. "Do you want to dance?"

Separating myself from that warmth was like stabbing myself in the heart, a pressure building in my eyes. "No."

"Why are we here, then?" An irritation entered his voice, a noticeable contrast from how soft it had been all day. After the kitchen incident, his voice was tender and his eyes comforting. A sea I could easily get stranded in.

"Marie asked for me to bring her. That's why I am here. You are here for your own reasons." He didn't have to come tonight; he knew of the king's announcement and was given the evening off since he wasn't going to get many in the upcoming future, but when he saw me getting ready, he started to get ready as well.

He shifted so his eyes were swimming in my vision. Without the heat, I was able to see the hurt that I had engraved into him. That hurt reflecting into me tenfold, another shadow added to my darkness that was sure to berate me later.

My darkness had yet to reform into the wall, so it was as it used to be a lingering pit that was begging me to fall into, and to evade another slip into the void, my vision pivoted away from the warm blues.

"Vina." His whisper a loud sound that rattled my soul. "I'm here because I want to be with my family."

You don't want me as your family anymore.

It was a funny thing how illumination brought shade. In the presence of my sun, I was sure to fall into those tiny pockets of shadow. "I think I do want that drink," I said as I abruptly made my way to a staff member carrying that delicious tart liquid. Dominick always served good wine at his court ordered parties. The blood to alcohol ratio was almost perfect, but not as perfect as Ginger's.

It had been too long since I last got drunk. Marie's sixteenth birthday was the last time I glutinously indulged. Sixteen was the legal age for Seelie fae to drink, and that night we let Marie have her first glass. The violent level of alcohol and the exhilarating first taste of human blood quickly had her eyes drooping and she went to bed soon after her first sips. Darius and I finished the bottle, it was expensive and we didn't want it to go to waste. Then we drank another and another, ending the night in a drunken, aggressive fuck.

Tonight, I did not want an aggressive fuck. I wanted to find sanctuary like I normally did when I fell into the clutter of my mind. My armor from the darkness before I had learned to work with it.

"When those horrors come, let your darkness in. It will protect you from succumbing to madness."

"Corivina," Dominick rumbled. A sound that would never even fluster my body. "Darius."

A bow came from me, low enough to properly pay respect, but not as low as it had normally been over the last five years. "Your Majesty."

Darius gave a nod.

"I didn't see you at the announcements. Did you just arrive?" Dominick talked directly to me, completely disregarding Darius, and his now heated appearance.

"Yes." I nodded, sipping my wine. I wanted to devour it in seconds, but I needed to keep an image with Dominick if I wanted to be a piece in the war.

A pleased grin made its way across Dominick's face. His eyes sparkled with calculations, a trait the cunning king often carried. "You don't mind if I steal her?" he said to Darius.

The air thickened and Darius's resolve hardened.

"He doesn't."

His head snapped to me, betrayal hidden in his stony expression. The edges of which cut into me like glass.

Another sip of my wine to soothe the sting before I set the glass down and followed Dominick. I had no care for Dominick's company tonight, but being away from Darius was less painful than being near him.

The king brought me to the room located behind the dais—his fuck room. He didn't currently hold any females, but he was known to hold a harem off and on during his reign. There have only been two females who have kept him to themselves. Camila, Prince Fredrick's mother, who only held it for the duration of her pregnancy. And Magdalena, Prince Karnelian's mother, who held it for twenty-ish years before she left Dominick. With all of the Party King's female drama, everyone knew this room was where he brought them to fuck.

Darius definitely knew that, his gaze burning into my back as I entered the dimly lit room, and a four-poster bed dressed in gold sheets.

"You are quite despicable at times, Dominick," I chided.

His lips quirked up to the side, not at all ashamed of his conduct. "I like to win, Corivina."

I rolled my eyes. "I am not a prize to win. As well as you have already lost, Darius and I bound our blood about a hundred-and-fifty years ago. You were there."

He raised a finger. "That is actually what I wanted to talk to you about." He reached into his pocket, pulling something out before lowering to one knee.

My eyes bulged as the male revealed a gold ring inside a red velvet box. "What the fuck are you doing?"

"Proposing," he said with heavy confidence.

My eyes narrowed on him. Mouth slightly parted as my brain tried to form the words to convey that this was a lost cause. I flirted with this male and might have been over generous with my attention, but as I just clearly stated to him, I was married.

"You and Darius are getting a divorce, are you not?"

I stiffened, shock spreading through my bones. "How do you know that?"

"Darius sent the request forms for my approval a couple weeks back. Which, of course, I will approve." He lifted the box, holding the gaudy ring for emphasis.

Shadows cast by my sun swarmed my being, wrapping around my heart and giving a generous squeeze. "He did that?"

Dominick nodded, his fingers finding my limp ones. His warmth not penetrating my cold. "Corivina, I know you don't love me, but I want you as my queen. You hold strength and power in every fiber of your being. When you speak, people listen. You spark fear in others even if you've never been known toward violence. You are an upstanding lady, and I have always thought that way of you. To be frank, I've fancied you since I first met you during your training. It would've been inappropriate of me to have an entanglement with a student, and you were marked for most of your time here, so I didn't pursue. I regretted that decision when I saw you on Darius's arm many years later. I know you love him, and you will always love him—I get that, I find myself in that position with another as well—but we would make a good team. So, Corivina, will you marry me and become my queen?"

His words were at war in my mind.

Darius sent the request forms for my approval. Versus. *We would make a good team.*

The breaking of my heart versus the pending victory of my vengeance. The loss of the love I never deserved versus a loveless marriage with a male whom I reluctantly called a friend.

"Would you want to mark me?" The question seemed to come automatically, straight from my tattered soul.

"Would you allow me?"

"Just answer my question."

The grin on his lips widened to show porcelain teeth and sharp canines. "I won't do anything you do not wish to do. We don't even have to consummate our marriage, though that is something I would wish to do with you."

My mind was a jumble of weeds. Invasive and over consuming. There wasn't a right choice. Darius wanted an end. He had already started it without even informing me. Whether I liked it or not, my marriage was over. *But should I tie myself to the king?*

"I... I need to think about it."

He stood, his face glowing with male arrogance. "That isn't a no."

"It isn't a yes."

A snort exited him before he leaned in to press a kiss to my forehead, a picture painting in my mind. A time when I feared being touched by other males, but I craved the warmth from Darius's forehead kisses. There was so much care within each one, care that wrapped around my heart, slowly soothed away my fears.

This kiss provided nothing. It was a grace from Dominick, warm only because his body temperature, not an ounce of care within its depths.

I pulled back, a tight smile holding back the preening emotions.

Dominick's hand still grasped mine as he turned my palm over to press the box into it. "Take it. Wear mine when you are ready to say yes."

My throat dried. My eyes locked on the object, carrying the gaudy gold ring. Pretty but not a resemblance of me. Not like the silver band adoring my finger with a simple diamond.

I didn't meet Dominick's eyes as I nodded and turned to exit the room. Immediately, I was faced with Darius's heated gaze. He hadn't moved from where I left him. His arms folded, and the corners of his lips pointed down.

The edge of the box dug into my palm as I made my way over to him, my steps slow and weighted.

When I moved out of the path of his gaze to position myself at his side, his eyes stayed pinned to the door. "What did he want?"

My face was stoic. I wished my heart was encased as well so it wouldn't feel like it was about to burst. "I'm going home."

His blues cut to me, the heat losing its simmer, his face coloring with concern. "I'll go with you."

"No, someone needs to wait for Marie and I'm tired."

"She is fine. She left with Karnelian. He will bring her back home when they are finished."

My brow rose in question. The last time she was with that male, it hadn't ended well.

"She said she was going to be fine."

My breath in was sharp. The instinct to worry over my babe overpowered from the raging emotions within. "I'm going to the inn," I said, turning to walk away from Darius. His hand wrapped around my arm, stopping me and knocking the box to the floor.

Darius bent down, picking up the box, his eyes studying it before he peeled the lid open.

He jerked back as his eyes landed on the ring. His face went blank, revealing no emotions, a trait a commander would have perfected.

A small snort exited him, the sound sad and mocking. "Of course, he'd do that." He closed the box, his eyes flicking to mine, not warm, not heated, but cold, more so voids of blue, almost gray in color. "What did you say?" A flat response, not an edge of harshness hidden within. Just flat and dull.

"Nothing."

"Nothing," he repeated, and I knew Dominick's words were ringing in his ears. *That isn't a no.*

My throat was too hoarse at this point to even bear another word. My eyes dry, itching with tears.

Biting my cheek, I held out my hand for the box.

He gave no emotions as he closed it and placed it in my hand. His fingers sliding against mine, not a modicum of warmth exiting him.

He looked me dead in the eyes. No, he looked into my eyes as if I was dead. A ghost he was seeing through. "I hope you're happy." Then he turned and walked away.

TWENTY

MARIE

I walked through a sea of colors. Mostly gold, but there were greens, pinks, and blues. Waving through the people, I looked for one who dressed in the absence of color like myself. The one my body craved and captivated my mind. But I didn't see him towering over the Seelie fae. No devilry or havoc being curated. Nor wicked smiles or devious smirks being thrown about.

Many eyes were on me, hushed whispers of my title sang in the air. Their presence didn't bother me none, my body forcing my focus on my heated core. Which was riotous, especially paired with the decaying organs within. My stomach churned, ready to flip at any moment and my hands were littered with sweat, but I was able to handle the feeling. Either because of my brief relief last night or my body knew tonight I planned to give in to its desires.

Red velvet appeared in my vision, stalling my course of action. Black raven hair sprawled down his back. He stood with confidence but that of which stemmed from arrogance. A smile, big and bright. A bit too big and the brightness a little too dull.

My steps were quick—hurried as I made my way over to the male dressed in the ridiculously lavish suit. He always wore overly flashy clothes. His presence not easily missed because he purposefully drew the eye. He didn't like you to ignore him, and he would challenge for the attention of those who did, just like the day we met in Alirick's bar. He walked into my field of vision with that easy smile edged with harsh lines, agitated that my awareness wasn't on his show.

My fingers tapped his shoulder, but he didn't turn away from entertaining those he had managed to catch in his web. His voice ebbed and flowed as he told his exaggerated story, laughs emanating from his current patrons. G was a comedian—when he wasn't dealing drugs, I supposed. I wasn't fully sure, but that was how we met. Him doing a set at Alirick's bar, me not laughing because I couldn't and him giving me drugs to lighten my mood. Drugs that slowed healing and abated my heat.

My second tap on his shoulder was harsh, bordering on a poke.

An exasperated sigh left his mouth as he turned, leveling his tilted eyes on me. His skin was a bit more tan than most, carrying olive undertones. His eyes were black, the lids of which held no crease. I always got this sense of familiarity when I was around him, he reminded me of someone, but I couldn't put my finger on exactly who.

His bitter smile loosened and spread. "Sunshine!" G's voice performative and lined with gusto. He was loud—an off-putting trait for a drug dealer to hold.

My mouth fell open to speak but my words halted as a female stood up next to G. Her wide brown eyes capturing me, my neck arching to meet them. She was tall for a fae female, an inch or two taller than G, who was of average male height. Freckles scattered across her face, and her mahogany hair streaked with natural blonde highlights. There was an otherness about her as she came off more ethereal, more fluid. Her beauty softer than a normal fae.

It was the eyes that made me pause, bigger and rounder, making me feel at peace in her presence. An unnatural feeling for a fae, triggering me to stiffen in defense.

A hand on my shoulder startled me, my feet taking a cautious step back. G's brows were furrowed. He turned to the female, pressing a soft kiss on her delicate cheek. "I'll be right back."

We headed to the corridor that Karnelian had brought me down when last I was here, the hall vacant of others just as before.

"I don't have much on me, Sunny," G said.

"How much do you have?"

"A couple days' worth, maybe a week if you rationed yourself." A hint of judgment inhabited his voice—which was comical. He was the one who introduced me to the drugs. He still supplied me, greedily taking my money to fund his comedy career.

Ignoring his jab, I asked, "When can I see you again?"

"I'll be in Lightwood the next few days. I can swing by the bar and leave your supply with Al." Al, also known as Alirick, was the bartender/owner at the best bar in Lightwood. He also knew my father and respected him, and even if Alirick did shady dealings with G, he probably wouldn't hesitate to tell on me.

"Could you meet me?"

His chuckle was light, carrying a mocking tone. "Why, *princess*? Also, not cool not disclosing who you are by the way. I could get in a lot of trouble dealing to you if anyone found out."

I tried to paint a sympathetic look on my face. What he said was true; dust was illegal. If he got caught dealing poison to the princess who wasn't supposed to die, he would probably be killed. "Sorry," I mumbled, brushing a strand of hair behind my ear. "But can you meet me?"

He smirked; his black eyes were razors cutting through my façade. There was something sinister about G. A misery hidden under his jester's mask. "When?"

"I don't exactly know."

He scoffed, crossing his arms. "You expect me to just wait around for you? Why can't I just leave it with Al? He's a trusted ally. He works for my boss, so he won't fuck with the product."

"Al knows my father. He will tell on me."

"I'll tell him to keep his mouth shut. He won't tell if he knows what's good for him."

A frown lined my lips.

G's brow raised. "Do you want the dust or not?"

"Fine," I grumbled, reaching into my pocket to grab the coin.

"Double this time."

My frown deepened. "Why?"

"Because you are interrupting my evening, Sunshine."

I rolled my eyes, pulling out more coin and placing it in his hand.

G handed me a small pouch. "It was nice doing business with you, Sunny," he said, straightening out his velvet suit. "We really need to set up some type of meeting time." Another false smile and he was walking back into the ballroom with a backward wave goodbye.

Huffing, I checked the pouch's contents. If I did ration myself, I could make it last for a week. Hopefully, I would be able to sneak out to Al's within that time.

I don't have to break my heat with Karnelian anymore.

Something about the thought left me a bit hollow. A feeling I didn't want to evaluate, and would like to drown away with dust and wine if I could snag one before we left.

Tucking the pouch into my pocket, I made my way to the ballroom. I scanned the room for my parents, not finding them where I left them. I continued my search, straining my neck to see over the crowd of people, until my body seized its action, stiffening. Eyes were on me, not the eyes of those who whispered hushed rumors of the Unseelie Princess. Eyes I didn't have to turn my head to know the color of, but I did anyway.

Silver hazel eyes. Burning, silver hazel eyes zeroed in on me.

My lungs forgot how to pull air to breathe, my core clenching as my heat intensified to a new height. My body drenched in sweat, my clit pulsing with intensity. I knew in this moment; I wouldn't be able to deny it anymore. No amount of dust would be able to stifle its will. Tonight, I would break my heat with the male who carried the blood of light and dark. A sinful male who danced with demons and partied with hellfire.

Every morsel of my body tensed as he took a broad powerful step toward me, his eyes pinpointing me like prey. What a foolish prey I was. All instinct of survival thrown out the window as the baddest beast in the world stalked after me.

When he was close enough for me to sample his delicious scent, his hand extended out toward me. My fingers were slow to raise and slid across his rough ones, the connection causing a full body shudder.

My head raised in time to catch his smirk—smug and arrogant, edged with his wickedness.

Hand in hand, we walked. Karnelian leading and me following, but his steps slow as to not overshadow me. Though my body was tight, I felt light, filled with relief, letting him guide me, there was a peace. No screams permeated my ears, no whispers of guilt or grief. Just Karnelian and Marie.

We entered the study where he had first helped me breathe, the warmth of his hand leaving mine as he walked over to pour two glasses of his drink.

He handed me the tumbler filled with the amber liquid, those fingers brushing mine before gesturing for me to sit as he leaned against the wall.

We studied each other in silence and for the first time I let myself compare him to my mate.

Karnelian was nothing like him. Karnelian was something else. Loud and outspoken, always taking up space. Karnelian was deadly, it was in the dominance that he held in himself. He was the most powerful fae, though, no one knew the preciseness of his power level, we could sense it. Sense that he owned the room if he so wished.

Then there was physicality. His hair was the color of wheat, his skin bronzed from the sun, tiny little dusting of freckles over the bridge of his nose. He towered over the crowds of already tall fae. His shoulders broad, and muscles built like a warrior, but somehow still slim and ethereal as any fae. His suits black like onyx, cut perfectly to his body, regal but rough.

And lastly his eyes. Hazel—his pupils lined with a rusted brown, a green outer ring that was so faded it shimmered like silver. His eyes didn't suck my soul out of my body, but instead lit a fire within, a chasm of energy from those bright orbs.

With all those differences, you'd think that he'd be the last male I would want to break my heat. That my heat wanted someone to replace or hold the space of my mate. Even if that was what I wanted, there was no way Karnelian would ever hold space for anyone.

The silence was broken with the sound of the whiskey swishing in a glass as Karnelian brought it to his plush lips. His eyes still intent on me as he swallowed and let out a hum. "You're in heat."

The reminder had my already taut body clenching tighter. My beast fully prepared to pounce on Karnelian, taking every last bit of my will to hold back.

"Why didn't you tell me?"

His voice was like wood, rough but still somehow smooth. Each lull of which scraping against me and aggravating my heat more.

I shifted in my seat, shuddering at the friction of my panties rubbing against my clit. "It's embarrassing."

A soft chuckle. "I don't think you understand how a fae male's dick works. We'd get hard at just the idea of our females going into heat. Only a few of us are lucky enough to enjoy that."

I shook my head. "I didn't tell you because I want *you*."

"I'm guessing that doesn't make me very special, you'd fuck anyone at this point." His bottom lips found purchase under his teeth, amusement coloring his face as he took in my disheveled state. "My father said you're moments away from breaking."

My nostrils flared with my shaky breath in. "My heat wants *you*. It would settle for Kolvin or any other male, yes. But you're the reason it's so bad, my beast selected you, causing the heat to get worse the more we were around each other. She doesn't want Kolvin, she wants you."

The corners of his lips spread out into his devilish smile. The smile that did foul things to me. "So, how long are you thinking about holding out?"

I forced my eyes away from the temptation, settling on my drink I had yet to touch. "I... uh... came here to ask you."

In an instant Karnelian was there, his fingers gliding under my face and lifting my chin. Cold lifeless black meeting steely hazel. "Are you sure that's what you want?"

A nod was all I could manage.

His thumb brushed over my lip. "Say it, little bird."

My body began to tremble, my lips parting under his thumb. "I... want you to fuck me."

His thumb traced my lips as if savoring the words, his eyes hooded and a soft smirk adoring his face.

That smirk spread into a smile, wicked, evil, but full of grace. "I'll fuck you."

My core clenched painfully, my creature screaming at me to take all my clothes off and fuck the shit out of him right now. I opened my mouth to speak but he pulled my chin, securing my lips with his thumb.

"*But...* I want to make a deal."

My eyes connected with his, chaos brewing within. The devil stood in that hurricane, crazy and maniacal. Plotting and planning, waiting for when the opportunity arose, but I had no idea of what I could offer him. "A deal?"

"Yes." His fingers trailed down my face over my covered neck. "A real one too, not a he said she said. A deal bound in blood, little bird."

"What do you want?"

"I want you to marry me."

I stilled, my eyes going wide. "What? I..."

Karnelian stepped back to lean against the wall, his face becoming serious. "I was born to the crown and had it taken away from me when it was discovered I was a disgrace. You are an opportunity for me to have it back without murdering my father and brother for it."

My eyes were practically popping out of my head at this point. "You were going to murder them?"

"No, but that was my only option, until you."

I released a breath I didn't know I was holding. "Oh."

"If I marry you, then becoming king is a guarantee. My father won't be able to take it from me."

My teeth gnawed over my bottom lip. "What if Markos has a babe before I get the crown?"

Karnelian folded his hands in his pocket. "Then we won't marry, and I'll let you die."

"So, we will marry but only after I have the crown?"

A quick curt nod was his confirmation.

"What about after that?"

"I will be king, and you'll be queen."

"But what about an heir?"

He shrugged. "You're in heat. Seems like it won't be a problem for us to bear one."

A sadness stole over my heated body. To return to my mate and relieve the ache in my soul, I would have to bear a babe. A babe that wasn't his and wouldn't know the love of their mother. "And then you'll let me go?"

"I'm not putting that in the deal, but possibly."

A wrinkle formed on my forehead. "Possibly?"

He blinked, his face offering no argument. He was the Silver Blooded Devil; deals were his thing. Being fae, I understood deliberately leaving things out of the deal. It protected him. I mean, what if our child died before birthing their own heir? The fae would be left with no Unseelie heir and chaos would ensue.

"And until then, you'll help with my heat?"

"Yes, that will also help with people believing that we actually like each other, and I'm not taking advantage of you."

"I do like you," I blurted out, not really thinking about it.

He smirked, sweet and sultry. "I like you too, little bird."

"But not like... romantically. There won't be romantic feelings between us, just sex."

"I won't fall in love with you, but I'm not binding that in blood." Karnelian must have read a confused expression on my face because he continued with, "Little bird, feelings are unpredictable. Did you ever think you were going to stop crying when he died?"

Dull, lifeless midnight eyes flashed in my mind, threatening to undo me, but the steely hazel ones kept me grounded. "No."

"But you did. Feelings are not something I add to my deals because they are unpredictable. I will probably care for you. You will be my wife and I will treat you as such. I'll be fucking you so I will have some feelings for you that are more than friendly." He smiled that sinful smile, the lust from before filling his eyes for a brief moment. "But, I won't fall for you. Even if I did believe in love, I wouldn't be stupid enough to fall for a female who's currently only breathing because she is forced to. That being said, I can't predict my or your feelings. Let's say it takes us a thousand years to bear a babe. A thousand years bound together might blur lines and the smallest bit of love could break the deal."

"You won't be bound to me," I said, shrinking into myself. "You can have other lovers as long as you satisfy my heat."

"All you want is for me to satisfy your heat? Nothing else? What I'm asking is pretty big."

At the current moment, all I wanted was to be rid of my heat. "No... I... I want you to make me come at least once a week."

Was my request very calculated? No, but the last few years had been a heated mess, and that was all my lust fogged brain could come up with.

A pale brow rose. "Can you not do that yourself?"

Shamefully, I raised my hand, flexing my fingers to show off my claws. "I can't stick them..."

His hand covered his mouth, amusement coloring his eyes. "You can't finger your pussy?"

I shook my head in annoyance. I could rub my clit but even then, I had to be careful not to cut myself.

"Why not just cut them?"

I scoffed at the atrocity of his statement. "Have you ever asked a being with claws to cut their claws off?"

His brow furrowed. "No."

"It's quite painful to cut them—extremely painful. We have nerves in there. *And* even if I wanted to, I couldn't because of your brand."

"So, you want me to make you come once a week and satisfy your heat. Anything else?"

"*Unless denied*. I want you to satisfy my heat and make me come once a week unless denied. I don't know exactly how much sex I want after you satisfy my heat."

He nodded. "You know I don't do vanilla, little bird. I fuck hard and rough, and I don't hold back. You really think you'll want that?"

Yes, gods yes! I fucking want that. Is what I wanted to say but all I offered him was a meek nod.

He stared at me for a moment, eyes assessing me before he spoke again. "I want something else."

"Hmmm?"

"I want you to wear the ring I give you." His eyes dropped to my left hand.

My stomach clenched and I looked down.

I fucking hated looking at it. I hated the reminder of one of the happiest days of my life that quickly turned into one of the worst. But over my feelings, it was a gift from him and taking it off would be another betrayal to add to my conscious.

I took a steady breath, staring at it, hearing the wails of my soul when I did, seeing his dead, lifeless body. This betrayal will get me closer to him. It wasn't the last thing I had of him either, I had my clothes and his claim even if it was another wretched thing.

Pulling off the ring, I offered it to Karnelian. "Keep it."

His jaw worked as he took the ring, examining it for a moment before putting it into his pocket. "Okay, little bird." He pulled his dagger, silver with an eclipse on the hilt.

"How are you going to cut me? I can't..." My eyes drifted to the dagger, the sharp point glinting against the fae light.

"It's my magic that binds you, Marie. I control when you are harmed."

His statement had me sucking in a breath, a wave of arousal falling over me. He held out his hand for mine, and setting my glass down, I took it. He pulled me to standing then maneuvered my hand, so it laid palm up in his.

His dagger was inches away from me when I spoke. "Wait." Karnelian stilled, eyes curious. "I have a question."

He pulled back, his face neutral as if he expected me to stop him. "Yes?"

"Will I take your last name? Wouldn't it be a little weird if there were two kings with the same last name?"

A small, surprised chuckle escaped him. "I'll take yours. It will be expected of me since you're the heir."

"*Karnelian Shadawn*. I think it will make you seem even more intimidating."

A grin lined his lips as he regrasped my hand. His eyes met mine, silently asking if I was ready and I answered back with a nod.

Pain, sharp and burning, traveling from my hand, and ringing down in my toes. Sweet, delicious pain that reset my being, and left me feeling alive and less hollow. The cut throbbed as red blood poured from the wound. Karnelian then cut his palm before joining hands with me.

"I, Karnelian Lightfire, promise to satisfy your, Marie Shadawn's, heat when it occurs and make you come." He suppressed the smile at his words. "Once a week. Unless denied by you."

"I, Marie Shadawn, promise to marry you, Karnelian Lightfire, if I become queen of the Unseelie Territory."

Silver veins began to crawl up my hand disappearing under my sleeve as black vines traveled up Karnelian's.

When it was done, he pulled out a handkerchief, wiping both our hands clean of the mixed blood.

His eyes met mine, and the questioning look that adorned my face. "What, little bird?"

"Don't you have a female? Shouldn't you have told her about this before we…"

"I have been with many females, but I have never called one mine. Until you."

There was a little flip in my stomach that I ignored, my mouth quirking to the side. "What about Charlotte?"

"Charlotte?"

"Yeah, the female you begged your father for."

Karnelian held up a finger. "One, I do not beg. Two, Charlotte is not a female."

My brows pulled close together.

He gave an easy smile, sin coating the arch in his lips. Karnelian stretched out a hand for me to take. "Come, little bird, let me introduce you to Charlotte."

TWENTY-ONE

MARIE

Karnelian and I found my father to tell him we'd be leaving. His focus was fiercely pinpointed to some door and my mother was nowhere in sight to badger us with questions, so Karnelian wasted no time grabbing me and magically transporting me without warning.

Walking through a regular portal was different than Karnelian's way. You never felt like you left this world. With the regular way, in the span of a step you'd be in a different place but when Karnelian portaled you, it was like you left this plane before you got to the desired destination. The disorientating feeling left one's being rattled, which I assume was Karnelian's intention.

The chill of fresh cool air brushed against my face when solid ground manifested under my boots. Karnelian let go of my waist, leaving me alone to grasp my bearings. Thankfully, I didn't puke and after a few breaths of the summer's night air, my stomach settled.

"Meet Charlotte, little bird."

A gasp escaped me as I took in the building. A huge sandstone castle covered in vines set in front of a thousand stars. There was a beauty to the building that one could only describe as love. As if this humongous castle was built with the objective of making it a home. The intentionality was seen in every brick laid and every arched carved. Though the building was old—a couple thousand years—the architect's vision still showed. Great care had been given to the place over the years. The memories made in this castle left the place lively and one could feel the heart of it beating in the waves of the air.

"*Charlotte Manor.* I've lived here for years but it was still technically my father's. I wanted the deed."

I blinked, still in awe of the place. "This is not a manor. It's a whole fucking castle."

He chuckled lightly as his fingers found mine, tugging me in the direction of the manor.

The grand wooden doors opened before we even were close, revealing a warmly lit foyer. Karnelian directed me towards a hall, not stopping to let me take in the beauty of the inside.

Some of the walls were made of the same sandstone of the outer building, a gold like substance used as grout in between each brick but most were painted in a light cream. Candles lit the area offering a warm light. The best part was, the vines that decorated the outside had found their way inside and draped across the walls.

"Why is it called Charlotte?" I asked as we started up some steps, Karnelian taking one step at a time.

"It's been in the family for thousands of years. Charlotte was a past queen."

My fingers reached out to play with the vines on the banister. "It's breathtaking."

"Why do you think I wanted it?" I glanced to see Karnelian's grin. His smile always did something to me, not like my mates had. My mate's smile was rare and seeing it brought joy to my face because I lived to please him. Each one of his smiles only ever for me. Karnelian's openness made it clear that he was haunted with demons, but he still smiled. The smiles easy, sometimes sensual, and sometimes not fully reaching his eyes, but he still smiled like none of his pain mattered. Like he wouldn't let his demons overcrowd that part of his soul. The youthful part that just wanted to smile when he felt happy, and I admired that. I adored even more that each one of his smiles was only for him. Not for me, not for anyone, just for him.

After a few flights of stairs and a couple halls, we stopped at a nondescript door. "This will be your room."

A crease formed between my brows. "My room?"

"You are my fiancée now. You should definitely have a room at my house. You don't have to stay here, but I might as well give you a room. I want people to think what we have is, in a way, real."

I nodded because it was a good idea for people to think we were in love with another, or just liked each other enough to get married politically.

Karnelian let out a heavy breath before tugging on my hand and continued down the hall.

A few doors down, we paused. "This is my room." Karnelian's voice had become slightly strangled, not in anger but in nervousness. The sound was soft, lacking his normal roughness. Something that had me pinching my brows because he was never nervous.

We stood there in silence that quickly started to stretch with whispers of madness. My soul's wails became dire, as if I would simply die if I did this. I wished I'd die but I knew that was the least likely case. What would happen was relief, and distraction from those wailing screams and midnight eyes that haunted my dreams.

Without waiting for Karnelian, my fingers found the gold nob, cold against my heated flesh. A turn and then a push had my soul quieted, from surrendering defeat or being drowned out by my body's need I wouldn't know.

The room was simple, but elegant. More Seelie than I would have thought from Karnelian, but somehow the room wasn't a surprise. The focal point were the windows, there were more windows than wall space, looking out to the night covered lands of the estate. Vines curled around the windowsills, twirling down to the post of the bed that laid in the center. White cream sheets, four pillows for resting one's head. Bedside tables, and a dresser crafted of lightly stained wood, and then plants. So many plants. Plants that did well in pots, which served no purpose than to add vibrance to a room.

There was one thing that stood out in the room, and not that they were out of place, but they were personable and had my curiosity piqued and my feet moving.

Three medium-sized frames sat on of the bedside table. All the photos—magical painted pictures that held the preciseness that a painter could never capture—were of Karnelian at different times in his life. The first when he was fully grown but was of a time before me. His hair was longer like his father's was now and a little boy, skin colored similar to mine, sat on his shoulders. Fredrick, his brother. The next was when he was younger just older than a babe, hair still long, hugging the female with chestnut hair and big brown eyes I saw earlier tonight. She smiled down at Karnelian with love that only a mother could hold. The last photo was of Karnelian and his father. He was a faeling at this point, nowhere close to adulthood. The king placed a gold crown upon his son's head. Karnelian's face was bowed and obscured, but his father's face was filled with pride and joy.

My perusing was interrupted when Karnelian came up behind me and flipped the photos upside down. A frown garnished my face, aimed at him. "Why hide them when I have already seen them?"

He leaned down, his face coming into the croak of my neck, his body becoming flushed with mine. "I don't want them to see how I am about to tear you apart, little bird." The rumble of his voice brought my skin to a pebble, a shiver racking my frame.

His hands came over my shoulders, offering a light comforting squeeze before he kissed my temple. The act not sexual in the slightest but still had my arousal peaking to a new height. "I'll go slow the first time."

I twisted out of his grasp, locking eyes with him, intensity pouring from my gaze. "I don't want slow." I wanted hard and fast. I wanted him to tear me apart like he stated moments ago. I wanted to forget my name, my body, my whole existence and be fully filled with his.

He smirked, a dimple forming in his cheek. "Are you sure? I tend to be hard and brutal to the females I fuck." His hand came up to stroke my cheek. "Leaving them sore in the best way."

My core tightened to the point of pain, and it was an effort not to rip his clothes off right then. "I want that."

He leaned down, my breath hitching as his mouth came within inches of mine. He halted there, not moving, and letting the buildup build and build. Our breaths, heated and scented with whiskey, fanning over each other. I realized he was waiting for me to fill the gap. For me to prove that I did want this as much as my body did.

I lifted on my toes, my fingers brushed his chin, the light prickles of his shaven facial hair scraping across my skin. Then I pulled his lips to mine.

This kiss was much better than our rushed first. There was lust like before, but there was also solidity, safety, comfort.

Karnelian was sturdy and strong but broken as I was. He could handle my pain like he handled his own, he had proved that many times. I didn't fear I'd ruin him or puncture his heart with the shards of my tattered soul. His heart was cold as was mine, unable to beat, unable to be broken.

He was the devil who danced with his demons and inspired me to want to dance with mine. To be able to smile with a cloud of darkness over my head and revel in indecency.

He took control, prying my lips apart to swipe his tongue. His hands moved down my body, pressing his hardening cock into my stomach, and extracting a moan from my throat. My nipples stiffened, rubbing against his chest as I lifted higher on my toes, to further deepen the kiss. Our height difference was apparent but didn't stop us.

He sat on the bed, pulling me into his lap so I straddled his hips, our lips only leaving another's for a brief minute.

His sensual scent entered the air, his hands traveling up my outer thighs to grip my ass and rock me into him. His pained groan echoed into me, buzzing against my being and heating my blood.

Those hands trailed up my back, climbing under my curls until he found the zipper that rested against my neck. I froze, my mind pinging with unaddressed information as Karnelian broke the kiss.

His eyes met mine a question in their steely gaze and I took a deep breath in before answering, "Um, could we... turn out the lights?"

A ghost of a frown appeared on his lips as he stewed on it, and I bit mine as I sat in wait. I knew what he was thinking, the room was lit perfectly for sex. Not too bright to kill the mood but just bright enough for us to see each other, which was the problem. I didn't want him to see me.

A shake of his head accompanied Karnelian's, "No." Finality flaring in his eyes.

"Please?"

"No. I want to see you while I fuck you. I want *you* to see *me* while I fuck you."

With a heavy sigh, I pushed off him.

"Marie, we made a deal."

I had my back to him, looking out one of the windows, the moon half full, the stars shining bright. "I know... I just need a moment."

I clenched and unclenched my hands before taking off my boots to avoid the inevitable. A concoction of nervousness and embarrassment mixing with my raging lust as I found the zipper of my dress.

There was a reason I wore clothes that covered me neck to toe. A reason I made sure my mother stopped watching me as I bathed. A reason I suffered the Seelie heat blaring down on me while I already had a heat blaring down on myself.

I swallowed the lump in my throat when the zipper had reached its end, pushing the dress off my shoulders. The fabric hit the floor, leaving me standing in underwear, a garter, stockings, and the necklace that covered my scent. I removed my bralette, hoping my breast would serve as a distraction from the horror that would enter his eyes when I turned.

When I met his hazels, they were trained on my body, still covered with the marks of my mate.

"How?" he said, his eyes still not meeting mine.

Marks lasted about three months on the average fae body, but since I was half fae, they lasted longer—about a year. When they started to fade, and everything within me started to panic. I had to find a way to keep them. That urge had a broken, barely functioning, me sneaking out of the manor to go to the bar in search of something I knew would stop my healing. "Faerie dust."

It wasn't foolproof; my marks were slowly healing but they were still noticeably marks after years of rotting my insides. I probably had a few more years of the dust fighting with my fae healing before they disappeared fully.

All the lust left Karnelian's face, his features turning hard and lining with fury. "That shit literally harms you, little bird."

"Loophole. The deal was I cannot cause harm or intentionally put myself in harm's way until the brand is removed. My intention is never to cause harm; it is to keep my marks. The harm is a byproduct of the dust *after* I've already taken it."

A muscle ticked in his jaw. "So, the clothes?"

"To keep them hidden."

He studied my body, his eyes still not meeting mine. That penetrating gaze made me feel awkward standing there half-naked, so I covered my breasts since he didn't even seem remotely interested in them.

The action drew his eyes to mine, and he cocked his head to the side. His small reveal of anger dissipated, and his devil mask slipped over top. "You won't get pregnant while on that."

I glanced at my toes. "Hopefully... we can find another way? Mating made me the heir. Shouldn't marriage make you the heir too?"

He snorted. "If that was the case, King Markos would have just married someone by now. Mates are under a special clause, because the magic is tied to the soul of the heir, so when you two fused, it became tied to yours."

"Oh... No one ever explained to me how I became the heir."

His lips thinned, an expression akin to disappointment ghosting his face. "Why would they?" A pause. "I'm guessing you don't want to stop?"

I looked away, pushing my hair behind my ear.

Karnelian sighed. "If you take too much, you can die. You know that, right?"

I nodded, still not looking at him. "I only take a teaspoon a day. Twice a day recently because my heat has been so bad, but you'll relieve it so I can go back down."

"You will. If you die, it's not just screwing me over. It's screwing over the whole race of fae."

"I know," I whispered, meekly. "You probably don't want to fuck me now, huh?"

"It won't be a problem." A yelp sounded from me as his hands came around my waist, pulling me to straddle his lap. Our eyes met. Something akin to concern filtered into his as he untucked the curl trapped behind my ear, twirling it around his finger before letting it go. "You are beautiful, Marie," he whispered it like a secret that he wasn't supposed to share.

"Thank you." My fingers came up to trace his freckles. "You are too."

A slow smile spread on his lips. "Thank you." His fingers found their way under my chin, his face coming closer to mine. "We'll worry about all the technicalities later, okay?"

"Okay."

Then his lips were on mine, heat flooding through my veins as his hand gripped my ass.

I moaned, wrapping my arms around his neck, grinding my hips into his hard length. The urge to push him on his back ever prevalent, but I wanted him to dominate me. Which he did, flipping us so he lay above me before he stood to remove his suit jacket, and rolled up the sleeves of his button up, his eyes trailing my body hungrily as he did so.

His hands found my arms, the calluses on his fingers scraping across my skin. He found the silver brand on my arm, tracing the eclipse and sending tremors through my body. Something about the brand made me feel more aroused, the connection to him feeling like a bandage to cover my bleeding wounds.

His fingers continued down, lightly trailing my body until they skimmed past my panties to my garter belt. "These are sexy as fuck," he murmured as he unhooked my stocking from the belt. He pulled them off, leaving me in wasted underwear and the necklace.

My fingers found the necklace, his eyes connecting with the action before he pulled it out of my grasp, swiping his thumb over the reddish-orange stone. "Karnelian."

I raised a brow. "You?"

He smiled, sensual but mocking. "The stone, it's Carnelian. I always use it when I need to bind a spell into something."

I examined it again, realizing I never attempted to figure out what kind of stone it was. "It's beautiful." And it was. It was chaotic and calm, soft and seductive. A great representation of Karnelian as a person, grounded but eccentric.

He batted my hand away. "We'll leave it on for now." His eyes cut through me, his beast energetically telling me who was boss before pressing his lips to mine, harsh and consuming, pouring himself into me.

His fingers trailed to my panties, brushing across the black lace.

"I..." I said between kisses. "I didn't prepare for this."

"Baby." Voice breathy and rasped. "I'm a beast. The more wild you are, the fucking better." He kissed me again, but I was slightly distracted by the word—*Baby*. It was a human word, something they called their babes and their loved ones. Some fae did call their loved ones that, but it wasn't normal. But hearing it from Karnelian's mouth made me feel warm inside, filling me with an appreciation that I decanted back into my kiss.

He broke the connection abruptly, suctioning his mouth with my nipple. My back arched at the unexpected action, causing a relieved moan to spill from my lips. His tongue swirled around the nub, his teeth lightly biting. I found purchase in his blond strands, pushing him into me, eyes rolling closed to savor the sensation.

He left my breast, a sharp slap stinging my skin soon followed. My eyes opened, connecting with Karnelian's. His fingers rubbing out the pain he caused, teasing my nipple. "Keep your eyes open, little bird."

He hurt me.

He hurt me and I fucking loved it.

My eyes fell closed again, reveling in the left over tingles of pain that flared as he soothed it out. Another slap, this one harder, causing a strangled moan to escape me, my thighs clenching together at the sweet, sweet pain.

"You like that?" Karnelian whispered, his breath flowing over the area, little blossoms of pain following.

I nodded, humming as he stroked the tender flesh.

"Be a good girl and I'll give you what you want. Open those pretty eyes for me."

I obeyed and he rewarded me with another slap. This one harder, racking through my body, causing me to grit my teeth.

He smirked down at me, his features sharpening with sin. Smug, like he just discovered something he was prepared to exploit.

His fingers hooked in my panties, pulling them down. Slowly. Ever so slowly, like he was unwrapping a present. When I was fully bare, he kneeled, spreading my legs wide. He bit his lip when he took in my swollen flesh. "So wet for me," he murmured. "Have you had a problem keeping dry around me?"

His eyes met mine, demanding I answer, so I gave a quick nod.

"Words, Marie."

"Yes."

"Yes, what?"

My nostrils flared and his face painted with a cocky grin. "Yes, I've been wet for you."

His grin widened before he returned his gaze to my core. One hand on my leg, while the other trailed my inner thigh.

"You'll come to me when you're dripping like this, okay?" I nodded greedily as his fingers skated closer to where I wanted them. "So fucking messy I could drown in you."

Karnelian's fingers continued to taunt, drawing this out more. Just fucking teasing.

"Please, Nelian," I moaned.

"So fucking needy." And finally, finally, his fingers brushed my heated flesh, my back arching enough to break.

He soaked his fingers with my arousal, sliding them up and down my slit, drawing little figure eights against my entrance, but never entering. He groaned as he continued playing with my core as if it was his favorite toy. It felt like hours of his teasing, each light flick to my clit driving me to madness.

He pushed a finger into me and I was lost. I hadn't had a finger inside me in years, and just his knuckle had me breaking.

My screams bounced off the windows, my walls tightening around his digit as he pushed further.

He hummed in approval as he lifted my hips, fucking his finger as I climaxed. He soon inserted another finger fucking me slowly and drawing out my pleasure.

"You sing so perfectly, little bird."

I bit my lip to hold back my moans, embarrassment I had never felt before coloring me at how loud I was. His fingers left me, a harsh slap on my clit, my body jolting at the sweet hurt.

"Don't hide from me," Karnelian said, voice stern.

I whimpered as he used his thumb to smooth out the pain.

"Answer me, Marie."

"Okay," I said, my voice barely above a whisper, my breaths panting, body exhausted in the best fucking way.

I didn't know what the fuck was happening between us, but I liked it. I liked his control, it was calculated, authoritative. His demand was like a rule I must follow, but not overbearing or forceful. I liked his slow perusal of my body. His eyes hooded with deep lust as if saving each detail of me for later. I liked his pet names. Little bird. Baby. Words connecting me to him, echoed with the rough rumbles of his voice.

He removed his fingers and brought them to his mouth, eyes rolling to the back of his skull as he tasted me.

Spreading my legs wider, his face came close to my core. "Eyes on me."

Then his tongue, wet and hot, made contact with my needy flesh.

I bit into my lip hard, the action not conscious. My whole attention on him as his tongue did things I didn't know tongues could do.

That tongue, that fucking tongue. I was starting to think they called him the devil for his sharp, wicked tongue.

No one should be allowed to have a tool like that. Pointed and long. Able to lap at me properly. My claws cut into the sheets as I choked on my own blood, the iron taste filling my tongue as his did wonders.

My eyes never left his. His silver irises tracked me as I became a bloody mess. A pain I could only have because he distracted me with that tongue. It increased my pleasure as my venom entered my veins. The effects not as powerful as if I was to bite another, but still affected me enough to come four times while he feasted on me.

When he was finished, that tongue met my chin, licking up the blood there. He let out a groan that bordered on being a growl, the sound igniting my creature and making me ravenously hungry for him. I pulled his mouth to mine, devouring him. My legs wrapping around his waist, my growl entering his mouth when my thighs met fabric.

I was fully a beast then, my fingers finding the neckline of his tunic and ripping the fabric apart, buttons raining down on me.

"Yes," Karnelian said through our connected mouths. "Rip it, baby. Show me how badly you want it."

A rumble in response, I tugged at his shirt, cutting the fabric away with my claws. His exposed chest was revealed to me, covered with blood from accidentally cutting into his flesh. I cleaned his wounds, soaking my tongue with him. The taste of him extracting another growl from my beast.

He pushed me back roughly, my head hitting the bed, fire dancing in his eyes. "Lie at the head." He grunted, voice full of anger but in the sexiest of ways.

Karnelian walked to the end of the bed and started to undo his belt buckle, eyes trained on me like a beast tracking prey.

I took in his naked chest, noticing the tattoo that lay in the center. It was a simple black eclipse, mirroring the silver brand on my arm. The dark striking ink against his bronzed skin made my core clench. I never had a thing for males with tattoos until I saw it on him.

The pop of his pants button glued my attention to his fingers. He pushed them off his hips, his underwear coming with.

Then panic entered me.

In my opinion, all the males I had been with were well-endowed. My mate was slightly bigger than Kolvin but not enough to tell. It didn't matter to me because my mate fit perfectly. He was the perfect thickness, perfect size, perfect shape, and I thought he was huge.

Karnelian was redefining huge for me at the moment. The male had a fucking monster attached to him. I was sure my fingers weren't going to wrap fully around that and definitely not fit inside me.

My breath was fast and fluttering as Karnelian crawled to me. His motions of a predator. That big thick angry cock coming for me.

When he was before me, my fears were tampered with the press of his lips. My beast happy to be split open by him.

His weight came over me, his cock kissing my core. He brushed it through my wetness, hissing as I coated him before he pushed in, pulling back so his eyes met mine.

Twined groans escaped our mouths as he entered further. He went slow, but his fingers definitely hadn't prepared me enough for him. There was pleasure, but mostly pain, blissful body-shivering pain.

Another light shove in and Karnelian paused, his abs flexing with his harsh breaths. His sweat covered brows pinched; nostrils flared. "Fuck, your cunt is tight."

All I could do was whimper, my walls clenching around the invasive intrusion.

He sucked in a sharp breath and thrust into me, shoving more of himself in. I winced as agony pushed through me, closing my eyes for the briefest second to revel in it.

His fingers found my chin, squeezing harshly. "What did I say earlier, little bird?"

"Keep my eyes open."

He kissed my temple as he pushed more. "Yeah." Then he thrust the last part of himself into me, and a wrangled scream ripped from my throat.

Pain... so much fucking pain, and I loved it. I knew I was sick and a little bit mad, but I didn't think I was masochistic.

He stayed still, holding himself so I could get used to his girth, which I doubted would ever happen. Not even if he fucked me all night.

After five years of horrid heats, I didn't care to wait. All I wanted was his cock pistoning in and out of me.

One hand wrapped around Karnelian's neck, pulling him down to me, the angle change pushing his cock deeper. Our mouths met, tongues dancing, while the other hand wrapped around the cold stone on my chest, pulling the necklace off me.

TWENTY-TWO

Karnelian

I was a male who liked to be in control. Kissing Marie, I was in control. Tasting her savory pussy—in control. Pushing my cock into her tight, wet cunt—in control. Even if I wanted to get lost in the obsidian darkness of her eyes, I floated, resisting their pull. Then she took off that necklace, and I was no longer in control.

My monster was.

Every muscle in my body tensed as I breathed in her spiced daisy scent. A sweet, sultry drug. A growl ripped from me, anger, lust, and confusion swirling into me as my hand found her neck, squeezing enough for her to bruise as my cock slammed into her core.

My thrusts were savage and uncontrolled, tearing into her with every bit of might I had.

Her sweet cries rang in my ears, eyes locked with mine, claws dug into my back, holding on as I destroyed her.

I couldn't hold back, everything within me was telling me to breed her, her scent clogging my nose and edging me faster. She didn't want me to stop though. Her legs were wrapped around me, caging me until I did my job, her beast battling mine with her hips upward movements.

The hand on her neck squeezed tighter. Her features went soft and serene, her tight cunt strangling my cock as my hand cut off her breath.

My mouth crashed on hers, being the air she breathed as my hold loosened. Our teeth scraped, mouths consumed, and moans scratched our throats as she came undone.

I pulled away to watch her. Her curls a mess on my pillow, her arousal painting the bed, her cheeks flushed, shimmer glimmering in the candlelight.

"You shine like a fucking star when you come on my cock, Marie." The sight had me thrust harder, balls tightening and liquid fire traveling through my veins.

I roared as my seed painted her walls. Each spurt violently ejecting out of me, spurring my hips to continue as if I couldn't stop until I filled her.

With one violent thrust, I emptied fully. Marie squeezed around me again, milking me in and taking me into her womb.

I lost feeling in my arms at that, falling on top of her plush body. Together, we twitched and squirmed through the aftershocks of our climaxes.

I was a bit hazy when Marie's limbs wrapped around me, her hand pushing my head into her neck, my teeth aching to bite into her flesh.

"Thank you," she whispered, her grip tightening with her shaky breaths.

A nod was all I could manage, having to hold the urge to claim her after breeding her like that. She held me there for the same reason—a primal reaction. The chance we created life was slim, but our beasts didn't understand that. She was in heat, and I relieved it. I needed to claim the possible mother of my babes for safety, and she needed the father of hers to do the same.

We laid there for what felt like forever. Long enough for the unchecked emotions from our fucking to filter through. How I lost it and was rough with her, rougher than I had ever been with anyone, bringing her to the edge of death. How I knew she liked it. How I liked that she did. How that was probably the best sex I had ever had in my life.

How this was all a terrible idea.

Marie softened under me, her hold loosening, but she still cradled me like I was something precious and valued.

No one had ever held me like this.

Another reason this deal was a terrible idea.

I extinguished the lights with my magic, leaving the moon to illuminate the room. I flipped us so my back was against the bed, and used my magic to clean the wet spot before returning her back down on dry sheets.

I stayed on top of her, not moving, not wanting to leave. I wanted more and I knew I wouldn't get enough of her. The next week was going to be hard as I waited to taste her again, feel her again, have her begging again. Have our eyes locked together, her capturing me, and threatening to swallow me into those deep soulless abysses.

I wished she had stopped this. She could have but she didn't. I thought she would, but she wanted this—me.

And there they were—the whispers ringing in my ears, loud, too fucking loud.

I pressed a kiss to her head, the act too soft for a monster like me, but my monster was a fluffy fucking kitten at the moment, urging me to give her more than just a kiss. To make sure she was cared for and fully content.

A gentle kiss was all I'd offer. Care wasn't a part of the deal.

I broke from her hold, a whimper sounding from her throat as my cock left her, the sound making me want to shove it back in and never leave her unsatisfied, but I resisted and laid next to her.

Our heavy breaths were the only sound in the room. I spent that time tamping my monster down. It was already trying to attach itself to her, claim her as ours. She would never be ours, ever.

Her face relaxed in the most tranquil expression I'd seen since the day I branded her. I traced each one of his marks with my eyes. She took faerie dust just to keep them, to keep him, killing herself slowly for him.

I was going to have to deal with that later.

Before I could get up and aid her to her room, a soft mew rumbled from her. She rolled over to me, her face burrowing into my chest, her arm wrapping around my torso, her breath relaxed in slumber.

I sighed, tired. I could have carried her to her room, but I didn't. I just let it happen, my arm curling around her waist, my monster breathing in her scent. A feeling settling over my blackened heart that I didn't want to think about. I didn't want to think about how nice it was to have a female warm my normally cold bed. How nice it felt that it was her who did it.

I woke with the morning sun streaming through the windows, the pinks and oranges reflecting over the cream walls, Marie's breaths softly tickling my skin.

I had never slept with a female before. I cuddled with a few but often that cuddle time was spent negotiating a deal that the other party wanted.

My fingers found her curls, playing with the hickory strains. She looked happy; her dreams peaceful, the sun twinkling against her bronze shimmer.

The image conjured another picture in my mind, an image from that day. An image I ignored. My focus needed to be on why she was here—power and the crown I deserved. But with her in my bed, the morning calm and relaxed, my mind couldn't stray from this moment to plan or deceive. All I could do was just be.

My fiddles with her hair eventually woke her, little sleepy grumbles sounding from her as she rose. Her knuckles rubbed at her eyes before she looked up at me, blinking a little as her lips spread into a smile.

Fuck.

Everything stilled within me as I took it in. It was just the upcurve of her lips and it was fucking tilting me off my axis.

Her nose perked up, cheeks swelled and full, and her eyes, her cold soulless eyes sparkled against the sun's rays.

Her smile, her first one in five years. Something she chose to grace me, the devil. The male who was a monster, an abomination, she thought worthy of her smile.

I had to smile back and it wasn't a smirk with my cocky bravo, or one tainted with trickery. This was a smile I hadn't given anyone in seventy years. Pure and filled with joy.

Then she leaned up and brought her soft lips to mine, kissing me sweetly, like I was a lover, not a male who was only fucking her so I could get a throne. The kiss slow and lazy and full of gratitude.

She pulled back, smiling again. "I slept."

I mirrored her. "You did."

Her smile widened, her teeth showing and I couldn't help but kiss her, thanking her for letting me be the first to see it.

She giggled slightly as I pulled her over me, deepening the kiss. "Nelian," she murmured over my mouth.

"Hmm?"

She pulled away, lying back at my side. "I want to sleep more."

Another soft kiss to her head I shouldn't give. I prepared to get out of the bed that felt so warm with her in it. "I have work anyways. You can sleep in, and I'll take you home later."

"No," she said, her arm tightening around my waist. "Stay."

That soft side I was rediscovering with her took over, and I relaxed back into the bed. "Just for a bit. I have stuff to do today, little bird."

She sighed, her features slightly disappointed. "You have meetings?"

I shook my head, brushing her bed-ruffled curls behind her ear. "Just paperwork."

"Paperwork?"

"I do most deals on paper. Makes it easier to keep up with and not have to remember them. Some of my deals are just signed in blood, making the implications less dire. As well as, most people want silly things, a portal mirror, or a fancy dress, and they are willing to trade their soul for it. I normally have those people sign in ink."

Marie's fingers came up to trace my tattoo with the tip of her claw, being careful not to break skin. "I'm getting the ins and outs of your business."

"You will be my wife." My dick hardened a bit at the word—*wife*. I maneuvered myself a bit so it wouldn't touch her silky thigh inches away. "The deals won't go away when we get married."

She spent a moment tracing the tattoo, over and over again. "Could you do the paperwork in here?"

"I supposed I could."

"But for a price?" she said, her brows pinched in question.

A smirk graced my lips, my hand finding her arm, tracing her brand like she did me. "No."

"No?"

I got out of bed, maneuvering over the discarded clothes from last night to get a pair of sweatpants from the dresser. "I'll be back."

I went to my office, grabbed the papers I needed to review today, and returned to her sitting up waiting for me, a smile tinting her lips.

Settling back in bed, a bed I never brought a female to, she rested her head on my lap and curled herself around me, and I began working.

TWENTY-THREE

MARIE

All my air was cut off, my eyes ripping open to see Karnelian holding my nose close. A violent awakening from my blissful sleep. My instincts quickly kicked in, my creature fighting for life, but Karnelian let go with a low chuckle.

"I need to piss."

I glared at him. "There wasn't a nicer way for you to wake me?"

"I grew tired of hearing your snores, so I thought I might as well kill two birds with one stone."

My eyes narrowed into slits. "You're a dick."

He shrugged, looking at me with that arrogant smile. "Move."

I grumbled but moved from where I rested on his lap, watching him get up and go to the bathroom.

Out the window, the sun was preparing to set, meaning I slept the day away. I didn't know how but I could feel Karnelian's presence as I laid near him. An awareness of him near, a distraction to my mind, allowing me to slumber peacefully.

A discovery my soul didn't love, but my body and my mind were content, delighted in their own disheveled way.

I got out of bed, rummaging through my clothes for my dust. Over to Karnelian's dresser, I pulled out one of his button ups and a pair of his boxers.

For being a female who held curves, Karnelian really made me feel small. He was so tall that his clothing practically dwarfed me, his boxers were a bit tight because of his slim waist but they still fit well.

I was tucking the dust into the waistband when Karnelian exited the bathroom.

The gold hues of the dying sun lined his form, casting shadows that chiseled his abs. His wheat-colored hair glowing, ruffled and unkept, a way I'd never seen him. Those sweatpants, low and baggy, doing little to conceal what laid underneath, and his eyes trailing me like a hungry beast.

Images from last night swirled in my mind. Him fucking me hard and bruising, his hand around my throat suffocating me, making my lungs burn in the most pleasurable way as he plowed into me.

Heat pooled in my core, not heat, desire, desire for him.

Our eyes locked. Scorching. The room filled with tension. Sizzling.

Our breaths huffed after another, the air thickening.

He predator, and I prey.

He took one step and I panicked, not in the way of a prey who wanted to get caught. In a way a prey should. Karnelian noticed this and pivoted, heading to the bed, and I scurried to the bathroom, slamming the door shut.

His lavish cinnamon scent filled my nose, stronger in here than it was in the bedroom.

I leaned against the door, taking in short, shallow breaths to attempt to calm my rapidly beating pulse that beat in tandem with my throbbing core.

More images of the night filtered through, his deep voice, and hazel eyes. Connected, me and him, coming together in an attempt to create life.

You will be the father of my children. I promise—Another broken promise to my mate. Along with—*For eternity.*

I wasn't burdened with heat, nor was I tired with sleep and my body was free of poison, leaving my mind clear for the first time in five years.

My descent to the floor was unconscious as tears burned in the back of my eyes.

The lust I felt for Karnelian was real, not discerned from my heat. A real emotion from me, and another betrayal to my mate. For the first time in almost five years, I smiled, felt delighted, maybe even happy, all because of another male who wasn't tied to my soul.

I fucked him—begged him to—and I enjoyed it. I was too weak to sustain the tortures of my heat, tortures I deserved, too weak to sustain the torment from my soul along with them.

I was always so fucking weak.

A weak little flower who got him killed.

My soul's shards cut into me, letting me know who should be alive and who shouldn't. The phantom scars tearing apart my being until the sound of running water from the bathroom faucet brought my attention to blue powder resting in the crevasse of my claw.

Snorting two hits of dust was a reflex to the agony, my body taking over to protect me from sufferings of my soul, because unlike my soul, my body wanted to live.

I was a creature born with the instincts to survive. My body was tired that the soul it house was constantly trying to kill its host so it took control, my mind letting it drive, snorting back the blue dust like my whole sanity depended on it.

The sharp lacerating pain burned my nose, and soon the wails of my soul were quieted.

I splashed my face with water, washing away any traces of dust and shed tears before exiting the bathroom. Karnelian sat on the bed leaning back on his arms. When my eyes met his, my core fluttered. The ache from his carnage last night filtering through my body, the pain relaxing my bones even more.

He was a drug all entirely by himself. Enough to drown out my soul's misery with just his presence.

My eyes were once again feasting on his torso and low hanging pants when he spoke, "Are you hungry?"

My head snapped up to his face, blood rushing to my cheeks. I expected there to be a cocky smile teasing his lips, but instead his face was masked with seriousness.

I looked down at my bare toes, brushing a curl behind my ear. "I could eat."

"I sent Rico home for the day when it was apparent you were going to sleep through it."

"Who's Rico?"

The corner of his mouth kicked up, his head tilting, mind seeming to be caught in a remembrance. "My father's best chef." His eyes returned to me, features suddenly guarded. "If we want to eat anything, we'll have to go to the palace. We can go there now before it gets too overcrowded, then I can drop you off at home."

My stomach settled in disappointment. He wanted me gone, but I didn't want to leave. I wanted to stay with him. With him I could smile, with him I could sleep. He was my distraction, and I always wanted to be painted in his illusion.

"Do you have a kitchen here?"

"I do."

"Can you just take me there? I don't want to go out in public at the moment."

"I suppose we could snack on whatever is in there."

Karnelian rose, and I averted my eyes. Him relaxed without an impeccable suit covering his gorgeous body was doing things to mine.

We walked through the manor in silence down to a small quaint kitchen. "If you don't find anything you like, there's a bigger one on the other side of the manor," Karnelian said.

I nodded and pulled open cabinets in search of food.

Karnelian searched the chilled cabinet, finding a bundle of grapes and popping one in his mouth. "The fruits are in here. Not much else in here to eat."

My brows pinched together as I took in the cabinet full of food. I would have to prepare it, but there was tons of food. I didn't know why Karnelian would even go to the palace to eat if he had all this food.

Then it dawned on me.

I covered my mouth to hold in the small giggle that escaped me, Karnelian's eyes snapping to me. "What?" His voice urgent and concerned.

"You don't know how to cook, do you?" I couldn't stop the teasing smile that tickled my lips.

His eyes locked on my mouth as he rubbed his chin with his hand. "So?"

His defensive tone made me giggle more. "How old are you?"

"I'm not answering that."

"You're at least over a hundred. How do you not know how to cook? Can't you at least make scrambled eggs."

He huffed, his jaw set tight, eyes heated and locked on my lips. "I'm rich. I don't need to know how to cook when I can just pay someone."

My laugh this time was a full bloom, but soon was cut short when hands gripped my waist, hauling me on the kitchen island.

Karnelian pressed his lips to mine, a startled moan sounding from me before I wrapped my arms around his neck and yielded my mouth to his.

His kiss was harsh and bruising, consuming me like he was starved of my taste.

"That smile is driving me fucking crazy," he whispered. "I don't think I can wait a whole fucking week to be buried in you again."

"I thought you wanted me to go home."

Another bruising kiss. "I don't." *Another.* "All I could think about all day was how your face was inches away from my throbbing cock." *Another.* "I didn't piss in the bathroom. I went to relieve some pressure."

He pushed his hips into me, his cock hot and hard behind his pants. "It didn't fucking work." His hands started to remove the shirt that covered me. "You slept in my fucking bed. You're in my fucking clothes. Your scent's tainted with mine, clogging my nose. Then you keep fucking smiling for me. Keep doing it and I won't be able to fucking hold back."

I smiled over his mouth, bringing my legs to cage him in.

Karnelian ripped his mouth from mine, tearing the shirt off me, then the boxers next. I went to grab the satchel of dust that fell, a little puffing out in his assault.

I met his eyes, panic filling me because I knew sooner or later, Karnelian was going to make me stop. "I know when you do it."

My brows furrowed.

"There's a pain when it burns through your nose. I've felt it before, but eventually I started to ignore your small pains. Since you found a loophole in my deal, it never triggered the brand to alert me that you were harming yourself."

"You felt it?"

"The brand notifies me when you're in pain. If you are in danger of dying, I can find you and save you."

"So, in the bathroom, you knew what I was doing?"

He nodded.

"Are you going to stop me from doing it?"

"Don't know yet." He shrugged.

I frowned at his answer.

He sighed, irritation and maybe a bit of impatience coloring his features. "Little bird, can I just fuck you now and then we talk about this later?"

My frown deepened. I didn't want to talk about this at all.

"Do you seriously want us to talk about it while you're sitting naked, dripping on my counter?"

Later was better than now, and I did want his huge cock ripping into me, so I shook my head.

A slow, sensual smirk lined his lips. "Good."

He grabbed my face, smashing my mouth to his. His rough, calloused hand traveled over my skin. The movement soft and slow, gliding from my waist to my thighs, before he spread me wide and found my wet core. He used his fingers to tease my soft flesh, a small whimper escaping from my mouth at his light touch.

"My come is still in there, isn't it?" he asked, sticking a finger inside me, and pulling it out to find his seed covering his finger. "I filled you up good, didn't I? You're going to be dripping with my come for days."

He pushed two fingers back into me, thrusting back and forth, stroking that spot that left me shivering in pleasure.

My head rolled back, my breast thrusting out towards him.

He pulled my nipple into his mouth, sucking lightly before blistering pain formed around the sensitive numb.

"Nelian!" My body filled with tension, my claws digging into his neck. He pulled back and I looked down at my nipple, seeing the bud free of blood. A relieved breath leaving me at the site.

His fingers roughly grabbed my chin, connecting my eyes to his. "The only time you're allowed to close your eyes is when your mouth is pressed to mine. Any other time, I want those voids glued to me. You understand?"

I nodded; a pained moan sounded from me as he shoved another finger into me.

As a reward he slapped me, gentle enough not to cause real damage but hard enough to leave a sting, causing me to clench around his fingers.

Karnelian smiled wickedly, his aura filled with satisfaction. "You're such a slut for pain, aren't you?"

"Yes," I moaned, as he started to thrust his fingers harder.

He pushed me, so my back hit the counter, the action violent and pain searing my being. "You're a masochistic little slut, aren't you, baby?"

"Yes!" I moaned, almost fucking there.

He started thrusting his fingers in me faster, jabbing them roughly.

One had to be fucked up to enjoy this. Insane, in fact, but I did enjoy this. I always loved being controlled, my creature submissive. But Karnelian wasn't dominating me—not in the normal way. This was his wickedly psychotic way. He was bending me, pushing me, playing with my limits. I didn't know I even had limits until I could feel myself approaching them, soon to break. I didn't know what was on the other side of that line, but my beast was excited to find out.

The second I touched the edge I was snatched back when Karnelian pulled out of me, thrusting his fingers in my mouth, and making me choke on my taste. Then his cock was thrusted into me, hard and brutal, tearing into my aching core.

The scream that sounded was quickly smothered when Karnelian moved his hand around my throat. He squeezed down, cutting off my air. My lungs soon burned, desperate for life, leaving my mind foggy.

I wasn't scared though. Silver eyes held me, face filled with furious lust.

His thrust became harder, banging into my cervix and ripping into my being. Then one last powerful thrust that had me transported way across my limits and Karnelian was spilling into me.

But he didn't stop.

His hips kept moving, fucking me raw. My overused flesh sensitive after my orgasm, the pain becoming overwhelming and my lungs screaming for oxygen. A deep primal part of me woke and panic licked my spine, triggering me to react in survival.

My eyes bulged, silently telling Karnelian I needed to breathe as my claws slashing into the hand on my throat physically communicating it to him.

He didn't let go, continuing to break me apart on his cock until it became too much, and my core somehow tightening around him again. He allowed me to breathe then, but I only got one sip of air before my body exploded, my muscles tightening to an extreme, the world coloring black, my being floating in limbo.

Something about the experience was serene, but also terrifying. He somehow managed to make my body come alive, connecting me to the beastly aspects I had learned to ignore—while making me face death. It was raw, primitive, savage. He reduced me to my most basic form, and I felt more vulnerable than I ever did in my fucking life.

Karnelian slammed his hips into me, letting another dose of his seed paint my walls before he slumped down, resting his head on my chest as I gasped for breath and the sensation subsided.

My body felt strange, my surroundings strange, I out of place—off-kilter.

"Karnelian?" I whispered, brokenly.

He pulled out of me and straightened, his eyes meeting mine. "You're okay, little bird."

"I…" I shook my head, tears filling my eyes. I had no idea what was happening, but everything felt too real, too crisp, too severe. He had broken me, but somehow, I was whole, not cut into pieces.

His hands went under my arms, pulling my limp body into his chest for me to cradle. "I got you, Marie. Don't panic. You just need to feel safe after that. What you're feeling is perfectly natural."

I nodded, whimpering against his skin. My nose buried into his neck to breathe in his warm luscious scent, my limbs clutching him tightly.

We stayed like that for a few moments, his body swaying us, his hand stroking down my back. Eventually I felt like myself—but more alive. I felt safe, more than safe, I felt…secure. Like this was where I belonged in this movement—cradled in Karnelian's arms.

Even as I could feel the shards of my soul once again cut at my being, I still didn't let go, taking my dose of Karnelian and letting him encapsule me.

"Are you still hungry," Karnelian whispered into my hair.

I nodded against his neck, taking in more whiffs of his scent.

"Is there anything you want?"

I didn't answer because I couldn't voice what I wanted out loud. In this moment, all I wanted was him.

TWENTY-FOUR

MARIE

I stared at Karnelian's sleeping form. It was morning, the rose-colored sky reflecting in his soft blond strands. I found myself mesmerized with the scruff on his chin, and the tiny hairs growing on his chest.

Though he was in a vulnerable position in his rest, he was still intimidating. The power he held wouldn't fade in his slumber, he was still the all-powerful hybrid that possessed silver blood. But there was a gentleness in his sleep. One, I was sure not many had ever seen. For him to allow me to see him in his weakest state, ensued trust. A male whose only goal was to obtain power, definitely wouldn't allow someone to see him like this unless he trusted them. An honor that spread warmth within because I trusted him too.

Karnelian may be a master deceiver, but I knew he was one to hold his word. By technicalities, I was his female, and he seemed to be honoring that. He spent the last night caring for me after his rough fucking. He held me, fed me, bathed me, then he read to me in bed until I drifted off to sleep, grounding me after he had thrown me off my base. The experience somehow more restorative than it should be.

Karnelian's breaths went from even and rhythmic to controlled and deep, then his hazels opened, gently taking me in.

We stared at each other for a while. My head propped up on his chest, each beat of his heart slapping against my palm. His arm draped around my waist, creating little figures on my skin.

The moment was too soft for us, my soul's shards poking into me. I never expected to be held like this by anyone other than my mate, and though a part of it felt wrong, another part of me was just happy to have a tiny moment of peace.

"Are you okay?" Karnelian whispered, voice groggy from sleep.

My eyes left his to look out at the dew painted field as I ruminated over the past. "Last night was… intense."

He pushed a curl out of my face, bringing my attention back to him, the act quieting my mind. "I didn't intend to take it that far. I just… got caught up in you. I guess I enjoy sex with you a little too much, little bird." He gave a cocky smile, but it was guarded—fake.

"I enjoyed it too," I whispered. "But after… what happened?"

"Sometimes during sex, especially when it's rough and intense, it can leave a person feeling… off. And they just need to be comforted after."

"Have you done that before? Like, with other females?"

He shook his head. "I never go that hard. Other females don't often like to be choked or hurt." His fingers trailed over my neck and I winced as he passed over the sore and probably bruised area. "I hope I didn't scare you."

"I was scared, but it was more of an instinct, my creature coming out and taking control to fight for my life."

"My creature was in control too, which is why I didn't stop. I'm sorry I made you feel like that."

I smiled. "You did stop, just waited until I had an orgasm that ripped me apart."

His fingers came up to trace the curve of my lips, his eyes locked on that action with an intensity before he leaned in to kiss me. The act simple and soft, clear with the intention that it was just for this moment and nothing would come after. My eyes fluttered closed, and I enjoyed it, deepening the kiss, and clouding myself in his energy. He made me feel free. I wasn't a pretty little bird locked in a cage with him. With him, I was free to fly, him the air that helped me soar.

He pulled away, resting his head on the pillow. My fingers trailed up his torso, coming to the eclipse tattoo, tracing it, the motion rooting me further in the moment. "How did you know what to do after?"

His hand found my arm, his thumb tracing my brand. "It was instinctual. Primal even. I just knew I needed to take care of you, so I did. Like I said, my creature was in control."

"Don't you think it was all too much for two fae who are just supposed to have sex with no feelings?"

"Do you love me after having sex with me twice?"

My eyes connected with his. "No."

"I don't love you either, and I won't. The sex was amazing, probably the best sex I've had. But in all sex, there's an intimacy you can't just ignore. It's another idiocy of the fae—polyamory. We can't go around fucking devoid of claim without it driving us a bit insane. We want to own another; we want something primal and deep. All sex, no matter how much you try to push the emotions away, is intimate."

I went back to tracing the tattoo, the room filling with silence as I gathered my thoughts. "I don't want to care for you," I mumbled. "I don't want to care for anyone. I can't care for anyone."

His fingers found purchase under my chin, tugging it so I looked at him. "It's just sex, Marie. Sex that is all about you. That was our deal. Last night was crazy and a little out of hand, but we don't ever have to do it again. We are only together so I can get a crown and you can die without wiping out a whole race. The sex is only for your benefit. You can deny me all you like. We don't even have to have sex. The deal is for me to make you come, not me alongside you. I can take care of my needs elsewhere and you get access to my tongue or fingers when you need. You are in control, little bird."

I rested my head on his chest, listening to the even beat of his heart. "I like how we did it last night."

"Did what?" I could hear the smirk entering his voice.

"Had sex."

His arms circled my waist, pulling me up so his mouth was against my ear. "Did you enjoy being a greedy little slut for me last night?"

I shivered, pulling back to meet his wicked eyes and devilish grin. "Yes."

He pressed his lips to mine, moving my hips back enough so I could feel his hard cock.

A moan slithered from my throat as I ground my hips into him in invitation. An invitation he didn't hesitate to take. His cock pierced me slowly, a hiss leaving me. My body was rotted out from faerie dust, having not healed at all and leaving me exponentially sore.

I broke the kiss, my claws cutting into Karnelian as I slowly speared myself with his cock. My eyes squeezed shut as the sweet trimmers of pain rippled through me.

His hand cupped my face, thumb gently rubbing back and forth against my cheek. "Open your eyes, baby."

I did, whimpering, because for some reason that simple action was torture, harder to face pain with your eyes open, easier to disconnect.

My hips rolled when I bottomed out, his huge cock filling me and pressing against my tender flesh. I ate it up, basking in the agony as his hand guided me up and down in slow movements.

One of his hands cupped my breast, his fingers pinching the nub, a pained groan leaving me.

"Did I hurt you last night, baby?"

I nodded, whimpering more.

"Do you like it when I hurt you?"

"Yes," I moaned, as he twisted it harder.

Every time I felt pain, the ache matched the agony of my soul, canceling it out. The feeling made me feel lighter, able to breathe, able to fly.

"You're such a dirty little pain slut," Karnelian whispered, continuing to slowly guide me across his cock.

Being with him, his cock stretching me too full, his sadistic mind, his sexy as fuck voice, was like a dose of dust but better. More visceral, prolonged, and idyllic.

It didn't take long for me to break apart on top of him, crying out as I stared into steely hazel eyes. Karnelian grunted, thrusting up into me, the sharp bit of pain adding to my orgasm as he emptied into me.

I fell on his chest, shattered in the best way and he held me, rubbing my back until I was able to piece myself back together.

After a while, Karnelian spoke. "I have to work for real today. So I have to get ready soon." He kissed my head, further comforting me. "Do you want me to take you home or do you want to stay?"

My hands tightened around him, burrowing myself into his chest. "I want to stay."

TWENTY-FIVE

CORIVINA

Swords clashed, each clang reverberating through my bones. Kolvin came at me with full force, not giving me a second to rest before striking his next blow. His twenty years of combat training an unfair advantage on me, but I had a disadvantage as well.

Pivoting away from him, I fired a blast of light. My magical technique wasn't skilled in the slightest. Even after Kolvin spent years teaching me, I was sloppy when it came to casting spells, only good at ones centered around heating objects, but manifesting my magic had become akin to breathing for me.

It had never been hard for me to manifest. In the past, my emotions often called out my connection with the sun, my veins flaring gold when I wanted to cause destruction.

The sun provided me a wealthy supply of magic. He was fiery but sensual, angry but delighted, aggressive but calming. My magic was best for battle, best for blasting, best for destroying. The gods made me a weapon, because wasn't I destined to cause ruin? Which was what happened when my blast singed the grass and part of Kolvin's shirt before he moved out the way.

The amount of light I threw at Kolvin was too grand for even him to capture and control, taking my light to use as his own as Markos did with Marie when he killed his son.

It had been two days since Marie left with Karnelian, and both I and Kolvin needed to let off steam for different reasons. We've been out here for hours. Our bodies lined with sweat, breaths heavy, pulses thundering.

We were so lost in our battle, trying to keep away from the wars that brewed in our minds, that we didn't notice when he approached. His calm but commanding voice called out and stilled our bones. "So, this is where you two snuck off to."

My head snapped to Darius standing a few paces away. Looking at him was worse than staring directly at the sun. He didn't burn my retinas but my soul, my heart, my being. He created an ache that I wished didn't exist. An ache I wanted to ignore but couldn't because I, as any other being, couldn't live without the sun.

Still, I ripped my eyes from him, trying to glare at Kolvin who tensed under my gaze, hands raising in surrender. "I didn't tell."

"He didn't have to tell, Vina." *Vina.* The word a magnifier, and I, the ant to be obliterated by the sun. "You aren't the type of female who'd get mud caked on her shoes or calluses on your fingers. I've known for a while now."

I met his eyes, warm, soft, loving, but heartbroken. Eyes that held me like no other did, eyes that were always perceptive of me. Of course, he knew.

"Marie called."

I straightened. "She did?"

"Yes. She broke her heat with Karnelian."

My inhale was sharp and was mirrored by Kolvin's. "She did?"

Darius nodded, hands behind his back, stance stoic. "She is planning on staying with him for a while longer."

"How much longer?"

"She didn't say."

"Why didn't you ask?"

He took a step closer. "Because she is an adult, and she can make her own decisions. I know Karnelian will take care of her. He is a respectable Lightfire, unlike the one you like to accompany."

Rolling my shoulders, I took a step back. "Thanks for letting us know."

I raised my sword, locking eyes with Kolvin in signal to begin.

"Denmor, leave," Darius commanded. The command brought my creature to the forefront, practically pawing inside me to go to Darius.

"We aren't finished," I said in rebuttal.

"He is." Darius shrugged out of his tunic, revealing his sculpted, taut muscles. Muscles I ached to outline with my tongue.

"What are you doing?"

"You want to train, you're training with me."

"Darius—"

"Corivina, he's going and I'm staying. He's not allowed to train you anymore. None of my men are, so it's me or no one."

I knew what he was doing—edging my beast. She didn't like force, for obvious reasons, but pushes got her riled up and ready to fight back. He was challenging me, and being a fae, I couldn't turn down his challenge. "Fine."

A smirk lined Darius's lips, He held out his hand for Kolvin's sword as the male made his way to leave. Head low, shoulder hunched, my daughter's actions causing more damage to his psyche.

Darius didn't waste the opportunity to charge while I was distracted. I blocked, our swords clashing, keeping his body about a foot away from mine.

His eyes burned into me as he stepped back. "You don't seem mad about Marie."

We began circling another—orbiting another. "I'm not."

"But you aren't happy."

"I don't understand her need to be dependent on a male. I didn't raise her to be like that."

Darius snorted, pivoting his direction so now we turned counter clockwise.

"What?"

"She isn't dependent on just males, she is—was dependent on you. You made sure she was."

"What are you saying?"

"Corivina, how many arguments have we had about me making a decision over Marie without asking you?" The question prompted me to stop and think, which was a mistake on my part as Darius charged again, giving me only a millisecond to react and block. "You never disagreed on what my decisions were, you were only upset that I didn't run them by you first." He took a step back, immediately charging with another strike. "Marie is dependent because you made her that way. She relied on you for everything. Over the last twenty-five years, you have spent more time with her than with me. It never bothered me that you did. I admire your dedication at trying to be the best mother for her, but in the process, you made her dependent on you, and now that she doesn't have you—"

Twisting, I crouched to strike at his knees. "She does have me."

He evaded my blow with a counter strike. "If she did, she wouldn't have clung to Karnelian so quickly."

"She could have clung to Kolvin if that was true."

"Kolvin may be a great soldier and dedicated to protecting Marie, but he isn't dominant. Marie's creature wouldn't choose him, even if Marie loved him."

"Since when did you start analyzing her love patterns?"

"I have to write a report on her every week, Vina. It is my job to watch her. It's not hard to see it. Her mate was dominant, you're dominant. Karnelian is an obvious choice since he carries more dominance in his left pinky than you and her mate combined."

"You're dominant. How would we work if I was."

He snorted, backing away, so we once again circled another. "I may be a male, I may lead our sexual encounters and have the power to keep you safe. But unfortunately, you have me by the balls. You're the queen I worship and will serve and protect."

There was an obvious double meaning to his words, and I refrained from responding so we wouldn't tumble down that path.

Darius knew me too well and knew what I was doing, so he shrugged. "Fine." His sword clattered to the ground. "Why didn't you ask me to train you?"

Losing my form, I squared my shoulders. "Kolvin was a better option."

With my guard down, Darius charged, tackling me and pinning me to the grass. "Lie."

Struggling under his grasp, I grunted out, "You are busy."

"So is he. He's a general, which means all the side tasks I have to get done get dumped on him and the other generals."

"You know why I didn't ask," I said, wiggling myself out of his hold.

He reinforced it, slamming me to the ground to keep me still. "I want to hear you say it."

Pushing at his chest, I screamed, "Because I can't be around you!"

"Why!"

"You are my weakness, Darius! You are the male I love, and when I am around you, I want to crumble. I want to cry out my darkness while you hold me." On cue, I could feel the darkness slither its way to the forefront, calling up the tears to line my eyes.

"And why would that be so fucking terrible?"

A darkness will come then, sweep you up and show you all its horrors. When those horrors come, let your darkness in. It will protect you from succumbing to madness.

"Because I need it! I need it to kill him! I need it to be strong enough to face him! I need it to protect me from the pain. The pain I get when I see our daughter broken and shattered and remember that it's all my fault she's like that. The pain I get when I look in your eyes and see the damage I caused you. I need the darkness to keep me going, and you unravel it, Marie unravels it. I love you both more than anything in the fucking cosmos, but I can't love either of you properly until he is dead."

Darius stared at me for a long moment, his brow furrowed, jaw clenched, then barely above a whisper, he said, "Do you think you'll stop loving him when he is?"

I stiffened, flinching back like he just struck me. "What?"

He released his hold on me, sitting up, so he kneeled in the grass. "Do you think him dying will make you fall out of love with him?"

I sat up, scooting back as a new form of darkness found me. "I'm not... I don't."

"Corivina, you love him." He plucked a weed from the field and flicked it away. "He's the darkness, Vina. He's thing that stands between us, not Marie, not Dominick, Markos. He's the reason that even though we've been together for two hundred years, we haven't fully connected. He's what stands in our way. And now, not only is he in the way of us, he's in the way of you and Marie. It's not that you can't be around me. It's that being around me makes you want to let go of him. We're ones, Corivina, my soul knows who I came here to be with. The second I saw you, I knew you were my one, but have you had the gods tell you I am yours?"

I shuddered, taking a deep breath to calm my quivering nerves. "Darius, I have told you my feelings about you many times."

"But when did you know?"

"Know what?"

"Know that I was your one? Am I even yours or is he? And you're just another curse I have stained on my soul?"

"He isn't my one."

"But am I?"

I looked at him, not able to fully process what he was saying. It confused my being and jumbled my emotions, leaving me feeling empty and purposeless. "You are. Ginger told—"

"No, Vina. Ginger wouldn't be the one to tell you. *They* would, and I don't know if you'll ever be able to hear them until you let him go and step out of your own way and let me in."

"I have let you in. You are the only one I have let in."

"I was there during your testimony. When you describe your relationship with Markos. Dominick originally kept you around for your intimate information on him. You let him in. Markos knows who you are. He knows a version of you I've never been able to see, a version you don't trust me enough to see."

"He knew me. Past tense. He knew me when I was a weak spoiled brat, Darius. He doesn't know me like you do and he never will. He was my first love. He was the one who broke me, and he left his stain on my soul as all first loves do. I don't hold your past loves over your head. I'm sure your first love broke you as well."

"She has, but I still love her."

"Then how can you be mad at me for loving Markos, when you still love her!"

"Because I'm looking at her."

I deflated, my eyes wide, my heart sputtering. "What?"

"Corivina, you are my first love. You are my only love. You are the only female I've ever been with. I didn't want to love anyone before you. I didn't think I was worthy of it, but then I did meet you and all I wanted was to be with you, make you feel safe, make you my wife. And stupidly I believed that our love would be like it was in the stories. That our love would conquer all. That our love would fill the gap you keep between us. But it won't, will it? Because you just admitted you still love him, and if you aren't going to let him go after two hundred years, I doubt you would let him go when he is six feet under."

Darius then stood, walking over to pick up Kolvin's sword and made his way back to the manor, leaving me utterly wrecked.

TWENTY-SIX

Marie

*K*arnelian stood, shaving his face in the bathroom mirror. I sat on the toilet, watching him glide the sharp blade across skin. I liked the stubble that grew on his face, but I enjoyed sitting here watching him even more.

We had formed a routine over the past few days, rough brutal sex at night, then aftercare that extended to a slow morning fuck. I laid in bed resting while Karnelian would shower, and after, I'd watch him shave. Then he'd leave me by myself.

I'd bathe and do a half a hit of my dust—a half because I was running out. A problem I would need to find a way to solve without alerting Karnelian.

There was an excuse I could use. I still had no clothes of my own, parading around the manor in his clothes, but I didn't want to go home and face my parents' curiosity and questioning. I was going to have to figure something out soon because when Karnelian wasn't here, the guilt consumed me, and I needed the dust to quiet the screams of my soul.

I was starting to grow bored here as well, spending most of my days waiting for him to return. A month ago, I would love the freedom, but I didn't want it; I wanted a distraction.

As I watched Karnelian, a longing grew within me. My body prepared for him to leave and me spending the day missing him. As well as preparing for the shame of yearning for him.

But today the longing was more intense, a few notches below desperate, my emotions all over the place. I truly didn't want to spend another day in this manor alone, waiting for him to come home.

Home.

I shook my head to clear my pending thoughts. That thread only led to a spool of hysterically crying on the floor, something I would avoid at all costs.

"What?" Karnelian said, gliding the blade over the curve of his neck.

"What?"

"You have that crease in your brow when you're thinking of asking something, but you decided against it."

The crease deepened at the fact he had cataloged my expressions. "I'm a… I'm a bit bored."

Karnelian's eyes snapped to me before he put the blade down and turned. "Do you want to go home?"

"No… I just want something to do when you leave me alone all day."

"We have lunch together."

I narrowed my eyes. "I still spend hours by myself with nothing to do."

Karnelian chuckled, combing his wet blond strands with his hand. "Sorry, little bird. I'm not used to… having someone around, someone I need to entertain."

"I'm not a child, just give me something to do. I can only stare at your plant collection for so long."

"And drink my whiskey."

I averted my eyes. I may or may not have been pilfering his supply to aid with the little dust I had.

Karnelian moved toward me, lifting my chin so my eyes met his. "You took a bottle worth eighteen thousand coin. There was no way I wasn't going to notice that."

"It was the youngest one. I didn't think it cost that much."

He smiled, sweet and a bit patronizing. "You can have whatever you want, little bird. What's mine will be yours, but don't think I'm not going to notice."

I quirked my mouth to the side, nodding.

"We need to get back to your training. Since I'm having later mornings, I don't have time in the afternoon. Not that I'm complaining about the why." He smirked. "But you liked the readings I gave you, didn't you?"

I nodded again in response.

"Little bird, words."

One of the only things I found annoying about Karnelian was the way he effortlessly took power over every situation by communicating to everyone like they were beneath him. "I just said I'm not a child, Karnelian."

"You act like one."

"I don't."

An arrogant smile lined his lips. "Look, now you're being a brat."

Groaning, I rolled my eyes. "Yes, I liked reading about magic."

"Good girl." He stroked his finger across my cheek in approval, something that made me uncomfortable.

The smile I gave was tight and didn't reach my eyes. I didn't feel worthy of his praise, and I didn't want it. I deserved to be degraded. I loved when he called me a needy little pain slut, and I felt like a slut for him. A needy little whore, who betrayed her mate because of her desires.

A ghost of a frown appeared on Karnelian's lip, but soon was masked. "I'll take you to the library later. I'll take the afternoon off and spend more time with you."

I hated that even though he was still talking to me like a child, I still perked up at the idea, desperate for his attention. Desperate to be lost in him at all times, my perfect distraction. I wasn't even this bad with my mate, but Karnelian was the only thing that fully silenced the screams, and mad as I was, I needed this small serenity.

"That would be nice, thank you," I said, trying to keep my smile light, though my cheeks ached for it to be wide and bright.

He pulled me into a kiss. A kiss I hated because I thoroughly enjoyed it. His lips soft, some of his unshaved stubble poking my skin, the shaving foam transferring to my cheeks. He kissed me like I was his, like he owned me, and I hated that a part of me was all for it.

My bones aching with each step, Karnelian and I walked hand in hand down the hall—not in a couple's way, in a friend's way. It was hard to explain, but when we held hands, it didn't feel like it did with my mate or Kolvin, like we were lovers, and we simply couldn't be apart physically. Karnelian and I held hands like we were holding on to a life raft. At least that was why I held on to him, a physical tether to ground me from whisking away into my soul's torment. For Karnelian, I didn't truly know how he viewed it, but there was a look in his eyes that spoke of need. When

Karnelian held his hand out to me, his eyes seemed to have a plea. Like he needed me to hold on to him.

We approached double doors, Karnelian letting go of me to open the door in a grand reveal.

He looked over to me with a wide egotistical grin that soon fell when he took in my non-impressed expression. "I thought this would be a female-like-you's wet dream, little bird."

"Then your ideology about me, devil, is way off."

It was true I had discovered a love of reading as of late, but I wasn't a female who would fawn over any library.

The room was nice, filled with plenty of books, calming like the rest of the manor, vines littering the walls and bookshelves. Two stories with comfortable furniture scattered about, but a great library to me had two things, two non-negotiables that would actually make me jump with joy.

He huffed, stuffing his hands in his pocket, and following me as I scrutinized the room.

I went to a few random shelves, the ache in my thighs flaring brighter with each step. I pulled out a few books I passed through, examining their text.

All the same sub-genre. Check.

The people who separated books just by author were appalling, I'd thought this back when I only read smut, and separating books into broad genre ranges was even worse. Separating your books by genre then sub-genre then author was the proper way to sort one's library, something I learned from my father.

I held my smile back as I scanned through the romances to find a divide in the stacks from boring closed-door romance to filthy one-hand reads. A female-like-me's true wet fucking dream.

I almost shrieked in excitement but held it back as I subtly grabbed a few books I had never heard of.

"Little bird, this is my library."

I turned to him, raising a brow. "Can I not borrow these? You said what's yours is mine, did you not?"

He chuckled, grabbing the books from me, and hauling them in his arms. "No, I mean, these are all my books. I put every last one in here, and I definitely know what kinds of books these are." He waved one in the air to taunt me, his eyes hooding with desire. "Is what I do for you not enough for imagination? You need more, baby?"

I blushed, dropping my head before trying to grab the books out of Karnelian's hand and failing miserably as he pulled them up into the air.

"Nelian!" I reached up. "Just give me the books back."

"Say please."

I folded my arms, frowning. "Please."

He smiled, handing me the books, but when I went to grab them, he snatched them back. I was about to protest but when I reached for them again, my mouth collided with his in a kiss.

Karnelian set the books down on a ledge, his hands encircling my waist and pulling me into him. We kissed for a long moment before his hands started to wander, unbuttoning the tunic I wore.

"You smell good," he said, inhaling heavy. "Really fucking good. I want to eat you."

For some reason, the comment threw me off and I was inhaling as well before freezing in place.

Karnelian pulled back, eyes examining me. "What's wrong?"

My drug-filled brain never thought things through. Every time I had my heat and failed to become pregnant, the same thing would happen. "I'm... I'm having my... bleed."

Karnelian's eyes widened before his features returned to his normal aloofness. "Okay, what do you need?"

Before my heat, I never had full-blown bleeds, just spotting for a few days every couple of months, but now I bled for a whole week and the cramps left me bedridden. "Um, I'll need underthings, the ones that have extra cotton for... absorbing. And pain tinctures for the cramps."

"Okay, I'll get it for you. Anything else?"

"No, wait!"

Karnelian looked at me with a mask of confusion.

He was leaving, going out to town to pick supplies. "Could I go? And could we go to Lightwood?"

"Why Lightwood?"

"I know where everything is there."

"You don't have any clothes."

"I can wear my dress. One of your maids cleaned it for me."

His nostrils flared, jaw flexing. "Fine, but you're wearing the necklace. Males will know you're fertile if you bleed this much, and even though you're covered with my scent, I don't want them scenting you out."

A light smile lined my lips. "Thank you."

It wasn't as hard to lose Karnelian as I thought it would be after we got the tinctures for my cramps, and it was time for me to get the undergarment from a female needs store. His mother lived in Lightwood, and he said he'd go say hello while I got what I needed.

I wasted little time getting my things and slipping into Al's Bar and because I was forever unlucky, Alirick was also currently working the bar today.

"Marie," Alirick grunted, his voice full of disapproval.

"Rick, you have something for me?"

He crossed his arms looking down at me. "I do."

"Well, can I have it, please?"

"Marie, if the male who gave me this wasn't my boss, I'd be telling your father," he remarked. "You're a good female. You shouldn't be messed up with this stuff, or those types of people."

"You're those types of people, Rick."

He grumbled. "You know what I mean. If I see you buying this stuff again, I'm telling your father, no matter the heat I'll face. You hear?"

I plastered a pained smile on my face, holding out my hands for my bag. I didn't have time to argue or plead with him over this.

He took forever getting it and when I finally got it, I said, "You just lost a customer, Rick."

He huffed, "Good. I don't want you coming around here."

I rolled my eyes, walking out of the bar and smacking into a hard chest.

Pivoting, I kept my head down, mumbling, "Sorry," and continuing on my way.

"*Oh, little bird?*"

I halted in my tracks, pressing my lips together as I turned to see Karnelian's silver gaze, a huge smirk lining his lips.

"What were you doing in a bar?"

"Uhm... I was just visiting. I know the owner."

His smile widened. "I know him too, very well. Maybe I should say hi. We could all catch up."

I scrunched up my nose. "He didn't seem to be in the mood today. You know Rick... kind of an ass."

"Hmmm." He eyed the huge satchel of dust in my hand that I hadn't thought to cover up. "Your nose twitches when you lie."

I pressed my lips together in defeat, waiting for a lecture or his disapproval, but Karnelian didn't poke, instead changing the subject.

"I got you a gift." I noticed his hands were hidden behind his back.

I raised a brow in question, and he pulled out a box wrapped in wax paper.

Taking it, I unwrapped it and revealed a box full of chocolate.

"I heard females like it when they are on their bleed."

For a moment, I swear my frozen heart beat, but it could just be me confusing my creature's pleasure in receiving a gift. Wrapping up the box, I smiled up at him. "Thank you."

I stepped up on my toes, and he leaned in to receive my kiss, my beast taking over, making sure he received my gratitude with the consuming press of my lips.

Karnelian moaned into my mouth, the sound urging me to deepen the kiss further, but he pulled away, eyes heated with lust. "Little bird, you're going to make me hard." He kissed my head, urging me to start walking, though we portaled here and the errands were complete. "If you really want to thank me, you should give me a treat that's just as nice as these chocolates."

"Yeah? What do you want?" I said, wrapping my arm around his waist as he laid his across my shoulders.

"You." He hummed, kissing my head again.

"Okay, when I'm done with my bleed, you can whenever you want."

"No, I want you now."

"What?"

"I want to lick your pussy now, little bird."

I stopped in place, looking up at him in shock. "You joke."

"No, I don't. I'm fae. We feast on flesh, draining our prey of blood before we dig in, and I want to do that to you."

I gave a nervous chuckle. "No way!" In truth, a part of me was intrigued but not enough to let it happen. I know we were beasts but having someone feast on my bleed was just... weird... right?

He pushed out his bottom lip, pouting. "I'll make a deal with you, anything you want—besides death."

"I have what I want from you," I said, my hand cupping his hard cock through his pants.

He pulled back, his face filling with challenge. "I'm not fucking you while you bleed, then."

"Uhm, the deal demands that you do." I gave a coy smile, though I definitely planned to deny him.

"We fucked this morning, and bleeds normally last a week, no? The deal demands that I make you come. And since you won't let me use my tongue, it will have to be my fingers. No cock for you, little bird." He smiled victoriously, that wicked glint flaring in his eyes.

"Fuck you."

"Not until the next week, baby."

TWENTY-SEVEN

MARIE

Quietly, I got out of bed and walked over to the bathroom while Karnelian still slept. I had woken up with dread clouding me. Even with the books to occupy my time during the day, I still felt Karnelian's absence. It seemed the more time we spent together, the worse it would get when he did leave and so I was dosing before the emotional weight fell upon me.

I exited the bathroom, wiping my nose to check for blood just in case. After my bleed, I felt even more emotional. So, I started taking an extra half dose, which soon became a full dose, making my nose prone to nosebleeds.

Karnelian had awoken, his eyes trained on the ceiling, lost in thought. I crawled on top of him, his hand automatically coming around my waist.

I pressed my lips to his. "I want to make a deal."

He stiffened a fraction. "For what?"

"I'll blow you if you stay with me today," I said, grinding my hips into him. We haven't had sex in almost two weeks. I had denied him last week due to my bleed and Karnelian had yet to initiate anything this week. Instead, we spent our nights cuddling and reading.

Karnelian relaxed, smiling. The gesture too pure for someone with his pseudonym. "You want me to stay?"

I blushed looking away from him, of course I did. He was my distraction, a drug better than dust. I craved him every second of every day to keep the screeching wails at bay.

His hand found its way under my chin, bringing my eyes back to his and demanding an answer. "I do," I whispered.

He kissed me, slowly like he was savoring my lips before he pulled back. "I can't."

My throat tightened, the phantom shards scraping into me, even though I had already had a dose of dust. A heaviness filled me, tears building in the back of my eyes, my world feeling like it was about to crumble.

I rolled off Karnelian and pushed it all back. I had gone two and a half weeks without a break down and I wanted to keep it that way, so I did my best to numb everything out. It was a battle between me and my soul, it whispering all my betrayals to my mate as I did my best to ignore it.

Desire for Karnelian.
Sex with Karnelian.
Companionship with Karnelian.
Love for others, especially my mother.
Five years separated in our eternity.
Being the reason the separation even existed.

Karnelian turned toward me, his finger rubbing against my cheek. I flinched, moving away. He could be my savior, but right now he was my tormentor. He could cure the agony, but instead he was the knife in my gaping wound.

"Please…" I whispered.

"Little bird, I'm a busy male. I can't just take off."

My soul wasn't crying or wailing, no screams echoed within me. It laughed, mocking me.

I focused all my energy on quieting it, but the laughs grew louder, my sanity growing weaker.

Karnelian turned my face to look at his. I gave him a dull expression, giving him nothing in the hopes he'll cave and give me everything.

But he didn't. Instead, he sighed, face filling with disappointment before he got out of bed and started to get ready for his day.

Panic coursed through me because I didn't expect him to do that. I laid there, confused and angry, because he didn't even seem to care. Which quickly turned to anger with myself because I wanted him to care, he wasn't supposed to care, and neither was I.

He took his time getting ready, or at least he didn't rush, not letting me affect him. It was like he was pouring salt on my wounds, not just salt but alcohol, making sure I burned.

He didn't need me, at least not like I needed him. He was the devil that could grant anyone's deepest desires. All he needed for me was to stay alive long enough to get his crown. It didn't matter how passionate our sex was, or how many late night cuddle sessions we had. To him I was a means to an end.

It shouldn't hurt, but it did. I tried to curl my palms to stifle my emotions but was stopped by his magic, making me boil more.

My focus zeroed in on my breath. In and out, slow deep breaths that kept me from bursting. When Karnelian was finally gone without a word to me, I sprinted to the bathroom. My next steps ingrained into my being—water filling the tub, clothes off, blue powder frying the insides of my nose, pain ripping through my body canceling out the shredded scars of my soul, then my skin burning from steaming water, the world fading away until I was nothing and there was nothing.

My body was jerked with force. "Marie." His voice harsh and cold, gyrating against my senses.

I squeezed my eyes shut to clear my utterly lost mind. Cold water slashed against my skin, racking me with shivers. I sat up, studying the now dusty pink water, hastily wiping my nose. Dried blood crusted my lower face and chest, a lot of it.

My reaction was automatic, a protection of my freedom. "I'm fine."

"You think passing out from blood loss in a bathtub and almost fucking killing yourself is just fine?"

I flinched at the harshness of his tone. "It was an accident."

"Bullshit, Marie. You took an extra dose. You have been taking extra doses like you said you wouldn't. Even if you use it as a drug, it's not one. It's fucking poison, and for it not to kill you, you need to heal. Or you'll end up getting bloody noses and almost bleeding to death in a hot tub."

I didn't say anything, my head bowed in shame.

Karnelian grabbed my face roughly, forcing me to meet his wild eyes. My creature stiffened, preparing for an attack. "You cannot die, Marie. I get that you need the dust and as long as you do it responsibly, I give you the independence to do so. I know being here alone means you get freedom from your parents' smothering, but I will hire you a fucking babysitter if I have to because you. Cannot. Die, Marie. It's not a fucking option, do you understand?"

I nodded and his hand tightened around my jaw forcing my mouth open.

"You said you weren't a child. Use your fucking words."

"I understand," I said, voice muffled.

He let go of me and stood. "Drink all you like, it won't kill you. But you're limited to one dose of dust a day. If you abuse that, I will alter the brand on your arm where it wouldn't even let you open the bag under the sink, don't fucking try me. They call me the devil for a reason, Marie."

I began to nod but he gave me a look. "Okay."

"Clean this up. I'll be back in a bit."

When he left, I couldn't help but grab a bottle of whiskey and take a shot to calm my beast. It was shaking, fearing Karnelian's wrath. Logically, I had a sense he wouldn't hurt me, but his beast was still a thousand times more powerful than mine, and scary as hell when angered.

I took another shot right after that because I felt ashamed. Not from my soul, from me. It was in my nature to please and disappointing Karnelian like that wrecked me, finally letting my emotions boil over. Tears, hiccups, and sobs stormed from me as I cleaned the bathroom before showering off the crusted blood on my body.

Something about this breakdown felt different than the ones before, because after the shower, I felt a bit lighter. I was still washed with sorrow and emotional turmoil but a tiny bit less.

Walking out of the bathroom wrapped in a towel, I saw Karnelian sitting on the edge of the bed wearing short and a short-sleeved tunic, a pile of clothes next to him.

Cautiously, I moved over to him, and when I was near, he pulled me between his open legs, his fingers rubbing up and down my arms. "You won't get your way with me. I make the rules and

I don't bend them for anyone. No matter if I stick my cock into you every once in a while. You understand?"

"Yes."

His sigh was heavy, and he pulled me closer, resting his forehead against mine. "We are friends, right?"

"Yeah."

"Friends don't let friends find them nearly dead in a bathroom."

I let out an equally heavy sigh. "I'm sorry."

He kissed me, slow and soft. "Put on one of these." His head moved a fraction, gesturing to the clothes. "Seeing you passed out was fucking stressful and I want to blow off steam. I'm bringing you along because you're my friend and I enjoy your company, but I'm still pissed at you for being so reckless."

I nodded, my hands finding his and playing with his larger digits. "Where are we going?"

"The beach to swim."

I couldn't help the slight frown on my face. "Well, in that case, you'll just be furthering my punishment."

His brows furrowed.

"I don't like the water, remember?"

He shook his head, his hand cradling my face to search my eyes. "What punishment?"

"Cleaning up. That was a punishment."

The crease in his forehead deepened. "I wasn't punishing you. You made the mess; you should have cleaned it up."

"Oh. I just thought..." A frown lined my lips. "Never mind."

"No, Marie. Speak."

"Just... my mate and I. When I didn't do something he liked, he'd punish me, and me to him. But others would think he was more extreme than I. The marks..." I looked at my body. "They were a punishment."

Karnelian sucked in a sharp breath, his hand scrubbing over his mouth as he assessed my marks. "You did that this morning. You didn't like that I didn't bend and so you were trying to punish me for it?"

I pushed a wet curl behind my ear. "Kind of, yes."

"Kind of?"

"It hurt that you wouldn't stay, and I didn't want to be sad. I ignored you to deal with… the feelings. It's also why I took the extra dose."

"Little bird…" His thumb started drawing little circles on my cheek. "Why?"

"Why?"

"Why did it hurt?"

I couldn't tell him he had become my new drug of choice. That I yearned to have his attention all the time. That if I could lock him up here I would, so I wouldn't have to spend another moment in the hell that brewed inside me. Instead, I could dance with him in his. I couldn't tell him I was sick for him, beyond obsessed. "I just don't like being alone all day."

Before him, all I wanted was to be alone, but after him, all I ever wanted was him. He kept me grounded in the moment, and I needed that to live, to breathe, to smile, without catastrophe.

"If you would have told me that, instead of shutting down, I could have assessed it. I can just bring you with me when I leave."

"Really?"

"I have an office in Solara where I do most of my dealings. There's a back office you can hang out in while I have guests. I won't be able to bring you with me every day because I have other affairs that require me to move around sometimes. But you can study while I'm there, and in between my meetings, you can play with me." A sinful smile lined his lips but it didn't stretch to his eyes.

"I'd like that," I said. "And we'll still have lunch together and our mornings and nights." I cringed at my words, feeling like the child I was trying so desperately not to be seen as.

But then Karnelian kissed me, brushing away my worry. "Yeah, baby."

TWENTY-EIGHT

KARNELIAN

*T*he waves carried my body. The sea calm today, unlike my being. Water called to me more than any other element in this world. It restored me, the waves balancing me out with its rhythmic movements.

Marie stayed on the shore, lying on a towel reading in the yellow bikini I got her. The sun made her glow, each sparkle of her shimmer eliminated. She had no worries about anyone seeing her marks because we were at my private beach that was magically protected from trespassers.

My eyes hadn't left her for a second since she refused to join me out here. I wished she did. I wished she didn't hate one of the most crucial things about me.

I had been out here enough for my fingers to prune, and I needed more time here, but I hadn't been able to fully connect to the sea with my concentration on her.

I left the water, my cock half hard, swinging as I walked out to her. Swimming naked kept me fully connected to my other home, but being naked near her was always a challenge, but my hard cock didn't stop me from tackling her with my wet form.

"Nelian! My book!"

"*My* book." I took it from her, setting it on the towel she had laid out for me. Something no one has ever done for me. No one, besides family, had ever come to the beach with me.

She wiggled under me. "Karnelian, you're soaking wet! You could have ruined it!"

A groan sounded as her thigh brushed my cock. "Look." I raised the book for her to see. "All of my books are magically protected."

"Oh," she said, inspecting it.

"Oh." I put it back down, then propped myself up with my arms. "You sure you won't join me?"

"I don't love the ocean. There are critters in there."

I snorted, not able to hold back the smile, real and genuine, less rare since her. "What if I make a deal with you?"

Her eyes narrowed, her nose scrunching up in the cute way it does. "What are you offering?"

"You swim with me, and I'll tell you a secret."

"A secret?"

"Yeah, a good one too."

"How good?"

"If it got out into the public, my father would lose his pants."

She giggled, the sound candy for my ears, and I kissed her to see if she tasted as sweet. "Okay, but I want to hear the secret first, and only for ten minutes. *And* you have to use your magic to make sure no critters come my way."

"How exactly are you going to tell time with no clock?"

"I can count."

I chuckled, mine causing hers which ended with another sweet kiss. "How about until sunset?"

"That's like two hours away."

"I promise once you get in, we will have so much fun you won't even notice."

"Fifteen minutes."

"Twenty."

She smiled brightly. "Deal."

I pressed another kiss to her lips before rolling off her and leaning in to whisper in her ear. "My mother is half water nymph."

Her head jerked back, eyes bulging. "What! Seriously?"

I nodded. It was rare for the child of a king to be of any other blood. It was expected for the leader of each territory to be full fae and even looked down upon if they held human blood—the most common species we mixed with. The Unseelie were more forgiving of being mixed with humans, but probably not a different creature.

"So, like do you have like *water powers*?"

"I don't think I'd be able to tell since I'm a hybrid, and my father definitely wouldn't want me to learn, but my mother can bend water."

"Wow." She took a moment to let the information swirl in her mind, an adorable look of wonderment embellishing her face. "How?"

"My mother's mother, my grandmother, was swimming. A water nymph caught her scent, pulled her down to the seafloor and they made my mother."

"He raped her?"

I shook my head. "No, they fell in love. I've only met my grandmother a few times because she lives down there with him. He uses magic to keep her alive. They actually have more kids now. I have two aunts and an uncle, but currently they choose to stay down there because… you know… fae."

"Creatures of chaos." Fae were an isolated species. We traded with other creatures but often the trades required that we use our human servants to conduct. Fae were feared or hated by most races because of our nature, and they chose to stay the fuck away from us. As well as we were the most powerful species beside the demons, so it was easy for us to manipulate them.

"I've never been there because of that. The only reason my grandmother is allowed is because her and my grandfather are believed to be mates."

Her eyes locked with mine. "Really?"

"They'll never truly know." Mating only happened if both parties were of the same race. It was believed that some pairs were born to different races and just weren't meant to join in this life for divine reasons. "But why else would a water nymph leave the ocean floor to follow the scent of a fae?"

The silence stretched. The little bird stuck in her head, probably thoughts of her own mate.

I would never want a mate, and I hoped mine stayed the fuck away in this lifetime—if I even had one. I could have never understood the toxicity of fae mates until Marie. She had relied too heavily on him, but I got the sense that was what he wanted. It was clear a part of her wanted me to fill his shoes, she had tried to manipulate me like she did him. It was an odd sight because no one would think the little bird could be sinister, but she did learn that I wasn't him. I wouldn't be manipulated by anyone, not after years of my father's manipulations before his betrayal. I wouldn't bend to her, no matter if I found her beyond beauty, or if she gave me that smile that she didn't give to others, maybe if she laugh—

I wouldn't bend to her.

I took Marie's hand, pulling her out of her mind as I brought her to standing. "You owe me twenty minutes."

She grumbled but came with, squealing, when the water touched her toes, those squeals causing my cock to stiffen more.

She shivered, fully submerged in the water, her teeth chattering. We were far enough out that she couldn't stand on her own, battling to keep her head above water. It was an instinct for me to pull her into my chest, my hands soothing her quivering body.

"Did you pee?"

The corners of my lips lifted as I pressed a kiss to her head. "I'm using my magic to warm you."

She looked up at me, her legs wrapping around my torso, a smile stretching her lips before she brought them to mine. "Thank you."

I didn't reply, and she moved her head back to nestle under mine.

I couldn't acknowledge how content I felt with her here with me. The waves just flowing around us. How I started to finally find my center with her here with me.

After I found her the way I did, seeing her passed out, close to dying, rocked me off my axis. It wasn't because if she died, she could be dooming all of fae, and I wouldn't get my crown. The thought of her dying threatened something deep within me, threatening my entire existence. The whispers became violent screams when the brand alerted me to her failing pulse, my blackened heart beating extensively. In that moment, I had to drop everything to go to her, and now that it was over, I couldn't excuse how I was already starting to slip.

She quickly took over my life. Not just my life, my every thought. Power wasn't my drive to get through the day, it was her. And often it was going back to her, making her smile, hearing her laugh.

She would probably take me over whole if I didn't pull back. We had gotten too close, too comfortable, too quickly. I had started to rely on her for… something, I don't truly know what it was that I craved from her. Her body, her scent, her smile, her voice, her words, her thoughts, her mind, *more*. Whatever it was, I needed to pull back. She couldn't be my base because she was instable, impractical, impossible.

Us not having sex over the last week and a half was supposed to fix the problem. It was too connective to be doing twice a day, let alone once a week. I have never felt as vulnerable with another being as I when fucked her soft cunt and choked the life out of her. We connected during sex, built a base of trust, and I couldn't keep strengthening that base. So, against my urges, I put an end to the unnecessary sex. A good idea in theory, but it just ended up bringing us closer and my desires for her grew even worse.

I would come home, and she'd be warming my bed. My monster's personal drug was daisies with a hint of pine, and the whole room would be suffocated with it. She barely left the room, making it hers. Books she wanted to read were piled on the floor. Pillows and extra blankets she stole from empty rooms—too many for two people—were piled on my bed like a nest.

I'd join my little bird in her nest and wrap myself around her small but plush frame as she read. She'd snuggle back into me, letting me know my presence was wanted and we would cuddle in silence.

I would read what she read, and I noticed her reading slower than usual after a few days of this. Eventually she only read a certain book in bed each night, saving it for me, so I wouldn't miss it even though the book she was reading I had already read twice.

No sex made it worse, so much worse.

Now we were in my favorite place, her just fucking holding me, having grown content after I used my magic to warm her. I couldn't help but wonder why. Why did she cling to me, why was I the only one worthy of her smiles and laughs. She had so many people who loved her, who truly loved her, and wanted nothing but to see her smile. Her parents begged my father to give her sanctuary in Seelie when her mate died and that was before my father even said a word about her being the heir. It was the first thought on their minds, keep their daughter safe. Both of her parents loved her deeply, I could see that in their eyes and feel it in their presence. With all that love, why me? Why the wicked, evil, Silver Blooded Devil, the abomination of a prince?

I pulled her tighter, letting the waves soothe me. Even though the water centered me, the water also had a tendency to bring out emotions, bringing them to the surface so they could be washed away.

Normally, I was good at not divulging in them, letting them rise but not engaging in the pain of the last hundred and thirty years. With her, I just couldn't hold it in. Everything just built, everything I had pushed down for the last seven years.

The whispers rang too fucking loud, whispering what they always did, but this time there was something new. Something new my subconscious strung together from the information found after I danced with her.

Stéla.

My Stéla.

My hand found her chin, raising it so I could smash my mouth to hers. My emotions too raw to hold back.

Her sweet moan reverberated through my mouth, her claw tipped finger poking into the back of my neck, consuming me back with equal validity.

My fucking Stéla.

The wave rose everything within me and I couldn't pull back anymore.

My hands moved down to her ass, gripping her ample flesh, grinding my hard cock into her core. My legs found their way to shore and to the two towels she had laid out for us.

I dropped her down on one, the action rough, just the way she liked it, the brand alerting me to her body sizzling with pain.

My Stéla loved pain, and I loved giving it out. I loved even more that I was the only one who could give her what she needed.

"Nelian," she breathed, fire dancing in her soulless eyes.

Fuck, I loved that name.

I had many names. Karney—Karnelian too complicated for my brother to pronounce as a babe, and now he uses it in taunt. My titles—the Silver Blooded Devil, the Cursed Male, the Uncrowned Prince, Prince Karnelian Lightfire. Big, flashy, and wickedly cruel.

Nelian was different. It was personal, connecting me and Marie. It was small, plain, hospitable. To her, I was just Nelian. A male with hazel eyes and blond hair. Nothing more, nothing less.

My lips smashed against hers, my cock rubbing into her soft flesh.

Being in between her thighs was my paradise. Her copious curves under me, my rhapsody. I had spent days aching for the sweet delicacy of her. A need I was tired of denying.

I pinned her arms above her head, calling upon the sun to keep her in place.

A hiss slithered from her barred teeth, her hips jerking up to mine as the light beams burned into her skin.

Her obsidian eyes locked on mine as she battled against my magic, those orbs threatening to drown me whole. Deep, dark, and bottomless. An ocean I wanted to swim in forever.

A sick trap set by the gods.

I would fall into those abysses and her soul would be found in the darkness's folds. The tattered thing it was, would obliterate my soul into pieces until I was nothing. But I felt no fear, staring into the depths of my personal inferno. My monster was never afraid of the dark.

No matter how badly I wanted to heed the warning, I couldn't stop myself. After seeing her in that tub almost dead, her blood spilling down her face. My monster needed to get absorbed in her, to be a part of her even if we got demolished. So today, I would let it. Just a dip of the toes, to soothe my beast of the chasm of worry it felt for her.

"We've been slacking on our magic practice, little bird." A nefarious grin tickled my lips, my beast fully out and ready to play. "Try to get free." The flex of her jaw and her muffled whimpers paired with the fear in her beautiful eyes. We both knew this was a game she wasn't going to win. It was more a play she was going to have to sit and enjoy as I enacted my performance.

She wiggled and writhed, the beams burning into her flesh, the horrendous smell assaulting my nose, but it didn't disgust me. It fucking intrigued me. My monster manic with the chaos of this, loving the sweetness of her torture. How she just fucking took it, how the fear in her eyes translated to excitement in her body, her arousal saturating the air. She was just as crazy as I, a heathen happily dancing in my devilry.

"Your shadows, Marie," I said as I peppered kisses down her neck, my tongue lapping at the salty sea water on her skin.

When I reached the swimsuit that covered her tits, I used my canines to tear it off her, sucking her nipples into my mouth when they were freed before moving down to her bottoms.

I wasted no time ripping them off, her pussy glistening up at me. A glazed treat I buried my face into, digging in and consuming it. Her taste so divine it made me rage with anger.

I fucking hated Levi.

I absolutely fucking hated Levington.

I didn't before, thought he was a fine male, but now that I had his female writhing under me, I hated him.

She tasted like the best fucking meal, not sweet, savory. So fucking savory I could fucking survive on her taste alone, but she was a meal designed for another male. Her succulent offering created for his pleasure. Not mine.

It boiled my blood. My monster hated that she was bound to another. That her body was littered with marks—his marks. The rage burning into me and screaming for me to kill, maim and disintegrate. The only thing keeping me here were her screams of pleasure and the obsidian eyes locked on mine.

She was such a greedy little slut for me. Obeying my command without ask, keeping her attention on me and only me. She would not think of him as I pleasured her. She would see me as she came on my tongue.

And she did come, again and again and again.

This wasn't for her. My monster was starved and wouldn't stop until it got its fill.

My hand roamed over her body, up to her soft pillowy tits.

Fae had a thing for humans, the imperfections about them drawing us in, loving the chaos in their creation. I tried not to be one of those males, being raised Seelie, you are taught to judge everyone and everything and appear fake. So, our craving for the flawed flesh was not an accepted fetish. And truly, I never had a problem with it until her. Before her, females were just pussy, I didn't care for their bodies, because they only cared for my might. After her, I was quick to realize I did care for things, her things. Her round frame, nice full ass, and generous breast, too big to even fit in my palm.

Her soft belly another thing I was amply enjoyed over. I found myself abandoning her pussy to press little kisses onto her abdomen, the action causing her to giggle, then cry out as she accidentally pressed herself further into her binds.

"Shadows, little bird," I said, sitting up, my fingers trailing her inner thighs.

"I-I can't!" she cried out, my fingers slipping into her cunt.

"Why not?" My voice remained controlled, carrying a note of curiosity as she wailed under me.

"Because..." she gasped when I hit that spot.

"Because what?"

"Your... it feels... I can't."

"Am I going to make you come on my fingers, baby?" *Baby...* A word that just slipped off my tongue and felt right, so I kept letting it slip out.

"Yes!" she screamed, her muscles tightening as she grew closer.

"Come for me, baby. Come on my fingers, like the dirty little slut you are." And she did. My derogation always an easy way to set her off.

I pulled my fingers out, letting her calm a bit, even easing the intensity of the light beams. Her gasping breath matched with the waves that crashed onto shore, but she was nowhere near her max. A place that broke her down into her rawest form, leaving her vulnerable and open. Broken to a state, she needed me to bring her back together. A task my monster was keen to take. It was depraved of me to enjoy doing this to her, but I was sick, twisted, wicked, and cruel.

I played with the outer lips of her flesh, the light touch making her shutter with aftershocks. My fingers slipped further down, resting on her little puckered hole.

I wanted to ask if he's been there, but by the way she jerked away from me as I neared, I figured the answer was no.

The fear in her eyes was pure. No arousal tinting it, just straight timid terror that had my lips spreading to a gleeful grin. My fingers pressing back to that virgin hole, circling the little bud.

"It will hurt, baby." She tensed, her hole flexing against my prodding finger. "When I shove my cock into this tight little hole, it will probably be the most painful thing I do to you." It was not if, but when. Today, she'd deny me, but I was going to fuck that hole. She liked pain, and I dished that out to her, but I liked dirty, disgusting, and depraved, and she would give that to me. I would fuck this dirty little hole and I was going to lick her pussy on her bleed, then fuck her cunt and use her blood for lubrication so I could fuck her ass again.

My finger pressed in further, almost breaking through, but she jerked again, moving back. "Karnelian, I… not there."

I gave her a look that told her of my future intentions as my hand moved up to gather some of the come that glazed her cunt. I shove my fingers into my mouth, groaning, when I got a taste of it. Her sweet ass enhanced with the taste of her savory pussy.

It set me off and I was moving up her, then shoving my cock into her.

She wasn't the sheath to my sword or the glove to my hand. She was better than that. Too tight to contain me, crying out as it pained her, but she still sucked me in, gripping me and sealing me in so I wouldn't leave.

My perfect paradise.

To me, it felt perfect. To me, she was perfect, but to her, I wasn't and I was reminded of that when she spoke out next.

"Fuck, Nelian. It's so fucking good."

So fucking good.

Good.

Not great.

Not amazing.

Not perfect.

Not him.

Just good.

My hips slammed into hers, my magic tightened around her wrist as it formed around her legs, holding her still for my battering. The sound of our damp skin slapping together cracked in my ears as I showed her this was better than good. Showed her how no one makes her come like I do. Showed her that I am the one who makes her sing to the point it damages her vocal cords. Showed it's me she fucking needed.

It didn't take long for her moans to become broken screams and her walls to tighten around me, squeezing me until I couldn't take it anymore and I came with a roar. My seed painted her walls to the point I felt it slipping out and dripping down my balls.

After a few labored breaths, my head cleared, slicing the past from the present. Because who I was five seconds ago wasn't me. It couldn't be me. I didn't get jealous, I didn't wish I was better than a dead male and I didn't wish to claim a female fated to die in a short few years.

But it was later, at my manor, and I'd finished the aftercare she needed—a time when my monster completely took over for me, caring and tending for the girl he sees as his female, even going to the length of applying a soothing salve to her burnt wrist and ankles, when it knew in a few hours, she'd heal on her own—that Marie rose from the bed, leaving without a word, only to bring back a bowl of grapes, washed and picked off the vine.

My favorite snack. I loved it more than whiskey.

She handed it to me before curling into my chest, and we lay propped in bed, eating the sweet fruit. No words expelled from us, but there were whispers in the air, letting me know that this female was poison fully spread within my veins, void of an antidote.

TWENTY-NINE

Karnelian

*T*hree hours late. I, Karnelian Lightfire, was three hours late, and not because I promised to be. I did plan to be an hour and a half late, but time slipped from me when I was with the little bird.

I blamed it on the fact that I had never kept a female before. I never had a person to plan around. People made their schedules work from mine, not the other way around.

Marie didn't do anything to make us three hours late, I just couldn't resist her. After the day on the beach, my head started to become crowded with thoughts of her. The only way to clear it was to give in to my monster's urges and have my way with her.

So, it was my fault we were late. I was the one who threw her on the bed and strangled her until her face turned blue and her cunt was equally strangling my cock. I was the one who spent the next hour after that caring for her. My monster enjoyed aftercare more than Marie did, and she thoroughly adored it, pressing kisses to whatever area of my body was in her closest vicinity in gratitude.

Right now, she was glowing from the oils I rubbed over her luscious body, but there was still an irritation bubbling in my chest that we hadn't finished the job.

My monster had definitely attached to her. Another problem I needed to deal with. Too many problems I had to deal with. Too many problems I avoided. Instead, choosing to hide in the harmony created with my little bird.

"Are we going to go in?" Marie whispered, drawing my eye away from the white double doors with gold detailing.

I could feel my family's presence on the other side. A familiar feeling with traumatic tragedy behind it. I haven't been in this place—me out here why they sat waiting in there—in over sixty years. I was always early. Always on time. Never having to be standing here like this again.

"I hate these dinners."

Her thumb rubbed back and forth against my outer palm, a sweet and warming feeling spreading through my chest. "Then why are we here? Why come to them if you hate them?"

"They are my family."

"A family you don't seem to like."

I stared at the door, letting my eyes trace the etchings carved within. "I love my mother and my brother."

She didn't ask it—if I loved him, and if she did, I wouldn't answer. Instead, she tugged on my hand, making me look back at her. A small mercy because my attention zoned in on her.

She had dressed for the occasion. We stopped at her home to get her clothes, thankfully missing her parents. She wore a beautiful black gown that covered her neck to toe, wrapping around her curves sensually. The gown had silver threads stitched through, matching the jacket I wore. A jacket she picked out so we would.

She leaned up on her toes, and my bend down was starting to become a subconscious act. Her lips met mine, the kiss soft and slow, not an ounce of lust within it. A kiss in comfort, like she was reminding me she was alive, and with me. Today, I wouldn't walk in there alone and when I walked out, it would be with her hand in mine.

A reassuring smile decorated her lips when she pulled back and I mirrored it, pressing a quick peck to her before entering the dining room.

60 YEARS AGO.

There was an eerie breeze that brushed through my shoulder length hair as I walked into the dining room. It set my creature on edge, but my creature was always on edge here in Seelie. There was only one person who soothed it, but that lion was in this den and lately he seemed to be making the hairs on the back of my neck stand as well.

I was late, just getting back from a trip to Unseelie. The place of darkness and despair was actually a haven. The children of the moon didn't shy away when darkness faced them. They embodied her and embraced it, lighting up in a way that didn't diminish the dark but still illuminated the world. There I was, still silver blooded, but I wasn't an abomination, still an outsider but they didn't shy away from my differences.

One could only dance with the Unseelie for so long though, they were unhinged. Fae were unhinged, but the Seelie hid their dirtiness. So, it was quite distraught to see Unseelie fae doing the most carnivorous acts—killing, raping, deceiving—out in the open. All I witnessed was to humans, but even if half of my blood was black, it was a bit too much for me to stomach.

Thankfully, I spent most of my time either with their professors, deepening my studies in Unseelie magic or in bed with some female deep inside her, oftentimes they were the same person. I had a few brief meetings with the king, something required of me since I was a prince. King Markos was quite different from the typical Unseelie. I think he's so popular here in Seelie because of how he never flaunts his darkness like past Unseelie kings. The darkness was still there in the creases of his eyes and the tightness of his skin but unless you were one fourth water nymph as I, you wouldn't be able to feel it looming in the air around him and choking him whole.

My family sat at the table, the eeriness thickening with each step I took closer to them. My creature wanted to riot and panic, but I did my best to not engage in the primal parts of myself when an appearance was needed of me as taught by my father.

They didn't speak as I pulled out the chair next to my mother. Fredrick, normally known for causing a ruckus when I arrived home, had his head bowed in shame. My mother's back was straight, her emotions concealed from me, but her face was cemented in disapproval. My father was the only one who looked normal, and somehow that was more off-putting than all the rest of their expressions.

The heavily lit room had the shadows around his face appearing faint, something I never took note of until today. Until today, nothing about my father ever put me off. My respect for him was practically a personality trait. I never once ever questioned his demeanor, trusting that the person I looked up to the most, would always keep me safe. But today, there was a small rumble in my foundation, a warning of an impending quake in my infrastructure.

My senses sharpened, the air stuffy and perfumed with sunflowers. The gold-plated room, gleaming like fire and burning my pupils. The grandfather clock resting against the wall, the only sound in the room. *Tick, tick, tick.* A countdown to my doom.

"Karnelian, I have an announcement to make," my father said, voice regal and kingly, each syllable in my name harsh and cold.

The final warning to my being came when my mother's hand found mine under the table, offering a gentle squeeze, not in reassurance but in solidarity.

My father cleared his throat, his emerald green eyes crystalized stone, no emotions reflecting through. Eyes of a king, but not eyes of a father. "I've decided to make Fredrick my heir."

It was a sliver of pain that ripped through my heart. It caused my blood to cease in its mission to pump through my veins. Thoughts filtered through my mind, fast like lightning, overwhelming like a heavy storm, bringing a well of tears lining under my eyes.

My anchor while I was stranded in the sea of my corrosive contemplations—my mother. Her hand squeezing mine to a point of pain, a pain that brought me back to this moment. "Dominick," she said his name as if spewing a curse. "Are you going to mention how you already made him your heir? How you did it while Karnelian was away."

"Magdalena. This is a royal affair." And his voice was a royal voice. "You are here because you—by association—are a part of the royal family. But that can quickly change if you think to speak out toward me again."

Magdalena. My father never called my mother Magdalena.

Unlike my father, my mother let her emotions shimmer in her eyes. Anger and anarchy littered within. "Do it, Nick. I am only here out of courtesy of you."

My father didn't divulge in her madness, instead turning to look at me. "I know the news may come as a shock, but I didn't want to alert you until I was absolutely sure about this."

So sure, he did it without even telling me. That was always how my father was, a planner, a narrator, an orchestrator. He taught me his tricks and I foolishly thought the master would never dupe his apprentice. A father would never betray his son. But a child's trust is blind, and I couldn't ever have had the foresight.

Not when my father and mother split soon after my blood was revealed silver. She removed his mark, not letting it fade, meaning her reason for leaving wasn't because they simply didn't want to entertain another, as I was told, but because he had possibly betrayed her when he told her of his plan.

Not when my father started to challenge King Markos for his informal title as the Slut King, sleeping around with as many females as he could. Not an act of a broken heart, but an act to conceive a life.

Not when he named that babe, my brother, a boy I loved so thoroughly it was braided into my core, Fredrick—*Ruler*. Karnelian was a stone, a pretty rock, but Fredrick was a ruler. A king, a worthy heir to the throne.

He compensated my worries with purpose, with distraction, illusion. Teachings of kingship and studies to strengthen my magic. It gave me hope, hope that one day I wouldn't have to be isolated from my peers, that they'd one day see me as a male instead of an atrocity. And my repayment to my father for this hope would be found within his haunting emerald eyes that I falsely thought secreted pride.

"Why?" A question I knew the answer to, but wanted to hear it pitched in my father's imperial tune.

"As a hybrid, the people see you as an abomination, Karnelian. Nothing you do will change that. It doesn't matter if you are the nicest male or the noblest king, they would never truly trust you. Some even distrust me for simply letting you breathe. For your safety and your virtue, it had to be done."

Abomination.

That sliver in my heart became a crater, a gaping wound, the pain searing through my being. I may have been ninety-two years old, but a deep part of me was still a boy. Hopeful and reliant on a male with the green greedy eyes, but that boy died in that moment.

Because If I was still a boy, still filled with that undeterred hope, I would have cried like I did the day of my sorting ceremony in this male's arms. No, I wasn't that boy anymore, I was a male who had felt the chill of isolation and the lashings of reality, so my tears would not be shed. There was grief, but there was not denial, anger, bargaining, or depression, just acceptance.

I accepted that my father cared more about his status than respecting his child. I accepted that I would never be valued instead I'd be feared. I accepted that I wasn't a normal creature. I was a monster. An abomination.

Laying my hands on the table, I stood, and he flinched. The all-mighty King Dominick Lightfire flinched at his hybrid son.

My fingers found the gold circlet that adorned my head, lifting it to place on mahogany wood.

"Fredrick." The emerald eyes of a seventeen-year-old boy met mine, tear lined and sorrowful. "You will be a good king, and I will always love you."

A nod of my head in respect of the little boy who held a part of my heart in his hand, I left the table, making my way toward the double doors.

"Karnelian," my father called out. "I am not finished."

"I am," I said, voice low, almost a whisper.

"You still have duties to me and this kingdom. Come sit back down so—"

"I am done, Father. I renounce my title as prince."

"Karnelian, you can't renounce yourself. You're my son."

I turned to look at him, my face void of emotion because my being had fully hollowed out. "You took away my birth right. Might as well take away my title too."

He walked over to me, looking up to my overly tall frame. "Karnelian, I'm doing this for the sake of our people."

"Your people. Not mine." They've never been mine, they never accepted me and neither did he. "I'm not a prince and I owe them nothing. I owe you nothing as well."

Turning my back to him, I left, going to the place where abominations were cherished and let to bloom.

And bloom I did because when I finally did set foot back in the Seelie Territory years later, I was the king of abominations and dirty dealings. The Silver Blooded Devil.

That eerie feeling was still stained in my bones, echoing when I walked into this room. It was a trauma response that only existed in my mind because the reality was, there was joy in the air. My family laughed as they ate their meal, having started without me.

Why would they wait for a cursed male? One who waited on them every month.

Their laughter quieted as we approached, their eyes pinning onto the little bird. Their noses twitching as they breathed in our mixed scent.

My father's brows were furrowed, my mother's head cocked, and Fredrick's lips were stretched into that easy smile, eyes gleaming at the mayhem of the predicament.

I offered no explanation, simply pulling out a chair for Marie next to Fredrick before sitting on her left and started to fill our plates.

My father cleared his throat. "Karnelian, you brought a guest?"

"I did," I said, starting in on my dinner.

"Why?"

I met those jeweled eyes, my face poised in disapproval. "Father, you'd think you would have some manners and at least let me introduce her."

"I know who she is."

"But you don't know who she is to me." My twisted grin lined my lips as I gestured to Marie. "This is Marie, also known as the Unseelie Princess. Sometimes I call her little bird, but as of recently I call her my fiancée."

My mother and Fredrick sucked in a breath. My mother's a genuine reaction, Fredrick's exaggerated.

My father's lips pressed together, those eyes attempting to pierce through me, but failing because I would never let him see a vulnerable part of me again. "Your what?"

"I'm not that far away, Father." I placed my hand over my heart in false worriment. "Is your hearing already getting bad? Need me to speak up?"

"Karnelian..." His voice bordered on a growl.

I sighed, deep and dissatisfied. "You are no fun with your old age. You used to be fun. Don't you remember when you lied to me for seventy years and pretended that I was still going to be your heir, but you were planning on finding a way to get me off the throne. Wasn't that just the best time? The jest of all jests." My father's nostrils flared, brows turned down, jaw set. "Well... Instead of killing you or my dearest brother, I found a loophole. A pretty little loophole packaged in a pretty little black dress."

"You are not getting married to her."

I laughed, big, loud, and menacing. "You think you can just demand me not to? You don't think I wouldn't get insurance or have crafted out a thorough plan? I'm a great planner, Father, literally learned from the best. My biography will mention how the Silver Blooded Devil constructed his tricks and thievery from the teachings offered straight from the Seelie throne." I took a drink of the wine set before me. "She will be my wife." My dick twitched at the sultry feel of that word escaping my mouth. "I bound it in blood."

"You made a deal with a mentally unstable female? You think the people are going to not cause a riot over you abusing her."

My body tensed, my features hardening as I leaned in, gaze penetrating straight into my father's greedy greens. "One, I don't give a fuck about *the people*. The people already see me as an abomination. Do you think I care if their already low opinion of me dropped lower? Two, she came to me. She opposed a deal, and I simply told her what I wanted, and she agreed to it. Three, don't ever, *ever*, speak about her like that again, or I'll rip out your fucking tongue."

I let my power rise to the surface, silver veins illuminating through my skin, engraving my threat in his psyche. I rarely ever challenged a person, let alone used aggression to get my way, but my father needed to know I wasn't a little boy who he could boss around anymore. He killed that part of me many years ago. Now I was a male, one of the only two males who could kill him, and soon I would be the only one. I was the bigger lion in this room, something he best not forget if he thought of disrespecting my female in front of my family again.

Marie's delicate hand found my shoulder, gently guiding me to sit back. "It's fine, Nelian."

My eyes connected with her deep orbs, and she nodded, telling my monster to stand down. Her creature didn't agree to aggression, and she let me know that in her eyes. It yielded to her, but only before one last glance at my father in warning.

Marie's hand found mine over the table, weaving our fingers together before she returned to her food.

"Is your relationship real?" my mother asked, nymph eyes analyzing us. She probably sensed everything that went down through our emotions, her powers greater than mine able to invade a being's aura without much thought.

Marie answered the question, "We are friends. Good friends. Intimate friends." The reply had my grip loosening, a reaction purely subconscious, but Marie noticed and tightened her hold, bridging any gaps I tried to set between us. We weren't a couple, but we were definitely a team, and we stood together. That was apparent in the reassuring gaze she gave before turning back to my mother. "Karnelian understands me, or at least he tries to when no one else does. If I'm forced to be queen, I'm glad to have him. I wouldn't choose another."

I leaned in and pressed a kiss on her head, an urge I couldn't hold back when hearing her words. I could feel my family's shock at my actions, their confusion, their wonderment. I never showed anyone outside of our family affection, and after I became the devil, my affection lessened to the simple kiss to my mother's cheek in greeting, and the stiff hugs with my brother.

The devil didn't show affection. He was detached and careless, cruel and wicked, but Marie didn't see me as him, so I didn't uphold his rules to her.

Her beautiful smiled shined up at me when I pulled back, and I really wanted to be anywhere fucking else at the moment. I wanted to take her and destroy her to nothing, only to rebuild her back up again after, but I settled for a simple press of our lips.

As I turned back to my meal, I sensed my mother assessing Marie. Something that made my skin start to crawl. I'd never considered needing my mother's approval over my female, but now that she was scrutinizing over Marie, I realized her approval was extremely important to me. Marie wouldn't meet my mother's eye, and her palm started to become clammy, but she pretended nothing was the matter. I knew my mother didn't have harsh intentions, but I still didn't like her judgment over Marie, making her uncomfortable and uneasy.

I loved to make people squirm, especially the little bird, but I didn't want others to make her squirm. I was prepared to divert my mother's attention away from her, but my father spoke up.

"Are you two planning on having a babe?"

One of the many problems of this ordeal I have been avoiding, if not the main one. Marie and I weren't on the brew, but the dust and the fact that she wasn't in heat kept me from having to think too much about it. If I did, my being would split into two opposing sides, excitement and dread. It was ingrained in a fae's genetic makeup to want a babe, and I had no problem with producing an heir one day, but if I had babes with her and then she left... "Time will tell."

"Have you not discussed it?"

My next breath in was sharp—annoyed. "We have, but it's not the most important thing at the moment."

"It's pretty important, Karnelian."

"So is the impending war and keeping Marie safe from anyone who is in Markos's favor. It's his head or hers if he doesn't have a babe soon. So is preparing her to receive that amount of magic when his head leaves his body. So are the arrangements we will agree to after the war is settled. The last thing anyone needs to worry over right now is a babe."

Marie's eyes met mine, communicating without words her fears of the future. She wanted to address this, but I didn't want to think about it, not after the bathroom incident a few days ago.

"It's important you have that figured out," my father piped in.

"And it's between me and my female, not you. *Especially* not you."

It was the squeeze of Marie's hand that had me realizing my slip of words. *My female.* A line that was not meant to be blurred, not as her friend—*good* friend.

My father huffed. "Markos doesn't seem to be trying to make an heir. He seems more focused on an attack or at the very least, a defense for an attack. You and Marie creating an heir is excruciatingly important. The war may take years to get into full swing and a babe will secure the Unseelie throne in case something happens to the two current upholders."

Before I fired my rebuttal, Marie said, "It is none of your concern." Her voice soft and demeanor non-threatening, but her soulless eyes locked on my father had him tensing. "Like Karnelian said, it's between me and him. Not you. Not anyone. No disrespect, but it's my body. You have already forced me to live in its confides longer than I intended. I understand why, *now*. Only because Karnelian took the time to explain. None the less, it's still a violation to me, and you had no right. So, I ask that you respect mine and Karnelian's decision to keep the matter between us as it should be. We plan not to doom all of the fae. That's all you really need to know."

Fredrick covered his mouth, trying not to burst into laughter, but failed.

My lips curved into an approving smile, my fingers finding her chin, pulling her gaze to me.

"Did I speak out of turn?" she asked.

"Fuck no." I pressed my lips to hers, kissing her passionately. Symbolically reinstating to my father that her and I were together, a team, a pairing.

THIRTY

MARIE

"We should probably talk about it," I said as I traced the tattoo on Karnelian's chest.

It was late into the night, the slice of the yellow tinted moon hung high in the sky. The stars sparked over the deep expanse like the light freckles that adorned Karnelian's cheeks. The night fell into the windows, the cool air brushing over us providing relief from the day's heat.

Karnelian had fucked me hard after the family dinner, so brutal I was left in tears and body was blistering in pain. His eyes were filled with triumph as he broke me. The sight of me wrecked, filling him with pleasure. It satisfied me to see it, to please him. An action that later would drive me with guilt because I wasn't made to please him.

After he cared for me extensively, repairing me, recentering me, grounding me. The sex always left me weightless and lost, but he'd hold me, massage me, bathe me, feed me, and eventually I'd find myself on a base that was more stable than the one I started on.

The session would always last long and we'd end up here, cuddled in bed, deep into the night, a calmness in the air.

"Talk about what?" Karnelian mused, his fingers equally trancing the brand on my left arm.

His calm voice didn't fool me. He knew the subject I was broaching.

The babe situation.

I had always wanted a babe. If I and Karnelian were a true pairing, no mates, deals, or seat on the throne, I would be more than happy to have his babes. If he treated our babes half as well as he did me, Karnelian would be a great father and I would be lucky to have him aid in raising my babes.

But that was a fantasy that would never come to light because there was a deal, a shiny onyx crown and my babes were supposed to be fathered by another male. A male I wanted to cut this life short to return to.

I didn't want to bring life to this world just to leave them motherless. I wanted them to experience the love that was given to me by my mother, but my soul was shattered, and my heart was cold, and there was no room for me to love another being.

"Karnelian..." I sighed, dragging my claw across the points of the sun.

His hand traveled up the expanse of my arm to my shoulder before resting in the crevasse of my neck, his thumb brushing against the tiny hairs on my cheek. "Not tonight, baby," He rasped, voice emotional, thick, and strained.

"We should have a plan at least."

"Not tonight, Marie." His eyes were strained, hard and piercing, shining more silver in the night light. His features were set in void but his body was tense, muscles stressed. "Later, okay?"

I nodded, pressing a kiss to his chest. It could wait. My soul may ache for death, but my body and mind were content to stay alive—as long as he was here. My guilty pleasure, my dark obsession, my personal drug—a male who smelled of cinnamon and whiskey.

As any addiction, I needed more. I didn't want to leave even if my soul berated me with horrific remorse. I had to have more. So, I could wait a bit longer. I could prolong the end.

"Can I ask you a question?" Karnelian whispered into the still night.

"Yes." Another kiss to his chest, my lips brushing against the tiny stubbled hair.

"It's about him. Your relationship with him."

My muscles tightened but were smoothed out by his hand on my back, the warm rough palm stroking up and down my spine.

I swallowed the lump in my throat. "You can ask but I may not answer."

The corners of his lips tipped up but didn't reach his eyes. "That's fair." He sighed. "Is he really worth your death?" A strained pause. "I've heard how he was as a mate. I'm not judging your relationship with him, but can you seriously not live without him? Do you think that he wants you to die after he sacrificed himself so you'd live? I get he is the other half of your soul, and you ache to reconnect, but is there truly no other option than death?"

His words sobered the high he emanated, my soul jerking within me, and hollering out all my convictions. The hollowness formed into my middle a reminder of who used to fill it, who I used to be pulled to and now I had no direction, no compass.

I had to look away from Karnelian's penetrating orbs, and gather my breaths to keep from the wave of emotion that started to rise to the surface. My eyes prickled, the tears wiggling under my lids and it felt like there was no stopping it, but then Karnelian pulled my head to lie on his chest. His heart pounding against my ear, a tune that would never match mine but vibrated through me until my breaths matched its steady beat. His cinnamon scent filled my nose, a balm, calm and warm, a lifesaving fire for my entirety.

"I'm not going to answer that," I whispered, voice choked.

Karnelian caressed my hair, twirling the end of my curls as we laid silent, until my muscles relaxed fully into his frame. "A different question. What did you want in life?"

"Me and my mate—"

"Not your mate. You. Just you. What did you want before him? Before you sorted and he took your independence away."

My head raised to meet his gaze. "He didn't take my independence."

"Little bird, there's nothing about you, that's just you. Everything I know about you has a little tint of him. What is something about you that has nothing to do with him? What did you desire in life before you sorted?"

My lips curved down as the thoughts swirled in my mind. Before my life was entwined with my mate's, my plan was to entwine it with Kolvin's, and before that it was entwined with my mother's. Marie Shweadawn, formally Foxglove, forever prepared to be another's shadow. No wonder my blood bled black.

Karnelian's thumbs found the corner of my lips, pushing them up so they no longer formed a frown, and as if sensing my thoughts, he asked, "Is there anything you were passionate about? A hobby that was just yours? I'll tell you one of mine, if you tell me yours."

"There is one thing," I said, my body becoming tight as I thought about it. "I've never told anyone about it, not even my mother. I would have told my mate one day but mates..." I exhaled. "Mates need to fuck, and the times we did talk, I spent most of it listening. That's what he needed, someone to listen to him. Someone who saw him just as him. Not a prince or a son soon to be king. So, he talked, and I listened. If I had known our time in this life would be cut short... I still would have listened."

A light smile lined his lips, a small snort sounding from him. "You realize I just asked you about you, and you found a way to make it about him."

I blushed, biting my lip.

He tucked a curl behind my ear, eyes hooded and gazing. "So, are you going to tell me?"

My chest tightened with nerves. "Could you tell me yours first?"

He nodded, kissing my head, the small gesture calming my nerves. "I love to swim."

I smiled, a giggle following. "I knew that already."

He pressed a soft kiss to my lips. "Yeah, but I love it. When I was a boy, it was pretty much all I ever wanted to do. Before I understood that I was due to rule the throne. I wanted to be a swimmer. You know, like, for sport."

My smile widened. "Wouldn't that be cheating because you're one fourth water nymph?"

"Totally, but my father would never let people know that. I don't have gills or anything, so they wouldn't have reason to believe I had gifts beyond pure talent."

"Does your mother have gills? I didn't see any at the dinner."

"She can hide them. It's a normal water nymph trait to disarm prey. Their larger eyes are a giveaway though, but you've seen my mother. If you didn't know, you'd think she just had big brown eyes. In her true form, she has it all, gills, webbed feet, serrated—scary-ass looking teeth. That's how my father found out about her. He wanted her to claim him, and for nymphs to claim, they need to be in their true form."

"That's pretty cool. I hope to see her like that one day."

"I hope you do too." His smile grew tight for a brief moment, but it was gone when he continued speaking. "So, tell me yours."

I blew out a breath, agitation building. "Don't make fun of me or anything."

The wicked gleam flickered in his eyes. "I make no promises."

My eyes narrowed.

"Little bird, you know I love to make people squirm. *Especially you.*"

An irritated growl left me. "Just... wait one day to make fun of me, okay?"

"Okay, one day. It's a deal."

"Music."

A crease formed between his brows. "Music? Why would I make fun of that?"

"Because... I... Well, I'm a bit of a nerd for it... I mean, I was. Any time I was alone, I was singing or reading music. Under my bed, there is a stack of sheet music. I got so good at reading it that you could give me any page and I could hum the tune for you without much thought."

"Really?"

"Yeah."

"Get up."

My face contorted in confusion. "What?"

"Get up."

I rose, moving away from Karnelian who stood from the bed grabbing his discarded boxers from the ground and pulled them up. He tossed me one of his shirts from the dresser and after I put it on, he held out his hand. "Come."

We walked through the maze of the manor, until we came up to an alcove.

Karnelian's magic lit the sconces, revealing the grand piano made of polished cherry wood and gold decals.

Mindlessly, I walked over to the beautiful instrument, admiring the care and craftsmanship before tapping on one of the porcelain keys. The sharp ping, reverberating through my body and clashing against my cold heart.

"Can you play?" Karnelian asked behind me.

"No." I raised my fingers. "Claws kind of get in the way of life."

Karnelian sat down on the piano bench. "There's a box of music over there," he pointed to the side wall. "Pick something out."

"Why?" My eyes flicked back and forth from the piano to Karnelian. "Can you play?"

A slow smirk formed on his lips. "Yeah, unfortunately. It's kind of a requirement as a prince to learn to play an instrument. My brother plays the piccolo because it is the instrument with the funniest name."

"Why did you pick the piano?"

He studied the keys, his smirk souring, eyes darkening. "My father played it, and I wanted to be just like him."

There was a stillness in the air as his mind traveled through memories he didn't share. Rolling his shoulders, he shook his head, eyes connecting to mine and focusing on me. "Go pick something."

I flicked through the music, excited to hear him play. It had been years since I enjoyed music, years since I even sang. The thought of getting to feel the harmonious hymns reverberating through my skin had heat flaring in my chest, forming right around my frozen heart.

I practically ran over to Karnelian, smiling ear to ear after finding a piece.

He took the papers, tugging me in to press a kiss to my lips. Slow, sweet, and tender. Then he pulled back and studied the page.

"Little bird," he chided. "I'm not a renowned pianist."

"It's one of my favorites."

The piece was from a famous ballet that covered one of the fae wars that wasn't civil. The Demon War.

Fae were creatures of chaos, but demons were creatures of carnage. The demons have this drive for power, their magic wasn't an ever-present stream that comes naturally, like the fae. They have to siphon their magic from a source. They siphon from the elements—Earth, Air, Fire, Water and Spirit. Sourcing from spirit is currently against demon law, but every thousand of years, a group of demons will come into power and declare it legal and then the demons will go on a killing rampage, sucking people's souls from their bodies. This piece pairs with one of the battle scenes in the ballet, it's violent and chaotic, but moving and sensual. One truly feels like they were there on the battlefield fighting against the demons as it plays.

The hand on my waist stroked up and down as Karnelian pressed a kiss to my brow. "I haven't played in years, little bird, but I promise I'll work up to it. Just, I'll need time."

"You're already pretty busy."

"I'll make time for it." He tucked a curl behind my ear. "Pick something easy for tonight."

I smiled and kissed him, before taking the sheet back and picking out something easier, it was a lullaby, a famous one every fae knew about the stars.

Karnelian took the sheets, warmed his joints up and began playing. The music flowed through me, my blood tuning to the rhyme, pumping in sync with the song.

He finished, looking over to me, my cheeks stinging from my smile. They got a reprieve when Karnelian bent to press his lips to mine.

"This time, sing," he said as he pulled away.

"What?" I said, my body tensing.

"Sing, little bird. You said that you loved it."

"I... uh... I've never sung in front of someone. Well, except my mother when I was little."

"Today's the day you do."

"I don't know... Can you just play it again, and I hum along."

"No."

"You can't force me to sing."

That sinful smirk and devious eyes adorned his face. "I can."

"How?" I crossed my arms.

"You owe me."

"What?"

"The night I saved you from bursting into tears in front of the whole Seelie Territory. You owe me for that."

"I didn't think you'd actually hold that against me."

"I don't joke about deals. If you don't let me cash it in, I'll make you pay in other, much crueler ways." His eyes hooded, but the heated gaze held anarchy that had my creature shrinking.

I swallowed the lump in my throat. "How?"

"Ever heard of edging?"

My nostrils flared, core tightening in a strange mix of alarm and arousal. "Yes."

"It can be hell to another if done correctly."

"You can't—You have to make me come once a week."

He bit his lip, his demeanor growing in arrogance. "Oh, I'll make you come but it will be so tiny and so unsatisfying that you'll feel worse than you did." He leaned in, hovering over me. "And don't think you can just rub one out while I'm not around either. The devil carries silver blood and can bound you to do whatever he does or doesn't desire."

Fuck. "Karnelian... I really don't like to sing in front of others."

"We're friends, are we not?"

"Yes."

"Best friends?"

Best friends? My mate was supposed to be my best friend, but he never felt like a friend. My lover, yes, but never my friend. Karnelian and I were lovers, our sex was extremely intimate, but we felt like friends. At the current moment my list of friends was quite short. My mother and I weren't what we used to be, Kolvin was more like family than friend, and Jessamine stopped sending me letters after two years of me never replying to them. In truth Karnelian was truly the only person I had, and even if I did have all those other people playing the old roles in my life, he was the only one I've shared this part of myself with. "Yes." I nodded. "I think you are my best friend."

He chuckled lightly. "You think?"

"You are. I just had to think about it."

"Well, as your best friend, you should feel comfortable around me to sing."

"You just told me that you loved to make me squirm."

Instead of denying it, he just shrugged. "At the very least, I promised not to make fun of you for a day. So, you're safe for now."

"That's really reassuring." I took a deep breath to try and calm my nerves. "Okay, just this once, because of the deal."

He smiled in triumph before cracking his knuckles and started to play.

Butterflies swarmed in my stomach and worms wiggled in my throat, but I looked over to Karnelian and I felt a feeling settle over, a calmness, a safeness and I started singing.

I focused on the music, each chime of the keys, guiding me through the lyrics.

The buzz that slithered between my lips as each syllable left my tongue, was like taking a fresh dose of dust, like a tart sip of wine sliding down my throat—exhilarating.

And that was when I felt it, my cold heart swelled in its confines, the frost beginning to thaw away.

Clarity settled over me, and for once I could truly feel a passion for life and see a future. One where Karnelian and I just did this. It wasn't anything big, but it was something to look forward to and it had me pouring myself into the song, my being harmonizing to the tune.

The song ended, the world coming back to me. The side of my face burned with awareness and I turned to Karnelian, a small pure smile blossoming on my lips, warmth filling my belly.

Karnelian's hazels beat into me, intense and engraving, exploring deep inside me and attempting to connect to the soul hidden with the shadows, trying to run away.

"You sing beautifully, Stéla."

I bit my lip, my face coloring red. "Really?"

He snorted, his fingers coming up to stroke my cheek. "I don't know why you would hide that, little bird. You are meant to shine, not hide behind others."

My soul jerked at his words, denial ringing within its hushed screams. "I didn't hide behind him. We were... we were one. Two beings sharing one soul, though I don't actually think that's how it works, but that's what it felt like. Like who he was, was just an extension of myself. I loved the things he loved because he loved them. I did the things he liked because he liked them. Seeing him happy made me happy." I took a breath. "To answer your question earlier, Nelian. It's not about him being worth my death, or if I should make the most of his sacrifice. It's that with him I feel right and without him I feel wrong."

Tears started to gather in my eyes as I felt his absence in my middle. "You know in most stories about the death of a loved one they talk about how you grow stronger, but for me, that's not the case, for me I am weaker. I was the weaker half of our pairing. I think if he had survived, he would have been able to rise up to his task and continue on. He wouldn't need a brand on his arm, or to shoot dust up his nose, or drink himself to oblivion." A shudder wracked my frame as the tears started to fall. "He could do all of this without me, but I can't, Karnelian. I can't do this without him. I wasn't designed to do this without him. There is no other option for me other than death." My hand covered my center where I felt my soul thrashing within me, confusion and chaos shrilling with it. "My soul can't stand to live another hour, but the only reason it does is because it's forced to. All it wants is to return to him, and it will not rest until it does."

Karnelian wiped away my tears, fingers angling my face to meet his eyes. "You aren't alone, little bird. You have me. All the shit you have to go through, I'll be there with you every step of the way. I'll be the strength you need when you feel weak. But know this, Marie, you are far from weak. You just think you're weak because when people see your softness, your vulnerability, they treat you like you can't handle anything by yourself. But you can and you are, believe that." His eyes penetrated into me, demanding I do.

I nodded, sniffling.

"Little bird," he warned.

"Okay," I said, wrapping my arms around him, my nose coming to his neck, breathing in a huge whiff of his scent to calm my creature. My soul still thrashed inside me, but I was able to tune it out as I burrowed further and further into Karnelian. My strength when I felt weak. My friend for when I felt alone. My ally against the twisted fate I had been dealt.

THIRTY-ONE

MARIE

The day before Mabon, Karnelian's work had him traveling around the territory, so I stayed at the manor all day practicing magic. I could manifest my magic at will now, but I wasn't able to cast a spell yet. That required me balancing my energy with a rock, something I was not good at unless it involved a person named after a rock. After trying for hours, I gave up and spent the day reading in bed.

I was so engrossed in the book that I didn't notice the stars lined the sky or that Karnelian had portalled into the room, until he tackled me, smothering me with his large body.

"Nelian…" I said, thrashing under him.

"Little bird…" Karnelian sang, throwing his arms around me and squeezing me into a bear hug, the air soon littered with my laughter.

Karnelian smashed his lips against mine, kissing me deeply, before breaking our kiss to set the book smashed between us on the bedside table. He attempted to continue devouring me, but I stopped him, noting something on his left hand.

"You got a tattoo?" I said, grasping his hand to study his ring finger.

It was a simple four-pointed star exactly where a ring would go.

Karnelian rolled away, sitting up. "Yeah, I made a deal with a tattoo artist. I'm not really a male who likes jewelry, so I thought why not."

My head cocked to the side in confusion. "You don't like jewelry, so you got a tattoo?"

Karnelian chuckled to himself before searching through the inside pocket of his suit and holding out something for me. "Here, for our marriage."

Then Karnelian, with no flare, just dropped a ring into my palm. Which I quickly realized wasn't just any ring; it was my ring from my mate, but modified.

"All the changes I did are reversible if you don't like it. I only asked you to wear my ring to see if you were bluffing when we made the deal. I know the ring means a lot to you, and getting a new ring just didn't feel right."

I felt another part of my cold heart thaw further as I took in the ring. The ring was the same band, the wolf chasing the rabbit, but instead of a rose gold, it was silver, and instead of a yellow stone, it was a black stone set between the two small diamonds.

I remained speechless, staring at the ring, an overwhelming feel of emotions—positive emotions, flowing through me.

"I used magic to change the band," Karnelian said, voice uneasy as he misread my blank expression. "Easily reversible. I have the original stone. I can just go back to the jeweler and get them to swap the obsidian back to citrine. The only thing not reversible is the engraving."

I turned the band, reading the engraving inside the ring. *My Stéla*.

"You called me that a few days ago. What does it mean?"

Karnelian smirked, his devil's mask hiding the emotion that swirled in his hazel eyes. "Look it up."

I huffed but wouldn't let him ruin the moment with his devilry as I handed him the ring.

"Do you not like—"

I held my left hand out to him. "Put it on for me."

A small genuine smile ghosted Karnelian's lips, cracking that mask. He took my hand in his, his roughness grazing across my softness, before he slid the ring onto my finger.

Something about it felt right, a feeling I hadn't felt in a long time. After my mate died, the ring felt like a tie to the worst day of my life, a tie to old Marie, whose favorite color was yellow and whose smile shined more than the sun. Taking the ring off was a relief but having it back now with Karnelian's changes was an unexpected gift. He didn't erase my mate, but he didn't illuminate the sorrow. He took something broken, and instead of trying to repair it, he made it into something new.

I looked up at him, tears lining my eyes. "It's perfect, Nelian."

Something flickered in his eyes, the silvery green darkening. "Perfect?"

"Yes."

There was so much gratification swelling within me, I didn't know how to cope with it. It was such a strange feeling, a warmth in my chest that spread through my being. Even though my soul felt deep sorrow, it was quiet, or at least my gratitude canceled out its screams.

That was when I felt it. My heartbeat. One small thump in my body, pumping a little bit of life into my being.

The next thing I knew, I was catapulting myself on Karnelian, my hips straddling his, our mouth fused.

Another thump.

My mouth traveled down his chin, his stubble pinpricking my lips. I kissed down his neck, an area our mouths never neared, and started sucking, licking, tasting.

Karnelian let out a pained groan, his hand finding the back of my head, fingers threading into my curls. He didn't pull me away, but he didn't push. He just held me, his hips rocking to mine, enjoying the pleasure of my tongue.

Thump.

My fingers fumbled with the buttons to his tunic, half cutting them off with my claws. His bare chest heated my palms, the taut muscles flexing under my touch before I was shoving off his shirt, and pushing him to lay on the bed.

My kisses perused his body, my tongue tasting every inch of his torso. I unbuckled his pants, using my claws to rip the ties, until his hard cock was in my hand.

Then my mouth was on him. My eyes rolling back into my head at the feel of his tip filling my mouth. His ragged moan had my eyes locking back on him, remembering his rule, remembering to please him.

His salty pre-cum filled my tongue and his husked cinnamon scent saturated my senses. I missed the feel of a cock in my mouth. I missed feeling a cock twitching on my tongue. I missed the feel of fingers threaded at the base of my skull, holding me there so I wouldn't stop giving pleasure. Most of all, I missed the faces, the crinkled brows, and panting mouths, satisfying the male to no end.

With my eyes locked on his, it made it more intense. His pupils dilated; lids hooded but irises lit with passion. He looked so utterly pleased with me. So content, so happy.

A look I was definitely a whore for.

Thump.

I sucked his cock deeper into my mouth, his groans covering my gags, saliva dripping down my chin as I tried to fit his monstrous cock down my throat. I could only get past a few inches before I was choking having to pull back, but I never fully left him. I wouldn't stop him from making that face, from creating those sounds. Instead, I sucked him hard, attempting to rip his skin from his flesh, focusing on the spot right under the head that had his eyes leaving mine.

"Fuck, Marie."

I smiled around his cock, my teeth touching his flesh making him flinch. Oh, he didn't know the pleasure I could bring with a slight graze of my teeth. Pleasure I so wanted to bring him.

No matter how much of a greedy little slut I was for him, for my drug, my distraction. I couldn't do that, but I would swallow him whole.

It took several minutes of me attempting to, my throat having to get used to his size and my body having to get used to the lack of air. My canines still scraped across his shaft, unable to hide them with his size, but the more I bobbed my head the more he seemed to like them dragging across his skin. Eventually my nose was tickled with raspy blond hairs and my mouth pressed against his pelvis.

Karnelian jerked when he felt me swallow him whole. I felt his cock swell in my mouth, then he did something I never could have imagined. Something I didn't think possible. Something I was told was rare for a male to do.

He purred.

THIRTY-TWO

Karnelian

Marie sucked cock like she was attempting to suck my soul out during the process. I knew she wasn't just good at this because I hadn't had this done to me in years. She was an artist, master, coordinator.

She watched my tells, adjusted to what I liked. The things I didn't like, she made pleasurable. She tested limits, pushing me, tethering my boundaries, sending my monster in a state of fear. Marie, the tiny female whose hand barely fit around my cock, brought my monster to fear by the drag of her teeth.

I've never had a female give me head this good. Never. The only thing even close to this was before I sorted, and the females wanted to secure a spot as princess with me. That was because head was only good when a female cared. If a female cared for you, or in my instance cared about the title you held, they put their whole being into pleasuring you. If a female cared for you, she'd make you feel cherished, and prized.

Marie went an extra mile. It was the look in her eyes that made it better. The gleam in her voids. The desire, excitement, euphoria. She looked like she wanted to dismember my cock from my body and have it permanently shoved down her throat.

She moaned at my taste, mewed at my pleasure, hummed at my satisfaction, her noises vibrating around my cock and traveling through my center.

Then there was the gagging. The fucking gagging. The suffocating, the gasping for breath.

The fact that she sacrificed her air for my pleasure had me reeling.

I was so lost in her—her noises, her mouth, her voids, that I didn't realize she was attempting to swallow me whole until her lips suctioned to the base of me—something none had ever attempted to do because none of them cared.

My body tightened, fire burning in my balls. I felt myself swelling and I opened my mouth to release another moan. But that was not what came out.

I stiffened, my orgasm stopping when panic filled my veins. I purred. I fucking *purred*.

Marie's eyes went wide, mirroring my expression with my cock still barred in her throat. I shifted, ready to pull her off and go. I had no idea where as long as it was anywhere away from her, but then she purred back.

My back arched as the vibration traveled through my cells, wrapping around my cock, and cupping my balls. A broken cry ripped from my throat, and my paused orgasm came to climax.

I grew lightheaded as she took my seed down her throat, my monster taking the reins and purring again in approval. She purred again, causing me to jerk and cry out again.

She pulled off my cock, showing me my mess in her mouth before swallowing and releasing another purr.

Her purrs were forced. My monster could understand them, not like we were speaking a different language, but there was a statement behind each purr. Mine were automatic, gratuitous.

Hers were purposeful, cautious, and reassuring. Marie controlled each one, not her creature.

Even if they were controlled, they were fucking euphoric. Ecstasy in my ears. The meek rumble echoing out of her made my softening cock harden to a point of pain, and I had to take her, I had to fuck her.

I grabbed her roughly, flipping us so she was on her back. I was fully animal at the moment as I tore one of my tunics off her frame and then mauled her plush breast.

Moving down her body, I appreciated every curve of her as my monster continued to purr. Now that it had figured out how to do it, it wouldn't fucking stop, and neither would Marie.

I wanted her to stop because the noise was driving me fucking mad, hysterical, on the brink of breaking.

My canines ripped into her panties, tearing them off and spitting them out. I buried my face into her pussy, sucking in her clit and letting my purrs vibrate through her.

Her scream was harsh, scraping at her throat, and echoing off the walls. She didn't stop purring though, not when I added my finger to the mix and made her screams become shouts. Not when I made her break apart into a thousand pieces. She continued to purr, answering my monster's calls with her sweet song.

My cock was hard as a rock as she laid panting and purring, her eyes hadn't remained on me because the sex was too explosive but as she rested, they found mine.

My reaction was instant, flipping her so she lay on her hands and knees and plunged my cock into her wet depths. Another forced purr from her, this one signaling pleasure and gratuity. The sound had me pumping harder into her. The wet slick sound of my balls slapping into her dripping core filled the room. I focused on that. I focused on making it louder, pain starting to bloom on my pelvis from the repeated slapping.

I stared down at her back, the expanse almost mark-less. I had never fucked her like this. Never not had her eyes on me. I couldn't drown in those depths right now because if I did, I knew I was going to be lost. I was already losing it. She had stripped me down, left me vulnerable, nothing to guard me. The sex was like I was under attack, her purrs, moans, and the whispers berating me. I just kept going at it, attempting to finish so this could be over.

I was able to claw my way to the surface as I examined her back, the one mark that lay there. Right in the center in between her shoulder blades.

My monster still purred, the fucker way too happy with the female, but I did my best to muffle them, letting that mark ground me.

That mark meant more than any of the other marks. Fae often marked on the neck, a visible place, a place of pride. One could always sense a mark if not visible but marking there was like a cherry on top, screaming to the world 'hey look who's mine.' Other places held other significance: genitalia, often done when the partner is extremely possessive or abusive; babes were often bit on the arm or hand for protection; and the middle of the back—impossible for the wearer to reach—to allow one to mark you there took trust, and a lot of love. The mark meant you surrendered yourself fully to your partner.

It had me thrusting harder, focusing on the feel of her, how perfect she felt for my cock, how she felt made for me. I pushed back the fact that no matter how she felt, she wasn't mine, or made for me. I focused on the feeling until I felt myself releasing, then pulled out immediately. I didn't bask in my orgasm, letting my come drip all over, not giving a fuck where it landed. I just wanted to leave.

I got out of bed and walked to the bathroom, closing the door softly so as not to cause alarm to the little bird.

I leaned against the door, my heart pounding in my chest, my lungs unable to take a breath. I felt outside myself, my limbs foreign, my reflection in the mirror a stranger.

I pushed the pants off, stepping into the glass shower and turning the water on.

A breath left me as the beads pelted my skin. My eyes closed, my head resting against the cold terracotta tile. The warm water soothed me, making it possible for me to take a few more breaths.

Slowly, in and out, in and out. I formed them like the sea forms a wave.

I lost time under the spray, my mind clear and focused on connecting to my second home. The creek of the bathroom door broke my serenity. Her soft patters grew louder as she neared, my body tightening with each step.

I didn't look at her as she entered the shower, staying turned toward the showerhead. I couldn't look at her. I couldn't let her see me like this, breaking apart, unhinged, exposed.

If I looked at her, I would spill everything out. I would tell her everything and let her hold every part of me, like my father once did. And like my father, she'd betray me, leave me, never accept me, a pain I knew would hurt worse from her.

Her limbs wrapped around me, her head laying against my back, her thumbs rubbing back and forth against my abs. A part of me wanted to push her away and another part of me wanted to pull her closer. So, I stayed still, letting her take control as I floated through my emotions.

She purred again, the action forced, my monster immediately answering, my body growing more tense. She purred more, her fingers soothing me, this purr telling me it was okay. That I was okay here with her, safe here with her.

It was rare for fae to purr. A fae didn't purr unless fully satisfied. I figured it was probably because of the disconnect we had to our beast. But Marie wasn't disconnected to that part of herself, because her purrs were more than satisfaction, they were communication.

She continued to purr until my bones knew her call and accepted it. Until I was relaxed fully into her hold and the purrs I answered her with were without restrain.

She held me for a little longer, the shower's spray the only song in the air before she untangled herself from me. The splash of water signifying her unknown movements until I felt the rough scrub of a washcloth against my back, and the smell of fresh soap littered the air.

She washed my back, arms, and legs before nudging me to turn. By this point I had gained a sense of balance enough to face her, but she didn't meet my eyes. As if she knew I was uncomfortable being this vulnerable with another being. She kept her gaze averted, focusing on washing my front with one hand, the other providing comforting touches.

It took me a moment to realize what she was doing. The touches, the comforting purrs, the holding me and the now washing me. She was performing aftercare to me.

Gratitude bloomed within me. My little bird was taking care of me. She had broken me and now she was putting me back together.

Being on the opposite side of this, I realized just how strong Marie was. She thought she was weak because she wasn't hardened against the world, but in truth that was why she was the strongest being I'd ever met. She was open, and didn't fear being vulnerable in front of others. She was able to feel deeply and not let it destroy her, and then keep doing it again and again and again. If she had confidence, she'd be an outstanding queen. Soft and powerful. I vowed then that I would try to get her there, to make her see how powerful she was just by simply being.

Marie finished washing my legs, making her way up my chest. When she reached my tattoo, her eyes met mine, a spark flaring in my chest.

I bent down and brushed my lips to hers, the kiss sweet and filled with appreciation. I pulled back, quickly turning to wash off before pulling her under the spray. She yelped, then giggled, the sound flaring in my soul and a smile blossoming on my lips.

On my knees, I pulled the cloth out of her grasp, filling it with soap before starting to repay her care with my own. She took the opportunity to wash my hair and gave me an extra long scalp massage, the sensation euphoric enough so I let out another purr. No fear came after the noise, just gratitude, and she responded in turn. Our eyes connected, her lips tipping up in a smile.

I finished washing her, standing, and grabbing the conditioner, pouring a generous amount in her hair before working it into the length. My fingers gently detangled her hair, working tip to root before I shampooed and conditioned again.

My arms encapsulated her after, her head to my chest, her arms around my waist. We swayed under the spray, letting our breaths come into harmony like when I connected to the waves.

"How did you know how to do my hair?" Something I have done many times before but a question she had yet to ask.

"I used to have long hair like my father."

"I know, but your hair is straight."

I kissed her temple. "If you let me finish, you'd know that my brother, who has hair of similar texture to yours, wanted to be like us when he was a boy and grew out his hair. Most of his childhood years were spent with his mother in a small village near the sea. She knew how to take care of his hair, but when he'd visit here, his hair would get tangled. So, I asked her to teach me how to take care of it."

Marie smiled up at me, and I pressed a kiss to those pretty pink lips. "That was sweet of you."

I kissed her again. "I'll kiss you anytime you want."

She growled, the noise nowhere near threatening to me. "I'm talking about what you did for your brother."

My grin was small but made my cheeks ache. "Yeah, well, that was a time when I was the type of male who did sweet things from the graciousness of his heart. That male quickly learned that when you do things for nothing in return, you'll end up being used by the person who makes the demands."

"You still do sweet things, at least for me."

I tucked a wet curl behind her ear. "You're my fiancée."

Marie's eyes studied mine for a brief moment before changing the subject. "Do you blame your brother?"

"Never. I love him, always will. He didn't have a choice to be born and he didn't have a choice when my father made him heir. He holds guilt over it that I have tried to sway but my disrespect toward my father makes him think I harbor resentment toward him. He tries to appease me by being angry toward our father and wanting nothing to do with the crown, but since I don't praise his effort, he thinks he hasn't done enough. There is nothing for him to do, he didn't hurt me, my father did."

"Do you hate your father?"

I shrugged. "I don't like him. It hurts to be around him because I used to trust no one over him, and he destroyed that. It's probably why I don't hate him because I know him so well. I know he wasn't trying to hurt me. He is never trying to hurt people when he acts, but the territory comes first for him, even before family. I haven't forgiven him. I don't think I ever will, but I don't think I hate him."

"I'm sorry he did that to you," Marie said, before pressing a kiss to my chest.

"There's nothing for you to be sorry about. You would never betray me, you can't. You hold nothing over me that I don't give freely. No one does." A part of me knew my words were untrue because she did. She held way too much of me.

THIRTY-THREE

Corivina

*T*he meal we ate was shit. It'd been too long since I'd cooked a full dinner for Mabon. Everyone said it was a lovely meal, but I could tell it was off, I was off. Everything was off.

Marie sat before me, quietly eating her dinner, her dominant hand tangled with Karnelian's under the table. She was off. She wasn't the female who was dead inside, like a few weeks ago, but she wasn't my flower who shined bright. Darkness still permeated her eyes which I did my best to avoid, but there weren't bags under her cold blacks, nor stiffness in her joints. She seemed calm, mellow, harmonious.

"So…" Jacoby spoke from the opposite head of the table. "You two are getting married."

The ring on Marie's finger sparkled then, black stone, silver band, similar to her mate's ring but not quite the same.

"We are," Karnelian said before taking a bite of his food.

Fire burned in my veins at this infuriating male. There was an air of condescension around him, much like his father but darker and unruly. He acted like this was no big farce, like the fact that they were betrothed and stained with another's scent was something that should have been expected when Marie disappeared a month ago.

"Are you two in love?" Kolvin gritted through his teeth. He sat next to me, eyes burning into Karnelian from across the table.

A smug smirk graced Karnelian's lips, hazel eyes gleaming as he responded with silence, taking another bite of his meal.

It was an effort not to roll my eyes at the males. 'The devil' got off on making people uncomfortable and Kolvin was too haughty to not engage with conflict. Tension raised between the two, stiff, humid and insufferably annoying. My daughter had fucked both of these males. Her attraction to arrogant assholes was something I will never understand.

The pissing contest was broken when Karnelian's attention was turned toward Marie from tugging on his hand. He didn't look at Marie like he looked at the rest of us. It was clear he respected everyone in here except possibly Kolvin, but he still looked at people like they were beneath him. My beast could feel it, his dominance, and annoyingly enough, my beast didn't feel threatened by it. He looked at Marie like an equal, his expression stripping off a few layers when connecting to her eyes. Something I would find appealing in a male for her if he wasn't such a dick.

They didn't speak, both keenly aware of their audience, but their eyes communicated. After a few moments, Karnelian yielded to her, huffing, and turning back to Kolvin. "No. We aren't in love. It's a deal."

The fire in my veins turned from a steady burn to scorching. "What."

Karnelian rolled his eyes before connecting to mine, the action causing my veins to flare gold just for a brief second. He was about to answer but I had enough of him to last a lifetime. My eyes pinpointed on my daughter. "Marie, speak."

Darius's hand covered mine, and I quickly shook him off. I loved the male, but he didn't make sense. He chided me because I coddled Marie too much and that was why she was so submissive letting males walk all over her. Now I was being too harsh, too strict, too stern.

"We made a deal." Marie cleared her throat, features settling into solidity, my anger having no effect on her. "He breaks my heat, and I agreed to marry him, if and when I ascend to the throne. And before you say anything, Mother, I do not want to be queen. My seat on the throne is another burden I would love to do without. Nelian was raised for the position and will be a needed ally if I ascend."

"Still doesn't seem like a fair deal," Kolvin mumbled.

Karnelian huffed out a chuckle, his grin villainous. "Oh, it's even."

Kolvin, a twenty-six-year-old male who still hasn't learned to keep his mouth shut, rose to the bait. "How?"

"Well, if you must know," Karnelian drawled. "The fine print states I must make her come once a week. *At the very least.*"

Kolvin white-knuckled his fork, nostrils flared. He didn't respond, maybe finally learning to think before he spoke.

"Nelian," Marie cursed. He bent to her, his eyes not breaking from Kolvin's as he kissed her forehead.

Karnelian jerked suddenly, hissing, eyes locking onto Marie's as he pulled his hand from her grasp. Little trickles of blood seeped from wounds made from her claws. A grin of approval glossing my lips that was quickly turned into a look of disgust when Marie licked his hand clean.

The act was too intimate for two beings who were just having sex. Their mannerisms were too intimate for two beings who held zero feelings for another. There was a harmony between them, they may not be in love, but they were on the road to it. I assumed both of them were blind to it though, especially when Karnelian pressed a kiss to her nose before petting her hair. His features apologetic.

HEART COLD AS GOLD

Their fingers interlocked, Karnelian going back to eating as Marie spoke. "The deal is as fair as it could be. I didn't want much and Karnelian provides what I need." Though I wasn't the one to ask, her words were pointed toward me, anticipating my judgment.

Darius's hand came over Marie's free one, stroking her palm. "Are you happy, flower?"

Her head cocked to the side, a small smile blooming on her face as she thought on it. She glanced at Karnelian, his gaze zeroed on her, intense and anticipatory. She looked back to Darius and nodded. "Yes."

Emotion built within me, my walls threatening to crumble as her smile widened. Bright as when she was a babe.

The image was stolen from me with a kiss—Karnelian's kiss.

"Are you staying for breakfast?" I asked, breaking their embrace.

Marie smiled at the idea. Before she sorted, Mabon extended to breakfast, our little family of three would wake and feast again. Marie loved having dinner foods for breakfast, often requesting them whenever asked what she wanted to eat in the morning. "Umm?"

She turned to Karnelian who pressed a light kiss to her lips before replying, "Whatever you want, little bird."

My eye twitched, my irritation rising.

"I guess, we will."

Dinner went on. Marie's smiles scarcely making an appearance here and there, but each one was stolen from view. Karnelian's lips pressed to it—every time. I hated it, but her smiles seemed to bloom brighter after each kiss, and I found myself growing grateful for him.

Soapy water soaked my hands as I washed the dinner plates. Darius normally acquired servants to clean, but with only seven people in attendance this year, it seemed a waste.

A weight pressing into my back caused me to stiffen, but an inhale of vanilla caused me to relax.

Darius and I had hardly spoken in the last few weeks. We even stopped sharing a bed—my choice, not his—though it felt like his.

He had been avoiding me after telling me I was the only female he'd been with, and I did nothing to correct the gap because there should be a gap. Darius deserved to be loved by a female who didn't allow gaps in their connection.

He took the plate from my hand, beginning to rinse the dishes under the tap.

"I can handle it," I said, turning the faucet off.

Darius shifted, turning the tap back on, shoulder brushing against mine. "You don't have to do everything alone, Vina."

My teeth ground, my darkness turning against me as it does. My emotions a whirlwind I could barely handle when he wasn't around after our last altercation, and with him around, they were on the edge of spilling out.

"Are you going to sleep in our bed tonight?"

The question added more tension to my body, and a roll of my shoulders didn't loosen it one bit.

There were four guest rooms in the manor. Two were currently used as storage rooms we kept saying we'd clean out, but never did. One was pretty much Kolvin's second bedroom, and the other was to be occupied by the Denmors tonight, taking my bed for the night away. "I will sleep on the couch in the main room."

Darius sucked in a breath. "You're not sleeping on the couch. You can sleep in our bed, and I'll sleep there tonight."

"It's your house, Darius. It would be rude of me to put you out of a bed. I'll just sleep on the couch, or I could just—"

Darius's head snapped toward me. "Don't fucking say go to the inn. And this is your house too. When we got married, everything of mine became yours, including this house. You'll sleep in the bed."

His assertion lately had me feeling like I was playing a losing game. He never asserted himself in our fights. Never dominated, always succumbing to my will. I never viewed him as submissive, just compliant, often finding medium ground with me. Now though, he wasn't yielding, not even an inch. It left me floundering for what to do because he never put me in this position.

"I thought you were avoiding me."

"I haven't been avoiding you."

"You have."

"No, I've been busy with the war. And you've been busy avoiding Dominick." That was true. I had been avoiding Dominick, avoiding the pain it would cause when I saw him again, and had to answer with a word my heart didn't want to say.

"Darius…"

Warm fingers grasped my wrist, tugging me closer, my eyes falling into pools of blue, an openness to them I hadn't seen in five years.

"What are you going to say to him?" His hand slid down to grasp mine, digits stroking over my wedding ring.

"I…" The look in his eyes gutted me, and the only thing that kept me from spilling was the knowledge that my answer would break him. I hadn't prepared myself enough to do that. So I turned those calm pools into blue flames. "It's not really your business."

His hand tightened around mine. "You are *my wife*. I think it would be my business if you married another."

"I won't be your wife for much longer." A harsh breath left me before I could continue. "Especially since you started divorcing me without even my knowledge."

"Wh—" He closed his eyes, taking a step away. "Dominick told you I put in a request."

"It was why he proposed in the first place. It was *how* he proposed." My throat grew dry, my eyes burning. Everything was right at the edge, threatening to burst. I couldn't even hold the tears back from lining my eyes. "It was a dream proposal. I always wanted to have a male offer me partnership, then tell me my marriage is ending."

Darius cupped my face, eyes softening. "Vina, you know that's not what I want. I was pissed at you after Marie's accident, and I just put in the request. It was just a request. It doesn't mean anything."

"It does mean something. It means you're done. You just don't want to let go."

And like I wanted, my words brought back the flame. "You don't want to give in. You don't want to admit you love him. You don't want to admit you fucked up."

"I know I fucked up, Darius! I realized that when my daughter was attempting to take her own life in front of my eyes! I have known!"

"Then why aren't you choosing to fix it? Why aren't you choosing Marie, choosing our family, choosing me?"

"I am."

"If that were true, you would have said no to Dominick. If that were true, you'd include me in your plans as I would include you."

I shook my head, a tear spilling down my cheek before I clarified myself. "I'm choosing to let you go, Darius. Because you're right. I probably won't let him go when he's dead. Finish filing, and when you get the papers, I'll sign them. I'm sorry I was a shit first love, and I hope you don't make the same mistake I did holding on to the hurt I've dealt."

"Corivina, don't."

"You don't! Darius, I am not your one. You must have been mistaken in thinking I was." The words burned through me, they felt like a lie, but I forced them to be true as more tears were forced down my cheeks. "I hurt you. I misuse you. I torture you. And I love you, but my love is tainted and toxic. And I can't keep handing it out anymore. I can't keep seeing you broken because of me. I can't keep fucking things up. You deserve better, and I want you to have better. So, get the papers and I'll sign them."

Before I could be faced with those broken blues again, I turned, walking out the kitchen, exiting out the back door that led outside. I didn't revel in the fresh air. Nor did I revel in the beauty of the moon. I walked, but I didn't go to the inn. I went to Marie's treehouse, holding up there for the night.

THIRTY-FOUR

MARIE

*I*n an armchair in the main room, I sat in Karnelian's lap. There were still open seats I could have sat in, but Karnelian pulled into his lap before I could even consider a different option.

Karnelian chatted with Sariah and Jacoby, Karnelian and Jacoby bantering like old friends, which I quickly found out they were. Once upon a time Karnelian was training under him and my father when he was a faeling. A requirement from his father to ascend to the throne.

I had no input, sitting on Karnelian's lap like a ventriloquist doll. A part of me liked it. I felt like I needed a tether to Karnelian and sitting in his lap, his chest against my back, hand on my waist, they were little reminders that he was there, and I was safe from my own torment.

Another part of me was annoyed with the power play he was inciting.

Kolvin was upset about the news and Karnelian intended on smothering his victory in Kolvin's face. I knew Karnelian didn't see me as a prize to be won, he just loved to rile people and Kolvin was his current victim.

His ambush was calculated and minuscule. Firstly, there was his energy. Everyone in the room knew Karnelian was the most powerful beast, we could sense it, but it was like he was pushing his energy out until the notion was stained into our bones. Then there were his mannerisms. Karnelian sat relaxed, laid back into the chair like he was a king and had no worries in the world. To those who respected him—Jacoby and Sariah—it wasn't offensive. To Kolvin, it was a slap in the face, telling him Karnelian saw him as no threat, no significance. There was also the way he acted toward me. His hold on me was loose—not possessive as if afraid to lose me. He held me like he owned me and if I left, he knew I'd come back. All these things, small little fuck yous aimed at Kolvin, edging his beast to come out.

The worst part was I did nothing to stop it, simply because a part of me enjoyed his toying. I found it enthralling, riveting. I wanted to play too, my beast piped up and ready to purr for Karnelian just to rub it further into Kolvin's face.

And after that thought crossed my mind I was colored with guilt. A thing I hated to feel even if it wasn't from betraying my mate.

I turned to face Karnelian, and he stopped talking mid-sentence the moment my eyes laid on him. "What, little bird?" His thumb stroked back and forth on my waist.

"I'll be back."

His fingers flexed but didn't tighten. "Where are you going?"

Our voices were hushed but everyone had quieted to listen in to our conversation. "Out."

A smirk spread on his face, his lip quirking to the side to hide a budding smile. "Don't be long. I like you warming my lap."

I couldn't help but smile which was quickly smothered by his kiss.

"I won't be long."

A quick kiss goodbye and I got up, meeting hurt honey-green orbs. I walked over to him, holding my hand out in command.

Kolvin didn't protest, and then we were walking outside to our spot, the pond next to the tree house. The place we made love, the place I broke his heart, the place I'd be nailing in the notion that our love died years ago.

We sat on a log near the bank of the pond, crickets chirping in the summer night. Kolvin sighed, voice hurt, heavy and exhausted. "Why, Marie. Why him?"

It was a simple question with a complicated answer. My beast liked Karnelian. It chose him to break our heat, but anyone could have done it. Karnelian was my friend, but so was Kolvin, more than, he was my family.

"Why not me," Kolvin asked when I still hadn't answered. "I… I love you, Marie. I always have. You say what you have with him is just sex, but why wouldn't you want someone who loves you? Who wants to take care of you and give you the best life possible after your mate?"

This question was a lot easier to answer now that he had spoken. "Because of that." I took his hand in mine, giving it a light squeeze in comfort. "I love you too, Kolvin. And I really did love you before all of this. My whole life's plan was to marry you, have your babes and live happily ever after, but that's just not how things worked out." A heavy breath left me. "If I would have chosen you to break my heat, that's all it ever would be. It would just be sex. That is what it is between Karnelian and I. We are friends too, but nothing more than that. Even if you are my friend, you are also in love with me. I know if I had chosen you, you'd hold out hope that there would be more, and there will never be more."

"You don't know that. You have gotten better. You've been getting better. We could have a second chance if you gave us a shot."

A sad snort left me. "That's why Karnelian. Karnelian doesn't hope for love. He's in this for the logistics, and he'll never feel more for me."

"He does."

I frowned, shaking my head. "He doesn't."

"Marie, look at him. Really look at him when he looks at you. Listen how he talks to you, how he touches you. He's under your spell. When he looks at others, they aren't even on the same plane as him, but he looks at you… he looks at you like you're his sun, his life source, the center of his universe. You may not see it, but it's clear as day to everyone else."

"He just… we are friends. He's not the type of person to have friends, so he just treats me differently."

"People don't look at their friends, no matter how many they have, like their source of life. My father has plenty of friends, but he only looks at my mother like that. Your father is the friendliest male on this planet, and he only looks at Corivina that way. Karnelian is not your friend, at least not in his eyes."

I was left speechless, my mind whizzing with the information and reprocessing everything that had happened over the last few weeks with Karnelian.

Last night, he purred. He, a male, purred. Purring didn't adequate to love exactly but it meant more than just friendship. It meant I deeply satisfied him. It freaked him out, when it happened so I purred back, but my purrs were forced, my creature educated enough on the manner to do it on command. I could tell Karnelian didn't want to talk about it, so I didn't push and I let the notion slip from my mind.

But he purred, and I purred, and my beast liked our harmonized vibrations.

If it was just the purring, I could disregard what Kolvin was bringing up, but there was more.

There was the ring. *My Stéla.*

I didn't know what it meant, but the few times Karnelian had said it to me, his voice deepened, eyes glazing over and pinpointing on me like they were trying to rip into my being. The word meant something deep, deep enough from him to permanently emboss it on the ring from my mate.

I knew we had crossed a few lines, we had sex daily, instead of weekly like I had planned. We slept in the same bed, kissed for no other reason than we wanted to embrace, and we held hands everywhere we went.

But we weren't in love, at least I wasn't in love. Infatuated? Yes. A bit mad for him? Yes. In love? No.

I shouldn't even be infatuated with him. I'm supposed to feel nothing for him, and him for me. I can't hurt another person when the inevitable happens, I can't leave another person.

"He doesn't love me," I said, voice hollow and holding no weight. "He just likes to piss people off and you're an easy target."

Kolvin's hand squeezed mine. "Okay." His voice took on the tone that had been directed toward me from many people over the last five years. The pity tone. The patient tone. The gentle tone, the ring of it clogging panic in my throat.

"I can't love someone else. I just can't. I can't hurt someone like that. I can't use them." My voice grew about three octaves higher. "You deserve better, Kol. You deserve to fall in love and have that person love you back and that's why I didn't use you when I could have. Karnelian knows I'm using him, so I can't hurt him because he knows. He agreed not to fall for me and he's the devil who never breaks a deal. It wasn't bound in blood but he's not stupid, loving me will only bring pain, and plus, he doesn't even believe in it."

Kolvin gave a curt nod, his eyes filled with empathy, sadness, and so much pity. He brought me into his arms, the hug not seeming like it was for him but more for me. I hugged him back, trying to find that ground with him, my childhood best friend, but I had a new best friend now. Another person to hurt.

THIRTY-FIVE

Karnelian

*T*he little bird's mind was muddled. After her chat with the general, she returned closed off and distant. I assumed he triggered her, and she was trying her best not to fall into the traps her mind created. What rubbed me wrong, was when we went to her room for the night, she shut me out, choosing to stew in her head instead of confiding in me.

I knew I shouldn't take it personally, but I wanted her to tell me every thought that passed through her little head. I wanted to know every secret she ever kept, her deepest desires, and darkest shadows.

After getting ready for the night, we laid in her bed, the yellow bedding contrasting to the lilac walls. A room for a girl I met six years ago, but not for the female who now laid turned away from me.

Cuddling was Marie's thing. She loved being suffocated with blankets and wrapping around my body like I was her personal life-sized teddy bear.

My monster couldn't stand the distance. I never thought myself clingy—Marie was clingy. I liked her clingy, grew used to it, anticipated it. Without it, I was sent reeling, an ache materializing in my bones, a stiffness in my muscles, tremors in my throat. Eventually, I couldn't stand it and I turned in bed, fitting my body behind her.

How could she not be made for me?

Her soft body pressed perfectly into my hard one, my arms wrapping around her waist and pulling her closer. The only thing separating my naked body from hers, an old white nightgown she threw on before climbing into bed.

Her curls tickled my nose, my head buried in her neck. Each breath of air I took in, tainted with her scent—daisies with a hint of pine—flowing thoroughly with mine.

"What is wrong, little bird," I whispered into her ear.

She shifted, her bodying growing stiff. "Nothing."

"I know you're lying. You're not really good at it."

Her tone took on a hit of offense. "I'm not lying. Nothing is the matter."

My hand moved from her waist, finding her thigh, and trailing down to the hem of her night gown. My fingers toyed with the frilled ends, pushing the garment higher up her leg. "If you keep lying, I'm going to have to torture the truth out of you."

"I like pain, remember?"

I brought my nose to her neck, tongue sliding across the expanse, her body racking with a shiver before tensing more. I repeated the action, this time her body relaxing into it, a small moan escaping her mouth. "Your parents' room is right down the hall... What, two doors down? The general that's so obsessed with you, right next to us. The lieutenant and his wife next to him. You're like a niece to them."

She squirmed as my hand slid her gown up, revealing her panties, my digits sliding under the fabric and brushing her soft hairs.

"What about them?" she said, her breath deep and heavy.

I pressed a kiss to her chin, then under her ear. "You're quite loud, little bird. Always screaming the most beautiful songs when I fuck you. I doubt you'd be able to hold them back." A kiss to her neck. "If you don't tell me what's got that pretty little head of yours all tangled up, I'll make sure they all hear how well I've been taking care of you these last few weeks."

Her legs pressed together, her toes curling against my shins. "I could deny you."

"Deny me tonight and I'll make the torture worse, baby. You remember what I said about edging."

"*Nelian...*" she moaned when my fingers slipped down further finding her hot wet flesh.

I flicked her clit, causing her whole body to twitch. "I can put up a sound barrier and fuck you until you come all over the sheets so only the housekeepers know how well I treat you. You just have to tell me."

A muffled moan escaped her, my fingers trailing to the seam of her opening, circling, and prodding at the entrance. Marie writhed against my fingers, shutting her eyes to deal with the pleasure.

I pulled my hand out of her panties and placed a sharp slap to her thigh. Marie jerked, another muffled moan sounding. "You know the rules, baby. Eyes open, eyes on me."

Her dark oases met mine, glimmering with lust. I shifted us so she was on her back, me still on my side. Quicky, I removed her panties, pulling her legs wide, one on the bed, one across my thigh.

My fingers found her wet heat, shoving two deep inside her without warning. Her eyes bulged, head raising from the pillow as she released a suppressed moan.

I fucked her with my fingers, hard and bruising, just like she liked it, her muffled whines growing louder with each thrust.

Agony painted her face, her mind now twisted up with the task of staying quiet and keeping her eyes on me as I pleasured her.

Both tasks against her nature in sex. She was the type of female who liked to have her eyes roll back and freely moan to her heart's content. The frustration at having both taken away had tears building in her eyes, and sweat forming on her brow.

My assault on her pretty pussy slowed, but only to massage her inner walls. Specifically, that spot that created blooms of pleasure for a female. A scream rang in her throat, and I added a comfortable heat from my light beams to add to the pleasure.

Her pussy tightened around me. One of her hands fisted the sheets, the other ripping into my shoulder. Her bottom teeth tried to find purchase into her plump lips, but my magic stopped her from harming herself adding to her frustration. "Come for me, baby."

She unraveled, a moan loud enough to be heard from the next room came from deep inside her, her come soaking the sheets.

My fingers left her wet heat and I fitted myself between her legs. With my cock in my hand, I ran it through her mess, her juices soaking me, her aroused scent almost bringing a purr from my throat.

"You can be louder than that. Sing for me, songbird."

Then I punched my cock into her.

Her back arched, a strangled moan exiting her mouth.

Not loud enough.

Her pussy was still too tight, her orgasm doing nothing to relax her enough for my cock. I couldn't pound into her like I wanted to, so my thrusts were slow, rubbing against her walls before sharply thrusting back in.

Another strangled moan.

Not loud enough. Thrust.

Thrust.

Thrust.

Thrust.

I no longer cared about what had her mind tangled up before. Now, only caring about making her scream.

I was a depraved beast, and she was a depraved beast disguised under the cover of a bird. My little bird. And all I wanted was for everyone to know how I made her sing.

She adjusted to my cock, and I was able to slide without restrain, my pace picking up, my thrust harsh and aimed at her innermost wall. Each one calculated, and bruising, fucking with the intention to break her perfect little pussy.

It didn't take long for her strangled moans to become screams that vibrated against the walls. For her to not give a fuck about how her family was listening to her come on my cock.

I could have put up the barrier then, but I wanted them to hear.

I knew it was sick, it was her fucking family, but I was sick, sadistic, sinful. I wanted them to hear their little flower come.

"You like that, baby?" I said, frantically thrusting into her, sweat dripping off my forehead onto her cheek.

She gave a curt nod, moaning in delight.

"Tell them, baby. Tell them how much you like it."

"Nelian," she whined, exasperated, her claws digging into my waist, cunt clenching around my cock.

"Yes." I thrusted into her. "Let them know who makes you feel like this. Tell them."

"Nelian," she panted. "Fuck, it's good. So fucking good."

I almost pulled out at the fucking word. *Good.*

Yesterday, I was perfect, today, I was good. Just fucking good.

I bunched up her gown, pushing it up until it revealed her succulent breast. I took her chocolate nipple in my mouth, swirling around the numb with my tongue, finger pinching the other.

"Tell them, baby. Tell them how I make you feel," I said as I switched to suck the other.

Her fingers found purchase in my hair, pushing me into her breast. "Good. Nelian, so fucking good."

A groan of frustration left me, and I abandoned her nipples, placing my thumb against her clit, and focused on fucking the life out of her.

But she kept saying it.

You're so fucking good, Nelian.

Yes, Nelian, that's so good.

You fuck me so good, Nelian.

I scowled at her lust-filled face that kept exclaiming how good I was, continuing my raid.

Stop saying I'm good. I don't want to be good. I want to be great, fucking fantastic. I want to be the best you have ever had. I want to be perfect for you. I wanted to say as I pounded my frustration out on her.

Tell me I'm better than your mate.

Her claws cut deep into me, body stilling, eyes bulging. "*What!*"

It was instinct that had me finally putting up the sound barrier. My thrust halting as dread filtered through my veins because I said that out loud.

Tell me I'm better than your mate.

My expression mirrored Marie's. "*Fuck.*"

A rule, boundary, that never needed to be stated, was to not speak of her mate while I was buried in her pussy.

"What?" Marie's face started to break, those tears that had built in her eyes from frustration quickly turned into guilt.

My hand cupped her chin. "Marie, I didn't mean that."

She hiccupped, tears starting to slip down her cheeks. "Get off me."

"Marie…"

She pushed at my chest. "Get off me!" she screamed.

I did, and before I could soothe her to make it better, she was out of bed, running into the bathroom, a bang sounding when the door slammed shut, the lock clicking soon following.

A ragged sigh left me. I pounded my head into the pillow a few times before rolling on my back to stare at the ceiling—waiting while water began to run in the bathroom, and a small burst of pain filled my nose.

THIRTY-SIX

MARIE

My soul was rattled—enraged—by Karnelian's words. The illusion cast by him had broken away, bringing me to face my demons.

Guilt, so much guilt, leaked through me. The wails bounced around in my head, each shard of my soul cutting into my being. My essence seeping out of the wounds and draining away with the tears that stained my face.

The screams were so loud, I couldn't hear myself think. So surreal, I was sure they were exiting out of me and bouncing off the bathroom walls.

Again, my mind and body saved me, finding the dust in the disregarded dress I left on the bathroom floor, not trusting one dose would be enough to achieve the silence that I so desperately craved. I didn't give a fuck if Karnelian scowled me for taking an extra hit. It was either poison my body, or let my soul poison my mind and drive me to madness where I would be even less of the shell I was when my mate died.

I'd be alive but lost, stuck in torment *for eternity*. I was already getting a taste of it, not conscious of any of the actions that happened after I locked the bathroom door, the shrieks too berating to even grasp the concept of focus. Instead, I watched through a window as my body reacted, only coming back to awareness when my fingers were pruned and I was sitting naked in the bathroom tub.

In the hazed silence created from faerie dust, I contemplated my safety. Seven little words. Seven little words had the ability to make me fall into psychosis. Seven little words gave my soul enough power to bury me whole. A confinement I barely escaped moments ago. What if I hadn't had the dust? What if the dust didn't work?

What Kolvin said was true. I don't know if Karnelian loved me, but he wanted more from me than sex, and I couldn't give him more. Giving him more meant, giving my soul more evidence to use against me later. Giving him more meant more pain, more guilt, more sorrow, more agony, and I just couldn't.

The thing was my soul was screaming the same thing over and over. One piece of evidence that was enough to push me back into a cage. A truth I couldn't face.

The truth I could face, Karnelian and I had crossed too many lines. Karnelian was supposed to be a distraction from my soul's reprimand. Another drug to escape into delusion.

But with any drug, I got addicted. Okay with the crossing of lines as long as I felt the high he provided. An addiction was just a disease packaged with a pretty shiny bow, infecting you in secret, in shadow, in slight. One only able to see the disease when it held you in its clutches, leaving you dangling over a cliff. That was when the high would fade away and you were faced with death right beneath your feet.

With Karnelian there wouldn't be death, but insanity, no blood, but rancidity.

I would not rot inside the confines of my mind for the rest of this life. I would rather live a hundred thousand years away from my mate than another day stuck in my mind.

Exiting the tub, I redressed in the night gown stained with the scent of daisies and cinnamon. My masochistic beast enjoyed the scent, but I could feel the thrashes of my soul trying to claw its way back to the surface, ready to deliver me more punishment.

Karnelian sat up when I entered the room. Judging by the moon and the dryness of my skin, I was in the bath for a few hours. I knew well enough to know he wouldn't have gone to sleep if I had stayed in there all night. That was who he was—no, that was who he was *for me*. He took care of me because he actually cared.

The notion made my heart swell and my soul scream, but I rolled my shoulders, preparing to let my heart re-freeze.

I climbed into bed, my back to him, energy stating to stay away.

"Marie," he whispered; his baritones soft but rolling on my skin like gravel.

I didn't respond, fisting the cover to fight against my body's ache for him and my mind's want for him. His voice was a simulant I could fall into, a song I could be lost in, the notes the perfect pitch to enrapture me.

Tell me I'm better than your mate.

Seven little words that were the poison to his pull and the tonic to my turmoil.

Karnelian didn't push, that wasn't him. He didn't bend, so silence littered the air. Exhaustion stole over me, and eventually, I was able to drift off and enjoy my last night of peaceful sleep.

My last rested sleep was short, Karnelian and I woke as soon as the sun crested the horizon. We dressed, ate dinner for breakfast with my family who were visibly uncomfortable. Karnelian put on his mask, pretending nothing was wrong. His hand held my limp one, he pressed a few kisses to my temple, my soul didn't react because we knew he only did it for show. No one seemed to notice the difference, taking the bags under my eyes and my silence as a sign of tiredness instead of hollowness.

That was what I felt, hollow, empty, airy. My dose of dust left me feeling lightheaded and an ache pierced my skull. I was back to floating through life with no ground to stand on.

We portaled back to the front step of Charlotte. Karnelian could have portaled us straight to his room, but he didn't. He was dragging out the inevitable with a few sets of stairs.

He let us walk in silence before he finally spoke. "Marie, I didn't—"

"I'm going to stay here while you work from now on." I didn't look at him as I spoke. I couldn't, a part of me didn't want to put space between us. A part of me was wishing we could go back to the day before yesterday when there was a pink cloud covering us.

"Okay." He gulped. "Do you want me to come for lunch?"

"It's not necessary."

"I know that, but I'm asking if you want me to come."

"No." A beat. "And I'm going to sleep in my room."

"Okay, and I'm guessing you're going to deny sex this week too?" He talked to me like a client or a business associate. His voice was even, no hint of hurt or offense, no sense of care or caution.

"Yes."

"Okay. If you need anything, try to cut your palm, and I'll come." Then he was gone, portaling out before we even made it to the rooms.

Just like with any drug, I had withdrawals, except the withdrawals from Karnelian were worse than dusk or whiskey. Life was colorless again, but I didn't even realize that it was painted in vibrant hues until the return of my gray view.

I missed him. Not like my mate, no tears sprung in my eyes, no lacerations opened in my being. There just was this cavity that used to be filled with wickedness and devilry, blond hair, and silver eyes.

I hadn't seen Karnelian in two days. He was in the manor, two doors down, sleeping on a mattress that was without bedding because I stole all of it earlier.

The heist was completely orchestrated by my creature. A need I couldn't resist. I missed him too much, I needed some form of a hit. So, blankets tainted with our scents were the fix.

The hollowness within me left room for my soul to sing in shame, but it wasn't a berate.

I sat in a foreign bed, suffocated with the blankets, each breath like a morsel of dust. The tiniest bit of joy sparking in my being before flaring out.

This was another form of insanity. I was high on caffeine, body tired from lack of sleep, sniffing a bundle of blankets I stole, just so if I fell asleep midnight eyes wouldn't haunt my dreams.

My body had grown used to sleep, so two days in and I was ready to crash.

I could easily solve my agony by sleeping with Karnelian, but I knew stepping in that room with him in there would just be like walking into a lion's den—the devil's den. I couldn't just sleep next to him, I'd cuddle his huge frame, cuddles would lead to kisses and kisses would lead to sex, sex would lead to more.

It was taking everything in me not to go to him. My body was one hundred percent team Karnelian, my heart ice with no say and my soul fire burning with rage. My mind flitted back between my body and soul and decided it wanted to stay sane.

I thought his scent would be enough, but it was soon or it was late, the time I didn't truly know, when tiredness stole over me, and I was fast asleep.

A sleep filled with midnight eyes haunting my dreams, suffocating me and telling me to not breathe.

THIRTY-SEVEN

Karnelian

A blood-curdling scream ripped me from sleep. I sat up, the white sheet pooling in my lap as I took a moment to figure my surroundings.

Another shriek, pitch from a voice that was branded into my bones.

I portaled to Marie's room, seeing her writhing in a nest of bedding. Her cries rang out, scraping against her throat, each filled with enough sorrow to fill the sea.

My monster acted, rushing for her, wrapping her in our arms. She wrestled against us, still stuck in slumber, but when my purrs started—a reassuring call—she calmed. Her hands clutching me, claws cutting into flesh.

Her cries and screams turned to sobs and whimpers. Her face buried into my chest, her tears staining my skin. Eventually she gained consciousness enough to respond to my purrs, an action completely primal, a thank you from her beast.

When Marie fully woke, she pulled back enough to figure out where she was and who she was holding before she pushed away.

She sat up and brought her hand to her mouth to cover a sob before proceeding to break down right before me.

My skin crawled with the need to comfort her, but I knew she didn't want that. She wanted space. I wasn't mad about it. I understood. I did the one thing I promised not to, I got too close, crossed too many lines until we were wrapped in a blurry mess of tangled strings. I would respect her need for space, no matter how much I ached to be near her, wished to hear her voice or see her smile. I needed space too.

The fact that I missed her, craved to have her in her bed, was disappointed when she took the sheets that were covered with our scent, was the reason I needed space.

Marie was a tragedy written in the stars. Her whole being was tragic. A true damsel in distress, drowning in a pit of misery. Poetic and pretty.

My beast loved the tumultuous pull of her.

And because I was fae, I could see her chaos but completely ignore it for the thrill of her. I could argue that she didn't in sight thrill, with her I felt joy, companionship, comfort. My fault though was not seeing it was actually dopamine, codependency, and complacency. She might have become my only real friend, but she was created to be toxic. A cataclysm to achieve disruption amongst the fae.

She was a mated faerie, designed for him, bonded with him, and fated to die for him. I wanted to give into the whispers that said differently, but I couldn't deny the facts. She had a mate and being mated was the only thing she could possibly offer this world. For me, she was a means to her end. A tool to get me on the Unseelie throne. I lost focus of that over this past month, and I needed to re-align myself to my goal.

First order of business: Kill Markos.

Killing him wouldn't be easy. My father and I were the only ones who could overpower him with magic by ourselves. If my father went head-to-head with Markos, it could kill him, seeing that they were equal in power. I wasn't sure if I'd survive myself. I knew I was more powerful than Markos, but it would take a lot of magic to overpower him which could lead to me exhausting myself. It was going to take more than one person to kill him, which unfortunately meant I needed to spend more time with my father.

I left Marie—her aura pushing I leave—and headed down to the pool in the manor. I swam until light started to thread with night, shaved and dressed, then portaled to the palace.

My schedule was mostly clear. I spent the last month planning for more free time. I would like to say it was because of what I was planning on doing today—I knew I wanted to be a piece in this war—but in truth, it was because of her, so I had more time for her.

I shook the thoughts of her off—a trick I had already perfected over the years—and readied myself to walk into my least favorite room in the palace—the war room.

My father had been spending his days trying to plan every detail of the war before it broke out so we could be prepared. My father always had a backup plan for everything, and back up plans for his backup plans. Dominick Lightfire was crowned the Lion King, but really, he was a snake dressed in lion's fur. If he had been unsuccessful in birthing an heir before I figured his true plans, I would guess his backup plan would be my death.

Karnelian, I'm doing this for the sake of our people.

I barged into the room. My father's spells easy for me to break, just a drop of my blood slithering through his enchantment, causing chaos and confusion, and I was in.

The chatters of the males halted, wide eyes pining on me, along with my father's greedy greens, and Darius and Jacoby's *you fucked my daughter slash niece too loudly and I wasn't okay with that* expressions.

"Karnelian," my father said. He and the members of the court—minus my brother who sat on the floor, reading a recipe book on wines—stood around the table adorned with the three-dimensional map of the fae territories.

I gave a cheeky grin. "Yes, me."

"What has you barging in here today? Want to steal another one of my top workers for something?"

"No, Father, just thought I would do my part, offer my services."

My father crossed his arms, eyes narrowing. "In exchange for what?"

"Nothing."

"Nothing. When have you ever done anything for nothing?"

"When I was your little lap dog, I used to run around here eager to do your bidding. Such a pathetic little son you used to have, one who loved you more than the sun and moon combined. I'm glad you fucked him up so he could grow up and get some balls." I smirked at my father's stiffening features.

A roll of his shoulders to dispel the air before he said, "What are you doing here, Karnelian."

"I happen to want to help with the war effort. You know... because I'm going to be the Unseelie King when it's over."

Hushed whispers reverberated throughout the room, my father's jaw cocking to the side and nostrils flaring. "So, this is for your gain."

My face expressed offense. "Don't be so condescending. Half of the males in here are only here to figure how they can get richer off the war. You know having me on your team is a gain for you. You could kick out all of the slimy males who are a pain in your ass, for one jackass with magic that has no bounds." I pointed at myself.

My father's emerald eyes stayed pinned to mine, a thousand thoughts flickering through them in his silence.

Then he nodded. "Fine. Everyone who isn't the commander, his males, or my son, get the fuck out."

The court members grumbled, throwing glares and annoyed faces at me on their way out.

I waved to them with petty. "Sorry, guys. I'm richer, more powerful and have way more resources. Maybe next war."

My father put his business face on. "Can you bring in Grayson?"

I threw my hands up. "Oh, now you want the guy who is fucking my mother around."

A twitch in his jaw. "Karnelian, can you bring him on or not."

"He does work for me."

"Good. Let's fill you in."

My father didn't want war as any good king would. War isn't good. It takes up resources, and puts a strain on our people, especially since most of our wars were civil. For that reason, my father didn't want Seelies to be the ones to start the war. Whichever territory started the war often ended up in debt one way or another, having to expend resources to recover damages. My father planned to wait for the Unseelie to strike, but it looked like the Unseelie's plan was to make it look like we were slowly killing them off, giving them reason to strike. Many soldiers have been found dead along the border, and not messily portal guards, top tier soldiers, some suspected of being Neeki. It seemed their attack would be coming soon because the clusters of soldiers that were stationed near Lightwood had moved north into the Wild Lands, meaning that we could expect attacks to come from the northern border.

The next two weeks were grueling. My days with my father, extensively going over every possible event that could occur in the war and our action to that. My evenings alone, her scent haunting me, though my room was stale of her. She still walked the halls and visited the library and kitchen whenever I wasn't around and left me a note to deny sex. And my nights were sleepless waiting for her screams.

They happened like clockwork, every two days, but my monster still anticipated she'd need me, so I barely slept.

When she started shrieking, I'd be there to calm her, purring until her purrs answered and she woke up, mortification and sorrow lining her face. Then I went to swim and did it all again.

I couldn't stand it anymore so I figured I should get more information on it.

"Darius, can I speak to you for a moment?" I said as we were exiting the war room for the night.

"Yeah, sure."

"In your reports on Marie, it said she used to have nightmares?"

His brow furrowed, worry starting to fill his aura. "Yeah, all the time. In the beginning, she was numb to the world, but when she came back, she practically had them every night. They started diminishing over the years to every other night, then every few nights. Before she left, she had them at least once a week."

I knew that from the file, but they didn't mention her reactions. "Does she... you know..."

"Scream like she's dying? Yes, every time."

"Huh?" I said, pondering it.

"What, is something the matter with her?"

"No," I lied, not wanting to worry him. The male looked haggard, his beard a bit longer than he normally kept it. His eyes were lined red. He had enough shit to worry about with the war and my father trying to steal his wife. "Thanks for the insight."

Later, sitting on the bed, I analyzed the information he gave, and the last month and a half spent with Marie.

I slept.

Her words the morning after our first time together. She made me stay in the room with her as she slept that day. After we formed a routine, she always got up when I did each morning, no matter how early, and she always waited for me to go to bed, no matter how late. The bags under her eyes had disappeared after a week or two of her being here, and she seemed less groggy, but I assumed that was because she was just getting better.

The fact that her nightmares used to happen every night then moved to every other night, stuck out in my brain. If they had simply diminished over time because she was getting better, they wouldn't be happening as frequently now.

The probable truth was Marie wasn't sleeping until she crashed, in an attempt to lessen the nightmares. She had figured out sleeping with someone stopped them, but now that she wasn't sleeping with me anymore, her nightmares were back, and she was back to trying to stave off sleep.

My body was filled with acid at this situation, I was tired, stressed, and my monster was filled with worry. I couldn't handle another night of her screams. I only wanted her to scream when I was deep inside her, and her cries came from a place of pleasure instead of terror.

Marie was due to have a nightmare tonight, so I cast out an energy field—a nymph trait—to check in on her. Her aura was diminished, telling me she was lacking energy, but her pulse was elevated. Blood pumped sluggishly, but in challenge, her body fighting to stay awake.

I undressed from the day, keeping my awareness on her as I changed into a loose tunic and a pair of underwear, then I waited.

It was late into the night when her nervous system shut down. Her breath evening out, her pulse steady in beat.

Entering her room, I found her asleep in the chair, book in her hand. I removed the book, pulling her into my arms. Her reaction was to wrap her limbs around me, face burying into my neck, little mews of comfort escaping her.

I laid her in bed, fitting myself behind her and pulled the covers over us.

The whispers sounded. I didn't push them away or ignore them, just accepted that a part of me was so broken it was delusional, whispering hopes of a lost little boy.

I didn't sleep, instead divulging my monster's allure to her, storing up on her scent, and the feel of her body pressed against mine.

When her breaths grew heavy, and her pulse quickened, my muscles tensed in anticipation of her rejection. I would leave, but I had to see her eyes clear and bottomless before I did.

I watched them flutter, then blink, before opening wide. A crease formed in between her brows, then she looked over her shoulder to me.

She was the most beautiful when she woke up, her face puffy and groggy around her eyes, but there was a peace about her that I never appreciated until knowing of her haunted nights.

Her eyes searched mine before she leaned up and pressed a soft kiss to my mouth, a forced purr of gratitude vibrating in her chest. I kissed her back, but didn't take over, letting her end it because I didn't think I would have the power to.

She looked out toward the room, resting her head back on the pillow, and I understood her silent rejection and began to get up.

"I dream about him."

I stilled, not knowing what to do or what to say. She turned to me, her obsidian orbs penetrating my gaze.

"At first, they began as dreams, blissful and full of love." Tears started to glisten in her eyes. "Then they turn to nightmares. Subliminal reminders that he's dead and I'm alive."

"So, you stopped sleeping."

"It was the only way to get them to stop... until you."

I cocked my head to one side.

She snorted but a tear slipped from her eye. "I don't know why, but when I sleep with you, I don't dream about him. I dream about you." She toyed with the blanket covering us. "I thought I could go without as long as I had your scent, but I need you and I hate it. I don't hate you, but liking you feels like betraying him, and it tears me apart. When you're around, my focus is on you, and I don't have to think about him. That in itself is a betrayal and then there's the sex on top of it. Which is why we can't be more. I don't want to betray him more than I have to. I can't care about you, Karnelian. The guilt I'd feel for betraying him, and then the guilt of hurting you… I just… can't."

I cupped her face, bringing her eyes to mine. "I'm not asking you to do that, Marie."

"But you said—"

"What I said was my beast. You're the first female I've ever kept, and it has grown an attachment to you. I just got swept up in the moment and let myself get carried away. It was a misstep on my part that meant nothing."

She eyed me wearily. She could probably tell that there was more, but I wouldn't offer the full truth. It wasn't like I could tell her without truly losing her anyways.

"We are friends, just friends. Right, little bird?" My voice was a bit more desperate than I would have liked, but wanted to confirm we were okay. She was the only person I could just be Karnelian—Nelian, with and I wanted to have that as long as I could.

She gave me a small smile, nodding her head. "Yeah. Of course, and the deal?"

"It's all you, Marie. We only have sex if you want to."

She chewed on her lip, taking it in. "I can sleep in your room even if we don't have sex for a while?"

I brushed a curl away from her face. "To be honest, that room is more yours than it's ever been mine."

"You still have your plants in there."

"Yeah, but you've been taking care of them."

Her eyes bulged. "Have they died!"

I chuckled. "No, I watered them the other day, but they aren't looking their best. You have a better green thumb than I do."

"Yeah, my mother loves plants, so I know my way around a watering can." She gave a bright smile, and I couldn't help but kiss it.

She moaned, and I pulled back. "Sorry, but that smile is my weakness."

"It's okay."

We laid there in the silence, her fingers coming up to trace my tattoo. That small action made me feel complete, like I needed her little fingers to trace it to feel ready for the day.

"You want to hear a secret?" I asked.

She smirked, eyes lazily gazing at me. "What?"

"I knew him."

Her brows furrowed, a small frown gracing her lips as she went back to looking at my chest. "I suppose you would. He was a prince, you're a prince."

"No, I knew him. I tutored him for a bit before he sorted. We were kind of friends... more so, allies."

Her fingers stopped, eyes meeting mine. "You knew him."

I gave a quick nod.

"How did you meet?"

8 YEARS AGO.

My back was pressed against the cold wall of the Seelie Palace. I was practically dragged into this secluded hallway by this female desperate to fuck me. Of course, she didn't want my cock, but my power. I could feel the greed oozing through her energy, could taste it on her tongue.

She thought she was fooling the devil, lusting him with her magnificent pussy. I wasn't going to break it to her that if she wanted to make a deal, I didn't trade in pussy because look how easy it was for me to get it. There were dozens of females like her for when I needed a fuck. If she wanted a deal, she could make an appointment with Grayson, this fuck was going to just be that—a fuck. An exchange of pleasure.

Her hand drifted down my torso to my belt loop when the rustling of paper sounded.

I pulled away from the female, looking toward the noise. A male faeling sat beside a credenza, obscuring him from view when I did my not so thorough sweep of the hall before the female shoved her greedy tongue in my mouth. He was hastily gathering his papers together, probably preparing to find another private place to view them.

With my interest peaked, I pushed the female away, heading over to the boy.

"Where are you going?" she squeaked, the sound halfway between annoyed and desperate.

"I'm bored of you," I said, straightening my suit out, back turned toward her.

"But... But..."

"*Leave.*"

She huffed and I heard the sound of her heels clacking against the ground in the opposite direction.

Debaucheries happened during my father's night parties. Fae weren't the type to hide that, but young children weren't allowed to attend the night parties unless they were above the age of sixteen. Which would suit the age of this faeling.

Confusion filled me as I got closer, taking him in. His hair was jet black, skin pale, clothes black. One thing I have never seen at my father's parties an Unseelie child, but it didn't take me long to figure whose child this was.

"Your King Markos's son." Markos was attending the party tonight. The only reason I was required to appear. My father wanted me here, so we emerged a united front. He even demanded I not wear black. Which meant I dressed in dark blue. My suit an almost perfect depiction of the night sky.

The faeling rolled his eyes, a scowl painting his face. "How could you tell?" His voice was dry, slightly vicious, and definitely annoyed.

I crouched, picking up a page he'd missed. He attempted to snatch it back. He was fast but my magic stopped him, a light barrier burning his tact fingers.

He hissed, "Fuck."

One edge of the paper was ripped, torn from a book, a Seelie book. It detailed a basic Seelie spell learned by freshly sorted faelings.

Holding my hand out, a butterfly made of light manifested. The boy was not impressed, features etched into irritation. With a flap of its wing, the butterfly turned from light to shadow in an instant. The boy's eyes widened; irises black with a subtle hint of blue locking with mine.

A devious smile adorned my lips, my brows raised with anarchy.

"You're the devil," he said, struggling to keep his voice in his 'I don't give a fuck about you' tone.

In mockery, I rolled my eyes. "How could you tell?"

I dropped the butterfly, snatching the papers from the boy and started leafing through the torn-out pages.

"What is your name again? I'm not really up to date on royal affairs," I said.

"Levington, but I go by Levi."

"I'm Karnelian and you already know my other names, I assume."

He didn't answer.

"So... you think your blood is Seelie?"

His scowl, that I was pretty sure was permanently etched into his face, deepened. "I don't know what I am, as my magic hasn't manifested."

"And it probably won't for a few years."

"I've read that you can get it to manifest early if you practice."

"Hmm? So that's why you stole all of these papers?"

He remained quiet.

"Magic isn't found on paper. As annoyingly cliché as it may sound, it's found from within."

"Okay, thanks for the advice, but I already have a tutor," he said, going for the papers.

He was met with another barrier singeing his fingers.

My head cocked to one side, fingers flicking through the papers as I discovered the magic seal. "You got these from my father's royal library?"

He glared at me but gave a curt nod.

Then I set the pages to fire, the disintegrated pieces floating to the ground.

Levi's eyes bulged, body jerking toward the remains. Then his eyes snapped to mine, his glare turning murderous.

I put up a hand. "Ah, ah, ah. No need for that look."

"You burned my pages," he growled.

"*My father's pages* that you stole." I wiped some of the soot off my knee. "But since I did you a wrong, I owe you a right."

"What?"

"Hold out your hand."

His nose scrunched up.

"Just do it. I don't like to waste my time."

He took a second to give me a questionable look before placing his hand in mine.

"I know I'm the devil, but you're going to have to trust me."

His brow raised a fraction, eyes suspicious.

"Just keep yourself open to me." Calling my magic, I pushed it into him, calling out to his. Only my shadows though, assuming he'd be Unseelie—the gods rarely had a person born where they weren't meant to be.

He jolted when we connected, and I sensed out his power level. It was hard to do when the body hadn't fully matured to take magic, but there was something there, the level it would grow to, unknown to me.

"Raise your other hand," I commanded, and he obeyed. "Try to match your energy to mine and feel out my shadows."

Being young and unfamiliar with magic, it took him several moments before his energy matched mine. "Okay, now try to push them out of your hand."

Analyzing his energy as he focused the shadows, it was clear he wasn't ready for this in the slightest, but maybe with extra practice he could be in a year or two.

A little tendril of shadow formed in his hand. He tried to hold it, a vein pulsing in his forehead, but lost it after a few seconds.

I pulled my hand away, smoothing out my hair. "Rookie mistake. Magic isn't a force that likes to be male handled. It's delicate and needs to be approached in a tender way." I shrugged, standing. "But now that you have a glimpse of it, you can keep trying."

I turned, making my way back to the ballroom when he spoke. "Wait."

My gaze met his, a questioning brow raising.

"Could... we do it again?"

"They call me the devil for a reason—I don't do things for free."

His lips flatted, eyes filling with disappointment. "I'm sixteen, I don't really have anything to offer."

"Everyone has something to offer."

"What could I offer you?"

"Trust. Dedication."

His eyes narrowed, brow furrowing.

"I'll help you manifest your magic quickly, but you have to trust me and be dedicated to learning."

"All you want is my trust?"

"It'd be wrong of me to draw blood of a faeling. But you offer an excuse."

"An excuse?"

"I haven't visited Unseelie in a few years and I need to, but my father gets cagy when I bring it up. He thinks I work for your father and insists I only stay for a short while or he'll start sniffing around in my business. You, little wolf, provide an excellent cover for me to do my dirty dealings. I'm very talented with magic." I manifested a silver orb in my palm for a brief moment. "I mean, I am the hybrid. Wouldn't you want to learn from the best?"

He sat there in silence, wide eyes gleaming before he nodded.

"Good, then it's a deal."

"You taught him how to manifest his magic?"

I nodded, wrapping my shadows around her, letting them slide over her skin for a second before pulling them back.

She shivered before her mouth painted in a smile. "He taught me that." That smile dropped, sorrow filling her eyes. "Almost exactly like that."

"We kind of became friends over that time. Eh… he felt more like my nephew than my friend because of his age, but there was a bond. We spent a year together until he finally manifested it. Then I came back here, and I…"

Marie's hand trailed up my chest, cupping my face to look at her. "You came back here and what?"

I met you.

She knew that, but our first meeting clearly didn't mean what it did to me as it did to her. Further proving my delusion. "And I went about my life. He'd portal mirrored me a couple times to ask me about some magical theories. But he was extremely intelligent, and did have good tutors, so I assume he only called to talk because often the subject would change to other things. He was a lonely kid, didn't ever trust anyone. I understood that because that's what it's like to be a prince. People often only want to be around you because of the power you hold, not caring to get to know the real you."

Marie's fingers stroked along my jaw. "Were you a lonely prince?"

"I wasn't nearly as broody, but yes, I was lonely before." *Before you.*

"Are you busy today?"

"I have places I should be…"

"But?"

"But if you asked me to take off so we could just lay in bed all day, I wouldn't oppose."

She smiled and kissed me. "Nelian, can you take off so we can lay in bed all day?"

"I thought you'd never ask."

THIRTY-EIGHT

MARIE

The smoky wisp of my shadows swirled in my hand. My channel opened and connected to the moon as I tried to control the tendrils. A wing manifested, an ache arising in my head as I attempted to form the second before the shadows muddied and I lost my grasp on them.

"Fuck."

I was in Karnelian's office in Solara. He had a few meetings today so instead of going to the palace where the males' discussed war, while Fredrick and I sat on the floor discussing his favorite drinks or the males he had been with recently, we came here.

His office was very Karnelian. Very shady devious devil. Firstly, it was above a bar. The same bar we came to a few months back when he taught me how to poison people. Secondly, it had a backroom with a bed. The second Karnelian brought me here, my creature immediately went to it, sniffing it for other scents. Karnelian laughed at me and told me he'd hadn't had a female back here in years, telling me the bed was here for when he decided to crash at the office when he was extremely busy. Thirdly, everything in the office was clean and impeccable but still dark and lavish, giving a chilling vibe to the place that probably set his Seelie clients on edge.

My magic abilities had sharpened over the last few weeks because me and Karnelian weren't having sex. The time we spent together was either filled with soft slow cuddle sessions, or magic training.

Even though I was best suited for technical magic, I wasn't able to fully form a single butterfly yet. I knew it would take time but with the talkings I overheard in the war room; I didn't have much time until my power source grew to a mass meant to fit a thousand monarchs.

So I'd been practicing getting comfortable with my shadows and playing with them anytime I could. It was draining and another stress on my body and I had yet to perform a spell. I needed to combine my energy to do that, and I wasn't good at bonding with rocks unless it was a person named after a rock. Karnelian wanted me to master rock bonding before I advanced to person bonding because binding with another would be more seamless if I didn't have to think about focusing my energy to align with the light.

A growl sounded as that thought entered my mind and I reluctantly picked up one of the carnelian stones that were placed all over the back office, some for decoration, some Karnelian used for clients in need of a charm. With a few deep breaths, I opened up to the moon, focusing on channeling her energy to match the vibrational properties of the stone. Not a second into my attempt, I was interrupted with the sound of a door opening, boots thudding onto the wood floors.

I turned, my brows furrowing when the male who stood in front of the door that led out to the bar, wasn't the male I was expecting.

"Sunshine?"

"G?"

"What are you doing here?" G asked, hands flowing over his luxurious navy suit. "Come to make a deal with the devil?"

My lips formed into a frown, brain whizzing with questions. Firstly, why was he entering through the door that only authorized personnel were allowed to enter. "No, uh… the devil is my fiancé. What are you doing here?"

G let out a cackling laugh, his uptilted eyes filling with tears. "I thought I was the comedian, Sunshine. Karnelian would never, *ever* get married." He wiped the tears from his eyes. "No, seriously, why are you sitting back here? Did you need more dust and think to come straight to the source?"

"What? No, Karnelian is my fiancé. What do you mean straight from the source?"

His face turned serious. "You're really his fiancée?"

"Uhm, we are really engaged." I flashed my ring.

"Fuck." His hand scrubbed at his chin. "Does he know you are on dust? Does he know who supplies you? If you're really his fiancée, he's going to cut off my balls."

I couldn't help but snort at his panic, my creature finding it amusing. "He knows I do it, but he doesn't know where I get it."

He blew out a breath. "Good, don't tell Karnelian."

"Don't tell Karnelian what?" G and I snapped our heads toward the door that led to the office.

Karnelian looked between us, eyebrow raised in question before settling his withering gaze on G. "Grayson?"

G—Grayson hesitated, eyes flickering with indecision, which quickly turned to panic when Karnelian came up to him, his tall frame towering over him.

"Nelian," I said, voice soft as if not to provoke his beast. Karnelian's gaze landed on me, alighted to a steely silver that just cut through a person, and set my creature on edge. "It's nothing. He sells me dust."

Karnelian's body grew tight, rigid. His head slowly turned back to Grayson, the air growing thick, taut, and chilled. "You're the one selling to her?"

The jester's mask was removed from Grayson. He didn't cower under Karnelian's gaze, his black eyes twinkling with depth, void and vulnerable. "I didn't know she was your fiancée." His voice was straight, serious—cold but in a wounded way. "You know you can trust me. If I had known, I would've."

"You are my second, not some lackey, Grayson. You knew I was combing through our dealers; you should have told me you were supplying. I thought someone was attempting to rival us or undercut us. You know I don't tolerate insubordination, and yet you are selling behind my back. To my fucking female, for fuck's sake. And what the fuck are you doing in Lightwood?"

"Your mother lives in Lightwood."

Karnelian's nostrils flared, his lip raising into a snarl that showed his canines. "So, while you've been fucking my mother, you thought you'd start dealing without my knowledge?"

Grayson's shoulders rolled and he took a step back. "No. I was doing a set and noticed her in the crowd not reacting to a single one of my jokes. I didn't know who she was or her relation to you. I chatted her up after the show and when I still didn't get anything out of her, I tossed her a bag of dust and left. I came back to the bar a week or two later and she begged me for more, so I continued to supply her and only her. I logged the cash under miscellaneous without thinking of it. I'd never steal from you, not after what you did for me."

Karnelian's anger dissipated a bit, but only a bit. "You still violated my trust, even if you didn't steal. We always vet who we deal to, you fucking know that. We vet so that shit like this doesn't happen. So, you don't end up poisoning the Unseelie heir and my future wife." He took a shuddering breath. "If your female was anyone other than my mother, I'd tempt her with dust until she was wrapped into its pull so deep, she couldn't stop. I'd show you what the fuck it's like to find her in a bathtub, breaths away from death. Except, I'd make sure she actually died so you understood that no matter what history you and I share, you don't skate around my rules, you don't disobey the devil."

His words had me sucking in a breath. Each sharp working of his scripture, cutting into my senses. The depth of them branding into my being and blazing the ice around my heart. I remembered the look in his eyes when he found me in the bathroom passed out, the harsh raw edges of him showing a vulnerability he'd had yet to reveal until then.

Grayson gulped, straightening his spine. "It was a mistake. I didn't think it through. I just… I got off on it. My beast liked her desperation for it, liked when she beg—"

"Shut the fuck up." Karnelian raised a hand. "Remember who you are talking about."

Grayson grimaced. "Sorry, boss. It's just…" He glanced at me, then back at Karnelian. "*You know*."

A muscle in Karnelian's jaw flexed. "Fine." He blew out a breath. "This is going to cost you."

"Yeah, I understand. But I'm not going to stop seeing your mother. I know it's weird, but I like her."

Karnelian shook his head, arms crossing. "My mother is happy with you, and I like her happy. You on the other hand… You are going to work under my father for the next few weeks."

Grayson rolled his eyes, the jester covering up the burdens stored within his soul. "I thought he just needed insights for what I know of King Markos's court. How is that a punishment?"

"Nothing is ever that simple with my father. He will want to pick your brain for every detail you know, but I'll tell him you're his until the dust from the war has cleared. Since you're fucking the female he loves, I'm sure he'll make your life more than chaotic."

"Fine," Grayson said, his eyes narrowing with faux scrutiny. "When were you going to tell me you were engaged or even courting a female? As your second, that seems like something you should tell me."

"You would have found out when all of Seelie did."

"Karnelian we are more than colleagues, we are best friends, been so for years. You should have introduced me to her."

I cut in then. "I'm Karnelian's best friend."

Karnelian glanced at me, a small smile ghosting his lips that didn't come near to reaching his eyes before he looked back at Grayson. "We are a good team, and you know I don't mix business with pleasure."

Grayson groaned. "You are so annoying! We are friends! I'll get you to admit it one fucking day."

Karnelian waved him off, his rage rolling off with it. "Leave."

"*Leave*," Grayson mocked before heading off.

Karnelian turned to me, but I spoke first. "So you deal dust."

"I deal with a lot of things."

"Is that why you never made me stop?"

"One of the reasons, yes. It would be kind of hypocritical of me."

"Hmm."

Karnelian made his way to me and kneeled down in front of me. His hazels pierced my blacks, his hands settling on my thighs. "Why do you take it?"

"I told you, to keep my marks."

"I know, but why do you want to keep them? You don't seem proud of them. You hide them. You don't get mad when I touch them. You never wanted them in the first place, right? They were a punishment from your mate."

My nostrils flared, body going on edge but then Karnelian's hands found mine, intertwining fingers and tying me to the present. "They weren't a punishment."

Karnelian frowned in confusion.

"They are a punishment... Still."

"I don't follow."

"It's... it's my fault." I said, voice cracking, tears filling my eyes.

"What is?"

"H-he died because of me."

Karnelian's expression turned to something akin to shock, his mouth opening to refute my claim, but I spoke first.

"Nelian, when you're mated, there's a need to please your mate. More so like a law between the two. They come first. Their wants, their needs, their happiness. And my mate..." I shuddered. "He upheld that law. In every decision he made, I came first. Even if I didn't agree with his way of seeing it. To him, everything he did was in benefit of me. Even these." I used our joined fingers to raise my skirt and reveal the marks on my upper thighs. "But... But the same wasn't true for me."

I untangled one of my hands to wipe the tears starting to flood my face. "There was always a person in front of him. First, it was Kolvin. The second I laid eyes on my mate, my soul's love for him unleashed within me and started to bloom, but I refused to hurt my best friend and tried to push my feelings for my mate away. Then it was my mother. I refused to let her go, insisting to visit her here. I refused to fully give into him like he did me because I wanted to hold on to them—my family. But if I would have just let them go... I would still have him." I winced, a hiccup racking me after.

Karnelian wiped the next set of tears, angling my face so I was staring straight into his soul. "Little bird..." His thumb caressed my cheeks in comfort. "I listen to everyone's testimony, you had nothing—"

"They wouldn't have come if I didn't beg them too. That dinner wouldn't have ended the way it did if I had just let my mother go."

His hand on my jaw tightened. "Marie, no. Your mother was the one who decided to escalate things by revealing her secrets in the way she did."

"She wouldn't have done that if I hadn't shown her the marks. Something I knew my mate would have never been okay with, but I did it because she was worried about me, and I wanted to appease her. But she thought he had… violated me, and in a way… If I hadn't gone to Seelie in the first place, I wouldn't have had the marks."

"Marie, it's not your job to control other people's reactions. Not your mate, not your mother, not King Markos."

"But my mate—"

"Stop, Marie. Just stop." Karnelian's voice was authoritative, his beast coming out to tell mine to heal. "The only person you should blame is Markos. What he did to your mother is atrocious. He traumatized her enough to get rid of her babe. A babe, Marie. Corivina loves you so fiercely you can feel it when you're in the same room together. She is overly protective of you because she is afraid to lose you. Her reaction was because of her trauma caused by Markos. It was Markos who pinned her against the wall. Markos who threatened to kill a Seelie female unprovoked. It would have been your duty to save her to prevent war. You did what you had to, and Markos was the one who escalated things further by attempting to attack you. There were only two other Unseelies in that room. You and his son. It doesn't matter if he was blinded with rage. He knew his blast would kill whoever he sent it back to. If your mate didn't push you out of the way… you'd be dead, and we'd still be going to war. Maybe even worse, there could be an end to the fae as we know it. There was no one in that room from stopping your mate from killing himself after seeing you die, if anything he might have attacked Markos and killed him before he killed himself, dooming our people and maybe even the world." A heavy breath sounded from him. "Even if you didn't cast that ball,

Markos would have killed your mother, and we would be at war. No matter what, Marie, the outcome would have been the same, someone would have died, and jeopardized the peace amongst the fae, and they would have died by Markos's hand."

Tears dripped down my chin, my lip trembling as I thought about the other outcomes, losing my mother would have destroyed me just the same. My mate and her losing me would still end with chaos ensuing. The gods had set a path and they made sure it would have been followed.

"It's not my fault?"

He leaned in, pressing a kiss to my forehead. "No, baby. It's not your fault."

My arms wrapped around his neck, pulling him in an embrace, as sobs started boiling out of me.

These tears weren't the same as ones shed in the past. Tears streaming from guilt and pain. These tears were filled with relief. A heavy burden exiting my being through the rain of my tears. Karnelian's body, the weight that held me from getting washed away with them.

After I poured out all that I could, I pulled back and attempted to clean my snot-covered face with the sleeve of my shirt.

Karnelian's hand found my thighs again, his thumbs drawing little hearts over my stockings. "Do you really need to keep taking the dust, baby? To keep punishing yourself over something you couldn't control. I know that it keeps you from seeing the horrors that haunt your mind, but… could you stop? Replace dust with whiskey or wine? For my peace of mind? I ask not as a lover, but as a friend—best friend." A corner of his lips turned up, but his eyes were glistening and shadowed with worry. "Could you stop for me? Please?"

Karnelian was asking me for something. A request. A query. A plea. Not a deal.

No, the devil wasn't kneeling at my feet, but Karnelian was. Doing something I knew he'd never done. Asking for me to give without something to receive, without blood being drawn, without binds being tied. Something out of the graciousness of my being, of my heart, that had been a few degrees warmer because of him.

His plea held reason. I didn't need the dust, not to keep my marks that I have never been proud to wear, nor to cloud my mind because I had him. My personal drug, my distraction, the male who held me down in the present time.

A smile split my face, increasing the temperature surrounding my heart as I nodded. "Yes. I'll stop *for you*."

THIRTY-NINE

CORIVINA

Sword on my back, combat boots in hand, bare feet on grass, I walked home from an intense training with Kolvin. Darius had quickly changed his mind about teaching me, and Kolvin and I had resumed as normal. Our daily training did diminish to weekly as Darius needed him in the war room, but Kolvin gave me stuff to work on alone during the week.

I didn't complain. Kolvin had become snarkier and broodier now that he knew Marie had chosen Karnelian as her male for the rest of her life, however short that might be. I had hoped he'd tell me what was going on in the war room and the plans for the war, but all the boy could talk about was how my daughter made the wrong choice and how Karnelian wasn't good for her.

Once upon a time, I would have thought Kolvin was perfect for Marie, but no matter how much of a dick Karnelian was, he was better than Kolvin. There was proof in the smiles he brought out in her and the twinkle in her eyes.

I knew if I asked Dominick, he would let me into that room, but I was avoiding the male still. If I saw him, I'd have to answer him. I was going to, I just… couldn't bring myself to yet.

Entering the manor, I was hit with the sweet scent of citrus with undertones of vanilla. My favorite food and my favorite person.

I dropped my shoes and sword in the foyer, making my way to the kitchen to grab a few oranges before going to take a nice hot bath and a nap.

I didn't make it to the kitchen.

Halting in the main room, my eyes locked on to the coffee table.

Pink roses.

Beautifully blushing pink roses.

Beautifully blushing pink roses sat on the coffee table in the main room. Beautiful blushing pink roses covered in *black blood*.

I lost my air to breathe, my pulse pounding in my ears, the wood floor starting to be lost to my feet.

My body didn't crash into the floor as expected; instead, I stumbled into a maid.

"Mrs. Foxglove?" The human's sweet voice chimed; eyes wide in shock as she helped me to stand. "Are you okay?"

It took everything in me to string a sentence together.

"Who brought these?"

The woman glanced to the flowers, disgust ghosting her face before she returned her eyes to me, face void of judgment like a human maid was taught to learn. "They arrived with the post about an hour ago. No note."

A cold sweat dripped down my spine, shivers beginning to wrack my frame.

"Mrs. Foxglove, should I call for Commander Foxglove?"

I shook my head. "No, thank you."

Being human, she didn't question me further, knowing it wasn't her place. She bowed her head in respect and went back to finishing her work.

My outstretched fingers trembled as I picked up the vase. Iron filled my nose, suffocating my senses. I looked down at the flowers, realizing that inside the vase instead of water there was blood.

Black blood.

My reality detached from me, all thoughts in my mind being lost, all feelings numbed out.

Vase in hand, I walked out the manor, the rough dirt sticking to my bare toes. Chatter filled my ears when I made it to the village square, finding my way to the portal pioneers.

The portals system was excruciatingly complicated for one to navigate without a driver—pioneer. They were complicated so the territory could profit off the convenience portals provided and commoners who couldn't afford a ticket couldn't hijack the system and ride through for free.

The vibrations of my voice were unknown to me as I spoke to the driver, my fingers unfeeling to the cold coin I passed him.

The next hour was lost as well. A blind spot in my memory as I sat in the carriage traveling across the territory from Lightwood to the palace.

It was the cold marble floors of the Seelie palace that brought me back to the tangy smell of blood that had dripped from the flowers to my arms.

Soon, I was running, running to the war room and banging on the door. Black filled my vision when the door opened, and I reared back in defense before my eyes found the hazel eyes of Karnelian. I pushed past him into the silenced room. I set the flowers down on the table, retreating a few steps back but eyes stayed locked on the harrowing gift.

"What is this?" Dominick's voice boomed.

I opened my mouth to speak but couldn't form the words.

Fabric smoothed over my arm, and I jerked away. My eyes looked for an assailant but found my babe, my flower, my Marie, a silver cloth in hand, and cold black eyes simmering with worry.

"Those are from Unseelie," she said, her hand finding my arm again and using the cloth to wipe up the blood. "From King Markos."

I nodded, my eyes fixing back on the flowers. The blood falling from the petals onto the table in sync with my heart.

Drip. Drip. Drip.

Beat. Beat. Beat.

With a shaky breath, I said, "They are from him. Sent to the manor."

"What!" Darius barked, his heat soon blazing into my side, his scent mixing with the tangy iron branded into my nostrils. "Who delivered them?"

"It's always just a Seelie postmale."

"What do you mean, always?"

"He... He used to send things, mostly these, but without blood. He knows that these are my favorite."

"How have I not known about this, Corivina?"

I shivered at my full name in his roughened tone. "Normally, he sent them to the shop."

Darius stepped in front of me, his heated blues full of fury replacing the bloodied flowers. "Another male has been sending my wife gifts. A male who harmed my wife, and you didn't think to tell me about it?"

My nostrils flared, his scent burning away the iron tang, his hostility rising a defensive fire in me. "It's not like I wanted the gifts." I seethed. "I burned every last one."

"Corivina, he knows where you work! What if something happened!"

"He wouldn't have done anything."

Darius crossed his arms. "He wouldn't have done anything? Are you seriously fucking defending him, Vina?"

"No! Fuck no! Markos wanted me to choose him. To leave you and become his queen. Which I didn't and would never do. I don't love him. He wanted me to love him again, and he knew forcing his way wouldn't work. The gifts were apologies, an attempt to manipulate me back to him by resurfacing memories of us. He wanted me to never forget him so even if I wanted to and live happily with you, he was always there, waiting for me to come back. He wouldn't marry another, not even the mother of his babe because the seat next to him would always be mine." My eyes found the roses over his shoulder. "What could you have done? He is the Unseelie King. You couldn't kill him, and you couldn't demand he stop. Even if you tried, he wouldn't have. Even now, he's never going to stop." My last words rang hollow like the toll of a warning bell, its echo reverberating around the room with sorrowed silence.

Dominick was the one to break the haunted hymns. "Have trade and post from Unseelie halted."

"Do you think we have enough supplies for the war?" Karnelian asked.

"What we have, they have more. A known cost when war erupts. They have more steel and ore, and a bigger population. We on the other hand have food, and gold which we can trade with other species. Hopefully our people stay fed while the Unseelie population diminishes from the lack."

"What about soil?" Jacoby asked.

"We have enough soil stored in humidified chambers to last a few years without drying out from the heat. If we run out before we are settled, we could steal from the fae wildlands or the humans."

"We are going to starve if it lasts longer than ten years, aren't we?" Karnelian snarked.

"If anything, we can eat fish."

"The nymphs aren't going to like that."

"We can bargain a deal with them. Your mother will negotiate. Having her as representation will help in our favor."

Karnelian snorted. "Maybe if you had actually made her queen. You're going to have to do more to get my grandfather in your favor."

Their words became mush to my ears. The only sound known to me was the dripping blood now littering the table.

Drip. Drip. Drip.

Beat. Beat. Beat.

18 YEARS AGO.

"Apple," I said to Marie as I started chopping up her predinner snack—an apple. She would often bug me while I made dinner grumbling about being hungry, so I gave her a light snack to settle her while I cooked.

"A-p-p-l-e," Marie said as she scribbled the word on the page laid out in front of her. At six, her penmanship wasn't great, but her spelling was. Her peers who went to primary school would be learning three to four-letter words right now, but since Marie was homeschooled by me, she could advance much faster without waiting for other students to catch up and was now working on five to six letter words.

"Correct. Maple."

"M-a-p-l-e."

I slid a saucer of half of an apple sliced into wedged pieces to her while taking a bite of the half I cut up for me. Her predinner snacking habits probably came from me as I often snacked while I cooked.

"You are doing very well, flower."

"Thank you, Mommy."

I pointed to the children's book next to her on the kitchen island. "Would you read that to me while I cook?"

Marie groaned; she didn't like reading out loud. She enjoyed being read to, but the reverse was very much not her thing. If it wasn't important for her to, I wouldn't force it, but it was, so I had to deal with my babe giving me the cutest little glare. "Okay…"

Marie began reading as I started on a simple dinner, one that didn't take long to make because Darius was due home soon, and Marie didn't hate—pasta.

It was about twenty minutes later when I was done with the food and Marie had read her book, switching over to singing a few of her favorite nursery rhymes as I plated the food.

Darius entered the kitchen coming up to me from behind and pressing a kiss to my cheek.

We got back together about a year and a half ago. Darius, being the perfect male he was, was persistent in getting me back without pushing my boundaries. It wasn't hard for me to feel myself letting my walls down for him and falling back into alignment. That didn't mean everything was great. I had forgiven him, but I couldn't forget it. Small things would trigger me to put up that wall again, and most of those small things were centered around the small faeling who sat at the kitchen island.

Yesterday we had a fight about him stepping too far into my babe's life before I was ready because he asked her to call him daddy without my permission.

I figured today he'd still be angry with me and want space until we both calmed enough to have a discussion, but he kissed me and a siren in my heart told me something was wrong with him, not us, him.

"Daddy!" Marie squealed when she saw him coming toward her.

He hugged her, placing a kiss on her head that warmed my heart but a smile didn't line his face. Instead, his features tightened.

I set his plate in front of him as he sat down starting to eat without a word.

"You said you were gonna take me with you today," Marie said between her food.

"Marie, please don't speak while you have food in your mouth," I interjected.

"Sorry, Mommy," Marie replied while stuffing her mouth with spaghetti.

Darius had offered to bring her to the field to see if she was interested in training. This was something he discussed with me. Everything in the fae royal system worked with heirs. Darius and I were married and technically it made Marie his daughter, and his heir. He inherited the position of commander when his brother died, who inherited the position when his father left after his mother died. If Darius wanted to retire, he would need an heir lined up. I was hesitant to let her go because I didn't want her to get hurt, nor did I want to push this on to her but if she was interested in training, then I didn't want to stop her from following that passion. If she wasn't interested Darius would have to make someone else his heir. I didn't want my babe to be forced into the position she hated.

"Sorry, flower," Darius said. "You were sound asleep. Couldn't bring myself to wake you."

He didn't look at her as he spoke, and Marie being six, couldn't read the cue that something was wrong, so she kept pestering him with questions that he did his best to answer, though something was off.

"Marie, eat your food, please," I said, diverting her attention from him.

"Okay…" she grumbled.

The rest of the dinner was spent with light chats between Marie and I, Darius remaining silent, tension radiating off him. Not heated tension. No, frigid, frightened, panicked. I barely touched my food waiting for Marie to finish.

When she finally did, I brought her plate to the sink and wiped her face with a towel.

I leaned over to Darius—whose plate was more full than mine—and whispered, "I'll meet you in our room in a few minutes."

His warm blues connected with mine. So many overloaded thoughts swirling within before he nodded, kissing Marie goodnight and headed up to our room.

It was too early in the night to lay Marie down so I climbed the stairs and walked to the nanny's room. After dropping Marie off, I made my way to the bedroom, opening the door to a stoic Darius sitting on the side of the bed.

I sat next to him, wrapping my arms around him. "Speak to me, my love," I whispered.

"I don't know if I can do this."

My first instinct was to freak out and run away, but I knew right now was his time to fear. "Do what?"

"This. Everything. I… What if I fuck everything up, Vina?"

Darius began to tremble, and I tightened the hold around him, putting my nose in his neck pressing a kiss to his mark. "Darius, you won't."

"I already did. I could do it again, and it's not just you who I'd lose, Vina. You're right it's too soon for her to think of me as her father because what if I fuck it up again, then disappoint her? I… Fuck, I already love her like she is my own, and it would kill me to know I disappointed her."

"Darius… whatever happens in the future. I will still love you. I never stopped loving you after you killed Maurice. I was just scared. And Marie loves you too, *you are* her father. Do hear how fucking cute it is when she calls you daddy? She talked about you all day, every time she called you that I knew it was right. I'm sorry I freaked out about that yesterday. I just wished you would have talked to me about it before acting."

His breathing increased, body tensing more. "That's my problem, Vina? I often act before thinking, don't I? I'm supposed to be this regal male who runs an army and is skilled at planning but in action, I don't plan. And it fucks me over."

I lifted my head, seeing tears dripping down his cheeks. I rubbed his temple with one hand, holding him with the other. "It is okay that you fuck up, Darius. I fuck up, you know this. It was a mistake for me to run away when you did what you did. That was my fuck up. And it was a fuck up for me to stay away. Even if things aren't like how they were before, I am still happier with you than without you." I kissed his forehead, pushing all the love I could into it. "Things don't have to be perfect."

"But—"

"Darius... we've talked about this." His biggest issue was needing to be perfect. To me, he was perfect. To Marie, to his friends, he was perfect. That didn't change how he felt, though. He felt like he wasn't ever enough, and the panic attacks would happen when the millions of unorganized thoughts rolled through that perfect brain.

In truth, Darius wasn't perfect. He had issues like me, issues he had only shared with me. Issues about his dead mother and brother, and missing father. And even at three hundred and eight years old, he was still dealing with them, avoiding them. He avoided them so much that eventually, like my darkness it became too much, and he was panicking. Sometimes his mind would separate from his body, and on the outside, he looked to be calm but on the inside he was gone, lost in panic, and that was when I would bring him back.

Because even though he was the one to heal me, I was the one to heal him as well. The one who could sort out his jumbled mind. It was why for two hundred years, I woke him for work so he didn't have to think about it, and I made his food and managed his finances and his employees outside the army. So, he didn't have to have so many little things on his plate to burden his mind.

We were both broken, just in different ways. Mine of sadness and his of fear.

"Tell me what you can't do, my love. Tell me and we'll figure it out, okay?"

He nodded, laying his head in my mark-less neck. A relieved breath leaving him before he spoke.

The edges of my vision fogged, darkness swirling around me, ready to swallow me whole. Their tendrils, dark, cold, and sinister, wrapping around my being, suffocating me in their ice-like grasp.

Frost spread through me, starting from my fingers, and licking up my arms. Its aim straight to my heart, freezing me to the spot, terrorizing me with the darkness hiding in my mind.

My raven.

Cor.

Kinder.

One whom you will destroy.

Flower.

Cold black eyes.

I want a divorce.

"Vina." Warmth spread over my frosted skin. Light-blue eyes, clear as the ocean on a warm summer day, filled my vision.

The ice didn't melt, instead it shattered, my emotions flowing out as the pieces fell from my being.

A small whimper escaped me, my body trembled, eyes filling with tears.

My arms folded around him, like he was driftwood, and I was lost at sea. My tears soaked his tunic as his arms held me in an embrace. His aura fell over me, calm, soft and soothing, his scent shoving out any of the iron tang.

In that moment, I didn't feel ashamed as I broke down in front of a room filled with people who were supposed to see the cold distant independent female. I couldn't keep that façade up in that moment. Not as the stuff hidden behind my wall learned how to climb and spill over the edge.

Darius stood there throughout my whole breakdown. Like a tree in a hurricane, rooted so deep and he couldn't be ripped out. He stayed still, holding me as rain pelted down all around.

When the hurricane passed, I was still holding on to that tree and he was holding on to me, stroking my back, head pressed into mine.

"You want me to take you home?" he whispered into my ear.

I nodded, feeling too weak to speak, too ashamed as the feeling of eyes on me manifested on my skin.

Darius's hands traveled down to my bottom, and he lifted me, so my legs wrapped around his waist. I hid my face in his neck, taking whiffs of his scent for security.

He started moving, his boots hitting against the floor in sharp thunderous booms, opposed to the dead silence that filled the air.

"I could create a portal straight there," Karnelian said.

I felt Darius nod and heard a blade being drawn, then we entered a portal that deposited us into our home.

Taking the stairs two at a time, Darius led us up to our room, setting me on the bed that smelled only of him.

My arms were cemented around him, unwilling to let go, so he came with, his weight settling over me.

"I have to go back, Vina."

A whimper left me, my arms tightening around his torso. The thought of being alone in this moment when I was at my weakest, most vulnerable state had my beast panicking with fear.

I didn't want to be alone in this empty house that was slowly losing all the ounces of love that was once placed in here. I didn't want to be lost in darkness without my sun.

"Could you…" I took a deep breath. I knew I had to let go but I wanted to have him with me and there was only one other way I knew I could. "Could you mark me… Just for a bit."

Darius's body tensed and he pulled back enough so we could lock eyes.

Primally, a mark was for safety and ownership. Asking this from him now was unfair of me because fae had civilized and so had the meaning. But just because you dressed a beast in clothes didn't make that being less of an animal. The mark still meant safety and it made me feel safe to wear his mark.

A small smile spread on his lips but didn't reach his eyes. He nodded, moving his head to the crook of my neck, and pressed a gentle kiss to the skin.

"I'll remove it later, I promise," I whispered to him.

Instead of replying, he fitted his teeth on my flesh and bit down. His venom coursed through my body, a pleasure I didn't delve into but floated through until I felt that small tether from his soul connect to mine.

A feeling so right, that later was going to be a forced to fight.

He licked the wound and pressed another kiss to my neck before he started to pull away. Tension filled my limbs, and he stilled before settling back down. His head notched between the other side of my neck, his teeth finding purchase into the skin, adding another mark for reassurance. The venom and the stronger bond relaxed me, my hands loosening their hold.

Darius leaned up to press a kiss to my forehead, the action soft and sweet and *everything*.

"Get some rest, Vina." He stood, grabbing a throw blanket, and draping it around me before he left me in the bed that was covered with his scent and his marks adorning my body.

The venom lulled me to sleep, and I woke later with him wrapped around me. Untangling from him was like ripping out my veins, but I had to leave.

I got up, removed the marks, showered, and changed before heading back to the training grounds by myself, because to truly destroy Markos, I had to be able to rely on myself.

FORTY

MARIE

*S*tepping up on my toes, I leaned over the sink to get closer to the bathroom mirror, smudging coal over my lids into a cat eye.

Makeup wasn't really my thing, but tonight was Samhain and it was practically a requirement to wear a costume to the party hosted at the palace.

My costume wasn't flashy, I barely thought it would count as a costume. I wore a black pleated skirt, a bralette that peaked through the sheer turtleneck that matched the spiderweb stockings that came up mid-thigh, combat boots, and my tiara Karnelian had asked me to wear tonight.

Today was the day of the dead, the perfect night to announce the engagement of the Devil and the Songbird—as Karnelian put it.

Finishing my makeup with black lip paint, I took a moment to look at my revealing outfit. Though little skin was shown, it was more than I had shown in over five years. My marks had started fading, barely visible at first glance. Every morning I looked at them in the mirror a small spark of panic flared in me, the shards of my soul jabbing into me, but I was able to push past it.

I would say it was because I justified that every betrayal to my mate was a step I had to take to get closer to him, but that wasn't true. It was that with every betrayal, no matter how cataclysmic my soul felt about the decision, my being felt lighter, my brain less fogged and rarely flashing with images of my trauma, my body healthier and less sluggish, and my heart less frigid with cold.

The withdrawals from the dust weren't that bad after a few days of puking, Karnelian staying home to take care of me through those rueful days. All I had were cravings every now and then, often when I was feeling emotional, something that was becoming rarer and rarer each day.

I stepped out of the bathroom, spotting Karnelian dressed in one of his suits laying on the bed, feet touching the floor, book in hand. He bookmarked the page he was on, setting the book down before sitting up.

He jerked when his eyes landed on me, mouth slightly parted.

His hand subconsciously adjusted the front of his trousers while his eyes traveled the length of me. When those silvery hazels connected to mine, Karnelian bit into his knuckles, muffling a pained groan.

I walked over to him, a smile painting my lips. When I was close enough, he pulled me in between his legs, hands stroking my thighs, fingers playing with my stockings.

"These are my greatest weakness. Fuck, little bird. I'd kill a male to have you naked in just these."

I snorted before fixing an out of place hair in his perfectly slicked back style. "I'm guessing you like my outfit."

He nodded. "I love it."

A spark flared in my heart, my body clenching at the omission.

Karnelian leaned up to kiss me, but I pulled back. "You'll mess up my lips."

"I want to do more than mess your lip paint up. I want it smeared all over your face and stained on my cock."

I tried to make an annoyed face, but my smile peaked through. Our foreheads met and I brought my nose to his, nudging it in.

Karnelian's fingers flexed on my thighs. "We're still doing this no sex thing?"

Forty days. It had been forty days since we last had sex, and we were both losing patience. At least Karnelian could take care of his needs with his hand. I was aching with the need to be filled by him.

I bit my lip with hesitation before I reluctantly gave him a nod.

He sighed in defeat, bringing his thumb up to my lips. "You got it on your teeth."

A giggle escaped me before I smiled, and he used the opportunity to wipe the lip paint off.

"Thank you."

"You're welcome."

A silence fell over us, one filled with harmony and glee. Eyes connected, smiles mirrored until Karnelian stole a kiss.

I jerked back. "Karnelian!"

He smirked, his lips paintless, causing me to frown.

His brows raised with zest. "Magic, little bird."

I rolled my eyes, before fixing them on him, mischief churning in their depths. "Speaking of magic… close your eyes."

His eyes narrowed with suspicion; brow raised in question.

"Just do it. And no peeking."

He closed his eyes, but I didn't trust him not to peek, so I covered them with my hands.

A smirk formed on his lips, his hands finding their way around my thighs to play with the stockings before trailing up to my ass. A groan left him when he found my cheeks bare because of my thong.

I smacked his shoulder playfully. "Stop. I have a surprise for you."

"Fine," he grumbled. "Hurry up."

I growled at him in irritation before recovering his eyes and concentrating on my shadows. Without the dust clouding my mind, my grasp on my magic was easier. I could feel the moon like I was a part of her. I fully understood why the fae were children of the orbs that floated in the sky because the moon felt like my mother. Not my mother—Corivina. Like an omniscient divine being that watched over me. She was cold but loving, wise but callous. Actually, kind of like my mother, and every time I felt the moon's essence within me, I was reminded of her.

Seeing her break like that last week was an assault to my heart that I truly never expected to feel. It wasn't guilt, but care and protection. She was a rock, and she was crumbling, and I hated it. Hated it enough to double down on my magic practice, and finally form a butterfly, then a snowflake, then a rose. I wasn't an angry person, but I was finally beginning to hate King Markos for what he did to my mother, and I'd aid in any way I could to help take him down. That meant becoming a queen.

My shadows were flared out around me, and I formed them into the shapes I'd been practicing over the last few days before taking a step back and standing on display for Karnelian.

"I thought we'd go as devils." I smiled. Technically, we were demons. The devil was a human belief that made no logical sense. He was the king of demons who lived in a fiery pit, called hell and I believed he was all red. The real king of the demons was named Jeroc and he had a pale skin tone like most Unseelies. He also recently had a son—Xadrien about four years ago, and I was sure the devil couldn't have children. He and the rest of the demons lived north of the human lands, their lands were mountainous and many of them lived in the snowy peaks—so no hellfire.

Twirling, I showed off my tail of shadow, adorned with a little point at the end that matched the tiny horns on my head. "Do you like it?"

He was silent a moment, taking in my outfit, his expression blank. Then a genuine smile spread his lips. He grabbed me, pulling me into a soul stilling kiss, that warmed my insides and the confides around my heart until there was no ice left.

"You're a magnificent creature, Stéla."

I smiled against his lips, kissing him back. "You're a magnificent creature, Nelian."

"The Silver Blooded Devil, Prince Karnelian Lightfire! And his fiancée, The Unseelie Princess, Marie Shadawn!" The announcer boomed as Karnelian and I crested the grand staircase of the Seelie Palace.

Every eye was on us, wide and bulging, as the two devils walked hand in hand down the staircase.

No trembles permitted my body, my creature calm and without panic. No, instead, I walked with my head raised, honored to be at Karnelian's side and proud to have him at mine.

There was terror hidden in the people's eyes. Not the terror that comes from a true haunting. No, the terror that comes from envy, from looking upon something that was beyond you, something powerful.

The crowd gave us a wide berth when we reached the end of the steps. Karnelian turned to me, mirth sparking in his eyes as his fingers lifted my chin, urging me to my toes to meet his lips. The kiss wasn't a peck. No, it was another heartwarming kiss, that had me curling my toes.

He pulled back, his smirk light, but his eyes penetrating. "Can I have this dance, milady?"

I snorted before nodding and I was whisked onto the dance floor that soon cleared just for us.

Even though I knew eyes licked every inch of my body, in that moment Karnelian was the only one who existed. It was just me and him, smiles on our lips, sparkles in our eyes, devilry in our atmosphere.

Our mischief only lasted one song because we were interrupted by King Dominick, features tight, eyes alight, steam fuming out his ears.

"Karnelian," he gritted out.

"Dominick." Karnelian grinned.

I patted his arm. "I'm going to go get some wine." I stepped up on my toes and kissed his cheek, more so his chin because of his height.

I attempted to leave but his arm snagged my waist, and he pressed a kiss to my head. "Don't go far." And then he let me go as his father berated him.

The snack table was dressed in all types of treats. I grabbed a glass of wine, sipping on it as I tried a few treats. I didn't get Karnelian a drink, not seeing any whiskey around, and instead filled a bowl of grapes, then started my way back.

It wasn't hard to spot Karnelian since even though it was the day of the dead, no Seelie would be caught in black. Seelies only wore black when someone died and Unseelies only wore white when blessing their child for life. So, when my eyes landed on the male whose clothes matched mine, instead of seeing him standing alone waiting for me or with his father as I'd left him, he was standing talking to a female. A gorgeous female, tall, blond, blue eyes that were hooded with lust and aimed at my male.

My muscles tensed as I looked at her standing with Karnelian. How she was the perfect height for him, how they looked good together. The sight brought me to agony.

Jealousy was a foreign feeling to me. I never felt jealous with Kolvin because even if I didn't know his feelings for me when we were young, all of his attention was always on me. Even when my mate slept with another to make me mad, I wasn't jealous, more so wronged. I knew in my heart my mate was mine, but Karnelian wasn't truly mine. He wasn't my mate, he didn't wear my mark, nor my scent and, in truth, our relationship was fake.

Panic filled me and anger trailed after as I watched the pair. How Karnelian's attention was fully on her, swirling his glass of whisky aimlessly as she talked. How her fingers grazed his suit and her spine arched more to show off her breast.

Abandoning my wine on a random table I started making my way towards them. My beast practically ready to claw this female's eyes out and stake my claim on Karnelian.

When I reached them Karnelian didn't even grace me with a glance, still entertaining the female whose laugh was sensual, elegant, and graceful.

"Here, baby," I said, holding out the bowl of grapes. The words were awkward as they left my mouth. I felt like a child vying for Karnelian's attention, shame filling me without it being tied to my mate.

He turned to me then, an eyebrow raised, a smirk on his lips. "Hi, baby." And I hated even more that the second his attention was on me, all my stress floated away.

He handed his empty glass to the female like she was nothing and took the bowl from me. He then popped a grape into his mouth before pulling me into his side and pressing a kiss to my head. "Thank you."

A blush spread across my face, Karnelian's admiration feeling like a reward, like a shot of dust.

He looked back to the female, his voice filtering into his business tone. "You have to find Grayson if you want to bargain another deal."

The female's cheeks flamed in embarrassment. "I didn't have to last time. Last time all I had to do was get naked in your bed." Her eyes narrowed on me with disdain.

"*Grayson*," Karnelian growled, the sound rattling my beast. "Find him if you want to make an appointment."

Her lips thinned, glancing at me again with murder in her eyes before nodding her respects to Karnelian and going on her way.

The giddy fog that fell over me dissipated and I pushed away from Karnelian, taking the bowl from his hands, and walking away.

He caught me quickly, hands turning me, so my scowl met his cocky fucking smirk. "Little bird... look at you all jealous."

My glare deepened. "Aren't we supposed to make people believe we are together?"

His smirk widened to a jovial smile. "We are."

"Then why were you letting her all over you?"

"I wasn't," he said, placing his hands in his pocket, his arrogance practically littering the air around him.

"I watched her touch you."

"She was touching me, so?"

"So, she shouldn't be!" I growled.

A grin broke out on his face, his eyes hooding over. "Little bird, she wasn't interested in me."

My eyes went wide then. "She just said—"

"She wanted to fuck me for a deal, not for her interest in me. Many females have tried the same. They think their pussies are more valuable than gold and that I'd make a deal with them for it."

"She said she had already fucked you."

"No, she said she was naked in my bed."

"How is that any fucking better?"

"Baby..." Karnelian cupped my cheek, placating me. "She snuck into my back office years ago. Got naked and laid on my bed, thinking her body would be enough for a deal. I don't trade in sex. Drugs, money, and dirty deeds, yes, but not sex. She wanted money, so I made a deal for her to cut off all her pretty hair so she would feel as ugly on the outside as I was sure her insides were."

"She hasn't fucked you?"

His smile widened and he pulled me up to kiss my lips. "No. I don't even remember her fucking name."

My arms wrapped around his neck, grapes falling and glass shattering onto the floor as I smashed my lips onto his. His arms came around my waist, pulling me in as he deepened our kiss.

There was fire in this kiss. A hunger that overtook us after forty days without sex. My claws pressed into his skin and his canines grazed my lips. Normally I would fear them tearing my flesh, but I wanted it. I didn't even feel guilty that I did.

The fingers on my hips flexed and pressed me tighter into his chest. His hard length pressing into my stomach, his groan slipping into my mouth.

His hands found my ass and he hoisted me up, my legs wrapping around his waist. It was evident that neither of us cared if we had an audience. We had already dabbled in exhibitionism and these parties weren't shy of public fucking.

"Karnelian," I said between kisses.

"Hmm."

"Fuck me."

He nodded, not letting his lips leave mine as he started walking. I giggled and broke our kiss to look out to the people parting for us. Karnelian strolled through them with confidence as he pressed kisses along my neck, his tongue sliding against my skin, making me wish it was sharp enamel biting into me.

We made it into a darkened hallway abandoned of people when Karnelian's mouth met mine again. Music from the ballroom vibrated through the wall he pushed me up against, but they weren't as intense as the growls that started to reverberate from us, each of our beasts starving for another.

My claws had made purchase in his skin, holding onto him like he was my lifeline.

"You're mine," I whispered against his mouth.

Karnelian abruptly broke our kiss, his eyes connecting to mine, our noses fibers away from touching.

This close to him, I could see the constellations of freckles that dusted his cheeks. Something that made him seem innocent, exposed, pure. Nothing like the devil he'd been named.

He uttered no words, just stared into me, but there was something said in his look. Something that made a thump sound in my chest. Something that caused my heart to beat.

As if he had felt it too, his lips met mine, and he poured himself into me, his essence filling my body, entering my veins and being the reason my heart had to beat.

His kisses were harsh and bruising traveling down to my chin then to my neck. His hands tightened on my waist as if he was attempting to push me into the wall before he dropped to his knees and threw my legs over his shoulders. He kissed my inner thighs as one of his hands moved my thong to the side and then, gracelessly, he began to dine on me. His tongue wicked and vicious as he lapped at me, his lips sucking and teeth grazing.

My moan was hoarse as if my breath was stolen from me. My fingers threaded into his hair, halfway pushing him away as he attacked my clit, halfway pulling him into me.

His fingers slipped into me, sliding in and out to the beat of my heart, my hips rocking with the pump of my blood.

His piano fingers, roughened from life, perfectly knew how to tap my keys. Angled within me to rub against that spot, forceful enough to make me explode.

Tears filled my eyes and my toes curled in my boots, my teeth finding purchase into the flesh to hold in my scream. Karnelian continued to lap at me, pumping his fingers with more ferocity, giving me no mercy as I came.

Then I was falling, the wall behind me disappearing, gravity becoming unknown to me until my back was smacked down onto a bed. A bed that was stained with our scent.

FORTY-ONE

Karnelian

With Marie's come dripping down my throat, I portaled us to our room, slamming her onto the bed.

My mouth still suctioned to her pussy, I took a few last licks in an attempt to get my fill of her, a task I doubted was even feasible.

Standing, I hovered over her. Her curls splayed around her, her lips smeared with blood and black lip paint, her eyes hooded with lust and possession.

You're mine.

The tearing of fabric ripped through the silence as I started pawing at her clothes. My monster was in full control, but instead of fearing I'd hurt her or destroy the world, I felt free. Wild but free.

My monster wasn't alone though, my little bird had become a little beast as she sat up and started cutting my clothes off me with equal ferocity. It took seconds for us to discard our clothing on the floor, and used my magic to remove her makeup off her face.

She was beautiful with it on, and later I definitely wanted it smeared all over my cock, but right now I wanted her bare, raw, nothing between her and me.

She was ready to savage me when I was done, but I stopped her, pushing her to lie back. Not only to tell her who was in charge, but because I just wanted to look at her like this. I wanted to see the female I spent every second thinking about. The one who captured me at that Solstice and has yet to let me go. The one who I would bend for, just to see her smile. The one…

I let my fingers trace over her marks, her fading marks.

You're mine.

A whisper I wanted to hear. A whisper I would gladly let ring in my head every day.

I grabbed her, carrying her to the head of the bed. Our mouths sealing together before I laid her down. Chest to chest. Kisses hungry and wet. My hand in her hair, her claws in my back.

My cock found her soaked pussy, slowly sinking into her, letting her feel every inch of me.

Our moans harmonized against another, and when I was fully sheathed within, I didn't move, instead basking in the feel of her.

I pulled my hips back before ramming back into her, sparks prickling up my spine as I did it again. And again. And again. Movement slow, but still forceful and hard. There wasn't a game to be played today. No tricks, just treats. Just her creature and mine. Her hips gyrating against mine. Sex raw, messy, and primal.

The squeaks of the bed sounded with each slam into her, growing louder as my thrust grew faster, harder. My cock plunging into her so brutally, I wouldn't be surprised if I was ripping her perfect cunt.

You're mine.

I wanted to rip her. Rip the tie her soul had with him and then forge it with mine. I wanted her connected to me deeper than a brand on her arm, deeper than a mark on her flesh, deeper than blood bound and sealed. I wanted to make her truly mine and I hers. I wanted her soul braided into mine, weaved so tight that nothing could break it apart and we were bound together forever.

I wanted her to be my mate.

My hips stilled, my lips leaving hers. Something souring my stomach as I looked at her. The moonlight made her shimmer sparkle. Her lips puffy, eyes delirious and vacant. Gone. Unable to house a soul.

I made a mistake when I made that deal.

I thought I could ignore fate, ignore the gods and their divine messages. They rarely gave fae messages, rarely, and I thought I could ignore it.

I couldn't because I realized I was fucking falling for her.

The broken female, who was reduced to rubble—that tiny, little, defenseless bird had sunk her claws in deep, and now she was bleeding me out.

I was falling for the one female I could never truly have. The female who was only alive because she was forced to live. The female with void eyes and a shattered soul.

Her hand came up to my chest to trace my tattoo. Her action, an action she had done a thousand times, an action I loved, another sign from the gods.

I moved her hand away, her deep soulless eyes connecting with mine. An abyss deeper than the ocean that had caught me in their wave, drowning me until it got ahold of my soul.

You're mine.

I was.

I was hers.

My hips started moving again, my mouth meeting hers simply so I didn't have to see those eyes. I pounded every part of me into her, giving her everything, because I was stupid enough to fall into her wave, a wave disguised as a comforting nest.

Her perfect pussy was too perfect, her cunt too wet, her flesh too smooth. And then she had to start convulsing around me. Her siren's song sounded through our lips and went straight down my throat to capture my heart.

It was all too much for me and a trimmer wracked my frame, my mouth disconnecting from hers to let a roar rip from my throat, my spine arching and my come shooting out of me. Her perfect pussy milking me for everything I was worth.

My body seeped into hers. Her sweaty skin flushed with mine as her arms wrapped around me in embrace. Her labored breaths brushed against the side of my face as she pressed a kiss to my cheek.

We stayed like that for hours, until I gained the ability to pull away, my cock leaving her heat. Her whimper at the loss made me want to shove it back in but I refrained and let my back hit the mattress.

Of course, she followed, her soft body wrapping around me, her head burying to my chest, a soft purr leaving her, it was forced but my monster still answered, satisfied to hear it.

I didn't sleep.

Instead, my mind wandered, twisted, clouded, misted. I was falling for her. The devil, a male with a dark and wicked heart, was falling for a fragile little sparrow.

And would it be that bad if I did let myself fall completely? To love her while I had her for however long that be?

I wanted her, and she wanted me.

You're mine.

Her claim felt right. She felt right. And maybe I could be right for her.

She woke when the sun was high in the sky, the morning edging to noon. She rubbed her face into me, breathing me in before a small groggy yawn exited her. Her eyes opened to mine, and she smiled just like when we had first slept together. Just a small lift of her lips that undid me in ways that it shouldn't.

She moved up to kiss me and I returned it with a small peck, hoping she wouldn't be able to sense the turmoil in my mind.

There was a glow to her, that had nothing to do with her skin and she seemed oblivious to my mind's troubles, laying her head on my chest, starting to trace. Over and over, the small motions hypnotizing but abruptly she stopped, her claw nicking my skin, her body tensing.

Her eyes were trained on something, and I followed them to the tattered pieces of our clothing.

Her movement was so fast, I barely felt her leap over me to the floor. She gathered the pieces, her beast panicking as it started to separate my clothing from hers.

Her fingers trembled as it went over the mesh pieces, tremors racking her body.

It didn't take long for me to realize where the clothes came from—who they came from.

Marie buried her head into the fabric when her sobs started. The cries muffled but still gutting to the ears.

She cried for moments before whatever turned over in her pretty little head soured and she wasn't examining the clothes anymore but her marks, and then the bathroom door.

Something in me stilled, hardened, fortified.

It didn't matter.

It didn't matter if she grew jealous and claimed me with her words. It didn't matter that I was her best friend. It didn't matter if she let the marks fade for me, or married me, or bore my babe.

It didn't matter if I was hers, or if she was... because the second she was able to, she'd return to him.

FORTY-TWO

MARIE

Karnelian's hands gripped my ass, holding me still as he thrust into me. Our mouths were glued to one another, my claws purchased into flesh, my moans ripping from my throat.

We were fucking just like we did a week ago—slow but brutal, passionate but primal.

The inverse to how Karnelian has been toward me this past week—cold but present, avoidant but kind.

He put all his focus on the war effort, but even though that was a pressing problem, it felt like there was another reason behind his cold shoulder. He barely spoke more than a couple sentences at a time. His voice bland and his words often a command or an advisement. He barely kissed me, the kisses always pecks that lasted seconds and seemed forced. The worst part was when I held his hand, it was limp, inactive, like he didn't care to hold mine back.

It hurt. My freshly thawed heart scared it'd started to beat for a male who didn't want it. My mind whizzed with intruding thoughts as to why he didn't show me affection as he used to. My body taut and wanting, I was sure my creature was making my panties soaked with my arousal so he'd act, and yet he didn't.

I initiated it a few nights ago, giving him kisses he didn't return, my fingers softly stroking his cock, but he denied me, saying he was tired and went to sleep. When today came and Karnelian was due to make me come, I thought he would tell me he was too tired again and ask me to deny him. I would, of course. I wouldn't force Karnelian to have sex if he didn't want to, but he didn't ask.

It was awkward at first, the kisses foreign. It was like I could feel Karnelian trying to keep a distance between us, but as the kisses slowly grew passionate, it was like the week of distance didn't happen and we were back fucking sensually, putting an ease to my mind, body, and heart.

My soul still cried out for my mate, but her wails sounded muffled and distant. They had been dimming for some time now, even a week ago when I found the clothes given to me by my mate tattered, I ended up being able to handle her plight. I was tempted to use dust to calm her cries, but I didn't. I let the emotion of it roll through me and expel as I had done in the past when I talked to Karnelian.

After my sobs calmed, I planned on snuggling with him, wanting to be grounded in him, but that was when his aloofness started.

We finished at the same time tonight. We stayed fused together for a few precious moments before Karnelian rolled off me, his cock leaving me way too soon. After a few panting breaths, I moved to take up my spot curled into his chest but found the space lacking his body.

He sat on the side of the bed, back to me, head in his hands, breaths heavy and deep. His muscles were flexed, strung too tight for someone who had just had amazing sex.

I thought about comforting him, wrapping my limbs around him and holding him, but his energy warned my beast to stay away.

He pushed off the bed, striding over to the bathroom. When the door closed behind him, I heard the lock click and then the run of the shower.

He was there for an hour or so, and I laid waiting for him in bed, my eyes glued to the door. My heart stilled when he entered the room. His scent wafted over me, cinnamon and traces of soap, no hint of daisy, no hint of me.

It took a lot to remove someone's scent from you, a couple baths normally, or extremely hot water and vigorous scrubbing.

Tears filled in the backs of my eyes, and I turned away from him, pretending to go to sleep. He dressed in clothes for sleeping, he normally slept naked, but by the sound of his movements he wore sleeping shorts and a shirt. He fitted himself behind me when he got into bed, but it didn't soothe my trepidation. It was clear he didn't want to, but he did it for my benefit, offering a small comfort after knowingly washing off my scent moments after having sex. But there was no true comfort in it, his arm was draped over me like a dead fish, not holding anything, and even though his form was fitted behind mine, his body didn't actually touch me. Inches of space filled between our body, and those inches felt like miles. I had to shut my eyes tight to keep my tears from falling but one did, spilling down my cheek and falling onto the bed.

Karnelian was less distant the next day, but it felt like a farce, like he was over correcting. The worst part was how pathetic I was toward it because despite that I knew he was over correcting, I was happy when he held my hand with purpose, and he kissed me with a bit more passion than before. But deep down I knew something was wrong, there was a heaviness in the air, letting one know today it was going to rain.

There was a party at the palace tonight, so the king dismissed everyone for the day. It was ridiculous that he was planning a party, especially since he spent every day stressing over every small detail of the war. My father even commented on the absurdity of it, but the king explained that he needed to distract the people as much as possible until we actually declared war to keep unnecessary casualties to a minimum.

I spent the afternoon in bed, trying to connect to the carnelian stone I snagged from Karnelian's office, but of course my mind wouldn't focus. Especially since Karnelian hadn't said a word to me since we got back, his cold shoulder returning and a weight settling over my chest.

He came out of the bathroom dressed in a suit, his hair freshly styled, his body smelling of just him. Making his way to me, he placed a kiss on my head. "I'm going to go out for a bit."

That weight pressed down further. "Where?"

He hesitated, making my gut twist. "I'm going to the palace."

"I can come with." The words rushed out of my mouth, needy and desperate.

He noticed it and his voice turned patronizing—pity filled. "I think it would be best if you just stayed here tonight. I'll be back late. If you fall asleep, I'll be here before you have a nightmare."

"Why can't I come?"

"I'm planning on meeting someone."

"Who? If it's a client, then I'll stay out of the way."

"It's not a client."

"Then who is it?"

"I haven't met them yet." And there it was, a crack of thunder signaling a downfall.

"Oh." My voice fractured in my throat. "You're planning on meeting someone... to sleep with."

Hurt ripped through my heart, my freshly thawed out heart, that was prepared to beat for this male. The male with silvery hazel eyes that looked cold and distant at the moment.

He took a deep breath. "I'm allowed to be with others, that's a part of our deal."

"I know but..."

"But what?" he interjected. "It's a part of the deal."

"I thought... am I not enough?"

He shuddered, his eyes flicking out towards the window and a small part of this mask slipping before he tacked it back in place and those steely orbs penetrated through me. "No."

The tears started to fill my eyes and I blinked profusely in an attempt to hold them back.

My soul screamed then. Loud, proud, and mocking. I shouldn't cry over this, over him, and I wouldn't be crying if I had never assumed that he'd be mine.

"We aren't in a real relationship, Marie."

"I know that." My lips trembled with my words. My soul's taunts and my heart's sorrow berating down on me. "But... I thought I was satisfying you. I... I can do more." I couldn't lose him. The thought had me feeling like I was falling, and I would do anything to stay upright—stay grounded. "I can do whatever you want."

His jaw hardened, nostrils flaring. "You can't love me, and you're not supposed to."

His words triggered me to flinch as if he had struck me. I felt that hollowness settle over me and dread soon after. "I didn't know that was something you wanted. You never told me you did. You said you didn't believe."

"I would like to believe and I'm telling you that now."

"But why now? Why can't you wait? It should be more than a couple years until the war is over. Why can't you wait till then?" My words were pleas, beggings, prayers.

Karnelian snorted, but it was more of a harsh grunt. "You want me to wait until after you're dead till I find love?"

"I didn't say that... it's just..." My foundation felt like it was crumbling around me, and I was grasping at brittle roots to find any solution. "We... we're busy now and we both know I can't die until I have an heir."

"You're implying it, and it's wrong of you to ask me to wait for you to die before I can be happy."

Something in me snapped. My beast coming out to protect me from his harm, anger disguising my pain. "So what? You're going to go out tonight and meet the fucking one?"

He flinched at my tone, just a bit, but I caught it. "Probably not, but who knows."

"So, you really just want to fuck someone else?"

Instead of stating it, he let the wind whisper it to me.

My heart clenched, squeezing painfully just like the day my mate died. It had started beating for Karnelian and I was prepared to let it. I was going to give in to my feelings for him and... and now he was going to go find someone else. A female who would probably be perfect for him, tall and pretty and didn't have her soul tied to another.

I looked away from him, physically paining me to look at the cause of my sins. "Okay," was what I managed to reply.

"I won't be out that late. I'll be back before you have a nigh——"

"I won't want to sleep with you while you smell like another female, so don't bother."

"Marie, you can't sleep without me."

"I was doing fine before you came into my life." A lie I knew the second the words left my mouth, but I kept going as if I could convince myself they were true. "Honestly, if I had never met you, I would be perfectly fine. As much as you think I'm a damsel in distress, I'm not. I lost someone I loved, and it destroyed me, but I was getting better. You are just a cock to soothe my heat, and I could have found that anywhere. I didn't fucking need you then, and I don't fucking need you now." My words were an attempt to hurt him, but in truth, they just hurt me because everyone was right; I was a shit liar. No part of me believed those words, not my body, my mind, my heart or even my soul. Karnelian was the only reason I was able to get through each day. He was the only reason I could sleep at night, the only reason I smiled or laughed. He did more than just soothe my body; he soothed my soul, my entire being.

"I'll see you later, little bird."

I didn't reply and after a pause the air shifted, and his presence was gone.

I collapsed into the bed, desperately breathing in lungfuls of Karnelian's scent. His scent that was mixed with mine. Just how I liked it, how I craved it to be. Soon, it will be tainted with another's and maybe she will be his one, or even worse—his mate, and they will fall in love and I'd be left to the side. I'd bear his babe, then I'd die, and she would raise my child, and they would call her mother and they'd be a perfectly happy family, my presence not even missed by them. In fact, it will be a relief because who would want a barely alive female who only brings gloom around? Who was literally designed to bring chaos to the fae.

My tears soaked the bed, running like a stream down my face as everything just came over me.

The reminder that I was mated, and even if he wasn't here, he still owned my body, heart and soul. I owed that to him and I betrayed him by giving them away.

The reminder that I gave Karnelian more than I ever gave my mate because Karnelian had my mind. Held my secrets I never shared, my worries, my fears, my comforts, my salvations.

The realization that I kept my mind from my mate because I feared I'd lose it, drowning in the depts of him and that was why he was so fucking afraid he'd lose me. He never fully had me, because I never gave him the one thing I could choose to give him.

The realization that I chose to give it to Karnelian, and he didn't even want it.

My conscious swirled and spiraled with these thoughts, over and over, tumbling until I had fully broken and I was lost inside my mind again, my soul wails loud in my ears.

I just wanted it to stop. I just wanted it to end. I just wanted my mate back.

He wouldn't take you back, my soul screamed.

You betrayed him. You killed your mate and then you danced on his grave with the Devil.

The cinnamon that clogged my nose felt wrong, my body felt wrong, tainted.

My feet carried to the bathroom, and I removed my clothes, stopping when I caught my reflection in the mirror.

I looked at my fading marks, my punishment I deserved. The punishment I didn't have the right to be pardoned from.

You're the one who should be dead.

My knees hit the tile floor, cracking, but the pain didn't register in my mangled mind. I opened the cabinet. My bag of dust still there, waiting for me to realize my fault and continue my penalty.

I opened the bag, blue sparkling dust puffing out and littering the air. My claw dipped into the powder, the soft fluffy feel of it caking my skin. Then with my finger to my nose, I took a deep breath in.

FORTY-THREE

KARNELIAN

Whiskey swirled in my glass as I counted down the seconds until I could leave. This was my third whiskey in the last twenty minutes. It felt longer than that, but my watch showed it had only been twenty.

Now, twenty-one.

I drained my glass, hoping it would soothe the tightness in my muscles, stifle the agony in my heart, steam over the picture of her tear-filled eyes that shadowed my mind.

Tears that were probably already tracked down her face. Tears that were formed because of the lies that left my tongue.

I'm planning on meeting someone. Lie.

Am I not enough?

No. Lie.

But they were lies I had to tell. Lies that would put distance between us.

They shouldn't be lies though. I should be meeting someone else. She shouldn't be enough. She shouldn't be more than enough.

The problem wasn't her; it was me. I wasn't enough and I couldn't let myself get wrapped up in her. Couldn't feel for her, just for her to die and rip my soul to pieces like her mate did to her. So, I'd tried my best to put space between us, to be her friend but not her lover.

Marie was poison though. A few sips and I'd be okay, weakened but able to recover. I could kiss her once or twice, but a third kiss and I was done for.

I spent the whole week trying to wedge something between us, for her third kiss to glue us back together. My plan was to fuck her, I knew eating out her would be torture to me, and fingering her would be anguish. I had fucked plenty of females not to care for them after, I rarely kissed them while fucking but I had to kiss the little bird to keep her eyes from ensnaring me.

The first kiss, I was able to hold myself back. The second, I could feel my resolve wanting to break. The third, similar to an erupting volcano. The process of our clothes coming off and my cock buried inside her a blur, and once I was inside her every ounce of my resolve broke and I was swept into the moment never wanting it to end.

This time was better than the last. Like we were more connected, like more of me had been enraptured into her and more of her tangled in me. The sex more primal than before—growls, grunts, and purrs emanating from us. The kisses deeper, her tongue sliding against mine, her teeth scraping across my lips, her fingers in my hair holding me still. For a moment we were just so desperate to connect, so desperate for each other and then we came, and something sliced through my chest, a painful reminder that whatever I felt was one sided, imaginary, impossible.

Twenty-two.

My eyes scanned the room, the music too loud, the people too cheery. I didn't want to be here at all. My monster ached with the need to go back to her, but I couldn't—not yet.

"Can I get another," I hollered at the barkeep before looking out towards the ballroom.

My monster wanted her. Which is why I scrubbed myself clean. If I wanted to stay sane and not let my beast drive me to madness, I needed to rid myself of her scent. Rid myself of the small claim she had on me.

Her reaction to what I did to preserve myself had my monster even more riled. All day today, it was doing everything it could to reassure her that we were hers. It had felt her sorrow, and heartbreak. Noticed her tight muscles and erratic aura. The reaction was unexpected to me, and that brief moment of shock gave my beast time to take over.

Luckily, she had fallen asleep by the time my monster pulled her into our chest, light purrs sounding from us to offer comfort. The day was spent with me trying to wrangle back my control, and then my father reminded me of this party.

Glass clinking against the gold plaited bar top brought my awareness back to the stupid party.

Twenty-three.

My throat was numb to the burn my whiskey was supposed to provide, my jaw tightening as I remembered the desperation in her voice.

Why can't you wait till then?

She had no right to ask me to wait, and yet, a part of me was gleeful she did because even if I wasn't enough, she still needed me.

You are just a cock to soothe my heat, and I could have found that anywhere. I didn't fucking need you then, and I don't fucking need you now.

Her voice got squeaky, nose twitchy, throat hoarse from holding back tears. Her eyes unable to meet mine as the lie left her lips. She needed me, but she lied.

She needed me, but I still left.

I wanted to be with her, but I stayed put.

I wanted to be with her, but she had a mate.

Twenty-four.

A clap on my back jutted me forward, spilling my drink and splashing on my suit. I turned, fury quick to rise within my taut limbs. Green emerald eyes met mine and I was about to wrap my hand around the owner's throat before I registered the mahogany skin. The sight of my brother brought my beast to a heel, but fire still burned in my veins.

"Hello, brother." Fredrick smiled, cocky, arrogant, and jubilant.

"Fredrick," I said between gritted teeth.

His fingers squeezed my shoulder, before he rested his head on my other looking out towards the partiers. "I was thinking about going by Rick, what do you think?"

"Alirick goes by Rick."

He groaned. "*Alirick* is a lowly barkeep."

"He works for me, so I agree with you on lowly, but when you say Rick, I will think of him."

"Fine." He stole my drink from my hand, taking a sip before gagging and handing it back. "Ricky? I look like a Ricky, don't I?"

My lips pressed together, and I released an annoyed breath. "Fredrick you are seventy-seven years old, it's a bit too late for you to request a nickname. Besides, Fredrick is a good name for a king. It means—"

"*I know what it means.*" He frowned. "It's a boring, stuffy name and I tire of it. I can't just change my name. Father would have another pissy fit. Come on, Karney, you have a thousand names, can't you just spare me one?"

I rolled my shoulder, shaking his hand off me. "Those are titles, and I didn't exactly pick them out." I finished my drink, flashing the empty glass to the bartender for another. "But if you truly want one, how about Drix?"

"Drix?"

"It's close to Fredrick, but at the same time, different enough. I believe it means innovative. A good name for you."

"Drix..." He tasted the name on his tongue, a smile spreading across his lips that was genuine and not full of his princely charm. The sight had my shoulders relaxing just a bit. "Drix Lightfire. It has a nice ring to it, no?"

I snorted, my lips turning up in the slightest smile.

"So... where's your little bird?"

The corners of my lips dropped, my body returning to its taut state. "She's back at the manor."

"Hmm. I really like her. She's a great taste tester for my newest mixes. Her alcohol tolerance is through the roof. She can go one after another without even looking the slightest bit drunk. Her critiques are also actually helpful. She doesn't just say it's good or bad; she offers pointers and adjustments. You know she knows a lot about food? She looked over a few of my—"

"Fredrick, I'm not in the mood."

He tsked, eyes rolling at me. "No wonder she didn't want to accompany you tonight. Honestly, I don't know how she even stands you. Even if broken, she's sweet and soft and doesn't seem like she would be able to be with someone who's so *wicked*." He enunciated the last word with dramatics.

"She's just as wicked as me, brother," I said, grabbing my new drink. Thirty-three. "Her soft edges color your vision and she takes that opportunity to stab you in the gut while you're blinded."

Fredrick laughed. "You are already having marital problems and you're not even married?"

My jaw hardened, eyes narrowing on him. "Fredrick, leave me—"

Pain flared in my knees. An acute fiery sensation sourcing my right nostril followed soon after—Marie doing dust.

Thirty-four.

I was about to down my drink, but the pain didn't subside. Instead, it intensified and started to burn my left nostril.

"You good?" Fredrick asked, brotherly concern making his haughty prince façade wash away.

Rolling my shoulders, I turned and waved my drink at him. "After my drink, I will be."

A snake twisted around the base of my spine, finding home in my stomach, but I ignored the feeling. I wasn't going to go to her. So, she was doing dust… she hadn't done it in a month or so, and her body was probably close to fully healed. Her tolerance was probably lower, and she couldn't take her second dose through the same nostril because it started hurting.

I gulped down the drink, hoping the amber liquid would fog my mind enough for that to make sense. For the snake in my abdomen to slither away and my taut muscles to calm, but it didn't.

The pain in my nose grew, my sinuses inflamed, my throat hoarse.

The blood in my veins flared silver for a brief second, alerting me to Marie's raised pulse, the thrashing of her heart. A sharp crisp pain formed in the back of my head and her pulse started to fade.

My feet hit the bathroom floor before I could comprehend that I portaled to her. She laid against the tile, her body limp, blood streaming from her nose and head, knees bruised, dust scattered everywhere. The sight was like a knife to my chest.

The snake slithered up my spine to apply its poisonous bite to my heart and fill my veins with its deadly venom. I was frozen in place, just staring down at her—scared. Terrified.

For this brief moment, I was a boy again, feeling helpless when the blood in my veins turned silver. A lost male when his father broke his trust. Alone, helpless, afraid.

I returned to myself and rushed to the ground, pulling out my dagger and cutting into each of my palms. I sliced into her arms, the blood slowly oozing out of her body like there was little left, and then I pushed light into her, giving her life.

Her veins lit up, but she didn't react, as if she was already too far gone to accept my magic.

"Wake up, Marie!"

She just laid there, her pulse still slow and barely beating.

"Marie, wake the fuck up!" I said, pushing more of my magic into her, willing to give her every part of me if she would just show me those soulless orbs one last time.

Nothing. No response. No movement. No obsidian eyes. Just Marie lying too fucking still on the cold floor.

"Please, Marie. You can't fucking die," I begged. I never begged but I would for her. I would strike a deal with the gods. Anything for her, my body for her, my life for her, my soul for her.

"Come on, Marie. Please. Please come back to me. Please wake up."

I pushed my whole fucking self into her, everything I had, light and dark, day and night, life and death, all of it into her. The dark to kill off the poison, the light to heal the body. Silver lighting her veins like starlight.

"Please, my Stéla."

Her muscles tensed, then twitched. A cough sounded and she turned over to start vomiting blood, food and mucus all over the dust covered floor.

The relief that filled me was better than any high I'd ever felt. When she was done puking, I pulled her into my arms. I couldn't give a fuck that she was covered in blood and vomit. I needed to hold her, needed to feel her rapidly beating pulse competing against my equally thundering one.

She quickly passed back out, but this time, to sleep, my brand not alerting me to her pending death anymore.

I stood, walking out of the bathroom, and going straight to the bed. I laid down with her wrapped tightly against my chest, breathing in the rancid smells that covered us. My adrenaline slowly seeped away, it had burned up my alcohol, so I was left sober and jolted.

There was no rainbow after the storm. Instead, a pause before another rolled right through me.

My eyes lined with tears, body beginning to tremble. I pulled Marie's sleeping body closer to me as my tears tracked down my cheeks. I knew no matter how tight I held her, she would never be connected to me more than the tangle of our limbs, but I needed to have some grasp on her for the moment.

I shuddered and twitched, whimpers crawling their way out of my trembling lips. I hadn't cried like this in years, and if I hadn't been rattled to my core, I'd probably try to keep the tears at bay.

I sat there drying it all out, my worry, my sorrow, my pain, my lust, my passion. I let any emotion I stored for her bleed out of my heart because I could never experience that again. I could never be attached to someone so reckless. Someone who yearned for death. Someone who was only here on borrowed time. Someone who'd leave me broken if I could never see her eyes again.

So I cried out all the feelings I had for her because they had no business being held within me. I was not hers, and she would never be mine. She was a pawn in my game and nothing else.

I let go of her, emotionally, and eventually physically. I got up, went down the hall and scrubbed myself clean, used magic to clean Marie the best I could, then called someone who owed me to come clean the bathroom until it sparked brighter than the little bird's skin.

FORTY-FOUR

Marie

*M*y eyelids were heavy, body stiff, acid staining my tongue. I opened my eyes to a graying room, the rolling clouds in the sky forecasting rain.

The creaks of my body sounded as I sat up, me immediately clutching my throbbing head and releasing a groan.

Ice clinked against glass, but it sounded like the large bronze bells casted away in towers that signaled time changing, the gongs splintering pain through my head and bouncing around in my mind.

"Here." Karnelian's deep soothing tone filtered through. He pushed the glass of water closer to me and my exhausted limbs grasped the cup, spilling a little before bringing the refreshing water to my lips.

I sipped on the drink a bit before I gained the strength to raise my head and meet Karnelian's eyes, flinching when they reflected cold and distant.

Images from the past night filtered through my mind. Karnelian leaving. My heart aching at the thought of him being with another. The guilt of betraying my mate with my feelings for Karnelian. Dust, a lot of dust, then nothing… absolutely nothing.

My soul was quiet, as if it knew what it did was wrong. I didn't know what happened in the depths of the nothingness from last night to now, but her screams were gone. It was still shattered and its shards still poked at the edge of my being, but it was still, quiet, and taking a step back, leaving me here to clean up the mess it made.

"Karnelian, I—"

"Drink the water, Marie." His voice was firm, commanding in a way that didn't hold demand. As if his words were law and they were to be followed without question.

My creature knew its place from the notes of his tone, so I brought the drink to my mouth, slowly gulping back the cold liquid until the glass was empty.

He took the cup, placing it on the bedside table. My eyes zeroed in on the other glass that sat there as his hand clasped around it. This one was filled with red liquid, iron wafting my way as it came closer.

"Is that…" I whispered, saliva gathering in my mouth, my creature propelling me forward, my aching bones the only thing keeping me from not snatching the glass.

"It's mine, not human."

As soon as the glass was near enough for me to reach, I came alive snatching the glass and draining the contents, my core pulsing at the taste of Karnelian's blood, being able to connect to the primal parts of me, making me grow heavy with need.

A need that was quickly dispelled with Karnelian's cutting words. "If you need more, tell me. Your creature probably feels quite erratic after almost dying. Hopefully, this will calm it enough to prevent you from acting out again."

The edge to his voice had my creature drawing inside me to hide away with my soul. Both of the fuckers leaving me alone to deal with Karnelian's cold steely demeanor.

He took the glass from me. "You can't have any more dust."

I sighed, eyes down cast in submission. "I know. I'm sorry. I jus—"

"No, I mean, I altered the magic of the brand. If you try to snort it, drink it, touch it, the brand will stop you."

A shiver traveled down my spine when my eyes connected to his. "Karnelian, it was an—"

"I don't give a fuck what it was. You almost died and you're not fucking dying until I get my crown and you produce an heir."

I flinched at his harsh tone. Karnelian wasn't even angry, he was reserved, but somehow his withdrawal had a tightness developing in my chest. "I'm sorry. Can I just explain what happened?"

"No."

"No?"

"There's no need for you to do so." He straightened his suit jacket. "Stay in bed today, Rico will bring you your meals. Eat everything he gives you." Another law I must follow. "I'll be at the palace today, and back late."

Then he was gone without another word.

The day was spent watching the rain fall through the windows. Every meal was soup, besides a witch's brew. It was a cleansing tincture that had me visiting the bathroom every hour. The rain let up mid-afternoon but since it was technically winter the sun was already cresting the horizon. The brew, soups and my healing body left me exhausted and I spent most of the evening trying not to fall asleep. I wanted to wait for Karnelian, maybe to try to smooth things over but mostly in fear of haunted dreams. By the time the moon was high in the sky, Karnelian had yet to arrive, and I eventually succumbed to slumber's pull.

It was late in the night when I woke again. Nightmare-less because Karnelian's form occupied the bed. He slept on the edge, facing away from me, an ache forming in my heart.

Karnelian always cuddled me. Even when he was being distant last week, he still held me. He knew I enjoyed it. We spent tons of our time just cuddling in bed, but now he was taking it away.

A memory formed in my mind, a time when I slept facing away from my mate, ignoring him as punishment. But Karnelian wasn't a mated teenager, he didn't do games. Everything he did was clear, bold, and clean.

This action was a grand seal on a petition, a law being passed to incite change. Things from now on would not be as they were between us, and it panicked me, leaving me with intense regret.

My anxiety only worsened as the days passed.

I thought Karnelian was distant before, but he was still there, still giving me him and subtly keeping our bond alive. Now, the only bond we had was one bound from blood. Another one of the devil's deals he had responsibility for. He didn't talk to me unless necessary, often treating me like one of his henchmales, using hand gestures to tell me to go sit in the corner with Fredrick as he did business. He didn't kiss me, hug me, or even hold my hand. The ache in my heart, desperation, and sorrow had me trying once but he pulled away, and the sting of rejection didn't have me trying again.

My creature was ever frightened, the submissive nature of it being challenged. It had laid a claim to Karnelian and couldn't accept his estrangement. I rarely slept anymore, spending the nights staring at his back as terror filled my lungs and I was unable to breathe.

The day came for him to fuck me, and I didn't deny him. The panic state of my beast had me in some sort of survival mode and I would do anything to gain rapport with Karnelian.

Sex was what first connected us. Intimacy something established within seconds of our first kisses, our bodies able to speak to another without words, our beast able to find harmony.

But there was no harmony found from this encounter, instead it left us in a state of asymmetry.

"Sit." Karnelian gestured to the bed.

It was mid-day, the king had called for lunch, and Karnelian grabbed me and portalled us here. A calculation I hadn't planned for. I had hoped that we'd wait for night, but Karnelian had proven to me that I was expertly naïve.

With night, one could fall in the shadow of another. But with day, the light kept one from slipping, they were able to see, able to maneuver themselves in the direction they wanted.

I stared up at him, our eyes touching for the first time in over a week before he averted his and gestured for me to lie back.

On his knees, he spread my legs out, pulling me to the edge of the bed. My skirt was short, my legs mark-less and left no reason for me to suffer the Seelie heat anymore.

The act of him moving my panties to the side was mechanical and stiff, the uneasiness only worsening as he started eating me out.

Karnelian was exceptionally skilled at this. His technique probably perfected after years of tweaking. He ate me out like he was trying to scrape out my soul with his tongue. I would always come so hard I was sure he had accomplished the job and I was indeed left soulless. There was no soul stealing at this moment because there was no one who wanted to steal my soul. No passion, just technique, making my body react but my heart bruised at the hollowness of his performance.

He continued, even though no moans left my mouth, truly not caring for my enjoyment, only here to get a job done. When I was wet enough, he stopped, stood and flipped me to lie on my stomach, placing a few pillows under my hips so my ass was lifted.

His belt unclasped, jingling about as he undid the ties of his trousers. I felt the heat of him against my thighs before his cock was at my entrance.

With his size, it always hurt when he entered me. Karnelian made the pain pleasurable before, hurting me just right so it turned me on. Now, the pain as he split me open with is cock was nothing like that, it just hurt, the pain mixing with the agony of my tearing heart.

His thrusts were slow, and careful, as to cause the least amount of pain until my body had fully submitted to his intrusion. Then his movements were fast, his cock angled perfectly to send waves of pleasure rolling throughout my body, like he knew exactly where it was.

The pleasure felt outside of me. I was detached from myself, dissociating from the action as my body started to react. I didn't make a sound as my walls squeezed around him. I didn't bury my head in sheets, nor did my claws cut into the mattress. Karnelian didn't groan as his seed started to spill into me, his fingers didn't flex around my hips, nor did he give last little thrusts trying to extend his pleasure.

He pulled out quickly, rearranging my panties before I heard the motions of him redoing the ties to his pants and buckling to his belt.

We didn't even remove our clothes, like this was truly just some deal to be dealt with.

I didn't move. My body feeling wrong, my heart a throbbing wound. Tears pooled in my eyes. Shudders built in my middle, spreading out until I was burying my face into the mattress and sobbing.

My tears were filled with regret, a mix of hating myself for what I did and wishing Karnelian would forgive me for the clear mistake. It took me many moments before I was able to push myself up, turning behind me to see no one was there.

"Marie?" Karnelian called when he portaled back to the room hours later.

I shifted so he could hear I was in the closet, and his footsteps grew closer until his body filled the frame.

"What are you doing?"

I walked past him into the room, laying the clothes in my hands on the bed, next to my open suitcase that was already half filled with my things.

"Marie." I've never hated my name until now. More so, I hated my name on his lips. I missed the pet names he had for me, little bird, baby, Stéla. Names I hadn't heard in way too long. I would even be okay if he called me pup, just anything but Marie.

"Marie, what are you doing?" His voice wasn't angry, something I also hated. If he was angry at me, he would still care, but instead, he was calm, his voice critical and vacant.

"I want you to take me to my parents," I said.

"Why do you need all your things to go to your parents?"

I sniffled, an attempt to not start bawling again like I had all afternoon when I discovered he left me. "You don't want me here."

"When did I say that?"

"You didn't have to say it. It's clear you'd rather not have me around, or be forced to fuck me, or even look at me."

"Marie..." A tiny hint of vulnerability entered his tone, but a deep frustrated breath followed after. "Tell me when you're ready," he said, tone firm and dull without a hint of care.

My lip wobbled as I continued packing. It was frustratingly hard to keep my tears back as Karnelian just stood there watching me. Embarrassment edged those tears further, as I packed his nightshirts covered with his scent because I still wanted him even if he didn't want me.

When I was done, Karnelian grabbed the suitcase before I could. Eager to have me out of his impeccable hair.

He grabbed my wrist—not my hand—and then we were at the entrance of my father's manor.

He let go of me, knuckles preparing to knock on the door.

"I'm sorry," I whispered.

He stopped mid-air, muscles tensing.

There was a silent pause that became clear he wasn't going to fill so I spoke again. "I wasn't trying to kill myself. I just... I just..." I took a deep breath in.

He turned to me, eyes clashing with mine, cold and careless. "You what?"

I was starting to feel more for you, and it freaked me out. I didn't say that. I couldn't—shouldn't, so I said, "I wasn't thinking. It was a mistake that I regret and I'm sorry."

His nod was curt, callous. "Again, you don't need to apologize. You want to die. You want to return to your precious mate. I know that, and I'll make sure you can have that. When the war finally starts, I'll hunt Markos down and kill him so you can rise to the throne. As for a babe, hopefully your heat comes back in time, and then I'll kill you myself after they are born."

His words were knives cutting into me, making me suck in a shuddering breath before replying, "You're denied from your duties to me for the foreseeable future." Originally, I planned to deny him for a month, stupidly hoping time would fix this, but it was clear he was never going to forgive me, never going to let things return to how they used to be between us.

Karnelian's nostrils flared, his eyes boring into me. "Okay. It's your responsibility to get the babe, then." Then he turned to knock on the door, body stiff and annoyed.

"You don't have to come in. I can carry the bag or my father can."

Another curt nod and he set my suitcase down, then he was gone, portaling without even saying goodbye.

My breath was shaky as I raised my hand and knocked, my body trembling as I waited for my father to answer so I could run up to my room and cry.

My father didn't answer the door.

A blue ice-like shimmer glistened as tears filled my vision. A blurry image of my mother's face coming into my view.

My strength.

My rock.

My soil.

I crumbled into her arms and she caught me, her rose scent wrapping around me as a well of tears poured out of me.

FORTY-FIVE

CORIVINA

$\mathcal{D}$arius appeared beside me, gesturing to take Marie from me. I let him take her and pull her up into his arms as I went for her suitcase. Karnelian's scent lingered in the air, letting me know he just dumped her here on our doorstep like discarded trash. If my babe wasn't bawling in my husband's arms right now, I'd find him and cut his balls off for messing with my little girl, but she needed me here first.

I followed them up to her room, Darius laying her in the bed and stepping away for me to take the space. Darius would have stayed if Marie needed to cry, that was what he did. Held you while you cried, but we both knew Marie had cried enough and she needed me. She needed someone to talk to, someone to uplift her.

I hesitated for a second before climbing into bed. I didn't know if I could do that. I had spent the past five years avoiding this. How could I tell her to be strong when I wrecked her. How could I give her advice on how to handle this pain when I was barely handling it myself.

She cried for a few moments, clutching me tightly. Each shudder from her cut into me and threatened to break my wall.

The wall that has been keeping me from her.

I didn't want my darkness to be cast over my flower, but she had a darkness of her own, and for me to ease it, I had to push mine out the way, there couldn't be a wall between us. Not anymore.

My eyes drifted over to Darius who sat in the corner. Over the last weeks, a truce had naturally formed between us. We rarely spoke, but we didn't avoid each other. I started cooking dinner again and we ate together in a calm silence. If we did talk, it was of war plans or trainings. We both knew we were going to have to talk about what had happened a few weeks ago but the rising tension from the border closing busied us.

Marie's cries diminished and I brushed the hair stuck to her tear-stained face away. "What is the matter, flower?"

She whimpered; another set of tears preparing to fall.

"Marie, tell me what's wrong." Her sorrow wasn't heavy, it wasn't filled with demolishing torment that had become the norm for her. She wasn't a destroyed female in this moment. No, in this moment, she was the girl I had known for nineteen years.

"I..." She hiccupped. "I ruined it."

"Ruined what?"

She shuddered. "Karnelian."

"What happened?"

"I... hurt myself." Shame coated each word, and I was able to decipher that she had another one of her accidents. "I promised him I wouldn't, but I did and then he didn't want me anymore." Her words started to slur into sobs, and I pulled her closer to me, offering comfort.

"My flower." I kissed her head. "It will be fine."

"It won't. He doesn't care anymore."

I snorted. "He does."

"No, he doesn't."

"My babe, he wouldn't have gotten mad at you if he didn't care."

"He wasn't mad. He… He just became nothing. He offered me nothing. He wouldn't even look at me."

"Marie, tell me exactly what you did."

She took in a deep breath, hesitating. "He said he was going to sleep with someone else and I didn't react well."

"Hmm."

Marie could hear the criticism in my tone and replied, "It's a part of the deal. Our relationship isn't real. He deserves to be able to find love."

"But?"

"But… I have feelings for him." She then detailed what had been going on between her and Karnelian. I listened without judgment, knowing she needed me not to offer any judgment as she talked. Though it was clear she had forgotten her father was in the room, because she left no detail out, including her sex life with Karnelian. "I have feelings for him. I told him not to have feelings for me, but I still started to fall for him. It just became clear in that moment and my feelings scared me, consuming me with guilt for betraying my mate."

I pulled her into the crook of my neck, my head falling over hers. "I feel guilt too."

"For?"

"I feel guilty that I was never able to open up to you, to your father." I couldn't uphold that wall anymore. Not in this moment. I didn't care if Darius heard my confessions to Marie. They both deserved them. They both deserved more, and I hoped they'd get it. Marie with Karnelian, Darius with… "If I had told you about Markos, your mate would still be alive, and you'd be happy."

She was quiet for a painful moment, the silence cutting into me with shame and remorse for what my actions had caused her. "I don't blame you, Mother. He hurt you."

"I know you would never blame me." Though I still felt a tiny bit of relief from her condonement. "But that doesn't stop the thoughts from spinning, flower. And my shame made me shield away from you… from everyone and now I have more things to be guilty about."

"Like?"

My chuckle was small and filled with sadness. "Letting my need for revenge ruin every beautiful thing I had, being your mother, being a wife to a male who I will love till I die. My guilt, shame and fear, ruined those things for me, but you don't have to let it ruin things for you. Karnelian made you happy, didn't he?"

"Yes, but my mate—"

"Is dead, Marie. He isn't here and holding on to him makes you a ghost. I'm not saying to forget him, but Karnelian makes you feel alive. He makes you smile. He is the person that gets you through the day, and you shouldn't feel guilt that he does. You're forced to live, but you shouldn't be forced to live in pain."

"Karnelian isn't going to forgive me."

"Probably not right now, no. He needs time. If I had found you like that, I would've been ripped into pieces. He probably feels betrayed, confused, threatened. He needs time to deal with that. Give him that time, but not too much time. You are the one who is in the wrong, my flower. You need to be the one to make it up to him." I almost laughed at myself for how easy it was for me to see her problems so clearly, but I couldn't do that to myself until it was too late.

"How am I supposed to do that?"

"Tell him how you feel."

"What if he doesn't feel the same?"

I snorted. She was always obvious to males being obsessed with her. This was her at Eighteen again confessing to me about how she was in love with Kolvin and she thought he wasn't interested. "He does. It's clear in the way he looks at you. You're the sun to him, the star that he orbits, the thing that gives him life."

She nodded, her arms wrapping around me tighter. "Thank you, and you didn't ruin everything. Even destroyed, I will always be your flower, Mother. I will love you forever."

I kissed her head, taking in a deep breath of her scent. It was always easy with her. I had forgotten just how easy it was to be her mother, how right it felt. How she was truly a gift from the gods, making my life feel worth something. "I will love you forever too."

"Mother?"

"Yes?"

"Could you cook something for me?"

A smile lined my lips, the ache in my cheeks a reminder that I probably hadn't shown a real one far longer than her. "Of course."

We all headed to the kitchen. Marie and Darius took up seats at the island and I started gathering things for a grilled cheese and tomato soup—Marie's favorite rainy-day meal. There was no rain in the air, but the atmosphere was quiet, calm, mellow.

Marie and Darius talked about her progression in magic as I cooked.

When the meal was ready, I pulled up the chair next to Marie and we ate at the island together as a family. It felt normal between us, like it used to be, but it was a reminder that even back then, things were off.

After the meal, Marie went to bathe, leaving me and Darius to clean up.

"Corivina," he said, handing me the last dish.

I turned, a brow raised.

"Did you mean what you said in there?"

He didn't clarify but I didn't need him to. I knew him better than myself, was connected to him more than any other person. "If I could go back and change things, I would, but I can't."

"You can't." He looked down at the empty sink, eyes flickering with thoughts. "I will too."

"You will too?"

Placing the last dish to dry on the rack, he turned, heading out the room. "I will love you till the day I die."

FORTY-SIX

Karnelian

*A*nother fucking family dinner, the second this month. Today was the Winter Solstice, so technically it wasn't a family dinner, but same room, same table, same people. Only difference was my father had decorated the dining room for Solstice. Green garland twinging around gold decals. The stink of pine staining my nostrils and reminding me of her.

Drinks had been served, meals eaten, the only thing keeping me here was the wait for everyone to open their presents.

We stood around a solstice tree, everyone in the room—excluding myself—cheery and exuding glee. Giddy for the gift they'd gotten.

I wanted to yell at all of them. The thousandth scraping sensation across my palm, pushing me to teeter on the edge of acting on my urge. We weren't fucking babes or faelings. We were the richest people in the territory who could buy all these meaningless gifts on a whim.

"Karnelian?" My mother's voice filtered through my raged state.

A flock of waiting gazes perched on me.

My breath in did nothing to loosen the tightness in my chest, and the up tip to my lips was more grimace than a grin. "Everyone can have one deal, free on my part."

Drix groaned. "Seriously, Karney? A deal? Did you even bother to try and get us presents?"

Sipping on my sixth whiskey for the night—six becoming my new normal—I was definitely tempted to stretch it to seven tonight. "I've been a bit busy."

Haunting emerald eyes rolled with the cross of his arms. "Fine. For my deal, I would like you to bring the little bird to the palace during war play tomorrow. I miss her."

Tension pulled my shoulder blades together. The chant—*I love my brother, I love my brother, I love my brother*—keeping me from breaking his nose and staining his stupid emerald jumpsuit with blood. "I can't control other people, *Fredrick*."

Drix's look leveled in annoyance. He had been very insistent this last month that people called him Drix, and all but my father obliged. "She is your fiancée. You could just ask her."

That would require talking to her, something I was keen on avoiding.

As if he could read my mind, he then stated, "Just talk to her! She will probably say yes if you tell her it's for me. She *loved* me."

The phantom cut across my palm drew my free hand into a fist, my chant becoming quieter and quieter as the sensation continued to scour the area.

My father cut in, his voice adding to my agitation. "Fredrick, you are supposed to be helping with the *war efforts*. Not mixing drinks for a female who shouldn't even be in the room."

The crack in my neck was audible as my eyes snapped to my father. "Why shouldn't she be in the room?" I said, voice quiet but deadly.

My father didn't balk but his body still stiffened a hair. His creature alerted to a pending attack. "She doesn't know anything about war. The less who know of our plans, the better. I'm not saying that she would betray us, but who knows who she might slip the information—"

"Shut the fuck up," I growled. "Everyone needs to just shut the fuck up. Let's just get on with the stupid fucking presents so I can leave."

Slender fingers graced my arm and I jerked, connecting with my mother's huge doe-like eyes. "Let's go for a walk." Her voice was soft, motherly, and brought my monster to a heel.

My nod was more of a jerk, and she started out the dining room, me following close behind.

We walked in silence, my mother leading, steps light, energy peaceful as she always seemed to be. She was truly my father's opposite, the light to his dark. I thought my parents were—

I shook my head, not wanting to think of it, focusing on the clanking of my shoes on the marble floor as we walked up a few flights of stairs.

My mother finally stopped in front of golden double doors. Doors that were once a beacon to me when I was a faeling.

The doors opened to the saltwater pool my father made for my mother when she was pregnant with me. The pool I learned to swim in. The pool I practiced my backstroke in. The pool my family would spend free mornings in before any chaos had entered my life.

My mother walked to the edge and toed off her shoes, sitting down and letting her feet grace the water.

She turned to me, her chestnut hair streaked with blond strands flowing over her shoulder. She tapped the ground next to her, just two light taps, a suggestion never a command.

I walked over, removed my shoes and socks, rolled the ends of my trousers up and sat down, relief spreading through my body as the water touched my skin.

"It's an idiotic ideology that fae view themselves as two separate beings," my mother stated, eyes on the water. "We are beasts. We are not separated from that side of ourselves. It is us, and it needs to be nurtured or it will drive us to insanity."

"I know this, Mother," I said, swaying my legs back and forth, feeling the water glide through my toes.

She turned to me, her expression caring with a twinge of pity. "Then why are you being an idiot?"

"How am I being an idiot?"

"*The female*. You love her."

I dismissed the statement immediately with a shake of my head. "I don't love her. I have—*had* feelings for her, but they weren't love."

She scoffed. "Karnelian, I am your mother. I know my little boy better than he knows himself." Her fingers reached up to pinch my cheek.

I brushed her fingers away. "I'm not a boy anymore."

"But he still lives inside you. Just because you grew up and became a male doesn't mean that the boy died. He's in there, and he's in love, but the stupid male who ignores him is afraid to love."

"Are you reading my aura? It's cheating if you can sense out what I'm feeling."

"So you admit you're scared?" She grinned, eyes twinkling with triumph.

My brows turned down as I threw an annoyed look at her. "How could I not be scared to fall for someone who is not only mated and in love with someone else, but wants to die? That is idiotic, Mother. Which is why I put a stop to it."

"They call it falling in love because once you start, you cannot stop."

My lips pressed together in frustration. "Well, I never started falling. I just thought I could."

"You can't lie to me, Karnelian. I'm not your father." She smiled, and I reflected her with a frown. "I was there the day you first met her."

Confusion colored my face. "You weren't there when I put the brand on her."

"No." She rolled her eyes. "I know you know what I am talking about. The first day you met her *before she was mated*. I saw the way you looked at her. You were hooked then, falling for a female you talked to for three seconds."

The whispers sounded then, flowing with the rhythm of the cutting sensation inside my hand, calling me back to that night.

6 YEARS AGO.

Summer Solstice was a sabbat I truly didn't care for. Unlike Winter Solstice, where gifts were exchanged, the Summer Solstice was just a festival to celebrate the light. Which my father took to throwing a party inside the palace before a lantern lighting ceremony that symbolized a way to keep the day going when the light finally left on the longest day of the year.

The Seelie went all out for it, decorating everything in flowers and gold, even themselves. My father's party even had a dress code: everyone must be dressed in gold—especially me.

I have tried to go around it every year since my title changed to the Silver Blooded Devil, but my father told me he would kick me out of Charlotte if I showed up not wearing gold. He spent months planning the Summer Solstice parties and if I ruined it by being the only one in black, he'd follow through with his threat.

My back was pressed against the bar. There were gold glitters in my whiskey and Grayson was flirting with my mother.

Why put gold into a drink? It was a waste. With heightened senses, one could taste every fleck of metal in the two-hundred-year-old whiskey, just ruining the divine experience of the drink.

My mother laughed at whatever Grayson said, furthering my misery at being back here in Seelie after spending a year in Unseelie. The residual emotions spilling out her aura let me know she was enjoying his flirts, which was just fucking gross. Grayson and I were the same age, sorted at the same time and have known each other since the first day of training. My mother was only twenty-five years older than us, and age didn't really matter to the fae as long one was old enough to be sorted—which was the age of eighteen—but still it was gross.

I knew Grayson was just vying for attention, his way of coping after returning from having to deal with his father while we were away. He was never serious about females, he was never serious about life, nor was his little sister who was currently suffering at the hand of his father's cruelty. They were both whores for attention, and they'd do anything for it. So I knew his flirts were completely harmless, but still disgusting.

The only reason I was suffering through the gold flecked whiskey was in an attempt to numb out my mother's aura.

As I sipped on it, trying to avoid the metal the best I could, my eyes caught on a female.

She was short, extremely short. Her skin was caramel, that naturally shimmered gold as the light danced against her bare shoulders. Her sundress fit perfectly against her curves. It flowed with her body, and led the eyes to her bare legs, showing more of her soft and creamy skin that had my cock stiffening as my eyes trailed over her.

She sensed my gaze across the room, our eyes connecting. My chest tightened as a slow smile played on her lips. That smile made her a thousand times more beautiful, bringing a weakness to my knees.

She's the one.

The one.

A fae ideology, though other species believed in it as well. The belief was that there was a person who wasn't your soulmate, but you came to this life to live with them, to meet them, to spend time with them, to learn with them.

I thought it was a silly thing fae made up to make their current partners feel special. Mostly because, when I was younger, my father told me my mother was his one. I believed him because he looked at her like she was his personal sun. But then they split shortly after I sorted, and my father quickly started taking other females to his bed. So, I ceased to believe in it after that.

But as I stared into the black eyes of the female with the cute button nose that I strangely wanted to nip at, it kept whispering in my head.

She's the one.
She's the one.
She's the one.

My feet were moving without consciousness, walking towards her because I had to meet her, I had to know her, had to learn with her.

Two feet away from her—two feet I prematurely wanted to close—a smirk lined my lips, and blush tinted her cheeks.

"Hi." Her eyes flicked to the floor as she tucked a curl behind her ear.

My canine grazed my lip, my cock thickening more at her clear nervousness. No female ever had me hardening from just the look of them. "What's your name?"

Her eyes met mine once again, and that smile brightened more. "Marie."

Marie. Something about the name rang true in my chest. True to my monster, true to my being, true to my soul.

She's the one.

I held out my hand which her claw tipped fingers delicately slipped into. "Nice to meet you, *Marie.*"

Her nose perked up, her cheeks growing deeper in color. "What's your name?"

There was hesitancy to my answer. Thoughts to lie, so as not to scare her away. It was clear she was a soft female, her aura bubbly but still calm. But I couldn't bring myself to lie to her. "Karnelian."

Her hand still held mine, like I was an extension of her, like it felt perfectly natural for our hands to be clasped as such. "Uh, you're the prince." Her teeth found purchase into her bottom lip, eyes sparkling just like her skin.

Not the devil—*the prince.*

Then she did something even more unexpected, she bowed. Something no one had done in a while.

Her head came too close to my swollen cock. I was sure the outline was visible through these stupid gold trousers, but luckily her eyes stayed locked on mine as she lowered. Beautiful dark browns, soft but sensual, perfect to drown in.

She's the one.

"Sorry," she said as she straightened. "I... um... didn't know what you looked like."

That gave me pause. There were only two reasons a fae wouldn't know who I was: she wasn't from here and just sorted Seelie this past eclipse—improbable because I gave a lecture to the new students after their first year here and would have met her then—or she was due to be sorted at the next solar eclipse in about a year. She could be twenty-one, or she could be even younger... sixteen.

"How old are you?" The thought of me hinting on a sixteen-year-old had my stomach in a twist, but she was...

Before she could answer, her hand was snatched out of mine and Corivina Foxglove—the commander's wife—was before me. A sneer painted on her elegant face. "She's seventeen."

The resemblance was barely there, but it was there. The shimmer. The claws. The button nose. Corivina was her mother.

I knew the drama between her and the commander over the past years. It was big gossip at the time because technically it was illegal to kill humans, though not a soul policed it—especially against someone as respected as Darius Foxglove.

"I turn eighteen in a month, Mother," Marie said as her eyes flicked to mine, her face covered in shame. Cute, innocent, nowhere near ready to be with a male as damaged as me.

Corivina glared at me. "And even in a month, you still are not going to come near a male who calls himself *the devil*."

I raised my hands in surrender, missing them wrapped around Marie's. "Corivina, it's nice to see you again as always. You have perfected that glare since we last met."

"When we last met, you were at a bar gambling away all my husband's money."

"He's shit at games without you whispering in his ear. You shouldn't have let him go out alone."

She crossed her arms, narrowing her eyes. "Stay away from my daughter. She's off limits to you, I don't want her becoming one of your conquests. If I have to make a deal to make that happen, then I will."

"I may be the devil, but I'm not a perv."

Her brow raised, her face broadcasting her disbelief.

Smile wide, my canines flashing, I said, "Have a good day, Corivina."

I took one last look at Marie, our eyes connecting and fixing to another, the whisper going off again.

She is the one.

Maybe, but not right now.

"I watched you that night," my mother said, bringing my mind back to the present. "You never go for females, never. They always come to you, but you went to her. You looked at her like you were already in love." She patted my shoulder. "You didn't sleep with another female for almost a whole year after, and rarely did you take one to your bed after because deep down, you were waiting for her."

"It's alarming that you know when I fuck someone."

"You always scrub them off after and the smell of powdery soap throws off your scent. That, and Grayson couldn't keep a secret if his life depended on it."

I frowned at my mother. "It kind of does. He is my second. He sorts my deals."

She rolled her eyes. "You know what I mean. The male enjoys gossiping and causing drama."

"Exactly why are you sharing *his* bed again?"

"Don't change the subject. You've had your eye on this female for a while, and a part of you has been waiting for the universe to bring you together."

What my mother said wasn't exactly true. I didn't intend to wait for her. I didn't, but she was all I could think about for months, and no other female could compare. I would—at the very least—pump my cock once daily to the thought of her, and it satisfied me more than any female ever did. It wasn't a conscious effort for me to look for her at my father's parties, but I did. Or ask if the commander was to attend, but I did.

It took me a year to stop obsessing over her when I never saw her. Another few months to enter another female's bed. I pushed her as far back into my mind as I could, but I still kept her there, thinking of her at random times.

Then Prince Levington was announced with a mate born from Seelie and she was to visit and be received by the commander on Samhain. Curious, I went, standing invisible to others under the cover of my magic.

What I hadn't heard was that his mate was the commander's daughter. No, that relation was quickly made when she was stopped by twin blades' hand outstretched toward Darius. Levington not allowing her to even hug her father.

There she was, my one with her neck covered with marks from her mate.

She looked beautiful in black, but miserable with a tiara hanging heavy on her head. I didn't stay longer to see what would come of the situation, disappointment covering my being. I had felt stupid holding out hope that she was actually my one.

It was only two short months later that I saw her again, face stained with tears, recounting her mate's death. Her eyes cold and lifeless, the whispers loud and screaming.

She's the one.

Something I tried to deny.

"She is my one," I whispered.

She was. A fact grained into my being. My soul came here to be with her. Even though her soul was bound to another's and she was his, I came here to be hers.

My mother nodded. "It's looking that way."

"You're not a witch."

"No, but I am not an idiot like you. You are in love with her. You should be with her. *You are supposed to be with her*. She is the one who nourishes your soul, makes your heart beat, your mind race. Your beast is miserable without her, and you are making others around you miserable. You had Grayson miss three of our dates to go over the recipes for the war meals. You don't even know how to cook, Karnelian."

"Why are you not with my father if he is supposed to be your one?"

My mother didn't balk, just smiled with an energy that made her feel younger than me but still so much wiser than me. "Ones are not mates; they are more so lessons. They all teach us different things and we teach them. Your father taught me what I needed to know, and I refuse to stay with someone who would hurt my babe—even if I love him. Has he learned what he needed? I do not know, and I do not care, if the gods make us spend another life together so he does learn that lesson, that is out of my hands." Her hand came up to my cheek, her thumb caressing back and forth against my skin. "You're destined to be with her and it's clear that's all you want."

I stared at the glistening pool, thinking of the ocean. The depths that you could get lost in. The pull in my chest to drown in them, until my soul was hers. "I can't be with her. I am going to lose her."

"You already love her, Karnelian. If she dies, it will still hurt. Right now, she makes you happy, and you haven't been happy in a long time, my babe." She combed a few strands of my hair back.

I nodded, unraveling my fist, tracing over the phantom cut that flared against my palm.

"What's the matter?"

A small snort left me, knowing my mother could feel my indecision in my aura. "She wants me to come to her."

"Then go."

FORTY-SEVEN

MARIE

*M*y claw slid across my palm, the act more of a coping mechanism than a calling. There was no piercing into my flesh or blood spilling down my hand, his brand preventing me from doing so.

There was still pain deep inside my chest, an ache in my scream-less soul, tears dressing my swollen face, and tension in my trembling body. I craved comfort, haven, foundation. I craved Karnelian.

He said if I attempted to cut my palm, he'd come. If it was a month ago, I knew he would have been here the second my claw touched my palm. Not after hours of useless attempts.

Even if it was fruitless, I didn't have the strength to stop. My being still hadn't faced the fact that he probably wasn't going to come. That he didn't want to come. But I was desperately deprived, and I just needed to see him, hear his voice, breathe in his scent, feel his body against mine.

I attempted a cut across the unmarred skin, a sob bubbling from me when no one appeared.

"Please," I whispered, trying it again. "*Please.*"

The tremble in my body bubbled to tremors, a sob scraping out of me as I fell into a fit of tears. My face buried into the pillow, the wet fabric clinging to my skin, my air lessening as the pillowcase was sucked into my mouth with each shuddering breath, suffocating me, but this time I hadn't the desire to die. My soul didn't beg for it, it stayed stoic and silent. Been silent since I woke from my accident. The quiet more tortuous than any of its screams, a punishment worse than pain. Without the torment, I was left with nightmareless dreams. Instead, I had dreams of a blond male.

"I can't live without you," I cried, my words not directed toward my mate.

Just today, I just needed him today. Then I'd give him the space he needs; I would go back to attempting to get through the day without him. Just today.

I pressed my claw as hard as I could before the brand stopped me. Ready to try again, but then his voice filtered through.

"I'm here, baby."

His scent—more whiskey than cinnamon—hit me first, perking up my beast. I turned to see his tall frame, loomed over my bed.

A sob of relief broke loose before I pounced, throwing off the covers and rushing to him. I greedily breathed in, dragging him onto the bed. I pushed him on his back, straddling his waist, my shaking fingers rushing to unbutton his tunic.

"Woah, little bird." Karnelian attempted to stop me, but I didn't let him, my beast fully in control.

My vision was filled with a clear expanse of tanned muscle adorned with a black eclipse tattoo. My face buried into it. Hot, taut skin rubbing against my cheek.

I purred. It wasn't forced but automatic. My creature happy to be submerged into this chest, a place that had become a second home to me.

Tears dripped from my eyes and pooled onto his skin, my whimpers bouncing off his chest and echoing back into my ears.

My crying wasn't agony filled, each sob was relief, like I could finally breathe. My tears cleaned everything out of me until there was no note of sorrow holding me down, and I was just breathing in him, clutching him.

Karnelian's hand brushed along my back, up and down in hypnotically lulling strokes. He started when the first sob appeared and continued far after they left. He was just there, holding me, being everything I needed, because that was who he was.

He wasn't my drug anymore. No, he was my source for life, my air, my food, my sun, my moon, the eclipse over my tormented soul.

He was the reason for her silence, I don't know exactly why or how I knew, but I did.

I rose a bit, letting the moonlight that streamed through the curtains guide me to the tattoo. My finger, flowing through the motion that was practically ingrained into my being. My personal grounding practice, each swipe connecting me back to this world.

"It's Winter Solstice," I whispered.

My eyes stayed locked on the tattoo, but the small shift in the bed let me know of his nod. "It is."

"Officially five years without him." The emotions started to boil up again and I laid my head back down on his chest, taking tentative sips of his scent. "I'm sorry I called you, I just needed you today."

"I'm sorry I didn't come sooner. I just…" His chest moved with his deep inhalation. "You left."

I found his eyes that were more of a cloudy gray than his normal silvery green. "You left first."

His fingers tangled into my curls. "I had to. I couldn't stop, I tried to stop but I couldn't. I left in an attempt to force you out of me, but you're in there deep. Too fucking deep, Stéla."

"Stéla," I repeated. "What does it mean?"

"I told you to look it up." The tiniest smirk lined his lips, but it was enough to bring out his dimple.

"You could just tell me."

He shook his head, disconnecting our eyes. "I don't think I'll ever be able to say it out loud."

My brows furrowed, but he offered no explanation, the silence not filling his words either.

I slid off of him, finding my place against his side and started digging into the pocket of my slip. "I got you a present for Solstice."

"You did?"

"Yeah." I pulled the little piece of cardstock paper before handing it to him. "I know you don't wear jewelry, but I saw them and thought of you."

He angled the paper into the moonlight, the stud earrings flashing when the light hit them.

"They are little birds," I said.

"Are they steel?"

"No, real silver. They were way overpriced because of the sabbat but I wanted to get you something even if I didn't see you today."

Karnelian bent so he could kiss my forehead. "Thank you. I don't think anyone has ever given me a gift because they simply wanted to."

I moved up, fitting my nose against his, our lips millimeters apart. "You're welcome." I said before they connected in a kiss.

"I didn't get you a gift."

"It's okay, you've given me enough. More than."

"Everything I've given you was already yours."

My words were lost from me after hearing that. Unable to say that there were parts of me that were already his. He won me over piece by piece, every part of me except my soul.

"Do you want anything, little bird?"

You. I couldn't bring myself to say that, so instead, I said, "Can you take me to the snow?"

Outside the civilized fae territory, the weather wasn't controlled by fae energy but by nature. Wild fae roamed free through here, living as we were meant to as savage beasts who created chaos.

A silver magical shield surrounded us. Silver. The color fae should probably live by as that was the color created when dark mixed with light. The silver lining created through a partly cloudy sky.

The shield was a precaution. Wild fae weren't worse than civilized fae. They just lived in trees and hunted for food, the same beings just different lifestyles. They had the urge to play or trick just as Karnelian and I did, so the shield was necessary to keep them away.

My knees hit the slushy snow, water seeping through my silk slip. Karnelian's suit jacket rested over my shoulders as memories flicked through my mind.

Laughter was in the air, gravelly against sharp and sweet. Two kids, who just wanted to love another, played in the snow in the middle of the night. Their only cares are for another, their only worries for another.

The rabbit and the wolf.

A love story with a tragic end.

My gloveless fingers shifted through the fluffy snow. Tears clouded my vision and became icicles on my cheeks.

Karnelian sat down next to me, uttering no words, making no moves to comfort me, just sat there being with me as I grieved for my mate.

He let me mourn alone until my body trembled from the cold and he pulled me to straddle his warm body. His hands and magic lightly caressing me, warming up my skin.

My head found the crevasse of his neck, and I took time gathering myself to be able to finally speak. "I hate myself."

He pulled back and brushed the hair out of my face. "Why?"

"Because of you."

A small disheartening chuckle left him. "I tend to do that to people, little bird."

"No, I mean." I shook my head. "*Thank you*."

His features scrunched together, his head cocking to the side. "I'm confused. You're thanking me for making you hate yourself?"

I smiled, my first in a month. "I didn't want to live another day, not even another second before you came into my life and at times I still don't… But when you're around, my life is bearable." I snorted, chiding myself. "Not the most flattering thing, I know. But it's enough, more than enough, Karnelian. So, thank you."

"And why do you hate yourself?"

"Because… You shouldn't be anything to me and I shouldn't feel anything for you. It feels like I'm betraying him when I want you more than I should."

His eyes flared, his hand cupping my face. "You don't need to want anymore. I'm yours, Marie. Until death does us part, I'm yours." He pressed a light kiss to my lips, but I deepened it. An attempt to try and communicate what exactly I wasn't able to say.

His back found the snow, and a bubble of warmth surrounded us. My fingers undid his belt, his hands slid my slip up and then we were connected.

He wasn't my mate, but we were connected.

Not by a branching of our souls, but the willingness of our beings. He chooses me and I choose him, a hand out to grasp another, bound by the treads of our limbs.

Connected, but only in this life.

FORTY-EIGHT

CORIVINA

The zesty smells of beef stew wafted up my nose as I added a sprig of thyme to the mix. Footsteps sounded near and I turned my head to see Darius enter the kitchen.

"You going all out tonight?" he said as he took his normal seat at the kitchen island. A stack of papers was placed in front of him, and he began leafing through the contents.

"I'm just testing the recipe I want to cook for tomorrow."

He smiled down at his papers, his eyes not able to meet mine because they were glued to his work. With the borders closing, tension held in the air, people antsy for the fight. Darius was working from first light to late in the night. I knew he was exhausted, but he seemed to be handling it fine without any help from me.

"How is she?" Marie was my go-to safe topic to talk with Darius. She had officially moved in with Karnelian, and I was happy she was happy, but I also missed my flower. We talked once a week over the portal mirror, but I always cut it short, letting her go to spend time with Karnelian as I knew she wanted to. He made her smile, and I wanted her to smile.

"Good. She looks visibly better, you'll see what I mean tomorrow. Karnelian has a hard time concentrating when she and Fredrick are giggling in the corner while the rest of us are planning for the war. He loves her—a lot."

"He hasn't told her; she would have told me." I was grateful I knew that as the truth. Gaining that one part of Marie back was a divine blessing. I would never again take for granted being the one she consoled in. Never.

"Why would he tell a female who is mated to another male—who is afraid to even be with him—he loved her? If I were him, I would keep it to myself too."

A gnawing feeling settled over me and manifested with my bottom lip fitting under my teeth. He was that male. I knew he loved me. I knew a part of him wanted us to come back together, but we couldn't. We just… couldn't.

"When are we getting divorced?"

The papers crinkled, a burning sensation permeating the side of my face from Darius's gaze. "I was thinking we'd deal with that after the war, but if you're in a rush to go off and marry Dominick, then I'm sure we could expedite it." His voice was harsh, losing the calm, relaxed mood it held moments before.

My next words were constricted, but I pushed them out anyways. "We shouldn't wait. I mean, it's not like there's much to discuss."

"Not much to discuss," Darius repeated.

I tried to prepare myself before I met heated eyes, but they still seared through me, burning straight to my core. "Everything that was mine before the marriage will still be mine, and all that was yours will still be yours. I don't want your money. I have enough from the shop to get me by. I just think… it's not good for us to be holding out hope that this is magically just going to work because we love each other. It hasn't been working."

His eyebrows slanted, his jaw hardening with his anger. "You know why it hasn't been working."

The doorbell went off then and I began to remove my apron, but Darius interjected, "The maid will get it."

"Are you expecting company?"

"No, but we aren't changing the subject."

I nodded, knowing that this needed to happen so I could do what I needed.

"You aren't trying, Vina."

He was right so I didn't argue a fruitless point.

"Why? Why, if you love me as much as you say you do, don't you want to try and fix our marriage? Is being queen and married to a prick like Dominick more important than trying on us?"

"You used to love Dominick like a brother."

"Yeah, well, he tends to screw off the people who love him. Maggie, with trying to de-throne her child. Karnelian, with declaring a new heir. Fredrick, with the guilt of being the person used to hurt his brother, and me with trying to steal my wife."

"He isn't stealing me. I told you it's purely political."

He scoffed. "You're going to sleep in his bed, wear his mark, and ride his cock. You may even have his fucking babes. It seems to me like a real fucking relationship."

"I'm not interested in having more babes. I screwed up being a mother the first time, I'm not going to destroy another child."

A tense silence settled over the room. It was heavy, heavier than the weight of this conversation. I looked over to Darius, unable to stand the heaviness any longer, but instead of finding his eyes on me, I found them fixated on something behind me.

I registered the sounds of footsteps approaching the kitchen, then the smell of blood. My gaze landed on the entry seconds before the housekeeper walked in with a bouquet of roses.

Beautifully blushing pink roses once again covered in black blood, the vase clear and black liquid splashing in place of water.

"Mrs. Foxglove, these are for you." Her words distortedly entered my ears as I watched her set the roses down on my kitchen island, placing the card next to it before leaving the room.

The edges of my vision started to blacken as if the darkness was beginning to pull me under, and I stood there frozen, unable to keep it from happening as the roses dripped their blood on the kitchen island. My kitchen island.

I knew time had altered for me because before I knew, Darius stood, rushing over to the flowers, and opening the card.

"A rose for my raven, but one would never do. A dozen covered with who ceased to care for you. Another with whom she belongs to, and the last to leave for those who she withdrew."

Darius took a ragged breath. "What the fuck does that mean?"

Somehow, I was still able to find my voice. "You said the blood on the last batch of roses wasn't his?"

"Karnelian did a test. It was someone from Unseelie but, he has no idea who, or if they are dead or not."

"I received a rose, a single one."

"When?"

"About six months back. The night you asked for a divorce." My breath picked up, flowing in and out like crashing waves. "It was red, just left on the doorstep. I thought nothing of it and left it there on the porch."

"Who is someone who ceased to care for you?"

I shook my head, my mind blank, a flock of ravens riveting in my stomach and crawling up my spine. The only thing I could see was pink roses on my kitchen counter. Bloody pink roses on my kitchen counter.

The sizzling sound of water vaporizing to steam ripped my eyes from the sight, my stew, my perfect stew, boiling over. "Shit." I turned down the burner, moving the pan off the fire. My fingers shaky and trembling, boiling stew splashing out the pot and frying my luminescent skin. "Fuck."

The word came out with a sob, tears streaming down my face, and shudders emanating my frame.

Darius's hand wrapped around my waist, pulling my back into his front. "Hey." He petted my hair, as his other hand made comforting circles on my stomach in an attempt to battle with the ravens. "It's going to be fine."

"No, it's not. He sent those roses to our house, *after* the border closed. What if he's the one who delivered them? What if he's here? He only sent two dozen, he plans to send another. What if—"

"Vina," he whispered, his breath warming my cold body. "I'm not going to let anything happen to you." He pressed a kiss to my head. "After the sabbat tomorrow, I'll get guards on the manor. We will put more patrols on the border. He's not going to send anything; he's not going to touch you. I promise." His arms wrapped tighter around me. "Come on."

He guided me, keeping my head turned away from the roses, and we exited the kitchen. He brought me to the stairs, and we walked up to our room. Darius led me to the bed, and I started to break apart, my darkness swirling around me and clouding us both, like it always did. Like I never wanted it to.

I pulled out of his embrace. "I'm fine," I said, reining in my tears.

He sat next to me and pulled me into his chest, his vanilla scent clogging my nose and warming my cold heart. I tried to push out of his hold, but his arms tightened, keeping me trapped in his safe embrace. "It's okay to need me, Vina. It's okay to need someone. You don't have to do everything by yourself."

I pushed him away, standing up and putting a few paces between us. "I do, don't you fucking see that?"

"See what?"

"I ruin everything I touch. I ruined you. I ruined Marie. I ruined Maurice. I probably ruined Markos. I'll ruin whoever is next to stupidly get too close. I have to keep away. From you, from everyone. That's why I can't try to fix us. If I fix us, it will just break again, and I'll just ruin you more."

Darius stood, his eyes blazing with challenge, with the decree to fight. "Vina." His voice was stern, his steps powerful as he moved closer to me. "Look at me and tell me you want to live your life with someone else. Tell me it feels right to be with another person. You didn't ruin us, and you didn't ruin Marie. You fucked up. So did I. I killed Maurice and I betrayed your trust. I hate that my actions unfolded the way they did, but I learned to let the past go."

"Then let me go, Darius! Because even if I let him go, he wouldn't let me! Darkness follows me and I'm tired of hurting everyone with it."

"I'm not talking about that right now. I'm not talking about him."

"Then what are you talking about!"

"You need to forgive yourself, Corivina. You can't be perfect, remember. You can't do everything right. You fucked up, but it's okay. Because you didn't lose anything, you didn't lose me and you didn't lose Marie."

The tears that I had pushed back came in full force, starting to furiously fall from my eyes. And then I just crumbled, but Darius didn't let me fall, his arm wrapping around me and holding me up as I did.

"I'm so fucking tired, Darius."

"I know."

"I just want it to be over, I just want it to end."

He pulled me closer and pressed a kiss to my head. "Let me help you end it. Let me take on some of your problems so you don't have to carry the weight by yourself."

"But… I…"

"Corivina, you are my anchor on my worst days, the thing that keeps me going. You are my wife, my best fucking friend, my partner. Let me be those things to you. Foxglove is a poisonous flower, but it can also heal wounds and burns. Let me heal your wounds and burns, Vina."

One who will heal you.

I choked out a sob, clutching him tighter, lifting my head to fit in the crevasse of his neck. "I love you."

"I love you too." He let me cry for a few moments, pulling me back to the bed where we sat clutched together. After a few moments, he pushed back so my eyes met warm blues. "Stop with the walls, Vina. *Please*, stop. They do nothing, they protect you from nothing. They protect me from nothing. Instead, they just cause everyone pain. They are what bring you a rain of ruin. They are what bring us a cluster of chaos."

I nodded. My sun would share my darkness gladly, and I would let him because he knew just how to cast it away.

"Promise."

"No more walls, I promise."

His forehead fell to mine, and he let out a relieved breath, before pressing his lips to mine. His kiss started off light but quickly he deepened it, pressing every part of himself into it.

A moan released from me. My fingers found their way in his hair, pulling him closer as my back found the bed.

"I'm starving for you," he whispered between the kisses as he started to undo the ties of my apron. His mouth disconnected from mine and he sank down to kneel at the foot of the bed, hastily pulling my dress above my hips, then off me and spreading my legs wide.

"You are the most beautiful creature I have ever laid eyes upon, my love."

I blushed, my whole body tinting red and offsetting my blue shimmer.

"I also love when you blush, even if you hate it." He smiled before pressing a kiss to my inner thigh, this one closer to my core.

He trailed kisses up until his mouth was flush with me, sucking in the fabric of my panties along with my clit, and ripping a strangled moan from my lips.

A groan vibrated from him and through my body before he lifted his mouth and hurriedly removed my panties. "It's been too fucking long, Vina."

"Never again," I whispered right before breaking out into a cry as his hot tongue flicked across my flesh.

He knew my body. Knew how to tease me, then give me absolute pleasure. Knew how to curl his fingers inside me to make me come in a few short strokes.

Basking in the high of my climax, I watched Darius remove his clothes and reveal his tan sculpted body. His eyes met mine, his expression turning sinister, commanding me without words.

I sat up, and slowly sank off the bed and onto my knees, looking up at him like he was the god I worshiped. Because he was, and I had been strayed away from my faith, but I was thankfully guided back to his light.

My hand wrapped around his hard cock, stroking him, feeling him pulse between my fingers before I guided him into my mouth.

His hand wrapped in my hair, tilting my head so our eyes connected, his hips starting to move, grunts of pleasure emanating from him as he fucked my mouth.

He was selfish with his pleasure, stealing my air and choking me with his cock, but I adored every second of it, his pleasure was my pleasure and mine was his.

When he got his fill, he sat on the bed, pulling me to straddle his lap. His cock found my entrance and he slowly lowered me down.

My claws dug into his shoulders, strangled moans deriving out from both of us like we were starved beasts.

When we were fully fused, he rested his head on mine, his eyes closing, breaths heavy. I ground my hips into him, but his hands stilled my movements. "Just a minute."

"What?"

"Just give me a minute," he said breathlessly.

A giggle sounded from me, and he opened his eyes, his warm smile filling his lips. "It's not funny."

I rolled my hips, a pained moan escaping him as his head fell into the crook of my neck. "It's kind of funny."

His fingers flexed on my hips. "Stop, or I'll come."

I snickered, then pulled his head back so I could press a kiss to his lips.

He deepened my kiss, our mouths moving in unison, his body soon relaxing and his hand starting to guide me up and down his cock.

Our moans were pained and desperate. His calloused hands scraped against my back as his cock scraped my inner walls perfectly, so fucking perfectly.

"It will never be better than this," I whispered to him, and I meant it. With Darius I felt loved, safe, whole. No one had ever made me feel like this.

He nodded, his mouth inches from mine, our sweaty foreheads glued to another. "Never."

Our movements grew strained with each thrust as we grew closer to orgasm, pleasure spreading through every cell within my body. I kissed his lips and then his scruffy chin trailing down to his neck until my lips were against his pulse. His fingers threaded through my hair, urging me to bite but I held back. He stiffened in defense, but I kissed his throat and said, "I want to do it at the same time."

His lips pressed to my head before he positioned his teeth against my skin, and we both bit down.

Tears filled my eyes, a hoarse moan ripping from me as his teeth bared into my flesh and his venom spread through my system. It was nothing like the last time he marked me. He used little venom then. Now, he didn't hold back, claiming me thoroughly.

Violent bolts of pleasure rippled through me, my core tightening around his cock, his fingers flexing against my back as he groaned and released inside me.

Our mouths met for one quick sweet kiss, and I pulled back, a smile splitting my face to match on his. "Can I tell you a secret?"

"I want to know all your secrets, Vina."

I brushed a strand of his hair off his brow. "I see myself as the moon, and you, you have always been my sun, lighting me up in the darkness."

He smiled, his fingers rubbing up and down my sides. "I am the sun and you are my moon, letting me rest as you hold the night."

I nodded. "Yes, my sun."

"Yes, my moon."

FORTY-NINE

MARIE

Karnelian pierced his ears. Well, just one ear, it'd been a month since he did it and I still can't get enough of it.

The harsh tones of the midday sun fell over his sleeping form. We slept in as much as possible today for Imbolc—a minor sabbat that celebrated the light to come, and spring soon to approach.

I lightly drew little circles on Karnelian's shoulder, counting the freckles on his face. His body tangled with mine, both of us laying on our sides, our new favorite way to sleep since I moved back in.

My fingers walked up to his mark-less neck.

You don't need to want anymore. I'm yours, Marie. Until death does us part, I'm yours.

He hasn't said it since, and we avoided talking about anything related to the future, but he still treated me like I was his.

But he could never truly be mine. I couldn't mark him, even if during sex, I wanted to. My betrayal towards my mate was already enough, and I didn't want to cross that line. Plus, I doubted my soul would want to be threaded to him. It had stayed silent since that night, but I didn't trust its silence would last. I was just enjoying the peace I had for now.

Moving closer to Karnelian, I pressed a kiss to his neck. He deserved my mark, and I hated that I couldn't give it to him. Throat kisses were the best I could offer, and they were torturous because all my beast wanted was to bite into his flesh.

After another kiss, I moved up and nipped at his earlobe, the metal tang of his earring zinging across my tongue.

A groan sounded deep in his chest, his fingers flexing on my hip before his nose twitched. He took a deeper breath in before releasing a pleasure filled moan, then pulled me closer burying his head into my neck taking in another whiff of my scent.

His chest vibrated with his purr, which my beast automatically answered.

"Mmmh," he grumbled. "You smell fucking good."

I chuckled, wrapping my arms around him. "I smell like you."

"Yeah, and that's a good smell." Another deep inhalation sounded with his nose practically fused to my neck.

"Nelian, stop." I pushed away but he just pulled me back to drink in more of my scent.

Giggles erupted from me, the light whooshing of air from his nose tickling my skin.

Karnelian pushed me onto my back, his hard cock brushing against my thigh before he settled between my legs.

"My scent really gets you nice and ready, doesn't it?"

He breathed me in answer, grinding his cock across my flesh. He pressed little kisses over my neck, his tongue sucking and teasing the area before his teeth scraped skin.

My muscles tensed at the action, and he pressed another kiss to the area, reassuring me he was just teasing.

The kisses trailed up to my lips, our mouths fusing together as his cock slowly stretched me, and sunk in.

Our morning sex was always slow and lazy after nights of brutal hard fucking. The night was our chaos, but the morning was our peace. The sex was raw and primal but in a different way. Our beasts were out and instead of them playing or fighting against another, they worked together, connected with each other.

Today Karnelian gave more of himself to me than normal. His fingers found my clit, drawing lazy but calculated circles. His cock sawed back and forth in little thrust, grinding against my clit with each one. Purrs reverberated from him, which I answered, the vibrations adding to the pleasure. He made sure to make me come twice before he ever let himself come inside me.

When it was over, he stayed on top of me, applying a thousand kisses over my face and neck that had me in a fit of giggles. Eventually his head rested on my neck again, purring more as he continued to sniff me like I actually was a flower.

"Why do you keep doing that?" I asked.

"You smell good today, really good," he mumbled against my skin.

I waited for him to elaborate but he didn't and sniffed me again.

"Karnelian, we need to get ready," I said, pushing at his shoulder to no avail. The male was glued to me. I growled in warning, and he snorted, kissing my neck before raising up.

After a chaste kiss to his mouth, I got out of bed and made my way to the bathroom. Before I could even reach the door, Karnelian's arms wrapped around me, his chest at my back. His body bent over me, nose pressed to my skin, breathing me in.

"What are you doing?" I grumbled.

"Don't shower or bathe," he said between sniffs.

"What?"

"I don't want this scent to diminish."

"Karnelian, I have to bathe. I have your come running down my thighs."

"Just how I like it."

"*Karnelian.*"

His arms tightened around me, his body starting to sway us back and forth in a comforting embrace. "Please, just sponge bathe? I really like your scent." He pressed a kiss to my neck. "Please."

I rolled my eyes, though my stomach did a little flip anytime he asked me for something. "Fine."

"Thank you, baby." He gave me another kiss to the neck before letting go of me and lightly tapping my ass.

My eyes turned into slits when I faced him, and he just gave me that devilish smile before exiting to go use the bathroom in the hall.

After my whore's bath, I dressed in a turtleneck and short skirt. The turtlenecks were a regular again because with Karnelian stealing my air every night, it left a bruise that didn't heal till midday because of my human body. Knee socks adorned my legs because though I didn't need stockings, Karnelian had a thing for them, and I wanted to give him everything I could while I still had the time.

Karnelian portaled us to my parents' main room. Which was odd because he normally always portaled us to the front door, insisting we knock out of respect, but he seemed distracted with his face buried into my neck.

Heads snapped to us when we appeared, their expressions going from a jolt of shock from our appearance to relaxed, then straight to concerned. Their eyes wide, brows furrowed, mouths turned down.

The tension in the room had Karnelian pulling out of my neck, straightening, and pressing me into his chest.

My mother and father stood, my mother sampling the air before she spoke. "You're pregnant."

Karnelian stiffened, his arms going limp, and he stepped to the side of me. His reaction casting over any reaction I could have. I immediately felt him trying to put space between us, and when I looked up at him, he was looking at me with a guarded expression.

He ripped his gaze away from me, his features hardening as he took in my mother, who was adored with a fresh mark. A part of a pair, the other on my father. "If she was pregnant, I would know. The male is supposed to know first."

My mother gestured at me. "You do know. You are crazy about her scent, are you not? She smells like you but better. That is your babe, well, a sign of it. The scent put off by a pregnant female is an aphrodisiac to the male so he will always want to be around the mother."

Karnelian glanced back at me, his eyes flaming with anything but joy. His hand ran over his mouth, and he breathed in, but stopped mid-breath, pushing it out like the smell burned his nostrils.

"She didn't go into heat," he muttered low as if to himself.

"She doesn't need to. When she mated, her physiology didn't change. The heats are just a way for her creature to draw her male in for breeding, but as any other fae female, she can still get pregnant any time her body decides to accept your seed if you two are compatible for breeding."

With the not talking about the future aspect of our relationship, we didn't ever discuss the babe equation of this whole thing. We didn't discuss when we were going to have that babe, or if either of us was even on the brew.

Karnelian took a deep breath in, then remembered my smell was his personal catnip, and slowly pushed it out. "Do you have any whiskey?"

"Yeah," my father chimed in. "In the wine cellar. I can go get—"

"I'll show him," I said, taking Karnelian's limp hand in mine and leading him to the kitchen.

I guided him to the island, and he took the seat, his features sullen and grave. The door that led down to the cellar was next to the kitchen, so I quickly skipped down and grabbed a bottle of whiskey.

The amber liquid filled the glass I set down in front of Karnelian. The second I ceased to stop pouring, he snatched the glass and slammed it back. He took the bottle from me and poured another and slammed that one back too.

"You're not happy about this," I said.

"I'm just in shock," he lied, made clear by the roughness in his tone and the third shot of whiskey he took. "Are you happy about it?"

His question was more of an accusation, sharp with an edge that was aimed to cut. The truth was, I still hadn't come to terms with me having a babe and the implications of having one. "I'm happy it's yours."

Karnelian grunted, harsh and rough. "Great."

I didn't know what to say to that. I didn't know how to react to him not wanting my babe.

Karnelian took a fourth shot, me growing with envy because I needed one as well. "We'll figure this out tomorrow. Tonight, we will just enjoy the sabbat."

"Figure this out?" I didn't know why but a part of me hated how he was reacting to this. The rejection coated me with fear and a primal urge to protect the babe that had barely started to grow within me.

He sighed, the sound irritated and adding strength to that protective feeling in me. "We will talk about it."

Anger burned in my chest and tears built under my eyes. Disappointment and disapproval were all that was known as I attempted to leave.

Karnelian's hand found mine, stopping me as he laced our fingers. His hazels pierced into me, a storm of emotions forming within. "It's just a lot for me, baby," he whispered, pulling me into his chest, holding me tight to him.

My arms folded around him, embracing him close, our beast purring in unison as if they both knew we needed a hug.

"There's already a lot going on." Karnelian spoke into my hair. "I doubt you want to have a babe in the midst of a war. As the father of the babe, I can tell my creature only wants to tend to you, and I just can't do that right now."

"You don't want the babe?" I said, voice weak.

He pulled my head out of his chest, eyes locking with mine. "I do. If things were different, I would be fucking ecstatic to be the father of your babe."

I didn't miss the hidden double meaning, but I also didn't want to acknowledge it.

"Great." I gave a half smile.

Fingers grasped my chin, and he kissed me, soft and slow, filled with so much passion before he pulled away a small smile on his lips which I returned.

"You smile so beautifully for me, baby, and I love it."

He loves it.

My smile grew wider, and I pulled him into a kiss, pushing in a message I had yet to voice. Was afraid to voice.

Heat caressed my cheeks from the roaring bonfire, the sky

glistening with stars, and owls hooting in trees. An unrested peace settled over everyone, no one truly in the mood to celebrate.

I sat in Karnelian's lap, his body rigid under me, even though his position in the chair seemed relaxed.

Tap. Tap. Tap.

His finger on the wood of the chair. It was clear he wanted to leave, but he didn't say anything. In fact, he had barely spoken since we exited the kitchen.

Going around to everyone, my father handed out slips of paper. Imbolc was a relaxed sabbat, where you lit candles or in many other cases a bonfire when the day faded into night to manifest good prosperity in the coming season.

I turned to Karnelian, offering him his papers, but he shook his head in refusal.

The frown on my face had him sitting up and pressing a soft kiss to my head. "A piece of paper isn't going to fix my problems, little bird."

It was common to burn stuff on this sabbat. Many burned actual things, but most just burned two slips of paper. One stating something you wanted to get rid of in the next cycle of the year, and one stating something you wish to manifest.

It wasn't an appropriate time for me to prod Karnelian, and I actually wanted to do this so I turned back around looking at the blank paper in contemplation.

There wasn't anything I wanted to get rid of in particular. My life was the best it had been in the last five years, and for that, I was thankful. But there were still things I wanted to change.

I want to be an honorable person.

As many others, the end of my story was once fuzzy, but then my mate died and it became clear how it would end. Recently, it had started to blur again, not fully, but it wasn't a precise ending as it once was. That was all because of Karnelian.

He was honorable. Everyone respected him, even if some of that respect was in fear. The ones who actually knew him respected his character. I respected him, and since I did, I wanted to do right by him.

When this did end, I wanted it to be with honor. That I did everything I needed to do. That nothing was left behind unfinished and uncared for.

I want to be able to step into the role expected of me.
Princess. Queen. Mother. Wife.

I had no clue how to do any of those things, but they were all thrust upon me, and I was going to have to be them. I doubted I would become a warrior princess in the war, but I could be diplomatic. I could be a figure head, a chess piece that actually moves with impact. All the while, I could learn how to be queen, even if my reign wasn't that long.

A mother and a wife… they were things I needed to think about. To process, but for now, I still had time.

Standing, I walked over to the fire, tossing the paper to the flames. The slip disintegrated in the fire and quickly turned to ash.

And then there was no fire, my vision being consumed in darkness.

There were no stars that shimmered, not a moon that smiled. The world was pitch black and utterly cold.

Goosebumps pelted my skin and snakes slithered around my shins. They were frosted and made of ice and swirled up to my thighs, then my stomach, up and up, tightening in their hold.

Warmth wrapped around my middle, and I was pulled into a heated hard body, their scent of cinnamon. Silver starlight formed around us, the snakes falling instantly away, but outside Karnelian's shield, there was still darkness.

A scream screeched in the high pitch of my mother. I jerked, but Karnelian's hold was steel around me. Grunts and groans followed, then the darkness was gone, leaving us alone in night.

The fire flamed back to life with a wave of Karnelian's hand, and the image brought to my eyes stilled my freshly beating heart.

Kolvin, Jacoby, Sariah, and my father lay on their backs. Blackened veins swirled through their bodies as they twitched and writhed in pain on the ground.

A ground littered with a thousand roses.

EPILOGUE

Corivina
106 years ago.

"*I* hate you," I cried, tears in my eyes. "I really fucking hate you, witch."

Ginger wheezed, a smile spreading on her wrinkled face. Her gold eyes still glowing with life as she peered at me. "Fae, you are supposed to respect your elders."

Today was the day. I just fucking knew. She knew it too. There wasn't any fear in her eyes, which boiled my blood, and had more tears spilling from down my cheeks.

I wiped my tears frustratedly, attempting my best scowl but miserably failing. "You are only ten years older than me. And you're a blasted human. You're supposed to be filth to me."

Her grin widened, cracking open a cavity in my heart. "Am I?"

"No, you cunt." Shudders from my body had more tears spilling down my face. "You fucking cast a spell on me or something because I shouldn't be crying. I don't cry about silly little humans dying as they do."

"I am not the only human you'll cry over."

"I think your old age has made you senile because I'm not going near a human after this."

A horrid cough escaped her mouth, but her smile stayed plastered on her face. She pointed her ebony fingers toward the bedside table, and I grasped the tea, bringing it to her mouth.

"Be careful, it's still hot."

A snort sounded from her as she sipped the tea. "You know, fae, the gods don't tell me everything."

I put the tea back on the bedside table, a scowl painting my face. "I do not want to talk about the gods today. Seriously, you are going to die. You deserve one day off, for fuck's sake."

She shook her head. "A witch's soul is in servitude of the gods. Today isn't my last day to live. It's not even my last day getting to see you."

"We both know it is the last day, don't fucking lie to me."

She just smiled that knowing smile of hers, her gold eyes gleaming with universal wisdom. "They didn't tell me you'd be my friend. That you'd stay after you found a moment of peace with the one who will heal you. They didn't tell me you'd be caring, or loving, or gracious. They didn't tell me I'd come to love you, and you me."

My lip trembled, tears dripping off my chin. "I don't love cunt witches like yourself."

"I'm glad they didn't tell me—except with the playing cards. I wish the gods would have let me cheat because you are too good at games. Their favorite jester."

A hiccup wracked me before I said, "I cheat. That's how I'm so good. I count the cards."

She chuckled, a raspy sound coming from deep within her throat. "If I had known, I would have spiked your wine. You'd be shitting liquids for a month."

"Aren't I lucky you can't get out of bed without my help?"

She turned toward the window, her face drawing serious as she looked out to the looming moon. "Listen, fae." Cold, freezing fingers grasped mine. "And I really mean, listen."

"I listen."

"You hear, but you don't like to listen. It's why you will face more darkness than you will probably ever need. You don't listen to the lessons the gods try to teach you."

"The gods are all arrogant pricks who like to laugh at others' pain. Why create a whole race that literally is known for causing destruction."

"I'm not going to get into that with you again. I don't have much more time and I need to tell you this."

I growled but refrained from speaking.

"You once had the option to change the direction of your life. Something I wanted for you, but you didn't listen then."

"When?"

"Fae... *Listen*."

Rolled my eyes but nodded for her to continue.

"There were things you could have changed. You are very divinely tied to your path, but you could have avoided some heartache while on it. Unfortunately, the path set for you is solid as stone now. So let me tell you this so that you don't break from the chaos." She took a rasped breath, accompanied with a few coughs. "There will be a time when you feel like you have lost everything, Corivina. Though, you never lost anything at all. A darkness will come then, sweep you up and show you all its horrors. When those horrors come, let *your* darkness in. It will protect you from succumbing to madness."

"What the fuck, Ginger! This is not the fucking time to tell me that after you die, my life will be shit!"

A wheezing chuckle emanated, and that smile graced her face again. "You will be alright. I think."

"You think?"

"The gods do not tell me everything, remember?"

"I really fucking hate you."

She patted my hand. "No, you don't, fae."

PRESENT.

After a darkness overtook me, I woke cold on a hard floor. The sweet smell of roses tickled my nose, but the smell of chestnut and snow was stronger, branded into the furs that blanketed me.

A small fire flared, revealing a portable stove, a male crouching in front of it.

Shock seized me, then panic pulsed in my veins.

My instincts kicked in, telling me to run, but that was when I realized I was trapped, steel bars encircling me.

The male rose, turning toward me. The click of his boot sounded the countdown to my doom.

He kneeled; face shadowed in darkness as his hand gripped the bar. The little light illuminated from the stove played with my vision as I saw something slither on his skin.

"My raven," Markos breathed. Tone hollow, ghostly, haunted. "Do you like the cage I made for you?"

THE END, FOR NOW.

The next installment of

FAE OF THE SUN AND MOON

Petals of Foxglove (a *Fae of the Sun and Moon* Prequel)

Coming 2/2/24

&

Soul Made of Silver (*Fae of the Sun and Moon* Book 3)

Coming 04/26/24

Preorder here: https://bit.ly/442pVfa

For updates, sneak peaks, bonus scenes, and all things Jewel Jeffers: linktr.ee/jeweljeffers

OTHER BOOKS BY JEWEL JEFFERS

<u>Fae of the Sun and Moon</u>

Blood So Black

ACKNOWLEDGEMENTS

First thank you to my readers. Would I have written this book without your support? Yes, but it would have been a lonely process filled with imposter syndrome, doubt, and financial stress. So thank you. It's so hard to tell you how much you matter to me. To show how important you are. Just that fact that you post about my book, saying it's your favorite, it's a small reminder that my book matters to someone. That I'm not stupid to try for this. That even though I don't physically see it there are people who loved my book and are supporting me. Thank you for that love. Thank you for following me on my journey. Thank you for buying my books. Thank you, I love each and every one of you.

Thank you to Mariah for beta reading my book.

Thank you to anyone on my street team for helping in promoting this book. It is truly appreciated. You help more readers find my books and that not only helps fulfill my dreams of being a full time author but it helps others possibly find their new favorite book. For that I am forever grateful.

Thanks to my editors Zainab and Zoe, for whipping my book into shape.

Thank you to Hannah and Brittany. Y'all are awesome bosses for letting me write at work. Sorry I quit. You probably shouldn't have let me write my books at work or I wouldn't have the money to quit...

Props to Heather for listening to me ramble and introducing me to the term "whore's bath" so I could put it in this book.

Thank you to my mom, Donna, my Nana, Esther, and my brother, Michael, for supporting me and getting my books even though you don't have to. As well as for not reading them because if you did, I would die of embarrassment. I love you guys. Xoxo

To my bestest friend, Amanda. *Blood So Black* brought us together and I'm so happy to have you. You are like my older sister, always protecting me and building me up. And you exude Jessamine energy which I love. You are my go to person, and I'm thankful for the many days we've had together and I hope for many more. I love you so so much!

Jewel... Jewel, Jewel, Jewel. This shit was hard. Like do we love this book? Yes! We love it. But seriously it was so hard. So much stuff happened. This book was, at a time, your only break from depression. There were so many growing pains with this one, but diamonds are made from pressure and this book is a diamond. I love you. I'm sorry you had to go through what you did while writing this book, but I'm happy you had this book while you went through it. Thank you for pushing through. Thank you for being you.

The best for last, Karnelian.

I wrote your book. You can stop haunting me now.

But.. Even though you are fictional, you have been the thing that made me feel safe. Grounded. I'm glad you appeared in my mind. And I can't wait to finish your story.